I0562003

Shadow of the Wolf

Choronzon Chronicles Book Three

Tess Adair

Cover designed by Ravven (www.ravven.com)
Formatting by Polgarus Studio (www.polgarusstudio.com)

Published in the United States by Tower Park Press
ISBN: 978-0-9977500-1-0

If you would like to get access to free content and be notified when Tess Adair's next novel is released, please sign up for her mailing list by clicking here: https://www.tessadair.com/mailing-list-signup

Seven Years Earlier

Down in the dark, labyrinthine bowels beneath his familial estate, in a lab that had never once seen the light of day, Charles Logan was having a less than perfect day. He always knew when the day was about to be a bad one, because it would be heralded early in the morning by some household accident that always resulted in a tiny, unnecessary cut on one of his fingers. He wasn't normally a superstitious man, but this pattern had happened often enough that he'd long since taken notice. Today, he had cut himself no less than three separate times.

If anyone had been around to ask him, they might have ascertained that some of his unpleasant day had originated in a fight he'd had with his business partner the day before. The fight amounted to his own request for a certain piece of information, and his partner's point-blank refusal to give it to him. This rejection flustered him in a way he didn't fully understand. It confounded him that he had even needed to ask; since when did Hugh Knatt hold the greater mastery of any subject, let alone this particular one?

And yet, the truth of the matter was undeniable: Hugh knew things that Charles didn't. And he refused to share.

So, it was in this spirit of vexation and uncertainty that Charles Logan had begun his day. The first cut had come during his breakfast when, absent the usual help from his partner, Charles had cut into a loaf of bread using a knife that had absolutely no business being as sharp as it was. After that, Charles decided that eggs were likely too ambitious a project for a morning like this, so he contented himself with a single (somewhat bloody) piece of toast and a cup of black coffee.

The second cut happened in the lab. He'd been holding a beaker full of dark blue liquid when his hand had simply slipped. The beaker crashed to the ground, spilling its contents all over his shoes. Fortunately, this liquid wasn't particularly acidic, so the only tragedy in dropping it was the loss of material. After he believed he'd swept up all the broken pieces, he spotted one last piece on the ground. As soon as his hand made contact with it, he felt the sharp sting of a seam opening in the flesh of his thumb.

The third happened more than an hour later. By then, he'd already grown quite sick of all the tiny mistakes and inconveniences the day had already offered him. He knew that when one was attempting to do something that had never been accomplished before, one had to accept a certain number of challenges and setbacks as a matter of course. But he hadn't expected as many as had befallen him. He'd hoped to be much farther along than this by now.

He adjusted the flame beneath his concoction and added in an extra hunk of sage. His next catalyst test was nearly ready. He put a few more drops of blue liquid in, then waited for the bubbles to subside.

The words he knew by heart, perhaps to his own detriment. He readied his hand.

"*Capere tutto*," he commanded as he struck the match. "*Capere null.*"

With a shake of his hand, he let the potion spill out over the flame. Together, the two acted as the catalyst for his cast. The power they ignited reverberated through the room, shaking its very foundation.

The demon let out a short scream.

He'd had it trapped in the cell before, but now it was chained up in the lab so he could do his tests. Its mouth still hanging open, it tipped back its head, then rocked it forward, letting something loose from its mouth as it did so. Charles attempted to dodge out of the way, but he couldn't quite move his hand fast enough. The same hand that had already borne the brunt of the morning's assault now took a third hit, as a strange, spiny spike grazed past it, slicing open the back of his forefinger.

Fortunately for him, that seemed to be all the fight the demon had left in it. If he didn't know better, he would have said that the look the demon gave him now was one of resentment. But perhaps he was merely projecting.

Nevertheless, he recognized the slack hang of the demon's limbs, the way it no longer strained against its chains. In fact, it looked like it might slump to the floor at any moment. At last, his experiment could begin in earnest.

He checked the gun at his hip first, letting his set of keys clang into clear view. He had barely taken his first step when he heard a chime ring on the opposite wall.

It was the doorbell. He'd set it up so he could hear it all the way down here, just in case someone from the Order showed up unannounced one day. Experiments like his were best done in the dark, without interference from the outside world.

Were it not for the events of the previous night, he would have left the door to Hugh instead of allowing an interruption to his work at this crucial stage. As it was, he knew Hugh wouldn't answer anytime soon. He didn't even know if Hugh had come back home yet. So, with a sigh, he left the demon's chains in place and dropped his cast. Immediately, the beast's growling resumed, as did its attempts to strain at the restraints keeping him in place.

Charles locked his lab behind him as he went, just in case. It was best if nobody else went in, and certainly best if nobody else came out.

A few minutes later, he had traded out his lab coat for a sweater and made his way up the stairs, making sure to lock the door at the top, as well. One could never be too careful.

He stopped in front of a mirror before opening the door, just to make sure nothing looked amiss. Apart from the three cuts that now peppered his fingers, he looked just like any other man.

The doorbell rang again as he cut through the kitchen to get to it. At long last, he pulled it open. On the other side stood a young man with pale blond hair and a somewhat sickly look about him. The young man smiled broadly.

"Mr. Logan, I hope I haven't caught you at a bad time," he said. His voice had an accent, but Charles found he couldn't quite identify it. The man straightened his black tie, which sat neatly over a black shirt. "We spoke on the phone about a week ago—I'm following up on my father's research. You told me I might pay you a visit today. Does that sound familiar?"

"Ah, yes," said Charles, a vague memory emerging through

the mist of time. "I'm sorry, I must be having an off morning. Could you remind me of your name again?"

"It's Casimir Volkov, sir."

"Ah, Volkov, yes. Come in, come in."

Volkov smiled broadly at him.

Then he stepped inside.

Chapter One
A Hint of Smoke

They didn't have much time, all things considered. She knew it wouldn't be long before the Wolf came looking, or sent someone in his stead. She'd told Knatt they needed to collect Charles Logan as soon as she could, but she couldn't tell him *why* while there was any chance someone from the Order could overhear.

It was bad enough that Volkov had said the words out loud in Order territory: *I know you're a half-demon.*

There's never been anyone in the world like you.

H.C. Logan didn't need any more incriminating information floating around in Order-controlled airspace.

When they were finally in the car, heading north to collect Charles, she felt herself let out a breath she hadn't known she'd been holding. They didn't have any answers yet, but at least they were *doing* something. It felt good to do something. Even better that Knatt had let her drive, which meant she was free to skate above the speed limit as much as she wanted, her sharper demon senses on the lookout for signs of trouble—for once, of the mundane cop variety.

"Well," said Knatt, when they'd been driving silently for

nearly 15 minutes, "do you suppose you're going to explain what we're doing any time soon?"

If she'd been in less of a tense mood, she might have rolled her eyes.

"The Wolf has been visiting Charles," she said simply, her tone so neutral it surprised even her. Didn't she feel angry about this?

Or was the feeling closer to disgust?

"Are you certain?"

Logan nodded, her eyes never straying from the road ahead. "He knows I'm half-demon. And before this past summer, there were only, what, five people in the world who knew? Two of whom are untouchable eira Masters, and two of whom are you and me. So unless you're about to confess something pretty huge…Charles Logan is the weakest link."

Out of the corner of her eye, she saw him nod as he mulled this over.

"And if he was visiting Charles…who knows what else he might have asked him?"

"Exactly." She shook her head, barely keeping in a growl. "It's not like Charles is exactly practiced in the art of putting others' needs before his own. We need to get to him before the Wolf comes back for more…if there's anything left he hasn't already said, that is."

"Agreed."

Logan stared out at the road ahead. She supposed she ought to be grateful there was so little traffic. The road was slick with rain, the trees drooping overhead…as she slowed her speed in anticipation of the car that would soon pass in the other direction, a thought occurred. There was something familiar about all of this. Granted, that went without saying—she could no longer count the number of road trips she'd been on in her life. Plenty of them had gone exactly like this: her in the driver seat, Knatt in the passenger's side, both of them contemplating what parts of their upcoming case they might be missing. It had been a few years since Knatt had come with her into the field, but the memory of it remained intact.

And yet…she was sure that wasn't it. She was remembering something else entirely. The ambient sounds of the car lulled a piece of her mind into passivity, and she could just about make out another car, another arrangement.

She was a child, and her father was driving the car.

She wasn't entirely sure how she'd gotten there. She'd simply woken up already in the car, fully strapped in, her father at the wheel beside her, while miles and miles of evergreen trees zoomed past.

"Where are we going?" she asked groggily.

"Somewhere very special," he answered—authoritatively, not quite reassuringly. "I'll tell you all about it when we get there."

The memory faded out after that. She was sure it was real, but…she had no idea how it concluded. In fact, she had half a dozen memories just like that: road trips with her father that seemed to have no conclusion, no destination. They just stopped.

She glanced over at Knatt, who looked like he was deep in contemplation. It wasn't a rare look on him, and yet…she felt somewhat reluctant to interrupt. For some reason she couldn't name, she wasn't sure whether she actually wanted to ask him.

But she had to.

"Hey." Her voice seemed to catch in her throat until she

coughed to clear it. "Do you remember those road trips he used to take me on?"

Knatt's eyebrows knitted together in concern.

"You mean when he would take off with you in the middle of the night with no warning, and no indication of where he'd gone, or when he would bring you back? Yes, I remember."

"Did you ever find out where he took me?"

"Well, I never got him to *tell* me anything," said Knatt, his expression suddenly furtive, even guilty. "But I looked through his receipts whenever I could. Bank statements, as well."

"And?"

"He took you all over. California a few times. New Mexico, Alabama, Louisiana. And a number of times, he didn't even leave the state. He took you to the peninsula at least four or five times. Is there a reason you're asking about this now?"

"Not sure," said Logan, shaking her head. "Something made me think of it, is all. Road trip memories, I guess. Or, I don't know, maybe it's just…"

She felt herself trailing off, felt her mind automatically changing course, veering away from the subject it never wanted to broach.

"Just what?" asked Knatt, gently, and not gently, at the same time.

It was important to take a deep breath before falling far under the surface of the water. So she readied the jump.

"Every time I go to see him, I have to think about the things he took away from me. And since he's, well, not even himself anymore…I have to think about the fact that I'll probably never get them back."

She glanced automatically to the right, just in time to watch a sudden and unwanted thought dance its way across Knatt's face.

"What?" Her voice sounded louder, harder than she meant it to.

"Hm? Oh, nothing, I just—I wonder…"

"You wonder what?"

Knatt's mouth formed into a deep frown.

"I was just thinking what a particular irony it was, that your father's illness took his memories away, after what he did to you. How strangely poetic."

Logan didn't know what to say to that. She'd had a similar thought herself, more than once, but it had never seemed appropriate to say it out loud. She supposed that, despite everything he'd done to her, she still felt a sliver of pity for her father, and what had become of him. Pity enough to try to save his life, even.

She had to wonder if it would turn out to be worth it.

It was raining in northern Washington state. Savino Rossi had never been this far west in America, and as yet, he couldn't say whether he liked it much. All he had seen of it was rain.

That wasn't to say the countryside wasn't beautiful, of course. He stood under the cover of a line of trees at the moment, staring out at a lush, rolling green before him. These were the manicured grounds of a home for the wealthy elderly, but as far as he could see, they stood as a fair example of the rest of the province. The grass before him was still a deep green, and the tall coniferous trees stood green as well.

But beneath all that green lay an ever-thickening mud—and

it was a mud he needed to get across. He shifted his weight from foot to foot, his big, bulky frame working against him as the heels of his shoes sank into mushy earth.

The rain would make visibility harder for normal human eyes, but he knew he was far from invisible. He hunched as low to the ground as he could before setting off toward the sprawling, spiraling complex in front of him. His feet threatened to slide with every step, but with the help of his new, inhuman grace, he managed to keep himself upright and moving. Despite the difficulty, he made good time. He took cover against the red brick exterior in under a minute.

Another 20 feet, then a left. His Master had shown him the plans for the building, then had him recite his route over and over again, until they were both certain he had it memorized. There would be no second chances today.

He moved down one side of the building, then another, ducking beneath every window he passed. Thanks to their plan, there would be no further risk of exposure until he reached his target…which wouldn't take long at all.

There it is. Wiping the rain from his face, he peered around the last corner, right through the sliding glass door and into the room beyond. The first thing he could see was a roaring fire on the hearth, throwing long shadows against the other walls. After that, his eyes landed on the overstuffed armchair—and the figure inside it, pathetically huddled under a blanket.

That's him, thought Rossi, triumphantly. *Despite the Master's fears, the girl is as stupid as the rest. Today will be an easy day.*

In one quick motion, he crossed the small cement patio and pressed his palm against the groove in the door. It slid open without resistance. It was unlocked.

Victory swelled his chest, and a smile crested his lips. The air inside the room had warmed pleasantly in the presence of the fire. He stepped forward, sliding the door shut behind him.

"At last, we meet, Mr. Logan," he said. He stepped forward, sliding a knife out of his waistband. He doubted he'd even need the full extent of his brand-new power for this. "It is a pity I cannot stay long."

"There's only one Logan here," said a voice behind him. Unbidden, his blood turned hot. "And I prefer no prefix, thanks."

"*Shadow summoner*," he growled. Anticipation and delight flooded him: he would get his fight after all. "My master sends his greetings."

He whipped around, knife held aloft, expecting to see the cold eyes of the shadow summoner, his master's strange obsession, staring back at him.

Instead, he saw nothing.

"Where are you?"

Something seemed to waver at the right side of his vision, but when he looked for it, it was gone.

"Show yourself!" He whipped his knife back and forth, hoping he might catch her if she was too slow. "Come out and fight me!"

She did as he commanded. As soon as she crashed into him, he could see her. She sent him sprawling to the ground with the force of her blow, while she danced away and adopted a loose boxer's stance.

She grinned down at him, a naked taunt.

"Aw, gee, did you fall down?" she asked, laughter in her voice.

"Should I call for a nurse?"

The heat in his blood had turned into a boil, and he let it take him over. By the time he had leapt to his feet, he could feel every single one of his muscles bulging outward, surging with inhuman power. *Now* his time had come.

"I will tear you to pieces, you little bitch."

"Are you sure your Wolf daddy would be happy about that?" Her eyes were alight with glee. "I get the impression he wants me around a little longer."

"Accidents happen," he responded, a calculating smile spreading over his face. "Sometimes, one must take a risk."

With that, he launched himself at her, propelling his bulk forward with all the strength he had. Unfortunately for him, he sacrificed speed for strength. She slipped out of his grasp just as he thought he had her.

But she didn't go far. Whipping around at the last moment, she aimed a flying kick and hit him square in the ribs, sending him backward. He worked to regain his balance and glared at her.

"Perhaps you are stronger than you look," he muttered. "It will not matter, in the end."

He lunged at her again, and again, he missed. This time, she delivered several hard jabs straight to his solar plexus, effectively knocking the wind out of him. Before he had time to recover, she whipped around behind him and kicked out both of his knees, sending him down.

She grabbed hold of his hair and pulled back, exposing his neck. One forearm settled behind while the other wrapped around the front of his throat, pressing into his windpipe and locking him down. Just like that, she'd overpowered him.

"You are a short thing, to be so strong," he grumbled, forcing the words out around strangled gasps for air.

"Not sure those two correlate the way you think they do," she answered, tightening her grip. He placed his hands on her arm and started to tug, though he could feel his strength waning rapidly.

"Will you kill me, shadow summoner? I can feel how much you want to."

"You don't know what I feel. You don't know anything about me."

"But the Wolf does," he muttered, barely pushing the words past his lips. "He sees your potential…for violence. He knows how…far you could go. Why…why don't you give in…as you have before?"

He felt her grip tighten. *Good.* Perhaps his Master would prove right about her, after all.

"Do it," he hissed. His own fingers were beginning to slacken. "I know you want to."

To his surprise, he felt her arm begin to release. Was she letting him go?

Before he had the chance to answer himself, he saw the bundle in the armchair, several feet in front of him, get to its feet and throw off the blanket.

"That's quite enough, I think," said the figure. It raised a funny-looking gun at him and pulled the trigger.

He had just enough time to recognize his sense of disappointment before the world went black.

Logan let Rossi's body slump heavily to the floor, paying no attention to whatever injuries he might incur on his way down.

She could still feel her blood racing, her body wheeling like she'd just had the rug pulled out from under her.

Rossi was right. She'd *wanted* to kill him. She could feel it in every muscle, every fiber. *Every* part. Not just the demon parts.

Or...were they all demon parts?

When she'd had her arm around his throat, she'd known without a shadow of a doubt what it would feel like to kill him. She'd hungered after it. Her instinct told her to do it.

So, instead, she froze. She waited for Knatt to take the decision away from her.

She looked at him now, standing across from her, nothing but the body of her almost-victim between them.

"You did the right thing," he said, and she knew he was trying to reassure her.

"I didn't do anything." She shrugged. "Did you hear him?"

Knatt gave a heavy sigh. He sounded tired.

"You must not pay attention to shadows, Henrietta."

For a moment, Logan remained where she was, still frozen at the site of her indecision. Then she decided to put it all away, and she leaned down to grab a hold of Rossi's limp body. She swung him over her shoulder with ease and headed for the door.

"Let's get going."

The ride home had been quiet, punctuated only by the rain and Knatt's classical music. Knatt drove, while Logan watched the blurry outside world through the window and did her best not to feel like a petulant teenager. She couldn't help but remember every long road trip she'd been on with him—most of them on the way home from one boarding school or other, after her inevitable suspension or expulsion. If anyone had asked her then what drove her to act the way she did, she wasn't sure she could have provided any real kind of answer.

Was it any different now? Maybe she'd acted out because of what her father had done—all the times he'd locked her in a cell with a demon and refused to let her out until she'd killed it. Not that she could remember, then or now. Every time he'd done it, he'd taken her memory of it away. And every time he'd done that, he'd made it just a little bit harder for her to know who she was.

Maybe that's for the best, if who I am is a killer.

So, maybe it was the abuse that made her act out. Or maybe it was the life she did remember, where her father never stayed in one place very long and always did his best to avoid too much responsibility for his daughter, either by sending her to boarding schools or by leaving her with Knatt or, on occasion, her aunt Adele.

Or maybe it was neither. What if her actions were her own, motivated by nothing other than her own inhuman nature?

What if I'm just a broken doll?

The thought came back like a boomerang, visiting her every few minutes, until eventually the monotony of her own mind lulled her to sleep.

When they got back to the house, Knatt marched on ahead of her, opening up doors to clear the path. She shouldered a still-slumbering Rossi and carried him through the connecting garage door, then straight down the stairs, into the lower basement.

The basement at the estate had two levels: the first one, which held an in-home theater and bar area, and the second, which held her father's old letha laboratory, as well as a large windowless cage that locked from the outside.

It was into the cage that she dropped Rossi. She didn't take particular care, but nothing cracked when he hit the floor. For a moment, she stared down at his unconscious form.

Black veins had spread across his face as he'd started to change—he was Bound, which meant that, though he had begun life as human, he had been gifted with demon powers through the letha magic known as Binding. When the Bound used their full strength, they often physically transformed into a larger version of themselves, complete with spidery black veins spreading over their face. His still hadn't receded entirely, though he'd been unconscious for over an hour by now.

Logan thought about the purplish black marks on her collarbone, slowly creeping up her neck and down her arms. She thought about the four black diamonds on her forearms, where her spikes slid in and out. She'd been measuring them since they first showed up, like her own private science experiment, and her results were conclusive: they were getting bigger, all the time.

What would her face look like a few years from now? Would it look like his? Or would it look even more inhuman than that?

"Are you coming out, Henrietta?"

Logan turned to look back at Knatt. She'd almost forgotten he was there.

"Yeah. Coming out."

She didn't bother to look at Rossi again. Instead, she strode deliberately back to the door of the cage and closed it tight behind her, throwing all four locks into place as soon as she was done.

"You're sure this is the best option?" asked Knatt, glancing between her face and the door.

Logan nodded. With her left hand, she reached up to close the tiny barred window in the upper half of the door, shutting off the pitiful view it offered. It was the kind of view that could only drive a person mad, anyway.

"It'll hold," she said, with a shrug. Inhuman strength or no, Rossi wouldn't be able to get out of there on his own.

She would know.

Knatt looked at her, concern writ large on his face.

"Logan, perhaps you ought to—"

"Don't. Not right now."

Pushing his glasses up the bridge of his nose, Knatt gave a deep sigh and folded his hands primly behind his back. Logan shook her head and stepped around him, clomping back up the basement staircase before he could stop her. She knew he meant well. She knew that.

The kitchen lights were already on by the time she reached the ground floor, and she could hear the sounds of human movement from beyond the doorway. Her instinctual self-preservation kicked in immediately, the tips of her spikes rising just beneath the surface to press lightly against her skin. Then she remembered—Adele.

Right after the disaster at the Order of Shadows' headquarters in New York, Alexei Marin had traveled back with them, and he'd hung around as long as he could. Knatt and Logan had gone to collect her father from the home right away, but that wasn't the end of the task. She'd had a feeling the Wolf would send one of his lackeys for her father—or maybe even make an attempt to collect him himself. So once Charles Logan was safely home, they'd gone back up to the facility to stake it out and see who turned up. By now, their stakeout had gone on for eight consecutive days.

Alexei had lasted three. When he'd finally begged off for the chance to fly home, sleep in his own bed, wear different clothes—though to Logan's mind, he had enough clothes with him to last a lifetime—she could hardly hold him captive. They didn't want to leave Jude and Charles without protection when the Wolf might come after them at any time, of course, so she'd called her Aunt Adele, who had graciously shown up within the hour.

So it was Adele she heard moving in the kitchen. Even as she took her next step, she confirmed it: Adele's soft hum floated over to her through the short hallway. Her spikes receded entirely, and she crossed out of the basement.

Logan stood silently in the doorway for a moment, taking in the vision of her aunt. She was a short, curvy woman, with a magnificent mane of thick black hair that fell to her waist. At the moment, she was wearing an apron and covered in flour, with a look of utter contentment on her face. It almost made Logan wish she could be a child again, when the mere mention of her aunt was enough to excite her for days.

Logan stood ever so slightly in shadow, and Adele hadn't noticed her yet. She disappeared behind the island counter, then reappeared a moment later with a heavy tray in her hands. Logan chose that moment to step forward into the kitchen, a broad smile on her face to greet her aunt.

Adele shrieked at the site of her and dropped the tray. Logan was there in under a second, catching the tray almost immediately.

"Oh! Well done," said Adele as Logan handed the tray back over to her.

Logan shrugged. "What's the point of being a demon if I can't pull off stupid stunts from time to time?"

"You could always try *not* sneaking up on frail old women, of course."

"You're not a frail old woman."

"And you're not a demon."

Logan felt the side of her mouth quirk up, involuntarily.

"So, how are things going around here?"

Adele turned to set her tray on the island, as she had originally intended, then grabbed a cloth napkin from the other counter to place it gently over the two neat rows of rolled dough. When she was done with that, she gave Logan a quick once-over.

"You seem uninjured, which means it's my right as your aunt to demand a hug." She tilted her chin down as she gave Logan a wink. "If you're so inclined, that is."

"Not sure you get how this whole 'demand' thing works, Del." Logan returned her aunt's smile and stepped gratefully into her embrace. Somehow, the woman always smelled like a perfect mix of burnt sage and freshly baked bread. If Logan had been inclined to give the concept of safety a smell, this would be it.

Logan still struggled to accept physical affection from most people, but her aunt's hugs had been one of the first forms she'd ever grown accustomed to. Adele had provided her a home at Other Side when her own had proven untenable. And more than a few times after that, as well.

"It's good to see you, Henri," said Adele, still pressing her niece into her chest. With one final squeeze, she let her go. "And things *are* going well, all things considered." She began wiping some excess flour from her hands, then paused to glance at Logan again. "Oh, I'm sorry, sweetheart. I'm afraid I've turned you into a dalmatian."

Logan glanced down. Her black shirt and pants were now both dotted with patches of flour. She shrugged.

"Wasn't planning on going out, anyway." She grabbed a spare washcloth from the side of the sink and beat it against her legs and torso a few times, batting away the worst of it. "What did you make?"

"Just some chocolate almond croissants for the morning," she replied with a shrug, as though it were the simplest thing in the world. "And some special field roast pastries for you, on account of, you know…the *sugar* thing."

She'd lowered her voice when she said the word "sugar," like she was referencing some dark family secret. In a strange way, Logan supposed she was: it was her demon side that couldn't process sugar, and its effects on her were similar to the effects of drinking alcohol for full humans. Adele was trying to accommodate her dietary needs.

"Sounds delicious," said Logan.

"Delicious is Plan A," said Adele with a happy nod. "Plan B is that little diner in town with the really good blueberry pancakes." She turned away from Logan to wash her hands at the sink and put away a few lingering items. "And did you get what you were looking for, up north?"

Logan felt her smile deflate, but she did her best not to let that push through to her voice. Her mind went back to the dark cell below, and the eerie black veins criss-crossing Rossi's face.

"More or less," she said simply. She didn't want to dwell. "How's the kid?"

"Asleep at the moment," said Adele. Once she'd given the counters one last wipe-down, she pulled the apron off over her head and hung it on the wall, next to the doorway. "She passed out on the couch while we were watching a movie. I fear I may have exhausted her at practice today."

Logan heard footsteps echoing up the last few steps in the stairway, and her eyes flicked automatically in their direction. Knatt had finally caught up. She bit back her irritation.

Adele's eyes widened as she followed Logan's gaze. A moment later, he appeared.

"Adele." He smiled warmly, like everything was perfectly fine. "I hope we haven't kept you away from your duties too long."

"Oh, Hugh." Adele shook her head slowly at him, then wiped her hands roughly against her jeans before crossing over and wrapping him in an all-inclusive bear hug. He returned it without hesitation. "You made it home safe."

"Did you ever doubt me?" Knatt's eyebrows knitted together as he pulled away from her.

"Near constantly," she said, smiling brightly at him. "I have absolutely no faith in either of your abilities."

"Oh. How reassuring."

"I thought it might be." She turned back to Logan with unnecessary flare. "You were asking about Jude's studies, yes?"

"Yes." Adele had been training Jude Li in eira summoning on an irregular basis for months now. As Logan had learned on her daily check-in calls with her aunt, she'd taken this "extended sleepover," her words, as an opportunity to enroll Jude in a kind of immersion course, with daily meditation and summoning practice, in the style of the eira Masters at T'eira'han—or Other Side, as Logan usually called it. "How's she doing?"

"Quite well, actually. She has some trouble clearing her mind, which is hardly unusual for someone her age. But when she does manage it, her natural inclination for eira is…something to behold." As natural as an instinct, Adele reached over and pushed a stray strand of hair out of Logan's face. "She reminds me a bit of you, when you first started."

Logan did her best not to wince, but she knew that was a backhanded compliment at best. Adele had never quite forgiven her for abandoning her own studies at Other Side, even though continuing them had come to seem increasingly pointless.

"Still," Adele continued, "I think it'll be good for her to take a little break. Perhaps you could spend some time teaching her how to pace herself, hm?"

Logan felt her eyes widen in surprise, an unexpected disappointment flooding through her system.

"Do you have to leave already?"

"I can stay through tomorrow," said Adele, gently. "As always, you're welcome to come with me when I go."

Logan sighed, glancing involuntarily at the hallway beyond, where the entrance to the lower levels was.

"Duty calls, unfortunately." She crossed her arms over her chest. "Duty never seems to let up."

"I know the feeling."

Knatt cleared his throat, looking questioningly at Adele.

"How has Charles been, while you've been here?" He glanced

up at the ceiling, as if he could see Charles through it. "Has he come out of his room at all?"

"No." Adele let out a heavy sigh. "I've brought him food, every day, twice a day. He talks to me sometimes, but…I'm not always sure he knows who I am. But he hasn't made any attempt to leave his room—not as far as I've seen, anyway. I suppose it's possible he goes on night walks after we're all asleep."

Logan repressed a shudder at the thought. She found herself grateful that she no longer had to sleep in this house.

Knatt, on the other hand, just nodded. He seemed unbothered.

"Well, I must thank you for everything you've done to help us," he said, straightening up like he was coming back to his senses. She wasn't sure when he'd left them, herself; he'd seemed perfectly composed to her.

"Hey, what else are families for?"

The sentence seemed to hang in the air like a fog. Logan suddenly felt tired in every inch of her body—tired in a way that mere physical exhaustion couldn't encompass. It was the kind of tired that could leave her unmoored in time if she let it.

"On that note, I should head home." Even as she spoke, she was already drifting to the other exit from the kitchen, farther from the basement and closer to her own space. "I'll be back in the morning. Good night."

Without another word, she slipped out of the room and down the hall, moving quickly. She moved like she thought she could outrun what she knew was coming. She had almost reached the travelling room when she heard his footsteps come up behind her. She stopped, but she didn't turn around.

"Do we have to do this every time?"

"Not at all." Knatt's tone was easy. It suggested simplicity. "All it takes to end this conversation is for you to go up and see him."

Logan's bones were tired, but her muscles tensed.

"I already tried to ask him what he knows about the Wolf." She shook her head, unwilling to entertain the memory of her father's scattered responses and inconsistent panic. "Either he's suddenly the world's greatest actor, or he can't remember anything. He's too far gone to give us anything useful."

"I'm aware of that." Now his tone became careful, measured out in spoons. "And you know that's not what I meant."

"*Do* I know that?"

She felt his sigh more than heard it.

"What I *meant*…was that it might be worthwhile for you to check in on him. Not to ask him about the Wolf or anything like that. Just…to see him."

"And *why* would I want to do that?" Even to her own ears, she sounded harsh. "It's not my job to keep him entertained."

Knatt took a moment to respond, and when he did, his voice was quiet.

"I'm not asking for him." He took a few steps closer to her, but she still refused to turn around. "I'm asking for you."

"Then you can stop now."

"Henrietta. There may be things he can tell you about yourself that…that I don't know. Answers that I cannot give you."

"You're wrong." Logan shook her head firmly. "There is *nothing* I need from him."

"How can you know that?"

Logan thought about Rossi lying on the cold, hard floor of the cell in the lower level. She didn't want to remember what that felt like.

"Because I know him."

With that, she walked away from Knatt, and she didn't stop until she was safe in her own apartment, 20 miles and a world away.

Chapter Two
The Deeper Basement

She was sitting on a bench in the middle of a busy city. She did not recognize the city, but she felt like she should have. She was sitting on a bench, and her feet did not quite reach the ground. For the briefest moment, she held the cognitive dissonance of knowing that her body was not her body, and then just like that, she forgot. She was the size of a child because she was a child. She had never been anything else.

Out of the crowd of blurry faces before her emerged a woman. She knew she had a face, but she couldn't quite make it out. It was as if her face resisted being seen.

The woman knelt before her and reached for her hand. Logan reached out for her as well, and an intensity of longing overwhelmed her. She was absolutely certain that she had known this woman once—and she had missed her.

Something was burning, but she didn't know what.

Just as their hands were about to meet, the woman disappeared. The scene dissolved.

Logan still sat on a bench, but it was inside a darkened hallway. She had been here before. She stood and began to move, searching for the hidden light she knew was there. There, at the end and through a doorway, was a faint circular glow. She walked toward it, drawn in inexorably. Something was burning. As she got closer, she realized a pattern was emerging from the light.

It was the Choronzon Key. It wanted her to go through the doorway.

The scene twisted again, collapsing in on itself.

"I want to help you, shadow summoner." She knew that voice. "I only want to help you realize your full potential."

She felt herself shake her head, but she didn't know why.

"I don't need your help with that."

The words seared her. She wanted to tear at the skin of the world. Something was burning, writhing within her, screaming to be let out. She no longer knew where she was. All she could feel was pain, and she wanted to tear it away.

A voice inside her told her to do it. Tear it open, it said.

All at once, her vision came into focus again. She stood on stone—no, cement. And there was some kind of circular symbol painted beneath her feet, but she couldn't make it out. She felt trapped, but she didn't know why. Fire illuminated the night-dark sky, though her face was wet with rain—and possibly something else. She could see Volkov only a few feet away from her, holding what looked like a palm-sized piece of circular bronze.

There were bodies all around her. Were they the bodies of people she'd killed? She couldn't remember.

The voice beckoned. It burned happily, ready to be released. The pain in her body redoubled, and she doubled over with it. Before her, the Wolf let out a sigh. He bent down in front of her so she could see the sorrow in his eyes.

"Just remember, you brought this on yourself."
For a moment, there was silence.
Then every single nerve in her body caught fire.

Logan awoke with a start, well before her usual hour. The sky outside was still dark, and the air in her apartment was cold—not that she minded. The cold was a respite. She welcomed November with open arms.

She swung her bare legs out from under the covers and let her feet come to rest in the thick shag rug next to the bed. She took one deep breath, then another, but it did nothing to quell the pain that still lingered, along with the memory of the dream—or vision, if that's what it was.

Her back still burning, she clawed at the shirt she'd gone to sleep in until it came all the way off. Then she reached into the top of her dresser for the first two articles of clothing she usually put on—two slim ankle holsters for two of her throwing knives. After that came underwear, followed by a nice thick pair of stretchy black jeans, with just a touch of extra room around the ankles.

The cold air helped to calm her mind, but it did little to ease the continuous burning in her back. Fortunately, or maybe unfortunately, this wasn't the first time Logan had awoken in the middle of the night feeling like her entire back had been set on fire. She crossed to the corner of the room, popped open the small freezer she kept there, and pulled out a large ice pack fitted with shoulder straps. She slipped it on and sighed with relief as the cold pack came into contact with her skin.

Deciding to forgo a bra for the moment, she grabbed a loose

black T-shirt with the arms cut off and pulled it on over the ice pack.

She knew she had to decode the dream vision sooner or later, but she also had a task to complete. Before she'd gone to bed the night before, she'd come to a decision about what to do with Rossi. And she needed to get it over with before she changed her mind.

A few minutes later, she stood in her own kitchen, pouring boiling water over the coffee grounds in her French press. Her cell phone lay on the counter a foot away, waiting for her. When she finished with the water, she crossed to the fridge to pull out her cream, setting it down neatly next to the brewing coffee. Then she took a mug out of the cabinet and set it down, lining all three up in a neat little row.

You're stalling.

She poured a dollop of cream into the mug. She could feel the ice pack already starting to melt.

You already made the decision. You just gotta pull the trigger.

But did she really know what that would mean? It felt like a simple enough solution, but she knew from experience how wide the ripple effects could go.

It's not Atherton anymore. Maybe Clément will be different.

She picked up the phone and opened up her contacts. Marion Clément, interim head of the Order of Shadows, came up first thing. She'd called Logan a number of times over the last few days.

Clément answered after only one ring.

"Miss Logan," said the clipped, French-accented voice on the other line. "To what do I owe the pleasure?"

Logan kept her sigh to herself.

"I've got Rossi." She decided to forgo the preamble. "If you have the facilities to hold him, I'll hand him over to you."

For a beat, Clément was silent.

"Just like that?" Her tone was suspicious. "What do you ask in return?"

Logan wished she could will her coffee to brew faster.

"I'll have my partner send you an invoice," she answered. As she chanced to look down at herself, her eyes fell on the small tattoo inside her left elbow. *The field only reveals.* "And let's say you owe me one. Sound fair?"

"Quite." Through the receiver, Logan heard an audible sigh of relief. "To be frank, Miss Logan, I wasn't certain if the Order could continue to count on your aid in this matter, after you seemed so…reluctant to join in on our search efforts."

Perhaps it was the relative lack of sleep, or the burning at her back, or just dealing with the Order so early in the morning—whatever the cause, Logan could feel a headache beginning to form. She didn't want to stay in this conversation, but she didn't see an alternative to it, either.

"Well, as long as we're being honest…I didn't think your search was gonna turn up anything." She poked pointlessly at the French press. "So I thought I'd try my idea instead. Seemed like a better use of my time."

"I see." Logan could practically hear Clément tightening her mouth into a hard line. "Be that as it may, I suspect your readiness to hand Savino over to us will do much to enhance your reputation among the other Seers. This is a good step forward, for the both of us."

Logan would have shrugged if there had been anyone there to see her. As it was, she stood still and said nothing. After a moment, Clément cleared her throat.

"Unfortunately," she continued, sounding audibly uncomfortable, "we are still in…disarray, here at Headquarters. Well, everywhere, as a matter of fact. We have yet to elect a new High Prophet. In fact…we still need to select one more new Seer before the election can take place."

Logan wasn't surprised by this piece of information. After all, it had only been a little over a week since James Atherton, the last High Prophet, had died at the hand of the Wolf, as a result of the latter's interference with the Binding ritual Atherton had been performing at the time. Logan still held in her mind the image of him at the moment of his death. She tried not to dwell on it.

"Right," she said carefully. "So, you're saying you might not be able to take him right away."

"Precisely."

"We have him in a cell for now. I can't say we've tested it recently, but it should hold for a few days. How long do you need?"

"48 hours at most," she said. She sounded grim, and maybe even a little tired. "Are you certain you can wait that long?"

"Is there another option?"

Clément chuckled under her breath. It was a short, tired sound. "No."

"Then here we are."

"Here we are." Another audible sigh. "I must thank you, again, for your service, Miss Logan."

"You might want to hold off on that," said Logan, allowing herself a small smile. "You haven't seen the bill yet."

This time, the laugh that came through the phone was louder and more genuine. A minute later, Clément ended the call herself, leaving Logan where she was.

The ice pack was completely melted now, and the back of her shirt was soaked through. On the plus side, the burning in her skin had finally calmed to a low and constant irritation. She pulled off the ice pack and put it in the freezer behind her. As she pulled away, her eyes caught on the tattoo again, and she used her right hand to trace its letters.

The field only reveals. But what did this one reveal?

She walked back to her room, pulling off the now-soaked shirt as she crossed the threshold. She pulled open the door to the closet, revealing the mirror hanging on the other side, then turned around, so she could see her back in the reflection.

There she saw the winding form of the Choronzon Key—a maze encircled by a teardrop shape, spanning the breadth of her back. It burned red against her skin, though she could see the red beginning to darken back to its inert state of plain black. The Key had been a part of her life so long, she wasn't sure she still knew who she was without it. And yet she had no idea where it came from, and no idea why it chose her to begin with. She only knew that it sent her visions, usually to guide her to help save someone…though most of the time, she couldn't save everyone.

Who did it want her to save now?

At long last, her mind went to the vision: a field of stone, a battle of fire, and an artifact in the hands of her enemy. It was rare for her to see a vision through her own eyes. Most of the time, she saw them through the eyes of a monster.

So, how is this any different?

She tried to focus on the specifics of what she'd seen. A circle in the stone. Cement all around. The smell of the sea. Rain. The Wolf. An unknown artifact. And so much fire.

And the Key had been burning *in* the dream, too. It had been a different kind of burning—a worse kind. Usually, the pain the Key inflicted on her was strictly limited to the parts of her that it touched—as if it were, itself, physically on fire, every time it activated. But in the vision, the pain had spread throughout her entire body. It had felt like…like the fabric of the universe was ripping apart. Starting with her.

Maybe it was something the Wolf was planning to do. It didn't make sense to her how he was planning to do it, but…if the Key was showing her, then…

She needed more information, and she wasn't going to get that from staring at her own reflection. She picked out a sturdy bra and put it on, swallowing the discomfort from putting tight clothes onto her still-raw skin, then picked out a new T-shirt, indistinguishable from the last—apart from being perfectly dry.

Then she went into the kitchen. At long last, she poured herself a cup of coffee.

By the time Logan stepped out of the travelling room at the estate, the whole house smelled like baked goods. Adele had already set herself to work. Logan headed straight for the kitchen.

She heard the others before she saw them. Pausing briefly in the great room, she closed her eyes and listened. It was Jude's voice she heard first.

"Do you think she'll like it?"

"As long as *you* like it, I don't think it matters what anyone else thinks." Adele's tone was patient but practiced, like she was speaking words she'd already repeated more than once.

"I know, but…well, I think I'm a little nervous. It's been a few days since I've seen her, and…I don't know, I'm just nervous."

"I'm sure she'll love it, Jude. If she has any taste, that is."

Bracing herself for whatever she was about to walk into, Logan crossed the rest of the room and into the kitchen, determined to like whatever it was they were talking about.

She was greeted by the sight of Adele pulling a tray out of the oven, while Jude practically bounced on her feet right next to her, eager to help. Logan registered that something about her looked different, but for a moment she couldn't tell what it was.

"Logan!" cried Jude, turning to beam at her. "Hey, do *you* think Eliana will like my haircut?"

Ah. Eliana, thought Logan, as some small thing within her quickly and silently deflated. *Well, the hero-worship had to end sometime. Better it be sooner.*

Outwardly, she blinked, giving herself a moment to take in the change. Jude's hair had been waist-length the last time she'd seen her, though it was nearly always pulled back in a braid. Now it was quite short, with one side cropped close to the head, the other falling across her forehead, not quite long enough to tuck behind her ear. On the short-cropped side, Logan noticed another change, too: bright streaks of neon yellow mixed into her natural black.

She raised an eyebrow at Adele, who had already slid the tray onto the counter and was now pulling off her oven mitts.

"I let you look after my ward for a week, and you bring her back with shorn locks?"

"I asked her to!" Jude blurted out before Adele had a chance to respond. "It was all my idea!"

Logan let a small smile pass through her lips as she shook her head.

"Just teasing, Jude," she said. "It looks great. Can't promise what Blake will think. She signed up for the Order voluntarily, remember. There's no accounting for taste."

Eliana Blake had not yet ceased to be a point of contention between Logan and Jude. She was letting Jude go visit her for a few days, but she'd also made it clear that she still didn't trust or particularly like Blake. She didn't trust *anyone* who worked for the Order, and Blake had yet to do anything that might make her think twice about that.

For the moment, however, Jude seemed oblivious to Logan's hostility. She tugged nervously on the longer side of her hair, failed to tuck it behind her ear, and smiled.

"I'm just nervous. And excited." Her smile widened. "I can't believe I'll be in New York in, like, four hours."

Logan blinked again, her vague memory of their last conversation swimming in her mind.

"Is that today? Huh. Time flies."

"Which is why you both need to eat your breakfast," said Adele. Logan could see she had put the automatic coffee pot on, which was good, as it had been over an hour since she downed the French press, and that wasn't nearly enough caffeine to get her through the day. Not after the week she'd had. "I was hoping we might all get in a shared meditation session before Jude and I leave in the afternoon."

Somewhat involuntarily, Logan's eyes flitted over to the opposite doorway—the one that opened in the direction of the lower levels. Where Savino Rossi lay locked in a cell.

"Yeah," she said slowly, walking over to the kitchen island. "Let's eat now. I'll need to…take a minute, before we get started with the session."

Adele's eyes narrowed in suspicion, but she said nothing. Jude glanced between the two of them.

"Is this about the Bound dude in the basement?"

"Yes," said Logan. She grabbed a plate and pointed to one of the pastries. "Which one's sugar-free?"

"On the right." Logan grabbed the one she indicated, slid it on her plate, and hopped up on a stool next to the island counter. Adele watched her as she did, and when she was seated, she continued. "I don't think you should go down there by yourself."

Logan pressed a finger into the side of her pastry to test the heat.

"I'm just gonna bring him some breakfast. If a polite conversation develops…well, I wouldn't want to be rude." She tore off a chunk of pastry and put it in her mouth. The spicy bite of field roast cut into the light, buttery crust quite nicely. She decided to focus on that, instead of Adele's disapproving stare.

In the silence, Jude took a pastry for herself before sitting next to Logan at the island. After a moment, she coughed.

"I could go down with you—"

"No," said Adele, her expression changing to panic.

"Absolutely not," said Logan, barely a second later. She took a breath, smiling painfully at herself. "Sorry, kid. Maybe another time. For now…it's gotta be just me." She glanced at Adele, hoping her words might give her some reassurance. "I know what I'm doing. And I've already beaten him in a fight. An exchange of words is *nothing*. Okay?"

Adele nodded reluctantly, worry and uncertainty etched into her warm brown eyes.

"On second thought, that's probably better," said Jude, letting out a sigh as she glanced between them. "If I were any more nervous, I'd probably pass out."

Logan chuckled and took another bite of her breakfast. After a moment, she looked over at Adele again, who had finally sat down to eat herself.

"Where's Knatt? He's usually up by now."

Adele took a bite herself before answering.

"I believe he's with your father." She kept her eyes on her plate as she cut fastidiously into her own pastry with a fork and knife. "Charles got confused last night and wandered out into the yard."

"Oh. I thought you said he hadn't left his room."

"He hadn't, before last night."

"Oh."

She said nothing more about it, instead choosing to eat the rest of her meal in peace. Eventually, Jude began chattering about all the things she might want to see in New York, and Logan gratefully let her steer the conversation from there. When the coffee was ready, she poured herself a cup and began to drink it as she searched for their small collection of paper bowls. She found one, and promptly filled it with a packet of instant oatmeal and a dash of water, before placing it in the microwave. The bowl couldn't be long for this world, but that was the point. By the time it was ready, she'd finished her coffee and filled up a small paper cup with lukewarm water.

Without another word, she slipped out of the kitchen. She could feel Adele's eyes on her as she went.

The deeper basement felt 20 degrees colder than the rest of the house, which was already struggling to keep up with the frigid November rains outside. Even Logan had to repress the urge to shiver.

The cage was just as she'd left it. She pulled the little lever near the bottom of the door, which opened up a small slot near her feet. She slid the paper bowl and cup through, then shut and locked it again.

Straightening once more, she located the lever toward the top and slid it open, revealing a small barred window that looked right into the cage.

Rossi lay flat on his back on the floor, on the far end of the room. The cell was perfectly round, the floor sloping slightly down toward the center, which was marked with a stone grate, long since stained a troubling muddy brown color.

His veins had completely receded from his face, making him look mostly normal once again. He'd been a burly man even before his Binding.

Logan coughed, loudly.

"Brought you breakfast," she announced, letting her voice ring out. "You really oughta eat, you know. Might get weak if you don't."

Slowly, Rossi opened his eyes and turned his head toward her.

"Shadow summoner," he growled. "Where have you taken me? Why did you not kill me?"

Logan rapped her nails against the metal door, letting the sound echo for a moment before she spoke again.

"I'll answer your questions if you answer mine." She said it like it was a challenge. She supposed, in a way, it was.

Rossi pulled his way into a sitting position, his back against the stone wall behind him.

"You think we are here to make an even exchange?" He barked out a laugh. "You hold me in chains, girl."

"I've chosen to think of you as a particularly unruly guest." She used a single finger to point down at the paper containers. "You should eat before it gets cold. It won't be great either way, but cold? Personally, I'd rather starve."

For a moment, he seemed intent on resisting her, but by now it had been at least 18 hours since the man had eaten, and Logan imagined that the appetite of the recently Bound would be even worse than her own, especially one who had so recently transformed.

Slowly but surely, he rose from his position and crossed the room, taking care to give the grate in the center a wide berth. She didn't blame him for that.

He picked up the tiny bowl and stared down in disbelief.

"What is this...paste?" He scowled up at her. "Shall I dip back my head and dribble it into my mouth, like the dying and infirm?"

"If that's what you want to do," said Logan, perfectly nonchalant. "You could also eat it with your fingers, although unfortunately you won't be given a shower while you stay with us. Management extends its regrets."

She could feel the heat rising in him, the urge to call to his powers. But that would only make him hungrier.

"A man needs *meat*, little girl," he grumbled.

Logan blinked at him.

"I'm not forcing you to eat it," she said, her tone light and cheerful. "Throw it away for all I care."

With one last growl, he tossed back his head and let the slop of mushy oats slide into his mouth all at once. When he was done, he threw the empty bowl against the wall. Logan pressed her face a little closer to the bars, though still far enough that all he could really do was wiggle his fingers at her.

"What's the Wolf planning?" she asked, her tone neutral and cold. "What does it have to do with me?"

Rossi flexed impotently, black veins running up his arms for a flash of a moment before they disappeared again.

"If I tell you, will you bring me *real* food?"

Logan cocked an eyebrow at him. He wasn't about to give in that easily, was he?

"I might be persuaded."

Rossi grinned darkly at her, then exploded in a burst of speed, slamming his body against the thick metal door with a deafening clang. Logan jumped back automatically.

"I told you, shadow summoner," he hissed, gripping the bars with the only two fingers he could fit through. "My master only wants you to realize your true potential. That is his *one and only* goal. The rest of it is all up to you."

Logan felt herself darkening against him.

"The Wolf wants me to realize my potential. And he thinks

I'm a killer." This time, it was her voice that sounded like a growl.

"Oh, so much more than that," said Rossi, sounding delighted. He let out a sudden, surprisingly high-pitched laugh. "*You will rip open the skin of the world.*"

Logan kept her expression neutral, though her gut gave a lurch. His words echoed her vision too closely to be mere coincidence. Swallowing down everything else her mind wanted to throw at her, Logan stood up straight and stepped toward him, pressing a cold smile onto her lips.

"What do you know about the bronze artifact?"

At last, Rossi faltered. His grip on the bars slackened ever so slightly, and uncertainty passed over his face. Then he blinked and recovered, forcing menace back into his features.

"You speak nonsense, girl."

"Oh, I don't think so." She cocked her head to the side, put her hands behind her back, and took another step toward him. She didn't know what the bronze artifact was, but she was willing to bet that Rossi had some idea. She took a stab in the dark, hoping to throw him further off balance. "Why is Volkov looking for it?"

Her gamble worked. She watched his expression waver, and knew that she'd guessed correctly. Whatever it was, Volkov didn't have it yet.

Before her, Rossi snarled.

"I will tell you nothing," he spat out. "I am not some child, playing at a game. Why don't you let me out of here, so I can show you how much of a *man* I truly am?"

Logan raised an eyebrow at him quizzically.

"Resorting to threats of sexual violence, are you? Mr. Rossi, have you let a *little girl* get under your skin so easily?"

His fingers tightened around the bars, though it wasn't nearly as threatening a gesture as she was sure he'd intended. He pushed his face right up to the metal, letting it contort his features until he looked deranged.

"Pointing out your cowardice, is all. Easy to poke fun at a man you hold in chains, instead of facing him in open combat."

"But I already beat you in open combat." Logan blinked impassively before deciding to press her luck. "And now I've gotten a confirmation from you that Volkov is, indeed, headed exactly where I think he's going, so I'll be able to stop him."

Rossi growled. "The Order cannot stop him, and neither can you. It does not matter what you know—the Wolf is always one step ahead."

The Order can't stop him, huh?

"But, unfortunately for you, it would seem his followers are not." With a shake of her head, she turned to leave him. "Goodbye, Mr. Rossi. I'll see what I can do about sending you some dinner later. I make no promises, of course."

His roar followed after her.

"You will rip open the world, shadow summoner!" he called after her. "No matter what you do, you cannot change your fate!"

Logan didn't bother to turn back. She kept moving forward, toward the light spilling in from the winding staircase to the upper levels. The faintest trace of a burn still lingered in her skin, but she paid it no mind.

Thanks to Rossi, she now knew that her vision had, at last, provided her some actionable information about the Wolf. The bronze artifact, whatever it was, was real, and Volkov was looking for it.

And from the sound of it, he believed that the Order had it.

That was enough to get started.

Chapter Three
A Simple Bridge

Jude woke up early. Her room was dark and a little cold, and she could already tell that today was going to be another wet, dreary winter day in the Pacific Northwest. Luckily for her, she knew she wouldn't end her day here.

I'm going to see Eliana today. She still couldn't quite believe it, no matter how many times she'd had it confirmed for her. A part of her didn't think she'd believe it even when it finally happened.

She swung her legs out of bed and immediately began looking for some thick socks, but then stopped herself. What had Adele just told her?

If you want to take your eira studies seriously, you should begin every day with a meditation—no matter how brief.

She pulled her legs back and folded them into a partial lotus, tucking her toes away from the chill. Then she took a long, deep breath, and started to count as she let it out.

I wonder if Logan is coming home today. Another breath, and a small internal shake.

What if she doesn't get back before I leave?
What if she's been hurt?

Stop it. Everything is fine. She took another deep breath, but it was a struggle to stay concentrated on it. Another breath, another struggle.

I'm going back to New York today.

Her next breath came out in a huff. She'd woken up early from the force of her own excitement, and now she couldn't seem to shake it off her. Too much had happened, too much was still happening. She and Eliana had fought a *demon* together. At long last, she hadn't run away. She'd faced something head-long, and she'd made her stand—

And I summoned fire. Intentionally this time.

Adele had been fairly concerned to learn about that last bit. She'd told Jude that while that was an impressive display of power, she needed to understand more about the necessary balance that eira casting requires before doing any more unsupervised summoning. But that didn't seem like much of a problem to Jude. After all, she was supervised most of the time, anyway. If summoning while supervised was okay, then she would just do that.

She shook herself again, and once more tried to clear her mind. If she could just meditate for one full minute, maybe that would be enough for today.

One full minute later, she sighed and decided she might as well put some socks on. Sure, she hadn't quite managed to clear her mind at all. But she had tried, and surely that had to count for something.

The socks she wanted turned out to be tucked under the corner of her nightstand, and once she had them secured on her feet, she stepped out onto the nice but cold wood floors of her bedroom. She crossed over to her curtains and pulled them back to get her first look at the day.

It did, indeed, already look to be a gloomy day. It was too dark to say for sure if the ground was already wet, so she couldn't say for sure if it would actually be rainy or only cloudy. She had woken up to this same gray for several days in a row, and though she wouldn't say she was entirely used to it yet, it had finally ceased to bother her. Though perhaps that was simply proof that nothing could puncture her excitement today.

As she moved to pull the curtain back, she caught sight of the blue-and-white striped fabric and paused on it. She had picked out the curtains herself, and then Logan had bought them. For the briefest moment, her mind flashed to her ex-girlfriend, Amy, and the last conversation they'd ever had. Amy had chided her for running off with a complete stranger like Logan. She'd implied she might be a murderer, or some other kind of monster. But the truth had somehow turned out both more and less strange than that.

Logan was certainly different from other people. Jude's mind strayed to a conversation she'd had with Adele a few days before. It came back to her easily, probably because of just how frequently she'd been thinking about it.

She was the one who'd started it.

"You and Logan keep telling me that eira is about connection," she'd said, fully aware that she might be about to put her own foot right inside her mouth. "And, like, meditation and all that. But I feel like I still don't know anything about it apart from that."

Adele had been outside in the back garden, despite the chilly gray skies, wearing a cozy sweater and drinking tea. She set her tea down on the stone table beside her.

"What is it you want to know?"

Jude blinked, taken aback. She wasn't sure what she expected when she'd started talking, but...total compliance with her request wasn't it. She scrambled to recover.

"Uh, well, for starters—I mean, what's the easiest eira summon to do?"

She felt her cheeks starting to burn as soon as she'd let it out of her mouth. She knew she sounded like a little kid, begging for video game stats or something.

But Adele just smiled patiently at her.

"It's different for different people, of course," she'd said. "But typically, most people seem to grasp fire and water first. Ancient eira Masters claimed that it was because their substantial but transient natures made them more similar to the human spirit than the rest. But the truth is anyone's guess." She'd paused briefly, studying Jude's no doubt expectant features. With an indulgent nod of her head, she continued. "The next easiest is earth, though there are some important caveats to that. One must build one's strengths the same as if you were starting to lift weights with your own two hands, only you begin like an infant rather than a full-grown person. Years of practice may eventually allow one's eira power to be greater than their bodily limitations, but it takes true devotion. I have never known anyone to summon anything larger than a car...and even that was only once.

"Even harder than earth to summon are air and shadow. For most, they prove...difficult to pin down. Perhaps difficult to understand, in a way. Or perhaps our own connection to the immaterial is simply difficult to face, difficult to accept. As you might have guessed, eira Masters have contemplated the reasons some things come easier than others for centuries, and we have yet to come to a true consensus.

"The most difficult to summon for any extended period of time is light. Again, we theorize that light may simply be the hardest concept to understand, on a deeper level. Properties of particle as well as wave, and all that. Or maybe it's another reason all together. Mind you, I have seen a novice here or there manage a single bright flash in a moment of inspiration, but sustained light? Only a true Master can do that."

Jude took a moment to absorb all this information. She loved spending time with Adele, both because of her generally kind personality and for her incredible wealth of knowledge in a kind of magic that Knatt and Logan both seemed reluctant to discuss. But sometimes Adele's depth of information felt like a tidal wave, and she was left in its wake trying to sort out the connections hidden in the detail.

"Okay. So…I know Logan can summon shadow…and air." Remembering the time she'd actually seen Logan summon air, she stumbled. It almost felt like she was exposing a secret, even though she was sure Adele knew about the ability itself. She was less sure if Adele knew about the incident, but she wasn't about to explain that herself. She blinked and spoke again. "If those are almost the hardest…does that mean Logan is an eira Master?"

At that, Adele let out a hearty laugh.

"Oh, goddess, no." She'd picked up her mug again, almost like she needed to give herself a moment to recover, and took a deep sip. When she was done, she glanced at Jude over her cup, her expression regretful. "I'm sorry. That was—*abrupt* of me."

She put her tea back on the table and sighed. "The thing about Henrietta that makes her…unique…is not that she can perform two difficult summons when so few can. It's the fact that she can hardly summon anything else."

In the present, Jude echoed her previous blink, still somewhat confused by this revelation.

"Huh?"

"Henrietta never finished her training. She has come back to T'eira'han a few times over the years, but she's always gone away again before we manage to make any progress." She smiled, her expression a strange mix of sadness and pride. "After a while, I had to accept that the choice had been taken out of both of our hands. Every time she comes back, a vision takes her away again. Well, ever since the first time, anyway."

Jude turned away from the window, back towards the bed she had vacated with such haste. She knew her weak attempt at meditation didn't really count. She knew she should try again.

She had just reached the edge of the bed when she heard a noise coming from downstairs—from the kitchen, most likely. It sounded like either Adele or Knatt had gotten up. She glanced up at Mortimor, the stuffed moose sitting right next to her pillow. His eyes, as always, were doleful.

"You won't judge me, right?"

He said nothing.

She grabbed the pair of jeans poking out from under her bed, dragged them on, and went out the door.

After breakfast, Adele counseled Jude to give herself a few moments to digest and contemplate on her own before she joined her for their guided meditation practice. Apparently, Adele believed it would help them to clear their minds if they practiced outside. In the cold, gray outdoors.

Just inside the back door that led out to the garden, Jude watched Logan slip on her usual motorcycle jacket before reaching for her new windbreaker—which happened to be the same bright yellow as the streaks in her new, partially buzzed hair. On automatic impulse, Jude ran a hand through the buzzed section before pulling on her gloves, too.

"This is not gonna be comfortable, is it?" she asked, peering through the glass in the door. Adele was already outside, sitting in full lotus on the cold stone patio, a small overnight bag beside her.

"Eira Masters have their own idea of comfort," Logan responded, glancing up at the sky, as if wondering what the chances were they'd all be soaked within the hour. "If you can connect with the elements and keep them all in balance…you can never be uncomfortable."

"Really?"

Logan shrugged. "That's what they say. But honestly it could all be a front. There'd be no way of knowing."

Jude looked at her out of the corner of her eye, a small smile forming on her face. "You don't trust anyone, do you?"

"I really don't."

With a rueful shake of her head, Jude pushed the door open and led them outside.

Adele opened her eyes as they approached. She looked perfectly serene, despite the frigid air and visible dampness of the stone beneath her.

"Take a seat, you two," she commanded, pointing each of them where to go. "And make sure to face each other as you do."

They both sat down. Jude couldn't help but shudder as she did, and even though Logan was rarely as bothered by the cold as she was, she saw her barely perceptible flinch as she did the same. Logan folded her legs neatly into a lotus, so Jude did the same.

"I think we'll start with a lesson," said Adele. She reached into the bag and pulled out three candles, handing one each to Jude and Logan, and keeping one herself. "The candles will help to guide and center us, as they have helped eira Masters for generations."

Once a candle was placed between each of them, forming a kind of circle with their bodies, all three roared to life at the same time. Uncommonly large flames shot up from their wicks, unleashing a sudden wave of heat before settling back down to normal size.

"Eira is a natural magic," Adele continued, as if nothing out of the ordinary had happened. "To practice it, you must allow yourself to fully connect to the natural world, and you must learn how to understand its balance, and your place in it. As such, eira stands in direct contrast to letha, which is unnatural magic, and unnatural dominion. Where eira is balance, letha is imbalance. No true eira Master would perform letha, and no one steeped in letha can ever become a true eira Master." She turned her gaze to Logan. "Henri, have you told Jude the creation story?"

Logan raised her right eyebrow skeptically.

"Uh—you know I'm not much for mythology, Del."

"Well, not to worry," said Adele serenely. "Now is as good a time as ever. Close your eyes, both of you."

Jude closed her eyes first, and could only guess if Logan followed suit. For a moment, nothing happened. Then Adele began to speak,

"This is the story as it is told in the Temple of the Moon, known to most descendants of the dark faith. The story begins where all stories begin, whether they know it or not: in the Heart of the World. Some say the Heart is a forest, others say it is a garden. But the only thing we need to know for this story is that this is where the storm-eyed god Ishta lived before she created the many worlds, and left this one to tend them all."

Before Jude could even begin to wrap her mind around those words, a strange thing happened: without her trying, a glowing, hazy image formed in her mind. She couldn't quite tell if it was her own imagination or if somehow Adele had somehow put the image there, but her money was on the latter. The image showed her an arboretum of sorts, with twisting, twirling plant life growing all around it, and a being of pure light at the very center. Jude thought the image looked familiar somehow, but she couldn't say exactly how.

"Ishta, the Maker, was then as she is now—all things at once, and entirely alone. She has no equal, and as such, no natural companion. In her time before the many worlds, her loneliness became too much to bear. That was how she came to create our world—the first of the many." The garden faded, replaced by the Earth as seen from far above it. "But our world still held no equal for her, and so she tried again. This time, she created for herself two daughters. At T'eira'han, we call them Laleh and Evet—or, sometimes, Letha and Eira."

53

The garden in her mind remained, but now it held three figures: a mother and her two children.

"For a time, they lived happily together as a family. But Ishta knew when she began that she would not be able to remain with them in the Heart forever. She had too many duties that called her away from them. That was why she made two—so that when she had to leave them, they would have each other for company.

"When that time came for Ishta, she traveled to the very center of the Heart of the World, which was where she kept the Source of All Things. She took the Source and locked it away, and she told Laleh and Evet that they were to stay away from it and never, under any circumstances, let it out of its containment."

As she spoke, the woman in the garden picked up a bright ball of some unnamable substance, put it down inside a heavy-looking chest, and used her hands to shape her shiny magic, which slowly formed into a giant lock that snapped itself around the entire chest. Then her two daughters appeared, and she seemed to warn them away.

"For a time, the sisters were happy without their Maker. They played together in the Heart of the World, and they were as joyous and carefree as any children have ever been. But Ishta had made them in her own image, and like the human soul, Ishta's soul is a restless one. It was only a matter of time before they, too, became restless.

"When their games within the Heart grew tiresome, they tried to escape. They tried to enter into the true world—our world. But though Ishta had gifted them with powers, her own powers were greater than theirs, and so they could not cross the boundary she had made to keep them confined within the Heart.

Still, they were curious little girls, and relentless in their own way. They quickly discovered that though they could not enter the world, they could still affect it with their own powers.

"It is not known whether Laleh and Evet created the demons, or whether they simply opened windows in the walls between worlds, letting the demons inside from there. Whichever way it was, *that* was how demons entered into our world.

"While Ishta turned a blind eye, the sisters grew beyond the confines of their childhood. One day, the sisters went for a walk and found themselves in the very center—in the heart of the Heart. They had not been there for quite some time, and they had nearly forgotten what lay there. But as they laid their eyes on the Source of All Things, they remembered."

Two girls came to a stop in front of a giant shining object; the light coming off of it now shined so brightly that it obscured its true shape, if it still had one.

"Before they saw the Source, both sisters had held the same question: how could they escape this garden and make their way into the world that waited beyond?

"But as they gazed at the Source, a rift formed in the Heart of the World. For the very first time, the sisters' thoughts differed from one another. Evet thought: *The Source could make us powerful, but perhaps it is not wise.* And Laleh thought: *The Source could make us powerful, and I want to be powerful.*

"And so a rift was formed."

The two girls stood on either side of the glowing object. Light shot out of the object in two directions, seeming to split their world neatly in two, each on one side of the division.

"Laleh moved to free the Source, but Evet moved to stop her.

'We must not,' she said, 'for we do not know what it will do. What if we destroy the world?' But Laleh laughed. 'If we destroy the world,' she said, 'then we will create another. And what fun that will be!'

"Like her sister, Evet still wanted to leave the Heart, but Laleh's words frightened her. Perhaps they had already acted wrongly; perhaps they never should have come here at all. She tried to get her sister to turn away from the Source, but to no avail: the rift had already grown deeper than she knew. Already Laleh could not be swayed from her goal; already she resented her sister's hesitance.

"By the time storm-eyed Ishta sensed the rift in the Heart of the World, she was too late—just as Evet was too late. Laleh used every ounce of her power to break open the Source of All Things, and when she did, chaos itself was unleashed on the world. Chaos broke down the barrier between the Heart and the true world, and chaos let all manner of power out along with it. Laleh herself disappeared into the true world, and with that, she was lost to the Heart forever.

"Evet, on the other hand, did not choose to leave the garden that day. She remained behind to await Ishta's judgment, and together, they pulled back what they could of the Source, and they locked it away again.

"Before she reformed the barrier, Ishta turned to Evet to ask what had transpired in her absence. Evet confessed it all. 'To amuse ourselves, we sent terrors into the world, even though we knew it was your creation,' she said, finally humbled by her sins. 'It was Laleh who unleashed the Source, but it was I who failed to stop her.'

"Ishta heard her child's words and understood. 'You could not stop her because you wished to go with her,' the Maker proclaimed, and Evet knew it was true. Ishta knew what her judgment had to be, though whether it was a judgment on her child or herself, she did not know. 'You must leave the Heart as your sister has, my child. She has brought great power into the world, and so you must go into it, as a balance for that power. Only when the world has found a permanent balance may you return to the Heart, to spend eternity by my side.

"And so it was that Evet was cast out of the Heart of the World, to make her way in our world, instead. It is her eternal wish to reunite with her sister and her mother, but it is a wish that may never be fulfilled. And it is *her* connective spirit that we Masters channel. It is her spirit which you must channel now."

The images had continued moving with her words, but as she said her last, the images vanished, leaving a curious void in their wake.

"All right. Let's get started." Adele's voice pulled Jude back out of the darkness, though she remembered to keep her eyes closed. "You two have performed the bonding ritual before, so this shouldn't be as difficult for you as it is for most. You're going to use eira to connect."

In the brief silence that followed, Jude coughed.

"Uh, connect? What does that mean?"

"She wants us to mind-meld," said Logan. Something in her voice sounded reluctant, almost resentful.

"Mind-meld, like in Star Trek?"

"That's Henri's crude way of putting it, yes," said Adele, sounding a little irritated. "The bonding has created a passageway between your two minds. It has opened a door within each of you. If you're both willing, you can *use* that passageway as a bridge to communicate with each other without ever saying a word, no matter how great the distance between you."

"Perfect reception, now in all 50 states."

"Henri, please."

"I'm paying attention, I promise."

"Good. So, I want you both to take a moment to clear your minds. When the mind is clear, focus on creating a space for yourself within your mind—a place you can always return to when you feel threatened or overwhelmed. It can look like anything, so long as you are alone there, and safe."

Over the past few days of practice with Adele, Jude had gotten pretty good at this part. In her mind, she saw a bright, sunny field, full of flowers of every imaginable color. It stretched in every direction, as far as the eye could see. She hadn't exactly based it on anywhere she could consciously remember, though she got the vague feeling that maybe she'd been somewhere like it when she was a very small child. Whatever it was, it made her feel safe. And that seemed to be the point.

"Now, imagine a light in front of you, slowly expanding. Let it expand away from you, reaching beyond the confines of your space. Let it form the bridge."

Jude took a deep breath, giving herself a moment in the safe space before continuing. She could feel her anxiety creeping in, so she did her best to keep it at bay. One breath in, one breath out. Just like Adele had taught her.

Once she was focused back in on her body, imagining the light was easy. She saw it right there in her little garden, only a few feet away. As she watched, it grew and transformed, turning into a doorway. She imagined herself approaching it, and so she did approach it. It opened as soon as she reached out, and beyond it she could see what looked like a completely different world. It looked like a beach surrounded by tall, black cliffs…

But then it flickered. The door itself seemed to waver, like a television improperly tuned.

"Can you see the bridge?" asked Adele.

"Y-yes," said Jude. She didn't hear Logan say anything.

"Go toward it."

Jude took another step, willing herself to be certain. The door was right there, if she could only get through it—but as she stepped forward, it receded. She stepped again, and again it fell away. She reached out her hand, and it seemed to shudder and lose its shape.

"Uh, I don't think it's working," said Jude, hesitantly. "I don't think I'm doing it right."

"Can you see a bridge?" asked Logan, her voice only a few feet away in the real world.

"I thought I did, but—now I'm not so sure."

"Well, take a step back and try again."

Jude did as she was told. She stepped back, took a breath, refocused on the blissful peace of the flower field, and tried again.

And nothing happened. And nothing happened some more.

"Uh, I think it's just…gone. I don't see anything anymore. I don't know why."

Logan said nothing. After a moment, Adele spoke.

"That's all right." She sounded as calm and even as ever. "We'll try again another time. Henri, you can leave us, now.

Jude, let's go back inside. I have a book I want to give you before you go."

Jude opened her eyes just in time to see something cross over Logan's face. It almost looked like…satisfaction. Like she was pleased with something. But it was gone as quick as it came, and without another word, Logan hopped up from the table and walked away from them, disappearing into the house in a matter of seconds.

Shame settled into Jude's stomach, like it had always been there. Was Logan so disgusted with her failure that she didn't even warrant a glance backward?

She felt Adele gently touch the back of her hand and looked up.

"Let's go inside, Jude."

So they did.

When they began the ritual, Logan thought little of it. She'd done it before at Other Side, and though it had been awhile, the muscle memory remained. She knew exactly how to clear her mind and escape to her own secret space, and how to call upon the bridge that always waited.

She imagined the same thing she always did: a secluded beach on a gray day, high cliffs of blackened stone forming a wall between herself and the rest of the world. Nothing but the sound of the waves to keep her company.

She willed herself to stay focused on the cold sand, the waves, the gray sky, the black rocks. But into her silence, another voice spoke.

You will tear open the skin of the world.

Even in the cold, the Choronzon Key felt hot.

"Now, imagine a light in front of you, slowly expanding," said Adele, still guiding them along the way. "Let it expand away from you, reaching beyond the confines of your space. Let it form the bridge."

Logan imagined the light, as she had done before. She let it grow and twist and arc outward, until it started to look like a bridge.

You're a killer.

Her bridge flickered. She was already starting to wonder if it might be a terrible idea to let Jude see this place, see her true self. Her mind had never been a particularly safe place to be.

"Can you see the bridge?" asked Adele.

"Y-yes," said Jude, while Logan merely nodded.

"Go toward it."

On her cold, gray beach, Logan took a step toward her faltering, flickering bridge. Even though the movement was a simple one, and imaginary at that, her heart started to race. Perhaps she should have known Adele would want her to try this; after all, she'd been the main proponent of the practice back when Logan had stayed with her at Other Side. But it had been so long since she'd done it, and so much had changed since then.

Still, she pressed forward, again and again. She was almost on it now. One more step.

In her mind, her foot pressed onto the first step—only for the bridge to disappear completely.

She said nothing at first. Focusing back in on the protection of the silent cliffs all around her, she tried to call the bridge back.

A spark, then nothing. And more nothing, and more

nothing. One minute stretched into two.

"Uh, I don't think it's working," said Jude, hesitantly. "I don't think I'm doing it right."

Logan breathed a silent sigh of relief. Out loud, she said, "Can you see a bridge?"

"I thought I did, but—now I'm not so sure."

"Well, take a step back and try again."

She knew it wouldn't work, of course. If she couldn't connect on her side, Jude wouldn't be able to, either. Sure enough, after a few more minutes of silence, Jude sighed.

"Uh, I think it's just…gone. I don't see anything anymore. I don't know why."

Because I can't let you in, Logan thought but didn't say.

"That's all right," said Adele, perfectly calm. "We'll try again another time. Henri, you can leave us, now. Jude, let's go back inside. I have a book I want to give you before you go."

Logan stood up as quickly as she could and hurried away from the others. She wasn't sure if she saw Adele glance at her sideways or not, but it didn't matter. For a moment, she'd almost been embarrassed of her failure. But as she shut the door behind her, she told herself that it was for the best. Jude was still at a vulnerable time in her personal journey, and Logan couldn't say for sure what the impact of intimate contact with her own mind might do to someone at that age.

After all, the farther she could keep everyone from her demon side, the better.

Chapter Four
Big City

A few hours later, it was time for both Adele and Jude to take their leave. Logan and Knatt escorted them both to the traveling room, with Logan carrying Adele's heaviest bag for her. They entered into the large circular chamber on the far end of the west wing of the house, with its echoing marble walls covered in indecipherable glyphs and its many doors, each as heavy and imposing as the last.

Jude still had a slightly shell-shocked look of awe every time she entered the room. Logan hoped she never lost that.

"Well, don't forget to call your old aunt," said Adele, turning to Logan and stretching out her arms. Logan carefully hefted her bag to the floor before stepping into Adele's hug.

"You're not old," she said.

"Oh, yes I am," said Adele into Logan's hair. "But I like being old." She gave her a squeeze before she let her go. Logan felt almost certain that there was an extra meaning in her words, but she couldn't put her finger on what it was.

By now, she had turned to face Jude.

"Jude, until we meet again." She swept Jude into a hug, as well.

"Welcome to the family. And remember what we talked about, hm?"

"Yeah, of course. Uh, thanks." As Adele let her go, Jude turned bright red and began staring aggressively at the floor. Logan suspected that she wasn't quite used to Adele's brand of all-consuming comfort hugs.

"And Hugh." Adele turned to Knatt, her expression soft and warm. "Take care of the young ones, won't you?"

"Always." This time, it was Knatt who initiated the embrace.

At last, Adele shouldered her own heavy bag with surprising ease, while Knatt muttered words over one of the skeleton keys and placed it in one of the west-facing doors. It swung open to reveal a lush, untamed forest. Adele stepped across the threshold without hesitation, pausing only to wave happily back at them as the door swung shut once more.

"Was that Other Side?" asked Jude curiously.

"Not quite," said Knatt. "We can't actually open a door directly to T'eira'han—or Other Side, as you know it. The magic that permits its existence also prevents us from using *this* magic to access it. But Adele will have no trouble making the rest of the journey on her own, rest assured."

Jude nodded, then checked her watch. "I should probably get going. I was hoping to—ah, nevermind. Uh, I guess I'll see you guys in a week, yeah?"

"If you need us for any reason, don't hesitate to call," said Knatt, offering her a fatherly pat on the shoulder. "And do remember to stay safe, won't you?"

"Absolutely." Jude could barely contain her excited grin. "Gah, I still can't believe I'm about to see New York! I mean, for real, this time."

Logan let out a chuckle. "Bring us back a souvenir."

"I will!"

Knatt picked out a new skeleton key and muttered more inaudible words over it. This time, Logan caught the faint glow it emitted for just a second before turning back to normal. He walked this one over to an east-facing door and put it in the lock.

Jude's beaming face turned to Logan.

"Looks like your ride is here," said Logan, nodding at the waiting portal door.

"Yeah. Guess I should take off." For a moment, Jude remained where she was, looking almost expectantly at Logan. Then she reached out and gave her a quick hug, which Logan did her best to reciprocate. As she pulled back, she whispered cryptically, "Tell him I knew he would be late, will ya?"

Before Logan had fully registered her words, Jude took off like a light, running the rest of the distance between her and the east-facing door. Logan watched the door open up into a wide, carpeted, sterile-looking hallway. The door remained open just long enough for her to make out the crackling sound of an announcer's voice, forced out over a loudspeaker into an echoing space, before it shut tight once more.

"That was weird," said Logan, still staring at the now-closed portal. "Do you know what she—"

She never got to finish her sentence. Right at that moment, the Choronzon Key erupted on her back, and her vision went dark.

Remember what we talked about, hm?

Jude blinked on the other side of the doorway, Adele's words inexplicably ringing in her ears. She was pretty sure she knew what it meant, though technically, she could tell herself that it might have meant a number of things.

But she knew. She let out a sigh and shook herself, deciding to put the thought away for now. She had things to do, places to go. As she made her way down the airport hallway, she zipped her winter coat up all the way to her chin, her backpack slung snugly across her shoulders. She didn't think she was ever going to get used to the whiplash of walking from one side of the country to the other in the span of a second; she hadn't even asked Logan if the traveling room could take them to other countries, though now that she thought about it, there didn't seem an obvious reason why it wouldn't.

So weird. So cool.

Knatt had done his best to send her to a relatively empty section of JFK, and he'd succeeded. She'd been walking for nearly two full minutes before she came across another person.

Of course, that person happened to be a security guard. The part of Jude's brain that remembered that what she was doing was against the rules—she was behind the security line, but she hadn't bought a ticket—started to panic. But she reminded herself that nobody knew what a traveling room was, which meant nobody had any reason to suspect her of anything. So, she pasted on what she hoped was a nonchalant smile and kept on walking.

Still, she was beyond relieved when she finally saw the sign for baggage claim, pointing her to the outside world. Once she was on the other side of that, she'd no longer be bending any rules.

And Eliana will be there.

Her heart sped up again. To calm her nerves, she ducked into the next bathroom she saw to give herself a once-over. She smiled automatically when she saw her new haircut in the reflection. Her mother had decided how her hair would look for most of her life. Though she'd been allowed to make her own choice about it for months now, she'd had trouble believing it. It had taken a gentle nudge from one Sasha Ren, a self-professed psychic from Boston, to get her to take that last step into freedom.

She still didn't know much about styling, of course, so when she saw herself in the mirror, she had to settle for shaking one hand through the longer side, trying to create something like the artfully messy look Alexei Marin seemed to have down pat. It nearly worked for about three seconds, until she tilted her head to the side and it all fell flat again.

Even so, she got a rush of pleasure from how quickly her fingertips slipped through the ends. There was something about the lightness of her own head now that felt so good. It felt so *her*. It was almost like she'd literally cut away the last false part of herself and left it behind.

A few short minutes later, she saw the archway announcing the exit, and she rushed toward it. The airport was busier on this end, and she had a little trouble pushing through the crowds to get closer to the doors. Intent as she was on finding her way outside, she almost missed the sound of someone calling her name.

"Jude! Jude Li! Hey, Jude!"

Jude jumped in surprise and spun toward the sound. There, not ten feet away from her, stood Eliana Blake, grinning like a maniac. She wore the customary uniform for a new Adept of the Order of Shadows: black military slacks and jacket, with a small insignia of a sword struck through the sun embroidered over the left breast pocket. Right now, she had no marks on her sleeve and collar, but if she ever achieved a high enough rank, she might. Her long, shiny black hair was pulled back from her face in a high ponytail, and her dark almond-shaped eyes carried her smile home.

"Elli," said Jude, managing barely more than a whisper. She felt like someone had hit the mute button on the rest of the world, and the only people not affected were the two of them.

For what might have been an eternity but was probably only a moment, they both stood perfectly still, eyes locked like missiles. Then, without another word, they both stepped forward, their bodies colliding in an awkwardly chaste hug. Jude let out a small, involuntary giggle and prayed Eliana didn't notice. A weird electric current ran through her body, lighting her nerves on fire.

After a moment that was simultaneously too long and not quite long enough, they broke apart. Jude cast her eyes toward the ground, already sheepish and uncertain. She was moderately sure that they'd both gone in for that hug, but a little nagging voice reminded her that maybe she was only seeing what she wanted to see.

"Uh, hi," she said, glancing up at Eliana as boldly as she dared.

"Hi," said Eliana, her eyes wide as she took in all of Jude's features. "Hey, did you get a haircut?"

Jude's hand went up to her hair, automatically trying to tuck it behind her ear, even though it wasn't long enough anymore. "Uh, yeah." She had never felt so self-conscious in her life.

Eliana's smile was warm, like melted chocolate.

"You look good with short hair," she said.

An undoubtedly goofy smile drifted across Jude's marshmallow-soft face.

"You think?"

"Well, you'd probably look good in anything." She winked, and Jude felt a part of herself die. "So, did you have another bag, or should we get going?"

"Oh—uh—this is my only bag."

"Great." She grabbed hold of Jude's hand, sending another electric shiver through her body. "Follow me."

With that, they were off and running, Eliana directing them with practice and ease. One short taxi ride later, Jude got her first bona-fide New York experience: riding the subway. Already, Jude found New York to be exhilarating and terrifying, in equal parts.

"Sorry about this," said Eliana as she paid for Jude's ticket. "We technically could have taken a cab the whole way, but Headquarters only issues us so much for incidentals, and…well, this is way, way cheaper."

"No need to apologize," said Jude, staring in wonder at the subterranean platform ahead. "I've, uh…well, I've never been on the subway before. It's kinda cool."

"Really?" As she handed her the card, Eliana smiled again, a smile that melted a river in Jude's heart. "In that case, just consider this the first of many adventures."

She grabbed her hand again before leading them through the

turnstile. The rush of people and sounds and smells all around them was chaotic and indecipherable. Jude vaguely remembered every chase scene she'd ever seen set in New York, and she felt like she suddenly had a deeper understanding of the lack of realism. If Eliana weren't there to guide her, she knew she'd be completely lost.

As they entered into the first real subway car she'd ever gone on, she almost wished she could take a snapshot of her life right at that moment and show it off to everyone she'd ever hated in high school. In high school, she'd been the weird angry Asian dyke who got her clothes stolen out of the locker room. Now, she was a short-haired monster hunter running around New York and holding hands with the most effortlessly cool girl she'd ever met. She wasn't sure she could have come up with a better future for herself if she'd tried.

In reality, of course, she never wanted to see any of those people again, even if it meant showing off. Some doors were better left closed.

Fortunately for her, Eliana knew exactly what she was doing. While Jude focused on getting one foot in front of the other, Eliana had hopped them from one platform to another and was now charging them through the crowds, right onto the last car of a departing train, just before the doors slid shut.

"Here, let's grab these seats," said Eliana, already leading the way. Once they were settled onto the hard plastic seats, she turned to Jude again. "Wow, I can't believe I haven't asked this yet. How was your flight?"

Jude was so windswept by the day she was having that she'd nearly forgotten her own cover story.

"Oh, yeah, uh, it was fine," she said, with what she hoped was a convincing shrug.

"Direct flight?"

"Y-yeah, it was." She hadn't even looked up a specific flight to pretend she was on, so she certainly hoped Eliana wasn't going to pursue this line of questioning for long. Fortunately for her, Eliana seemed as uninterested in testing this story as Jude had been with fortifying it.

"Well, I know you came a pretty long way, but I hope you've got some energy left." She gave Jude a mysterious look. "If you're up for it, I thought we might kick off your first visit to New York in style."

Jude smiled, feeling the last remnants of her trepidation melting away.

"I'm up for anything. What did you have in mind?"

Eliana winked at her again.

"No spoilers. Don't want to ruin the surprise."

Exhilarating and terrifying, in equal parts.

Eventually, they ended up at an apartment in Brooklyn that Eliana referred to as her "walk-up," a term Jude only put together when they trudged up four flights of stairs to get to it.

"The nice thing about it is the easy roof access," Eliana explained, pointing to a metal door in the ceiling above them as they rounded the final landing. "If we get called to break up a nest, sometimes that's the fastest way to get there."

"Over the roof?"

"Yeah. Less traffic, fewer witnesses." She came to a stop in front of one of the identical metal doors leading off the cramped, drafty hallway they were walking through. She glanced back at Jude to give her a sly smile. "I run pretty fast now."

With that, she unlocked the door and swung it wide, letting them inside. Before she'd even stepped into the apartment, she could hear the fake fight sounds of a video game, along with the angry cursing of someone who wasn't playing it well. *Sounds like Fisher's home.*

When Eliana had first asked Jude if she'd wanted to come visit, she'd explained up-front that she and her best friend, and fellow Order Adept, Ian Fisher had already moved out of their shared dorm at the Order headquarters and into a two-bedroom apartment in Brooklyn. Apparently, they were subletting it illegally from two other Adepts who'd been sent on an international mission for a month. She said they'd find a permanent place as soon as they got their permanent assignments, but for now, they were just happy for the taste of freedom, even if it wouldn't last. Jude could relate.

Jude hadn't exactly made friends with Ian Fisher yet, but she was hopeful that would change on this trip. After all, at the very least, he had to have agreed to her visit, right?

As Jude squeezed into the tight entryway after Eliana, shuffling around to make room for the door to close again, she realized how small Eliana and Ian's borrowed apartment was. They passed the kitchen, which looked like it could fit maybe four people into it comfortably, provided they all stood absolutely straight and still. In the living room, someone had managed to squeeze a wall-mounted TV, a tiny coffee table, and a very low, slim couch, that could maybe fit three people at a stretch.

Well, good thing I'm the only guest, I guess. There's exactly enough room.

She realized, of course, how spoiled she probably was from living at the Logan estate. If you included her large personal bathroom and the wide hallway in front of her room, there was a good chance this entire apartment would fit in the same space as her room. Of course, it was far and away the largest, grandest place she'd ever lived. It blew her high school bedroom out of the water.

And yet, despite the cramped quarters, she couldn't think of anything better than this tiny apartment in Brooklyn. *And they have rooftop access! Am I gonna get to go on a rooftop in Brooklyn?*

"Can I take your bag, or did you wanna change?" asked Eliana.

All at once, Jude came back to earth. They were standing on the precipice of the living room now, and she could see Fisher on the couch, wearing the same beanie he'd worn every time she'd seen him, along with gray sweatpants and an open Order of Shadows uniform jacket over what looked like an indie band T-shirt. He didn't even look up from his game when they entered.

"Nah, I'm good. Unless, am I supposed to look fancy where we're going?"

"No, not at all. I just wanna make sure you're comfortable."

"Oh, yeah, I'm fine." She shifted her bag off her shoulders, made sure to grab her wallet from the outer pocket, and handed it over. "So, where are we headed?"

Suddenly, Fisher paused his game and glanced over at them.

"You're not doing what I think you're doing, are you?"

Eliana shook her head as she opened the nearest bedroom door just long enough to toss Jude's bag on the bed. Jude's heart seemed to speed up again as she realized her backpack was now sitting on Eliana Blake's own personal, albeit borrowed, bed.

"None of your fucking business, Fisher."

"It is! Man, you're a fucking cheeseball, Blake."

"What's it matter to you? You're not invited." She stuck her tongue out at him, and Jude was suddenly, briefly, reminded of her own little sister, sticking her tongue out at her little brother…

Not going there, she told herself firmly. *Memories of my family are not going to ruin my trip to New York.*

"Should we get going, then?" asked Eliana, motioning toward the door.

"Absolutely."

And with that, they were off again.

Jude wasn't sure how long it would take her to feel comfortable in the New York subway system, but she was starting to suspect that it wasn't going to happen on this trip. She followed Eliana blindly, grateful for every time that Elli grabbed her hand to make sure she didn't lose her in the crowd.

And despite how incredibly lost Jude was at all times, they still managed to make their way out again. As they emerged above ground in the middle of Manhattan, Jude found herself overwhelmed once more. There were so many sounds, so many people, so many giant buildings all around her. She was starting to feel like she was losing all sense of space and scale. She'd never been anywhere so *full* before. If she were completely honest, she'd admit that she was already feeling just a little tired of it. Feeling overwhelmed every 20 minutes was starting to exhaust her. Still, the excitement hadn't yet faded enough for exhaustion to take over.

They traveled another four blocks on foot, taking a simple route that Jude immediately forgot. Then they passed through one last crosswalk, and Eliana squeezed Jude's hand and pulled them to a stop, making a sweeping motion to indicate the area just in front of them.

Jude blinked several times, slowly taking in where they were and doing her best to keep her cool.

"Is this…is this Rockefeller Center?"

Not ten feet away from them, a metal railing demarcated a steep, man-made drop-off into perhaps the most iconic ice-skating rink in the world: the rink at Rockefeller Center.

"I told you we were gonna start in style," said Eliana, grinning at her.

"Holy shit!"

With their hands still clasped, Jude ran toward the railing to get as good a look as she could. She took in the shiny golden statue on one side, the giant cement staircase on the other, the various national flags all around. There were still tons of people everywhere, but for some reason, in the midst of this little pocket of wide-open air above the frozen pool, Jude found it a little less overwhelming. She *knew* about this place, even if she'd never seen it before.

As a bonus, plenty of people here were bound to be tourists. So, at least for today, there might be a few people around who were less cool than she was.

Deciding to take a chance while she felt safe, Jude gave Eliana a knowing smile.

"This is great," she said, "because, see, now all I gotta do is show up some Midwestern tourists."

Eliana cocked her head to the side.

"I mean, technically, you *are*—"

"Ah! See, *technically*, I'm a Pacific Northwestern tourist. It's a totally different thing."

Eliana laughed. "You're right, totally different thing. Well, wanna go show the tourists what's what?"

"Yes, I do!"

So, they made their way down the wide staircase and over to the desk to rent two pairs of skates. Jude couldn't even remember the last time she'd gone ice skating, but she didn't care. They were there, and they were going to have fun. That was all that mattered.

"Just a warning, I'm probably terrible," said Eliana as they laced up. "I was never any good when I was a kid."

"Then we can fall down together," said Jude.

As it turned out, Jude was correct, but Eliana was not. It took them both a little while to find their footing, and at first, they stumbled around the rink together, in sync in their clumsiness. But by their second time around, Eliana had already found her center of balance.

"You just gotta keep your ankles super straight," she told Jude, in what was probably meant to be a helpful tone.

"If I could do that, we wouldn't be in this situation."

Jude had barely managed to get the words out before one of her feet slid in exactly the wrong direction. She would have tumbled head-first into the ice if Eliana hadn't been right there to catch her before she fell.

"You know, I'm beginning to feel like you lied to me," said

Jude. She tried to sound more playful than bitter.

"Sorry," said Eliana sheepishly. "I...I think it's because of the Binding, as weird as that may sound."

Jude glanced at her quizzically. "The Binding gave you special skating powers?"

"Well, no, it's more like—I have a better sense of what my body is supposed to do now. You know?"

"You're saying you're supernaturally graceful."

"I guess, yeah."

"Great. Well, now I feel really confidant."

Eliana let out a gentle laugh. "Why don't we take a break and grab a hot chocolate, huh?"

"Yeah. Yeah, I like that plan."

Eliana took hold of her hand and began to pull her toward the exit, but the change was too much for Jude. She wobbled wildly, her other arm flailing to keep the balance. Fortunately for them both, Eliana's enhanced grace took over: she spun around and grabbed her by both elbows, pulling them both upright and face-to-face, with very little space left between them.

Jude sucked in a nervous breath, then prayed to her gods that Eliana hadn't noticed.

"Uh—thanks," she stammered.

"Don't mention it," said Eliana. Jude might have been imagining it, but she thought the Adept sounded a little more breathless than the situation strictly called for.

They both let out awkward half-laughs, then adjusted back to a skating position. As Eliana faced forward, she let her hand glide slowly down from Jude's elbow, tracing down the side of her coat until it found her hand again. Despite the layers of coat and glove between them, Jude found that her fingers left a trail of fire in their wake.

They made it to the gate without incident, and Jude quickly decided to switch back into the nice, faux-fur lined boots she'd brought with her. To her relief, Eliana followed her lead without comment.

A few minutes later, they both had hot chocolates clutched in their hands as they stood on the side of the rink, watching the other people go by. Jude felt a small rush of relief as she watched two other skaters fall flat on their faces in the middle of the ice. At least she wasn't the worst person out here today. She just hoped they'd never have to chase a demon across an ice rink— or that Logan was way better at it than she was.

She probably is, she thought automatically, then immediately chided herself for the thought. *Okay, I don't have to be negative about everything. If I really care, I can take lessons or something. Just…not in front of Elli.*

"Whatcha thinking about?" asked Eliana, her eyes alight as she surveyed Jude's face.

Oh, just how much I suck and how everyone is better than me.

"Uh—not much," she stammered, suddenly looking at everything around her but her companion. "I guess, just—uh, what's it like to live in New York?"

Eliana gave an almost rueful smile, casting her eyes down at her cup. "I'm not sure I'm actually the right person to ask. I've lived at Headquarters the entire time I've been here, and I might not end up here after this—all graduates get assigned to a team eventually, which usually means you go wherever they need more people. I could end up here, or I could end up in Guatemala."

"Guatemala?"

"Maybe, yeah. That's the joy of working for a secret international organization. You could end up in a whole different nation." With a wink, she raised her cup in a semi-salute. "Of course, I am the reigning Champion, which gives me a little more privilege in the process. Although it also means I'm more likely to get yanked out of any given assignment if there's ever a crisis."

"Because you're all big and important now?"

Eliana's expression turned sheepish.

"Well. Maybe I'm just trying to impress you." When she smiled, though, she looked more cheeky than chastened. "Is it working?"

"Maybe a little." Jude took a quick sip from her hot chocolate, hoping she looked calmer and more collected than she felt. Then she decided to ask something she'd been wondering about for a while. "So, hey, you never actually told me how you ended up working for the Order. I mean, how did you even find out about them?"

Eliana's expression shifted. Her eyes seemed to empty out and her smile seemed to sag. Then she shook herself a bit and straightened her shoulders, giving Jude a more serious look than she was accustomed to.

"The same way a lot of us end up here," she said. Her voice sounded almost resigned; her shrug seemed to imply futility. "I lost someone I loved to a demon."

An awkward silence stretched out between them as Eliana paused to drink from her hot chocolate. Jude didn't know what to say to that, and she wasn't even sure she should say anything at all, so she didn't. Luckily for her, Eliana chose to continue.

"You didn't know about magic growing up, right?"

"Nope," said Jude. "I, uh, read some stuff online about a year and a half ago. But even then, a lot of what I read was…well, obviously bullshit."

"Yeah." Eliana's glorious ponytail bobbed up and down as she nodded her head. "I didn't know anything, either. And neither did my parents. Or my brother." Her eyes softened and lost focused, like her thoughts were sliding her farther away. "We lived on the south side of Chicago. My dad was a doctor, running a private practice, but his patients lived in the neighborhood, mostly first-generation immigrants, and a lot of the time, they couldn't pay much, so…we never lived anywhere all that nice, you know?" Her faraway look twisted into something darker, but only for a moment. She covered it up like it was second nature. "You know, he changed his name when he went into private practice. When we were kids, he told us it was because Blake would be easier for his patients to pronounce." She shook her head. "It took me *so long* to figure out what a lie that was."

Jude thought of her own parents, running their Italian restaurant because they thought it might appeal to their mostly white neighbors in her hometown.

"Yeah," she muttered softly. "So…what was your name before?"

"It used to be Bahrom. I probably still have family out there who…well, doesn't matter. It's probably easier at the Order, anyway. To be a Blake."

She cleared her throat and straightened her back, like she hadn't meant to steer so far off course.

"So, yeah, uh, we lived in Chicago in a not-great neighborhood. It was just my parents, and me—and my older brother. He was basically my idol—and we were just close enough in age that he always put up with me following him around. Or maybe that was just how patient he was, I don't know. And…we probably knew we shouldn't, but we used to play outside a lot, even after dark—both our parents always worked long hours, and they always enrolled us in the magnet school program, so most of our school friends lived in different neighborhoods, far away. So…we just had each other. It was just the two of us, like always, the night he died."

From the look on Eliana's face, Jude guessed that she could see everything she was talking about, like it was playing out in front of her all over again.

"We were out too late, playing around in this shitty park near the apartment complex. I think we were taking turns trying to climb to the top of the swing set, since it didn't actually have a swing on it." She shook her head, but this time it looked like a gesture of shock, echoing through time with no signal degradation. "It should have been both of us. I still don't understand it. But somehow…it got him, but it didn't get me."

Jude felt like her body had frozen to the bench. What was she supposed to say to something like that? She couldn't even imagine it, really. She had to wonder how it would feel to lose someone close to her—like Logan or Knatt—but even then, she didn't think it was quite the same. The impulse was to reach out and touch Eliana's hand, as if that could offer any real comfort, but she couldn't tell if that was the right thing to do. Maybe there was no right thing to do.

Before she could really make up her mind one way or another,

Eliana cleared her throat and spoke again.

"I told the cops everything I'd seen, but they didn't believe me. They never do, right? They said there was no point looking for some lost boy from a bad neighborhood. They said he'd probably run off and joined an *extremist* group. So they wouldn't investigate any further." Her voice had taken on a dark, angry quality that Jude barely recognized...but she couldn't say she blamed her. "They were never gonna do a damn thing for us. Meanwhile, there was still a demon wandering around the neighborhood, and I was certain it was only a matter of time before it killed again. So I did the only thing that made sense to me. I bought a gun. And I went hunting."

Jude's eyes widened, and before she could stop herself, she heard the words tumbling out of her mouth.

"You just bought a gun, just like that?"

"This is America, Jude. How hard do you think it is? Guns are a hell of a lot easier to get your hands on than magic, I can tell you that."

A cold dread settled into Jude's stomach, but she did her best to ignore it. Then Eliana laughed.

"I was an idiot, obviously. I know that *now*. Lucky for me, an Adept from the Order of Shadows beat me to the finish line. In the end, I tracked that demon down just in time to watch someone else kill it, right in front of me." Her eyes settled on the middle distance; Jude saw the clear, hard outline of regret in them. "She must have been impressed by my tenacity, though. She told me I needed to learn how to do my research before I went hunting again. If I had, I'd have known that *this* demon couldn't be killed by a gun. And then she gave me a gift."

The dread in Jude's stomach seemed to double in mass.

"What was the gift?"

"It was a choice. She told me I could move on with my life, safe in the knowledge that the demon that killed my brother was gone, and I could continue living in the world that wrote him off as a tragic accident. Or I could turn my back on all of that, agree to distance myself from my family…and help her track down the person who had summoned the demon in the first place. She told me upfront that if I chose the second option, my life would never be the same again. There would be no going back."

Jude nodded, seeing the pieces fall into place. The knot in her stomach stayed put anyway.

"I guess the rest is history." Eliana paused to take another sip of her drink. "Once I saw what the Order did, what they could do…I knew there was nothing else I could do but this. Anything else would be a lie. You know, they even found a way to change the official police report on my brother's death. Now it says he was mauled by a wild animal. It's not much, but…at least my parents don't have to live with the world thinking their son was a terrorist. It's something anyway."

Jude nodded and mulled that over.

"Maybe they could have sued over that that, or something. For defamation, you know? I mean, obviously there wasn't any evidence."

Eliana let out a long sigh.

"They *could* have, but they never would. When I started looking for the demon…my mother told me to drop it. Maybe she believed my story, maybe she didn't. But she didn't want me to investigate at all. She said…she said we needed to move forward. That if we kept looking for answers, then…our family would be stuck, trapped living through his death over and over." She shook her head, looking rueful but resolved. "Honestly, that helped decide things for me. I love my parents, but…I couldn't live with that. The thing is…a part of me *is* trapped in that moment. Maybe I always will be. At least with the Order, I don't have to pretend it's any different. Every one of us is damaged one way or another. It's more honest this way. Besides, there's only one thing that really helps, you know?"

"Fighting demons?"

"Fighting demons." Her stormy expression finally broke, and a genuine smile stretched across. "At least I'll always know why I'm doing what I do, right? Not everyone can say that."

Jude returned her smile, but it felt brittle to her. Elli sounded so sure, and Jude envied her that. In more ways than one, she wished she could be more like her. Wished she could be enough for her.

But the pit in her stomach wouldn't go away.

And she didn't know what that meant yet.

Chapter Five
Demon Below

Eliana took one more deep drink from her cup before turning to toss it in a nearby receptacle.

"It's your turn, now," she said as she turned back. "How'd you get mixed up in this shit?"

Jude smiled involuntarily, though her smile immediately faltered as she remembered exactly how she *had* gotten into all this.

No time like the present to tell the truth, she told herself. She wished that could be enough to steel her nerves.

"It's not, uh, not quite as heroic a story as yours," she said.

"I wouldn't call my story heroic," answered Eliana, in a self-deprecating tone. "More...*stupid.*"

"At least your intentions were noble." Jude took a drink from her own hot chocolate and swallowed hard, almost wishing she had something a little stronger. "I guess my story has a couple parts to it. And the first part was, uh, when I was a little kid, and I, uh...accidentally set a girl on fire. By wishing it."

Eliana blinked in surprise. "Whoa. You mean, you performed eira...spontaneously?"

"Yeah," said Jude, with a nod. She understood *now* what what she had done was an eira cast, but she'd spent most of her life completely mystified by that memory, and half convinced she'd made it up. "I guess I did."

"Wow." Even after the story she'd just told, Eliana's eyes widened in shock, like she'd never heard anything like it. "I mean, I knew that was *theoretically* possible, but…the Order has no record of anyone alive who's done it."

This time, it was Jude who blinked.

"You don't know…*anyone* else who's done it?"

Eliana checked their immediate surroundings, like she was looking for someone who might be listening in. "Well, there's a theory that the eira Masters at T'eira'han know who they all are…and keep them hidden from us." She gave Jude an appraising look. "You know, if Logan hadn't found you…I bet the eira Masters would have come for you eventually, anyway."

The eira Masters. Logan had never mentioned this, nor had Adele, who should have known if it was true. But was it?

"You really think that?" she asked, hoping she sounded more curious than uncertain.

"I do," said Eliana, sincerely. "But I am the *wrong* person to ask. The Order doesn't exactly go big on eira education, you know? It's just not a cost-effective way to train your people if fewer than one percent of them are ever going to be able to master it."

"*Fewer than one percent?*" Jude could fear the shock in her voice. "That's how many people can master eira?"

"That's how many people can get to the point where they can reliably *perform* it," said Eliana with a nod of her head. "As for actual eira Masters? I think there are like...10 of them at any given time. You know, alive."

Isn't Adele a Master? Well...I guess that might explain why she had to go back so soon. Or, it would, if I had any idea what it means to be a Master.

"Huh. That's crazy," she said out loud.

"I *told* you you were special," said Eliana conspiratorially. "So, what's the next part of the story?"

Jude gave herself a shake as her mind came forcibly back to earth.

"Oh, right. Uh, well, a weird, creepy kid in my class summoned a demon, and it killed a girl. And then Logan showed up to fight it. She, uh, kinda thought it was me at first, actually."

"She did? Because you can cast, or...?"

"No, because I...I kinda hated the girl who died. And, uh, I told her that I wasn't sorry she died. Because I wasn't. I just knew...she was never gonna bother me again." Her head tipped forward, short hairs falling over her eyes. The old impulse to tug at her long braid was back, but there was nothing she could do to satisfy it. "Do you think I'm terrible?"

Eliana shook her head. "We can't control how we feel about stuff like that. The day after my brother died...I put on my running shoes and ran until I puked. You do weird stuff, you know?"

Jude wasn't entirely sure those two things were the same, but she also didn't want to spend any more time thinking about it than she absolutely had to.

"Yeah, I guess." She swallowed hard. A part of her wished she could just forget her own origin story. Every time she thought about it, she couldn't help but remember Amy…and her mother. It pissed her off to think about her mother, because she was absolutely certain her mother never thought about her. Taking a cue from Eliana, she cleared her throat before starting up again. "So, uh, I ended up going to this party in the woods, and the demon attacked. And I tried out this spell I'd read about online—I mean, I'd tried it before but it had never worked. But then it did, just for a moment—and luckily for me, Logan showed up, too. She chased the demon off and saved my life."

"Wow." With a funny half-smile on her face, Eliana leaned against the bench, then propped her bent arm over it, bringing her hand right up to Jude's shoulder. "So, tell me. Did you go to that party because of a girl?"

Jude felt the blush bloom across her entire body.

"Uh…yeah. I did." She stopped herself just short of apologizing for it.

"Yeah. I know how that goes." Her fingers brushed against Jude's shoulder, coming dangerously close to her face.

"That's pretty much the story. Logan killed the demon, and then she offered to take me out of town with her and train me to fight demons. And I couldn't wait to get the hell out of town, so of course I took her up on it."

"I'm glad you did."

Despite the relative innocence of the sentiment, Jude noticed a brand new intensity in Eliana's tone. When she met her eyes, she saw a soft light there as she studied Jude's face. Her eyes seemed to linger briefly on her mouth.

"Me, too."

Without breaking eye contact, Eliana reached up and pulled

the glove off her nearer hand. With that now bare hand, she reached up until her fingers grazed the side of Jude's cheek, coming to rest just behind her ear. Her skin was a little callused, probably from frequent weapon use, but it was warm, and to Jude, it felt electric.

"Is it okay if I…"

Her words trailed off, but her gaze fell to Jude's mouth again. Jude took her meaning, and, afraid she couldn't trust her voice to work, nodded.

And the world melted away. Eliana's lips pressed softly into her own, and all thought vanished. Every nerve in her body tingled as she kissed her back. For a few short seconds, they were the only two people who existed, and *this* was the only feeling that mattered.

Then, just as gently, their lips parted. Eliana looked roughly as dazed as Jude felt. Jude was shocked to discover that she was still holding her half-empty cup of cocoa; against all odds, she hadn't managed to drop it.

"Can I tell you a secret?" Eliana leaned in, her hand still resting on Jude's face. With her thumb, she pushed back one of Jude's stray hairs. "I've been waiting to do that all day."

Jude probably blushed all the way down to her feet, but it didn't matter. This time, she was the one who leaned forward and initiated the kiss.

When the vision first sucked her in, she momentarily lost who she was. This body was so different from her own; she could feel a powerful lower half, that didn't quite seem to be comprised of legs, propelling her forward with such grace that for the briefest moment, she thought she was flying. Then she recognized the cold, comforting press of water all around her and realized the truth: she was swimming.

Through these eyes, she had no trouble making out her surroundings, even though she could think of few places darker than this underwater depth. She had to be in the ocean, or something so big she couldn't tell it apart from one.

The being she now inhabited pushed forward, and she could feel its frustration, its growing panic.

It didn't know where it was, either.

Inside this alien body, she felt the current working on her, tossing her about. The creature looked everywhere for some hint of the direction whence it had come, but to no avail. It didn't understand these foreign waters.

The next roll of current brought it closer to land and, not knowing what else to do, it gave in and followed where the current led. Soon, it found itself facing a metal cave, jutting out into the water across a stretch of flooded sand.

That's not a cave, *thought Logan.* That's a pipe.

But the beast could not hear her. It went into the pipe and followed it inward, toward human civilization—though it didn't know that. With its impressive underwater eyes, it could make out the pitch-black insides of the pipe, and it had no trouble following its various bends and curves.

Logan glanced down at the being's hand as it pressed against one metal wall: it was giant, nearly three times the length of an average human hand, and four of its five digits were webbed. The fifth curled inward in a giant talon, perfect for ripping into its prey.

Eventually, it found its way into a large underground cavern. Once its eyes swept over a small cavern set off from the main one, *full of dusty old artifacts, Logan realized she knew where it was.*

But it didn't stay there long. It was hungry now, as well as confused and scared, and it moved toward the smells of the world up above.

She knew without a shadow of a doubt that it would devour whatever—or whoever—it found.

Logan came to a few minutes later. For several seconds, she was completely disoriented—in part because she'd awoken to find her head gently cradled by a soft feather pillow, while the rest of her body lay against a hard stone floor.

She blinked open her eyes to find the concerned faces of Hugh Knatt and Alexei Marin staring down at her. She blinked a few more times, giving her mind a chance to catch up.

"What are you doing here?" she asked Alexei, the words tumbling out of her mouth more abruptly than she'd meant them.

"Jude called," he answered, blinking his large, dark eyes at her. "Said she was leaving for a few days and thought I should come babysit you." He shook his head, wry amusement tugging at the corner of his mouth. "You know, I think it's bad feminist form to keep calling in a man to take care of you."

Logan grunted. "Well, someone needs to make the sandwiches," she said, propping herself up on her elbows. "And you boys are just better at it, you know?"

Knatt gave her a withering look. "And here I was, about to offer tea."

Logan already regretted moving away from the cold stone, which had done a nice job of muffling the burn of the

Choronzon Key at her back.

"If 'tea' actually includes a sandwich, then I apologize a hundred times," she said, giving Knatt her best mournful look. "Also, purely out of curiosity, do we still have ice packs in the kitchen?"

"I believe so." Knatt gave her an appraising look, possibly judging the sincerity of her apology. "I *was* considering making some egg and cress. I suppose I still shall. And I'll leave kitchen clean up to the two of you."

"More than fair," said Logan, forcing herself up into a full sitting position. With that, Knatt turned around and left the traveling room, presumably for the kitchen.

"Sorry," said Alexei, glancing bashfully at her. "Didn't mean to start drama."

"Oh, it's not you," said Logan. Almost unconsciously, she touched the tattoo on the inside of her left forearm. "We're in…disagreement at the moment. About Charles."

"Ah," Alexei nodded. One strand of perfectly tousled hair fell into his eyes. "Well. Families are hard."

"So I'm told." In one smooth motion, Logan stood up completely, then offered Alexei her hand and pulled him up to standing, too. "Thanks for the pillow, by the way. I don't normally get to wake up from a blackout in comfort."

"Anytime." Unzipping the top of a comically large rolling suitcase beside him, he slipped the pillow back inside. Logan had no doubt the suitcase was from some designer she'd never heard of, probably worth more than her entire wardrobe put together. Not that her wardrobe was worth much.

"So…Jude called you?" She beat roughly at her relatively

cheap jeans to clean them off.

"She did." He started walking to the door without his bag. She glanced at it, wondering if he expected her to take it. "She seemed reluctant to leave you alone with Knatt and your father. Can't imagine why."

An unexpected thought popped into her head.

Alexei knows now that we use the travelling room to get to my place from here. So, leaving it here is the most sensible thing to do…if he's staying with me.

She blinked, trying to let her brain register that information before she turned back to him. Then she realized it had nearly been too long since she'd spoken.

"Well. How do you feel about going on an adventure tonight?"

She left the bag where it was.

Despite Logan's clearly articulated warning that they would be spending a good chunk of their evening in an underground cavern with dirt walls, Alexei chose to wear a suit. The suit was a deep maroon, with a crisp charcoal shirt and French collar underneath. To appease her, Alexei agreed to leave the gold pocket watch accent behind, shaking his head as he acquiesced, and to wear a coat over everything. From the look of it, Logan guessed that it, too, was designer.

They suited up in her apartment, which was fortuitously well placed for where they needed to go. Choosing expedience over stealth, Logan put on her over-the-shoulder ax harness outside of her motorcycle jacket, while Alexei showed off a new toy from his favorite San Francisco retailer: a bespoke spring-loaded dagger which fit neatly under his suit jacket.

"You like it?" he asked, giving her a smile as he adjusted the strap near his wrist. "Watch this." He performed a quick thrusting motion with his arm, activating the device and shooting the blade forward, just beneath his own fist. "Of course, it only works as a surprise once."

Logan did her best not to roll her eyes as she slid her ax into place. "I think you're more likely to hurt yourself with that than you are anyone else."

"As long as I look good doing it."

Alexei had a long history of buying weapons for their aesthetic value over their practicality. She saw he had also brought with him an old favorite: a walking cane with a silver handle carved into a snarling panther head on one end, and solid steel tip on the other. Logan smiled as she caught sight of the tiny symbol carved just beneath the panther head, the only thing signifying the cane's true power: yakoshi demon power, Bound into the silver.

"Whatever makes you happy."

The place they were headed wasn't even far enough away to justify taking her Ninja, so they rode the elevator down to street level and set out on foot. Logan was well-acquainted with Seattle's back alleys and various underground networks; the city was small enough that it hadn't taken her long to find them all. The very first place she'd ever explored, back when she was a teenager skipping school to hang out on the waterfront, was the infamous Seattle Underground, a series of tunnels and caverns beneath Pioneer Square that had once made up the city's downtown streets, before they built the new city right on top of them. She'd been fascinated by them as a kid, and she had to admit, she still felt a certain fondness for them now. She'd even gone on an official tour once—though as she suspected, the tour covered less than a third of what she knew to be down there.

Of course, to be able to explore the Underground at all, she'd had to figure out how to get in.

Barely three blocks from her apartment, they stumbled upon her favorite entrance: an unused and forgotten cellar door, hidden beneath the giant trash receptacle behind a grimy nightclub. Logan had never been inside the club, but she certainly hoped it did enough business to survive, so nobody would ever have cause to examine the ground in the alleyway behind it.

As she pushed the trash bin out of the way, Alexei gave her a wary look.

"Are you sure about this?" he asked, his upper lip crinkling in uncertainty.

"I *told* you to change," she answered, crouching down over the ancient-looking door. "Demon slaying is dirty work, Marin."

"It's not that," he said, leaning his cane against the wall as he reached into an interior pocket. "I'm just worried about tetanus. And possibly tuberculosis, depending on how far back in time we're about to travel."

"Says the man with the walking cane." Her hand found purchase on the hidden handle, and she yanked the door open wide. It was heavy enough that human strength wouldn't have been able to open it, but it didn't pose much of a problem for her. "You ready?"

Alexei produced what he'd been searching for in his pocket:

a sleek pair of night-vision goggles, which he slipped onto his head. Logan assumed without asking that these, too, were bespoke.

"As I'll ever be," he said, and picked up his cane again.

"There's a bit of a drop," Logan explained. "If you wanna go first, I'll lower you down."

"Fan-fucking-tastic." He grimaced but stepped forward, looking beyond disgusted as he sat on the edge of the opening, letting his legs dangle in first. "If I die down there, you *have* to lie to the public about it, do you understand? Tell them—tell them I died in a brothel, of a drug overdose, or something equally acceptable. Will you do that for me?"

She patted him gently on the hand.

"Oh, Alexei. I'm definitely going to say you died on the toilet, and you can't stop me."

He shook his head at her as she grasped his forearm, and he dropped gracefully through the opening, until he was suspended by nothing but her strength. She loosened her grip slowly, letting him slide down her arm to her wrist, then to her hand.

"I'm good," he called up to her, and she let go.

After she heard him land on his feet, she gave him a moment to step aside, then jumped on down herself. Years of practice made her landing easy, her knees bending slightly as her feet hit the earth with perfect balance. It was already night out, but even if it had been mid-afternoon, the small entrance above wouldn't have let in much light. Unlike Alexei, however, Logan didn't need night-vision goggles to see in the dark: her demon side supplied her with night vision…and though she didn't like to think about it, there had been a marked improvement in that night vision in recent years. With one blink, her eyes adjusted to the darkness of the room, allowing her to see into the deepest, darkest corner.

The cellar wasn't particularly large, perhaps a little bigger than the average backroom at a bar. One wall was packed high with ancient wooden chairs covered in a thick layer of dust. A few boxes sat in the corner, also covered in dust.

On the opposite wall from the chairs, an indentation in the stone, about two feet wide, marked their path. The indentation hid a door made of wrought iron bars, held shut by a heavy padlock Logan had long since broken. She walked right to it and removed the broken lock, placing it atop the nearest box in the usual spot.

"After you," said Alexei, giving as extravagant a bow he could in the small space.

Logan pulled the door open and stepped just inside the tunnel, then turned back to him.

"Keep your weapon ready," she said. "And keep me in your sight at all times."

"I'm not your newbie sidekick, H.C.," he said, shaking his head at her. "Just because I dress well doesn't mean I'm helpless."

Logan shrugged. "I'm a worrier. Now let's move."

With that, she turned back around and started forward. The tunnel was made of round metal, and Logan figured it was either an old sewer access tunnel or a smuggler's tunnel from prohibition, or both. They followed it in relative silence for a few minutes, with nothing but the sound of their boots against the grimy floor to keep them company. Roughly 40 feet in, they were met with a crossroads. The metal pipe continued in front of them, but a new dirt tunnel jutted off to the left.

Logan went left. Based on what she'd seen of where the sea creature would go, left was their best option—closer to the larger caverns, and the remnants of the old city. Behind her, Alexei stumbled slightly and cursed under his breath. Deciding it was best to let him save face, she said nothing.

They traveled along the narrow dirt path for several minutes until they came to a spot that at first appeared to be a dead end—but on inspection, the wall before them wasn't a wall, but an old, heavy wooden door, so coated in dust and dirt that it had become invisible. Logan walked right up to it and pressed her ear to the ancient wood, listening for sounds of movement on the other side. It was late enough that the tourists had surely all gone home—so anything she might hear in the space beyond would be something that shouldn't be there.

Nothing yet. With a nod to Alexei, she reached for the handle and pulled up, jostling the door on its rusted hinges until it came free and swung open.

"Watch your step," she whispered to Alexei before she descended the short but steep earthen steps into the room beyond.

If the cellar they'd come through was old, this place was ancient. She was pretty sure this whole area had once been a part of the main tour, likely abandoned when it became too unstable for lawyered-up tourists. The room they were now descending into was a small storage area set off the main chamber and filled with artifacts from another time—bed frame, part of an old bank teller window, a broken doll. The walls here had been plastered over at least once, long ago, though they were just as dirty as everything else. She clocked a bit of spray-paint on the wall opposite them.

You're gonna die here, ha ha, it read.

Kids, she thought, rolling her eyes.

Alexei came down the stairs after her. He made for an odd sight, carrying his walking cane propped against his shoulder instead of using it to help him down the uneven steps. Of course, Logan knew that the cane didn't really work that way; in fact, using it like that would only dull the blade.

Once he was down, he stepped close to her and lowered his voice.

"Is it nearby?"

Logan motioned at the entrance to the next room. "It's going to come through there. I didn't get a precise time stamp, but…no time like the present."

With that, she strode through the storage room and entered into the cavern beyond. It was far wider and had a higher ceiling than anything they'd trudged through so far. Upwards of 30 people could stand in it comfortably, and Logan suspected they likely had, back when it was part of the tour.

Of course, just because it was big didn't mean it was comfortable. The floor here was made entirely of dirt, and Logan could make out bits of broken glass and rusted metal all around. Wooden support structures stood along the side, demarcating where the ceiling began to slope down, creating smaller caves on either side. On the far end of the room, a row of old windowframes had been hung from the ceiling, likely to demonstrate the former boundary of a building long since lost. The wooden beams probably originated with the same building. Beyond that, a more open tunnel formed, and Logan knew from memory that the tunnel extended in both directions, with rickety old wooden bridges available to carry you through the nebulous caves on either side.

"Uh, Logan?" Alexei's voice carried through from the storage room behind her. "My goggles don't work in here."

Logan paused, an uncomfortable realization sinking in: she'd *never* been able to see this well in the main chamber before—not without a little letha help, first. That meant her night vision really *was* better now than it used to be. *So, at 28, demon puberty has hit at last.*

She let out a small sigh and pushed the thought away. She had work to do.

"Just a sec," she whispered back to him, then reached inside her jacket to pull out a leaf of sage, her small puncture tool, and her lighter.

Moving the tool down her wrist to her arm, just above where her first spike would slide out if she called it, she pushed it down into her skin until a small bead of blood bubbled up. Then she used the lighter to torch the end of the sage.

"*Invoco potentiam de envathum,*" she whispered as the sage began to burn. "*Invoco potentiam de envathum. Invoco potentiam!*"

In a flash, the flame that enveloped the leaf turned purple and burst outward in all directions—but only for a moment. Then it was gone, and in its wake, a faint purple glistening remained. Every visible surface in the room glowed brightly purple for a moment, then faded into a light sheen. With a satisfied sigh, Logan tucked her tools away and walked back to Alexei to guide him into the main cavern. Goggles still in place, he glanced around in all directions, clearly taken aback.

"What did you do?" he asked, stepping deeper into the cavern.

"I summoned the power of an envathus demon," she replied. They both walked a few more feet into the cavern, taking in the details all around them. "Envathus can emit a small cloud of bio-luminescent microbes that will coat every surface in a given area. It allows them to hunt in caves so deep, they might never have been bothered by human encroachment...until the Order found out about them and nearly drove them to extinction, of course."

Even in his goggles, Alexei managed to toss her a sideways look.

"Thinking about joining the Society for Demon Preservation?"

She shrugged. "Just stating a fact. Hey, take off the goggles for a second."

They had made it more than halfway through the underground space, standing closer now to the far side of the room than the one from which they'd entered. Looking bemused, Alexei obeyed. Once the goggles were off, he widened his eyes to take everything in. Logan watched intently as his expression changed from surprise to awe. In the warm purple glow, he looked prettier than ever. For a moment, Logan wished she could forget about the mission tonight.

"Wow," he murmured, his eyes now roving the glistening, glittering cave around them. "Wow. I honestly can't say if this is beautiful...or creepy as hell."

She cleared her throat before answering and made sure to keep her tone as light as she could.

"No reason it can't be both."

Alexei let out a nervous laugh in response to that—then stopped cold. Logan did, too. They'd both heard the same thing:

not 20 feet away from them, the sound of wood snapping under too much weight.

The demon had arrived.

Chapter Six
Looking Glass

While Alexei scrambled to put his goggles back on, Logan crouched low and moved to the right, closer to the sound. With one quick shake, her spikes burst out of her arms—four on each side, hard and sharp. They slid out of individual black diamond markings, evenly placed along the length of her forearm. Every nerve in her body was on high alert. Her ears pricked for the nearest hint of sound, her eyes searching for movement. Alexei followed close behind her, cane grasped tightly in his fist.

Just then, a scratching, scrabbling sound met their ears—the sound of an animal struggling to find purchase on a too-smooth surface—but she couldn't say with certainty which direction it had come from. A moment ago, she'd been sure the noise originated in the tunnel to the right, but now the scratching sound seemed to come from right, left, and behind—the structure of the space created an endlessly rebounding echo and obscured the truth. Seeing few alternatives, she decided to ignore the new cacophony of information and go with her first impulse—moving forward. She pressed right up to the corner of the wall that separated them from the tunnel, and then leaned around to peer inside.

The bio-luminescent microbes had found their way into the tunnel, but only just—they sparkled here and there, coming just short of illuminating the whole space.

In fact, the patchy luminance created an adverse affect. Logan's eyes had difficulty adjusting past the faint purple glow. She could just make out the wooden bridge and the barest hint of the depth beneath it. She couldn't see the platform on the other side or the bottom of the cavity the bridge stretched over.

Fuck. If I hadn't done that cast, I could probably see right now. But, of course, the downside of that would be that Alexei would be absolutely blind. *Well, the Key didn't exactly tell you to bring him along, did it?*

She shook that thought out of her head and forced herself to look into the abyss anyway. The one thing she could make out was a single broken plank—right in the center of the bridge. She pulled back and turned to Alexei, still a few feet behind her.

"I don't see it, but I'm sure it was over there," she whispered. "Back against the wall and weapon at the ready, got it?"

"Logan—"

Alexei's tone sounded his obvious protest, but Logan didn't stop long enough to hear it.

Staying low, she strode out into the tunnel, keeping her eyes on the dark as she headed for the bridge. When she reached the railing, she crouched down and peered over the edge. She could see the beginning of the wall that went into the chasm beneath, but she couldn't quite be sure how far down it went—and it had been a long time since she'd decided to check out the underside of the bridge, if she ever had.

If there was one thing she knew about fighting strategically, it was that one generally didn't want to give up the high ground if one could safely avoid it. So, following her own advice, she decided not to travel into the pit, and to instead traverse the bridge that crossed it.

Over the bottomless abyss, it is, she thought. And she took her first step.

It creaked far louder than she would have liked, but the wood held. She walked all the way to the center without a problem, casting her gaze in every direction she could as she went. At the midpoint, she paused, knowing that her position made her about as vulnerable as she could be—and wondering if that might be bait enough for the beast. She didn't quite know how this thing could move, so she kept her eyes moving along the periphery of her vision, wishing again that she had forgone the cast and allowed her eyes to adjust.

She saw nothing. She heard nothing. Moments passed. Finally, she decided she had to keep moving. She took a few more steps across the bridge, toward the platform on the other side, which she was only beginning to make out. It was then that she felt a pricking at the back of her neck—the kind that told her someone was watching her. She whipped around, spikes raised, almost hopeful that she might catch it sneaking up—but there was nothing there. The bridge was empty. She kept going.

At long last, her feet made contact with the floor of the far platform. With most of the glimmer now behind her, her eyes suddenly adjusted.

She could see the platform. It was completely, ominously, empty.

Behind her, she heard Alexei give a strangled cry.

"Fuck." Self-loathing came on like a worn-in glove. How could she be stupid enough to leave him by himself? She spun around and ran at break-neck speed back across the bridge—only for her boot to catch on the broken plank, sending her sprawling.

Cursing herself again, she pushed back up and kept running, ignoring the brand new pain that blossomed in her palms and ankle. She rounded the corner just in time to watch the creature dragging Alexei to the ground and knocking his night vision goggles off in the struggle.

Though her Key vision had shown her the creature's hands and feet—mostly webbed, but with one hooked claw on each side—it hadn't afforded her a look at the rest of it. Its head was strangely rounded, with a bulbous dome protruding above the puckered, gasping mouth, and a spiky fin ran the length of its spine. It looked precisely like a fish out of water.

A fish out of water with the upper hand on Alexei. While Alexei was prone and vulnerable, neither goggles nor weapon near at hand, it slashed at him with those curved claws, slicing right through his delicate shirt to the skin underneath.

Her instinct took over in an instant. She leapt on the fish-man, using her not inconsiderable strength to wrap her arms around it in a mock bear-hug, pinning its pesky claws to its side as she rolled it away from her now-helpless companion. The sea-creature struggled against her unbreakable hold, then used its legs to force them to roll again, this time ending with her on her back. In that position, it gave a mighty jerk, and her head bounced backward, into the ground beneath them.

The world briefly blinked out of existence as her body threatened to send her into unconsciousness. A part of her brain chose this moment to remember that the oxygen in the caves was stale and sparse. Not recommended for anyone with a breathing condition, and certainly not recommended for passing out while trapped beneath a sea monster.

The sweet, quiet world of unconsciousness beckoned to her, but she pulled against it. *Alexei needs you*, she reminded herself, before swimming back to the surface.

The monster's trick had worked, of course. Her grip on it slackened, and it skittered away from her, heading south…toward one of the exits from the cave.

Toward normal, vulnerable people. She couldn't let it do that.

She ran after it at top speed, slamming into it again and sending it sprawling. This time, it spun around to face her. With a strange, high-pitched cry, it flew at her, slashing out with its talons at every part of her it could reach. Luckily for her, her thick leather riding jacket proved a better match than Alexei's fine dress shirt, and its attack failed to so much as break her skin.

As the creature realized the futility of its efforts, it seemed to freeze mid-movement—like it didn't know what to do from there. Logan had no such trouble. She bared her forearms and advanced, slamming her left arm into its chest so hard that her spikes ripped right through the skin, burying themselves into its surprisingly soft flesh.

Logan's mind went blank as her actions continued on autopilot. She made a fist and pulled her arm down, ripping through the fish-man's chest with ease, like it was made of tissue paper. And just like that, the fight was over. Its eyes went dead and its legs gave out. She watched impassively as it fell to the floor.

All of a sudden, Logan had the strangest feeling that she didn't know where she was, or how she had gotten there. She felt like a monster herself, moving on instinct instead of conscious thought.

Instinct. That's all it was. She shook her head as she forced herself to look down at the dead creature at her feet. *It wasn't trying to be evil. It was just hungry.*

The cavern had fallen silent as their fight came to its abrupt end. Into the silence spilled Alexei's uncertain voice.

"Is it over? H.C., are you okay?"

Oh, right. He can't see. Because he's *human.*

She stepped away from the dead beast and walked back to the other side of the cabin, where Alexei lay helpless, his night-vision goggles barely five feet away. She picked them up before she knelt beside him. Taking his right hand in her own, she pressed the goggles into it.

"How badly are you hurt?" she asked, her voice soft and chastened.

"I'll live, I think," he replied. He moved the goggles around in his hands, and then lifted them up and secured them over his face again. "Sorry. Looks like I missed the fight."

"Wasn't much of a fight," said Logan. Even to her own ears, her voice sounded hollow. "It, uh…it was out of its element up here. It never meant to be so far inland. I don't think it was built for life outside of the ocean."

Despite the fact that his eyes were completely obscured by the presence of the goggles, Logan could sense him giving her a concerned look.

"It never *meant* to be so far inland?" He sounded quizzical, and she watched him push himself further up on his elbows.

"It didn't. It was just trying to find its way home."

"I suppose it didn't mean to rip open my shirt and part of my chest either, hm?" With a grunt, he made a valiant effort to sit up the rest of the way. She managed to catch him right before he could fall back down again, and placing one hand in the middle of his back, she guided him into place.

"Are you sure you're okay? We should probably head to the surface anyway."

"I'll be fine. It just stings a bit." He glanced down sadly at himself. "This shirt, on the other hand, has gone on to meet its maker."

"I've got plenty of t-shirts at my apartment, if you need to borrow something."

"That's not funny."

"You mean the thought of you pairing your custom-fitted suit pants with a t-shirt stained with motor oil? It's a little funny."

"You're lucky I don't bill you, you know."

"You volunteered." Without meaning to, she glanced over at the sea-creature's unmoving body, and she felt the wince come over her face before she could stop it. "Come on, let's get going."

"Hold on." She felt one hand settle on her elbow as the other went to the goggles, pushing them up on his head. The purple light all around them cast the same soft glow over his already perfect features. "What was that look?"

"What look?"

"Don't tell me you feel *bad* for the thing that almost ripped me to shreds."

Logan shrugged.

"I don't know. Would there be something wrong with that?"

"Logan, it's a *demon*."

"So am I."

"You're also *sentient*," he said, a harsh edge to his voice. "There is a difference."

"How can you be so sure that it wasn't sentient?"

She watched the frown furrow his perfect brow. She watched his eyes slide past her, to where the beast lay.

"Would the Key have sent you after it if it was?"

"I don't know." She looked back at the creature, too. It still lay, unmoving. It would never move again. "The Key doesn't give me orders. Maybe I had another choice."

"But…demons aren't *from* this world. And they're dangerous, right? That's what we've always known."

Logan didn't want to shrug anymore. Instead she sighed.

"Hippos are dangerous. Their jaws are powerful enough to cut a person in half. But I'm not exactly about to go exterminate the hippos, am I?"

Alexei looked back at her, his jaw hanging slightly open.

"Can they really do that? Wait, not the point—the point is, it's different. Demons are like…an invasive species in this world. We *do* have to get rid of them."

"According to the Order of Shadows."

"Yes, according to the Order. And to every crypto-historian who's ever studied it. Demons didn't originate here. They come from somewhere else." His eyes searched her face, and she wondered how much of it he could really see. "What else can we do about them?"

Her right ankle, the one that had caught on the break in the bridge, began to twinge, protesting against the length of time it had born her weight in this crouch. She relaxed into a real sitting position, letting her ankle rest at a more natural angle. It would likely recover before morning.

"I don't know. It just…it feels like it's a choice I should be making. And I don't know if I'm making the right one."

It was Alexei's turn to let out a sigh. His eyes strayed back to the slain beast, but only for a moment before re-centering on her.

"Nobody ever does," he said. "Welcome to being human."

Being human.

Her ankle had already begun to feel better. Within a few minutes, it would be like nothing had ever happened. She'd had slower recoveries before, but lately it seemed like they were speeding up. Just like her eyesight, getting better all the time. She didn't want to breathe too deep down in the damp underworld, but even without it, she could smell the sharp tang of the sea creature's saltwater blood—as well as the rats it ate on the journey between the Sound and the cave.

She could see Alexei's face entirely, but he was blind down here.

The thing was, she didn't *feel* very human at all.

Jude was happy but tired by the time they took the train back to Brooklyn, back to Eliana and Ian Fisher's borrowed apartment. Now that she knew what to expect, she wasn't quite so taken aback by the miniature size of the place, which meant she could simply appreciate the novelty of staying in an apartment in New York City.

New York had never been a specific goal of hers, but it fit neatly into the goal she did have: to get the hell out of Montana and live somewhere as different from Wolf Creek as it was possible to be. She'd wanted out her entire life. And this? This was as out as it got. This was so far out, she wasn't even sure she recognized herself anymore. And as far as she was concerned, that was a good thing.

I kissed a girl at Rockefeller Center, she thought, incredulously, as she followed Eliana through the hallways and into the tiny apartment. *Today has been a pretty big day.*

Almost as if she'd heard her thoughts, Eliana whipped around to give Jude a mischievous grin.

"I hope you're not tired yet, because the best is yet to come." She turned away with a flourish and crossed the living room in a single bound, coming to a stop in front of the door to her bedroom. "We've got a few hours before we head out again, so if you want to rest a bit, you can take my bed."

There was something suggestive in the way she said that, and Jude felt the blood rush automatically to her cheeks.

"Probably not a bad idea," she said meekly, before ducking past Fisher, still sprawled on the couch, into Eliana's room.

There wasn't much space to walk around in there, but at least the bed seemed to be queen-sized, unlike the little twin beds Jude remembered from the Order's guest quarters. She moved her backpack down to the floor before pulling off her jacket and shoes and dropping them in a heap on top of the bag.

Privately, she'd been pretty sure her sustained excitement was going to prevent her from taking a real nap, but that turned out to be incorrect. Within moments of her head hitting the soft pillow on Eliana's bed, she was out like a light.

When she woke up again, it was to the feeling of weight pressing down the other side of the bed, then shifting as the unseen culprit leaned over her, the curling ends of a long ponytail brushing her cheek.

"Time to wake up, Li. We've got an adventure to go on."

Jude was disoriented for a moment, wondering how Eliana had gotten into her bedroom at the estate, before she experienced the unsettling sensation of realizing, all at once, that she was thousands of miles away from the bedroom she'd woken up in that very morning. She realized, of course, that airplane travel could have achieved the same affect, but there was something particularly strange about the fact that she'd skipped right over the hours a plane ride would have taken…to instantaneous, reality-bending magic.

She couldn't share that thought out loud, of course. The Order wasn't supposed to know about the Logan estate's traveling room. Something about the rarity of the magic that created it, and how it had been lost centuries ago. Jude had been too excited when they'd first told her about it to ask the right clarifying questions.

"Where are we going?" Jude asked out loud, now, as she pushed herself into a seated position.

Eliana's weight shifted off the bed as she stood up again and flipped on the light switch. Instead of a bright overhead light, a glowing pyramid-shaped lamp on the small bedside table turned on, bathing the room in soft, slightly rose-toned glow.

Eliana leaned into the doorway as she gazed at Jude, excitement burning in her eyes.

"We found a *nest*," she stage-whispered enigmatically. "Put on your best fighting gear before you come out."

With that, she disappeared, shutting the door behind her. Jude felt a small lump of anxiety form in her stomach as she crawled out of the giant bed, letting her feet land on the scant amount of floor space available to her. Fortunately for her, Logan had insisted, despite the light-hearted nature of her visit, that she bring comfortable, movable clothes and *at least* one set of light armor.

Stripping off her clothes from earlier in the day, Jude reached down to the bottom of her bag to pull out a pair of thick cargo pants with armored patches sewn into the shin and thigh areas. Pulling those on helped quiet her anxiety, though it didn't quell it completely. At least she knew she had some protection. After that, she pulled on an insulated Henley and grabbed the armored pads at the very bottom of the backpack. These she zipped into the hidden inner pockets of her winter jacket. Finally, she got back into the only shoes she'd brought: the nice new boots from Logan, which Logan had insisted she train in so that she'd be ready to fight in them. Despite how much she'd complained about the blisters the first few days, she was more than happy she'd done it now.

Her jacket had other hidden pockets in it, too, and those were already filled with a variety of letha catalysts, as well as her puncture tool and a refillable lighter. Even if she didn't quite know how to prepare herself yet, Logan certainly did.

The last thing she put on was the belt that held her knife sheathe. She'd tried to get used to some of the harnesses that fit under the clothes, like Logan wore, but she hadn't quite figured out how to get the weapons out fast enough for them to be useful.

So, she put on her perfectly visible belt and hoped that, wherever they were going, they didn't have to take public transport.

When she exited the small bedroom, she found herself briefly relieved, and then quite alarmed, to see that both Eliana and Fisher were visibly armed to the teeth.

The good news was, she doubted she had to worry about subway riders clocking her weapon. The bad news was that even bad-ass Eliana felt the need to stock up on weaponry for this expedition, strapping herself with multiple throwing knives, one sword, and what appeared to be a gun. Next to her, Fisher carried all the same knives and the gun, but seemed to have opted for a crossbow instead of a sword.

"The tenant here left us a van," said Eliana, dangling a set of keys in her right hand. "Said we could use it if the need arose. You ready?"

Super not ready, Jude thought to herself.

"Totally ready," she said out loud.

"Alright. Let's get this party started!" said Fisher, pumping his crossbow in one fist, like a foam finger at a soccer match.

He filed out ahead, slipping down the narrow hallway to unlock and open the door. Eliana ushered Jude out ahead of her, locking up behind them as they went. Once they were at the stairway, she turned sideways and caught Jude's eye.

"Fisher started tracking an irahu about a week ago," she explained, her excitement so obvious it bordered on giddy. "They're not much trouble on their own, but irahu demons tend to live in groups, and once a nest moves in, you gotta make sure to eradicate it before it gets too big. Sort of like a colony of much-bigger ants, you know?"

"Sure," said Jude, though she was fairly certain she didn't.

"Anyway, Fisher got a tracker on this one, and we started following its patterns. We were pretty sure we knew where the nest was yesterday—but I thought it might be fun to let you in on the action, so we decided to postpone the raid until today. So, I hope you're ready for a fight!"

Jude still felt like she was doing her best just to keep up, but she understood from the look on Eliana's face that the Adept expected a reaction from her.

"Oh—yeah, excellent! Yeah, I'm totally up for a raid. Uh, excited to see how the Order does it!" She hoped that sounded convincing. She wanted to believe that once the shock wore off, she really *would* be excited—but right now, she mostly felt like everything was moving too fast.

"Oh, almost forgot." Eliana reached into the small duffel bag she carried over her shoulder and pulled out an energy drink, which she promptly tossed to Jude. Taken aback as she was, Jude just barely managed to grab it out of the air before it clattered to the ground. "That should help you shake the sleep off, if you need it. I drink 'em all the time."

With that, she clattered away, leaving Jude on the landing, staring blankly as her fervent counterparts disappeared down the stairs. For a moment, Jude could do nothing but stand there, uncertainty and shock colliding to form a glue on the soles of her nice boots, holding her in place. She swallowed hard, and then glanced at the drink her hand.

Why does every monster hunter I meet have a caffeine addiction?

After two long, painful seconds, she decided to pop the can open and chug as much of it as she could. She wasn't sure it would help her much, but at least it gave her an excuse to dawdle for a moment. When the last drop of sickly sweet liquid slid down her throat, she let out a sigh.

Time to go.

It was easier to move now, though she wasn't sure if that was because of the drink so much as the fact that the others were so far ahead of her now that she no longer had a choice. Whatever it was, she made it down the stairs in record time. A few moments later, she caught up to the others right as they crashed through the door to the tiny, awkwardly shaped garage beneath the building. There were only five cars down there, and they seemed headed for the very last one—the unmarked black van right next to the exit.

Eliana clambered into the driver's seat, passing the bag over to Fisher. Fisher motioned Jude inside first, then followed her into the back of the vehicle.

The van appeared to be customized, with bolted-down racks of various weapons taking up the side walls, where normally there would have been windows. Jude and Fisher strapped into two individual seats in the back, the duffel bag of supplies resting on the ground between them. Jude had barely strapped herself into the seat before they were moving, the van rumbling and shaking over the uneven pavement as they made their way out into the night.

With Eliana driving up front, and the ambient noise of the van just enough to make them feel separated, Jude realized that she was, in a sense, alone with Ian Fisher for the first time. Fisher was Eliana's best friend and fellow graduate. He had become a fresh new Adept of the Order of Shadows alongside Eliana at the annual Summit—which already felt like it was eons ago, but in reality was only one week before.

Eliana had been at the very top of their class; she had, in fact, won the title *Champion of the Gauntlet* by defeating every single opponent in a dueling tournament, which seemed to serve as their final graduation rite. Jude's understanding of Fisher was that he had ended up somewhere in the middle.

And she wasn't quite sure he liked her, though she suspected that might have to do with the fact that he was used to having Eliana all to himself. He hadn't expected their duo to become a trio.

Jude glanced around the space again, looking for something she might be able to use to start a conversation. Eventually, she settled on the only thing that came to her.

"So," she started, trying to ignore how awkward she sounded, "this van is pretty decked out. Does it belong to the Order?"

"Nah, it belongs to Simons," Fisher replied with a shrug. He still had his crossbow in his hands, and he looked it over so carefully that Jude would have described the action as 'lovingly.' "But Simons is a good soldier. Always ready for anything."

He gave Jude a smirk instead of a smile. She got the impression that he was doing his best to seem like a bad-ass. She bit down on her anxiety long enough to give him a true smile in return. She couldn't shake the feeling that both he and Eliana were about to realize that she didn't belong on their mission—that she'd only lasted as long as she had because she always had Logan to protect her.

But Logan wasn't there during your last fight, she told herself, firmly. *Not for all of it, anyway. You did that yourself. You can do it again.*

She turned back to Fisher.

"Has the Order already sent you out on a lot of stuff like this?"

"Nah." For a moment, Fisher didn't look up at her, too consumed in whatever tiny flaw he'd just discovered on the side of his crossbow. Then he grinned at her, a slightly menacing look in his eyes. "They didn't send us on this one, either. Not all of us only do what we're told."

The truth hit Jude like a rock: this was *not* an Order-sanctioned mission. From the sound of it, the Order might not even know about it. Which meant, among other things, that there would be no one coming to save them if they stumbled.

Exciting and terrifying, all at once. Jude wasn't sure which feeling would win out.

Her hand hovered briefly over the inner pocket where her cell phone lay. She could tell Logan, right now, what they were doing. She could tell her, and—it would probably all be over, just like that. She'd be safe, yeah. Safe and boring—and probably back home at the estate, forbidden to go visit Eliana ever again.

I'll still have the cell phone, if things go bad, she reasoned with herself. *I don't have to call her right now, I can—I can call her if we get into trouble. Which hasn't happened yet.*

She dropped her hand. Thinking about the way Logan usually reacted to trouble, she did her best to imitate that strange, quizzical calm.

"If the Order didn't send you, how'd you find out about it?"

Fisher gave her a look then, like he was evaluating her. She did her best to meet his gaze and not to squirm. Just when she was sure the moment had gone on too long, Fisher broke into an unexpectedly friendly grin.

"Now, that's the fun part!" He leaned over toward the duffel bag between them, unzipped it, and pointed at a large piece of boxy metal that looked more than a little bit like an old-fashioned radio. "We've got a police radio scanner. Helps us stay on top of what's *really* happening in this city."

Jude knew that her role here was to be impressed with this feat, and not at all concerned with the legality of it. If she was honest, she didn't have to pretend too hard to pull it off. It was pretty impressive, even if a voice at the back of her head told her Logan might not like it.

"Cool," she said decisively, matching his grin with ease. She reached up to run her fingers over the short hairs on the shaved side of her head. Somehow, the soft insistence of the stubble actually did make her feel a little braver.

"Yeah, it's pretty sweet," said Fisher, leaning back in his chair. He adjusted his glasses as he did so, and Jude noticed that they still had no lenses. Upon graduation, new Order Adepts were often bound with a special power to help them fight demons. Eliana had chosen super strength, and had spent the night of her Binding demonstrating her new power to a small crowd of admirers. Fisher, on the other hand, had chosen something a little subtler: magically enhanced vision. His vision was perfect, even in absolute darkness, and he could see through certain magical illusions—and Jude had the distinct sense that he could see through solid objects, too. So the glasses, at this point, were an affectation.

"We intercepted some chatter about a lady calling in to report a cockroach the size of a small dog," he continued. "Obviously, the cops thought the lady was nuts, but we knew better. When we got there, I managed to tag the irahu before it vanished down a sewer." He pointed toward the front of the van, where Jude could see a GPS mounted on the dashboard, a blinking light indicating where they were going. "After that, it was just a matter of time."

The size of a small dog. She let that thought sink in, but she didn't let herself react to it.

"Awesome." This time, it was Jude who leaned back in her seat, more to cover her discomfort than anything else. "So, uh, I don't know much—or, anything, actually—about irahu demons. What are their weaknesses?"

Fisher just shrugged.

"When in doubt, go for the head. Not too many monsters out there can live without a head. Except chickens." Then he glanced at her out of the corner of his eye. "But, uh, irahu are water dwellers. They're sensitive to fire."

Jude felt an unexpected warmth in her stomach, rising through her chest. A smile passed over her face. Though she still wasn't confident in her powers, she couldn't help but feel like the universe had thrown her a bone.

Then the warmth, for a moment, flickered.

Adele's last missive came back to her. *Remember what we talked about, hm?* Jude remembered. Adele had told her not to summon without supervision. *You're at something of a crossroads,* she'd said. *It would be much too easy for you to lose your balance, especially with how you favor fire so. I know it feels powerful, but it's also volatile, Miss Li. We must be careful how we proceed.*

She knew she should obey. She knew Adele only told her what she needed to hear.

But she was already there. And they were headed into a fight, one way or another. Didn't she also have a duty to defend herself?

What other choice do I have?

Chapter Seven
The Mayhem High

They didn't talk much for the rest of the drive, which didn't last long. Before she was even finished steeling herself, Jude felt the van rumble to a halt. Eliana cut the engine and looked back at the other two.

"We'll have to go the rest of the way on foot," she said excitedly, leaning around the back of her chair to address them. "Everybody ready? Jude, you good?"

Even though she knew she was actually the least prepared for what they were about to do, Jude couldn't help resent the implication of it.

"Ready when you are," she said, despite how she felt.

"Excellent!"

With that, Eliana turned away from them and leapt out of the van, into the outside world. Before Jude could follow her, she felt a hand on her elbow. Fisher.

"Good luck out there," he said, looking more serious than she had ever seen him—not that she had much to compare it to. He pulled his lens-less glasses off, as if to drive home his point. "I mean that."

"Thanks. You, too."

"Before we go out there, I just wanted to say—I think we're kind of the same, you and me." He dropped the glasses into a mesh bag that hung off the back of the driver's chair. Perhaps he found them too much of a liability on the actual mission. "Or, what I mean is—I know what it's like."

Jude blinked at him; she wasn't expecting empathy from him, and she wasn't sure what it meant.

"What *what* is like?"

Fisher sighed. "To feel like a sidekick, I mean. Sorry, I don't—I don't mean it as an insult, it's just…I'm around Elli all the time, you know?" He gave her a sad smile. "And I'm sure it's the same with Logan. It's like—no matter what you do, you're always gonna be out-shined by the person standing right next to you."

Jude nodded but said nothing. She *did* want to prove herself, but that wasn't how she thought about her relationship with Logan. Still, she wasn't about to say that out loud to Fisher.

"And for what it's worth," he continued, "I think it's pretty cool that you decided to come out with us tonight. Us sidekicks—we've gotta show how good we are, unlike some people. And sometimes that means taking a risk or breaking a rule. Hell, sometimes it means getting hurt. It's better than the alternative, right?"

"What's the alternative?"

"Being forgotten."

Jude blinked, then nodded. She didn't know what *getting hurt* meant for Fisher, and she was increasingly sure she didn't want to know.

It's probably just macho fighter talk, anyway, she told herself.

Out loud she said, "Yeah, I guess you're right."

He didn't have another chance to clarify, because Eliana chose that moment to yell from outside the van.

"You ladies having a tea party? Get your asses out here!"

Fisher spared her a grin before he flipped around and pulled the van door open, tumbling out of it without another word. Jude followed close behind, her mind muddled with new uncertainty.

As soon as her feet hit the ground, she decided to put that conversation out of her head. They had a job to do; she could worry about the rest later.

Glancing up, she saw they had parked behind a row of warehouses on a dock somewhere. Thirty feet to their right, a waterway roiled, inky, dark, and unknowable. Eliana had already sprinted ahead of them, heading closer to the water with every step. Without a word, Fisher and Jude ran to catch up.

Eliana steered them toward the outer wall of the nearest warehouse, coming to a stop just around the corner, where the building would keep them hidden from anyone who might be passing by—though for now, there didn't seem to be anyone casually hanging out on the docks in the middle of the night. *Lucky break.*

They huddled up around the object Eliana held in her hand, and Jude realized that it was the GPS from the van. The blinking light had come to a stop.

"We've got to be right on top of it," said Eliana, raising her head to look around. After a moment, she smiled. "What do you want to bet that it's *underneath* us?"

Both Jude and Fisher looked over where Eliana's eyes were turned: a break in the railing indicated a ladder, leading down to the water below.

"Uh—I'm not exactly dressed for swimming," said Jude, uncertainly.

"Shouldn't be a problem," Eliana assured her. "Irahu live *near* the water, not in it." She glanced at Fisher. "There's probably, what, like 20 of them?"

"No need to guess when we can find out for sure," said Fisher, an unfamiliar gleam in his eye. Without another word, he took a step back from the other two and knelt down on the dock, staring unusually hard. Jude wondered if she was about to see the benefit of choosing to be Bound with something other than brute strength.

"They're definitely down there," he said slowly, his eyes still roving over the ground. "I count…maybe 25. A bunch of them are kind of on top of each other, so it's hard to be sure. But it's not many more than that."

"25 demons?" asked Jude, her heart now all the way in her throat. "Are you serious?"

"Oh, don't worry, irahu are really small," said Eliana. "They're about the size of a house cat."

"Oh, okay. And here I thought they were the size of small dogs." Jude's terror remained perfectly intact. Eliana didn't seem to notice.

"Alright!" She slipped her GPS into a leg holster and looked more excited than ever. "We know what we're headed into. Everybody ready?"

Fisher jumped up from his reconnaissance position. "Hell yeah!"

Jude let out an internal sigh as she pasted on a smile.

"Totally!" she said, with as much vigor as she could muster.

"Then let's do this!"

Eliana led the way, vanishing down the ladder so fast, Jude almost wondered if she'd jumped. Fisher followed right behind her, giving Jude a maniacal grin as he disappeared from view. Jude took a deep breath and held it for three seconds. Then she, too, went over the edge.

The stairs did come down over water, but an outcropping of rocky shore was only a short jump away. Jude climbed to the very last rung and swung herself to land with all the force as she had. The other two were already there, moving forward at a crouch, their guns drawn. Jude had never once seen Logan use a gun on a demon, regardless of size; she'd come to believe that guns probably didn't work on demons. But now she was beginning to question that thought.

Jude, for her part, pulled out her knife, and checked again to make sure her letha catalysts were only a quick grab away.

It took her eyes several seconds to adjust to the relative darkness beneath the docks. Water lapped at the shoreline behind them as they traveled deeper into this partly man-made cave. A few feet ahead of her, Eliana and Fisher had come to a stop, posing in a crouch with their guns at the ready. Jude came up beside them and re-gripped her knife.

At first, her brain couldn't quite make sense of what her eyes were seeing. It looked like she was staring at a colony of roly-polys...only they were far, far too big. Like Eliana had said, each irahu was about the size of a domestic cat. For one out-of-body moment, Jude couldn't help but feel like she'd somehow stepped inside an old black-and-white science fiction movie, and she was staring at a nest of bugs hit by gamma radiation or something.

"Ready, boys?" whispered Eliana. She raised her gun with both hands, and aimed. "One-two-"

Instead of saying *three*, she fired. Jude stood frozen as one of the nearer roly-polys partially exploded. *Oh. I don't think those are normal bullets*, a part of her brain whispered at her. The rest of her brain thought, *Oh, fuck.*

The effect of the shot was immediate. The irahu screamed into action, squirming away from their half blown-up brethren in all directions, their shining black bodies glinting strangely in the reflected moonlight. A number of them inevitably began running toward the encroaching humans, squealing all the way, and Eliana and Fisher wasted no time. Eliana fired right at the front of the line in rapid succession, blowing open one, then two, then three. Her fourth shot went wide, but Fisher's didn't. He hit all four in the next row, paused to let a fifth one wiggle closer to them, then popped that one out of existence, too.

For a moment, Jude felt the urge to run toward the mob of fleeing insect monsters, forcibly proving herself by way of sheer stupidity. Then she heard another gunshot, and realized it would be a better idea to wait until—

"Ammo's almost out, you?" Eliana asked Fisher as she fired another shot.

Fisher took out two more, which Jude judged to be his seventh and eighth kills, then nodded and holstered his gun. "Gone." Even as he spoke, he reached behind himself and pulled his crossbow around. "Now for the fun shit."

Eliana got off one more round before she, too, holstered her gun, and pulled out her second weapon—in her case, the sword. Jude had no reason to stay back now.

And wasn't it just her luck? A lone irahu began wobbling right toward her.

The irahu were still squealing, their high-pitched tones sounding almost mechanical, like the screeching of a million brakes slamming to a halt. This one squealed, too, getting louder as it advanced—it almost sounded like it intended to be intimidating, like it was letting loose a war cry. Jude re-gripped her knife, and, not a second too soon, lunged toward the ground, throwing her body into it as she came down on the beast. She felt, more than heard, the *crunch* as her battle knife cracked through its brittle exoskeleton, burying itself in the gooey flesh underneath. The irahu's scream abruptly came to an end, leaving a brief, eerie silence in its wake.

Jude didn't give herself much time to think about it before peeling her knife out of the dead demon and jumping into a crouch. Another irahu was on her in seconds, but this time, she felt more exhilaration than terror as she launched herself at it. Her knife punched through the hard exterior, but she could tell immediately that her aim wasn't quite true—though the knife had it momentarily pinned to the dirt, it only screamed louder and squirmed harder, and quickly dislodged the knife from the earth.

Swallowing down on her own panic, Jude grabbed the knife's hilt and yanked it free. She scrambled back from the increasingly angry irahu, but not far enough to miss the image of it finally rearing back its head to show its underside—and the row of sharp pincers and powerful-looking mandibles that waited there.

She still had the knife, and she held it out, in front of her chest, hoping she could at least keep herself safe, if she could do nothing else. Her other hand reached for a letha catalyst, but she couldn't remember the words to the cast it belonged to—

She only had to sputter for a few seconds, however. In no time at all, Eliana was there, like a conquering hero. She swung her sword down in one long, decisive arc, and chopped the demon clean in half. Pulling her sword back again with ease, she reached out a hand to help Jude get back to her feet.

"Looking good, Li." She offered Jude an audacious wink before spinning away from her, holding her sword high once more. Jude watched her for a moment before turning away herself. She ran after another irahu, slithering toward the water.

With the new influx of adrenaline running through her veins, her aim was true on the first try. The squealing ended, and she ripped her knife free and turned back to the fight. As she surveyed the damp little cave around them, she realized there were way more bodies now than living demons. She watched Eliana place her boot beneath the hilt of her sword, which appeared to be stuck inside her latest kill.

While she wrenched her sword free, a laughing Fisher slowly stalked one of the last fleeing demons, his crossbow held nonchalantly at his side.

"Hey, Elli, watch this!" He leaped forward, landing in a crouch only a few feet away from the irahu, which appeared to be scrabbling toward a hole in the wall. He laughed as he let loose an arrow, sending it right into the rear end of the demon.

All of a sudden, he froze, and the laugh died in his throat.

"Oh, shit."

He barely had time to stand back up before a tide of new irahu demons burst forth, swarming out of the hole in the wall like a giant oil spill. This, their mechanical screams sounded undeniably like a war cry—or an omen of onrushing doom. For his part, Fisher let loose a string of epithets as he fired his crossbow again and scrambled to reload, all the while running backward.

Eliana rushed forward to help him, but Jude suspected it was already too late. Fisher managed to fell a few in quick succession, but the crossbow took too much time to reload. Already, the wave of demons was at his feet. Already, they were climbing up his legs—

Perhaps it was the adrenaline coursing through Jude's veins that made it feel like time slowed down just for her. Or perhaps it would simply always be true that power and inspiration came more easily to her when she could see someone in trouble in the flesh. Whatever it was, in that moment, Jude knew without a shadow of a doubt that she didn't need her letha accoutrements to access magic. All she needed to do was clear away the cobwebs and unnecessary thoughts, and let herself go.

Her mind already wanted to go blank, so she let it. An image of a classroom on a cloudy day, and the feeling of helplessness, and the clarity of hatred. She called out to the fire, and the fire called back to her.

At first, the flame that formed in her outstretched hand was small as a pinprick. But within seconds, it had grown to the size of a baseball, then a bowling ball. She shot it toward the two irahu squirming up Fisher's legs, knocking them back. Before they even hit the ground, she'd formed a new ball of fire in her hands. This time, she held onto it a moment longer, walking forward as it grew and grew, until it turned into a raging wall of flame.

The darkness of the cave disappeared, replaced by an angry red-orange light, casting contrasting shadows in the farthest corners. In the periphery of her experience, she sensed Eliana yelling at Fisher to get out of the way. She paid it little mind as she directed her sun-bright wall of destruction to crash down on the irahu, crushing them as they tried to writhe and thrash away from her. Their squealing got louder, reaching a fever pitch, but she hardly noticed. The fire wanted to grow, wanted to burn. She knew if she let it get too close to the wall, it might find something to catch. And she might not be able to stop it.

But she kept her breathing steady, and she kept it in check. She pushed it down at the writhing irahu, and listened as their screaming finally died out. Just to be sure, she kept the fire going a few seconds more. Then she knew it was time. With one last flicker, the flames sputtered and went out.

In the wake of all that screaming and burning brightness, the silent dark fell back on them with a thud. Jude's legs lost their strength, and she dropped to her knees. She felt like she'd been hollowed out.

"Was that all of them?" Her voice sounded like a croak.

In a moment, Eliana and Fisher were at her side, kneeling down with her. The side of Fisher's face looked bloodied.

"That was all of them," said Eliana. She re-sheathed her sword, wiped off her hands, and gently took Jude's in her own. "You okay?"

"I think so." She pointed in Fisher's direction. "Did I do that?"

Looking bemused, Fisher reached up to touch the side of his face. His hand came away covered in blood, which seemed to surprise him.

"No. But I think you probably saved me from worse. Thanks."

Eliana squeezed her hand and gave her an encouraging smile.

"You were *amazing*. Are you sure you're okay?"

Jude wasn't sure *what* she felt. A part of her didn't feel quite real; it was almost like her body belonged to someone else, and she had only come to borrow it for a little while.

"Not sure." She glanced down at her free hand, then moved it up in front of her face.

She didn't know if it was a good idea or not, but it almost didn't matter: she *had* to see if she could replicate the summon. There wasn't any other choice. Not if she had any chance of getting better at doing it.

Closing her eyes, she called to the fire. And the fire called back to her.

She knew before she opened her eyes that a candle light of flame had appeared in her palm. She could hear Eliana and Ian's simultaneous sharp intakes of breath. She opened her eyes.

There it was. The longer she held it, the more she *felt* it. She'd been a little worried that a second summon might wipe her out, somehow, or even cause her to faint. Instead, it felt like the opposite was happening: she felt *more* energy, not less.

The fire is you.

A grin cracked its way across her face. By the time she let the fire go out, she felt like she'd downed three more energy drinks.

"So," she said, smiling merrily at the other two, "what are we doing next?"

When they got back to Logan's apartment, the first thing they did was clean and dress Alexei's wound. The cut turned out to be shallow, though it did span the length of his chest. Almost as soon as they stepped in the front door, Alexei deemed the shirt ruined, and he had it torn off and tossed aside not a moment later.

"You've got a med kit, right?" he asked as he sailed past the kitchen, heading toward the living room.

"Of course," she said, frozen at the doorway to the kitchen as she watched him retreat. "Maybe you should come sit at the table—"

But she could already see him flopping onto the couch in an unfairly graceful arc. With a silent sigh, she grabbed the sturdy red container off the top of the refrigerator and followed him. When she seated herself on the stool in front of him, he leaned back into the cushions expectantly, clearly assuming she would dress his wound for him.

The smirk on his face told her everything she needed to know about his motives. He was in one of *those* moods, no doubt. Those moods that were only dangerous if she was in one, too. The truth was, she couldn't tell if she was in one, or not. Lately, it felt like she *always* was, but maybe the events of the evening were enough to throw her off.

Better safe than sorry.

She opened the box and handed him iodine and a cotton ball. His smirk only faltered a moment before he accepted the tools…and proceeded to swab himself down with delicate care.

She barely let him finish, leaning forward to press a bandage over it while he was still dabbing gently at his own pectoral muscle. She was just placing a second piece of medical tape down when his hand closed lightly around her wrist.

"Thanks, doc," he said softly, looking up at her through curly bangs. "I appreciate the personalized service."

Logan cleared her throat.

"Can't let you die on my watch," she said dryly. "You still gotta make me a sandwich."

His laugh pulsed warm.

"I'd say a fight like that calls for pizza." He still hadn't moved his hand from her wrist, which meant her hand still rested partially against the bare skin of his chest. "Don't you?"

"Injured gets to choose." Ever so carefully, she slipped her hand away from him. "I'll call the place on the corner to see if they're open."

While Logan ordered an ungodly amount of pizza, most of it packed with goat cheese and artichokes, Alexei picked out an old zombie movie from Logan's haphazard collection of DVDs. Logan laughed when she saw his choice.

"You sure about this?" She motioned for him to sit up straight, and when he did, she slumped down next to him. "I'm sure I have at least one normal movie in there somewhere."

"What, you don't like it? Didn't you buy it?"

"Oh, I love it. I just can't promise any other living person will."

Alexei smiled.

"I like monster movies. I like seeing what the normies come up with, you know?"

Logan shrugged. "Your call. I bear no responsibility in this."

Almost as soon as she'd settled in, Logan felt the weight of the day beginning to slip away. She felt like she'd been on high alert for week—and, in fact, she had. Every move she made felt haunted—either by the specter of the Wolf, or by a persistent paranoia about the Order of Shadows. And undergirding even that, her father. What had he said? How much of her had he betrayed?

But as she watched a stupid movie with a resolutely shirtless Alexei, waiting for pizza…it all finally melted into the background. At least for a moment.

She didn't know which of them fell asleep first. Or how Alexei had ended up on the floor while she remained on the couch. All she did know was that when she woke up, her arm was dangling into the abyss, her fingers rested against something warm. She jerked fully awake when she realized what it was, and snatched her hand back, hiding it impulsively under her own body.

Alexei still seemed solidly asleep, one arm thrown across his face while his chest rose and fell in steady rhythm. She didn't let herself look at him too long, preferring instead to roll herself to the other end of the couch until her feet had a clear path. Then she got up and walked back to her own bedroom.

Moments later, she was safely tucked into her own shower, happily washing off what remained of the grime and stale air from the underground. She turned the water as hot as it could go and let it rain down on her, until it drowned out the faint residual heat from the Choronzon Key.

She normally kept her hair at chin length, slightly longer in the front than the back. But as she ran her hands through her hair, letting the hot water wash it clean, she realized the front ends now grazed her shoulders. If she'd had to guess, she would say it had been at least a year since she'd last bothered to get a cut, and as soon as she had that thought, she had the resultant rush of pessimism, too: *is that normal? Or does demon hair grow slower?*

She reached for the shampoo and wished it could scrub away more than grime. She felt tired.

Eventually her skin took on the softened feel of the exfoliated, so she shut off the water, squeezed out the slightly too-long ends of her hair, and pushed open the clear glass door. As she toweled herself off, her eyes fell, like they often did, onto the tattoo on the inside of her arm: *the field only reveals.*

It was a reference, and it was a reminder. When she'd first gotten it, she'd meant it to remind herself that the work was never done. With every demon she defeated, there were 10 more to take its place. And sometimes the real demon didn't turn out to be what she first suspected.

Did it still mean the same thing, now? Or did it only exist to remind her that misery had no end, either?

A knock sounded at the bathroom door. If she'd had human reflexes, she might have jumped. Instead, she had to force back her body's automatic impulse to unleash its spikes.

Her hair was still wet and tangled, the cold ends brushing against the hardened, purplish-black skin of her collarbone and shoulders. She could see now, without a doubt, that the armor-like skin was spreading. It had started to stretch in both directions, forming a little arrow at the top of each upper arm, as well as a collar creeping up the sides of her neck. Her robe would no longer cover it completely, but she reached for it anyway, and made sure to tie the waist before she opened the door.

Alexei met her on the other side, wearing nothing but silk pajama pants, though she was certain he must have gone into the guest room to change into them, and therefore could easily have found himself a shirt.

His skin was burnt sienna and perfect, of course, his frame lean and lightly muscled, like a model on a billboard. With a hard blink, Logan forced herself to refocus on his face and hair, though that wasn't much better: his cheekbones could leave a scar, and his dark, slightly curly hair had an extra hint of tousle today. *Like he could roll right back into bed at any—*

Good lord, Logan, she said to herself, with deliberate force. *Are we a fucking teenager?*

Immediately, a voice answered: *What if demon adolescence starts at 29?*

"Hi," she said out loud, doing her best to keep her tone neutral. "How's it going?"

"I got us a reservation for brunch downtown in one hour," he said. He cocked his head to the side as he gave her a smile. "Is there a second bathroom for me to shower in, or are you ready to share?"

"Down the hall, last door," she said. She decided it was best, for the moment, to ignore his second suggestion. "Might be a bit dusty, but it should be fully stocked."

"Perfect, thanks." He started to go, then paused to glance back at Logan. She couldn't help but wonder if he was giving her a moment to appreciate the movement of his unclothed back. "Not sure if the restaurant will love the black satin robe and no underwear look, but I personally think you should go for it."

Logan glanced down at herself reflexively, then shrugged.

"I think I've got a second one around here, if you wanna match?"

Alexei let out a laugh.

"On second thought, I should at least *try* to stay out of jail this time."

"This time?"

He didn't offer her an answer, not that she'd expected one. He was already disappearing down the hallway, toward the bathroom she was certain she'd already pointed out to him before.

She combed her hair out quickly and toweled it dry, deciding to forgo any attempt at hair care or styling. She rarely did either, anyway. Instead, she spent her time strapping on her most discreet weapons harnesses before finding a movable pair of black jeans and a high-collar, long-sleeved gray blouse.

For now, that was all she needed to keep her demon side hidden from the public. But if her body kept changing at this rate, she couldn't say how long that would remain true.

Chapter Eight
Back Down

Jude couldn't quite put her finger on the moment the whole night changed, though she was tempted to say that it was the moment her cast kicked into high gear. That was certainly the moment her own energy seemed to change—growing and twisting until she almost felt like a completely different person. It felt a little bit like the height of a particularly good game, back when she played soccer, only multiplied by an incalculable degree. Her blood sang and her limbs felt like wings; for the briefest moment, she felt so full and complete that she had no room left over for her own insecurity.

But was that the moment the night changed? She wasn't sure. The looks on the others' faces told her a different story. They were impressed, yes, but to be impressed with something inherently means to be apart from it. So, while they were impressed with her, that meant they were still separate. Still disparate units, waiting to be made whole.

It took her a few minutes to come back down to earth after she let the fire go out. It was like she could still feel the fire inside her own body, begging to be released—begging to *consume*. She heard the others talking, but her mind weaved in and out of what they were saying. After a few moments, she realized they'd started gathering up the charred irahu bodies—the ones that hadn't been burned away entirely—and shoving them into giant sacks Jude hadn't even noticed they were carrying. Once she figured out how to move her feet again, she helped get the last few remains picked up and put away.

A part of her wanted to ask if they were just clearing away the evidence to keep normal people safe, but she couldn't get the words to form in time before she'd moved on to a different thought entirely.

Their drive back to the apartment was a manic blur. She remembered the radio blaring a familiar up-beat song, and Fisher whooping out the open window and banging his fist on the roof. Cold air must have flooded the van, but with her blood still on fire, she hardly noticed. It was possible she had joined in on the noise-making; she couldn't say for sure.

They made an inexplicably whirlwind tour through the tiny apartment, stopping just long enough to each down two shots of the nastiest-tasting liquid Jude had ever experienced. She could *almost* see what it had in common with the beer she'd drunk in high school…but not quite.

To her dismay, Eliana insisted on pouring a third round—but Jude bowed out. She was pretty sure if she tried to swallow that awful stuff one more time, she'd end up throwing up, which seemed like a sure-fire mood-killer. The other two downed it in one, apparently unbothered by the taste and the burn.

And just like that, they were off again. Their first stop was a nearby dive bar, where they didn't get carded, and where Eliana bought Jude something called a *seven and seven*. Jude was delighted to discover that it tasted infinitely better than the shots had.

While Eliana and Jude got the drinks, Fisher wandered off into a shadowy corner Jude couldn't quite see from the bar. As soon as he walked out of sight, Eliana leaned in to whisper in Jude's ear.

"So…how would you rate our first date?"

Jude felt a blush that began in her toes and traveled the entire length of her body, landing on the skin of her neck. Partly to play the game and partly to cover, she leaned into Eliana's ear to answer.

"Five stars. Ten out of ten."

She had barely started to pull away before she felt Eliana's fingers brush her cheek, her hand reaching for the short side of Jude's hair, grazing the ends and sending shivers down Jude's spine.

She watched in amazement as Eliana's eyes fell on her lips, her head tilting forward—

Three heavy-bottomed drinks slammed down on the bar next to them, the bartender's grizzled mug swimming up between them.

"You starting a tab?"

With obvious, physical reluctance, Eliana forced on a public smile and turned to him.

"Yeah, under Blake. Thanks."

The moment summarily lost, they picked up their drinks and headed toward the back, eventually finding their way to Fisher in the far corner. As it turned out, the corner he'd chosen featured a dart board, and he held up nine darts as they approached him.

"I'm surprised you actually waited for us," said Eliana with a smirk as she set two glasses down on the high table nearest him. "Or did you already finish a game by yourself?"

"Nah." Fisher afforded them a wicked grin. "What fun is showing off if there's no one *important* around to watch you?"

Before Jude could ask what he meant, he picked out one of the darts with his right hand, turned to face the board, and proceeded to throw each dart individually, one right after the other.

Every single one landed in the middle of the bull's eye, creating a perfect, tight ring right in the center. Fisher turned back to them, adjusting his glass-less glasses like he was taking a bow.

"Not bad, not bad," said Eliana. She pushed one of the pints toward him. "Let's see how you do after a couple of these, huh?"

"Why don't we make it interesting? I'll drink all three of these and let you try to beat me sober." He picked up the nearest drink and tossed his head back, gulping down the liquid inside as quickly as he could. A thin trickle dripped down his cheek as he slammed it back down on the table. "I'm willing to lose if you are."

Eliana shook her head. "I've lost that bet too many times. Now, if you wanna arm wrestle—"

"I like all my limbs intact, thanks," he responded with a laugh. Leaning closer to them over the table, he lowered his voice to a whisper. "Wanna play the underwear game?"

Jude felt a ribbon of anxiety snake through her stomach. She clutched her drink to push it down.

"What's the underwear game?" she asked.

Eliana gave her a sly smile. "Well, you know Fisher's special vision can do more than just win a game of darts, right?"

"Uh—right." Jude knew that at his Binding, Fisher had chosen to have his eyesight enhanced, but in truth, she didn't *really* know all that might entail. She didn't even know the limits of Eliana's enhanced physical strength—or whatever lasting side effects there might be from the fact that the man who Bound her with her abilities, the High Prophet James Atherton, had died within days of performing the ceremony. And Eliana hadn't seemed keen to dwell on those effects, either.

But she didn't need to remind the two of them of any of that.

"So, we developed a game to play in bars," said Eliana, serenely pushing past Jude's unspoken uncertainty. Her voice was low enough that Jude was pretty sure nobody else could hear them. "We pick out someone at the bar and place bets on what their underwear looks like. And then Fisher finds out the truth."

For a moment, Jude could *feel* Logan disapproving of this in her head. But Logan wasn't there now, was she? Maybe it was only the fire in her blood, but for once, she didn't want to wait for her mentor's approval. She just wanted to have fun.

She gave Fisher a theatrically suspicious look.

"How do we know you're not cheating?"

Fisher chuckled. "You gotta take some stuff on faith, Li. Besides, don't I have an honest face?"

"Lots of people have honest faces," said Jude, shaking her head at them. On sudden inspiration, she added, "And then it turns out they're wearing *Batman* boxers under their regulation cargo pants."

"Are you betting on *me*?" he asked, feigned outrage in his tone.

Jude shrugged and took a drink from her cup. "I don't know. Wanna prove me wrong?"

Fisher pursed his lips and glanced between Jude's solemn expression and Eliana's attempts to cover up her giggles at his expense.

"I...would prefer not to," he responded eventually, giving his best attempt at a haughty, dignified expression. It seemed to involve a fair amount of eyebrow work.

At that, Eliana's giggles gave way to an outright laugh.

"She clocked you, didn't she?"

"Would you look at that? It's already time for another round of drinks," said Fisher, cheeks reddening, as he pulled away from the table. Once he was out of earshot, Eliana shook her head and got control of herself.

"That was good," she said, with a wink at Jude, "but we should play the game for real. You know, give him some cover for that humiliation when he gets back."

Right, cover. At the expense of an unwitting participant, Jude thought.

"Sure," she said out loud before taking a deep drink of her seven and seven. "Got a target in mind?"

"Always," said Eliana, gazing at Jude with utmost certainty. She pointed at someone behind her. "How about that fucking guy?"

Jude turned, following Eliana's point until her eyes landed on a man leaning over the pool table, several feet away. He was a giant of a man, bushy mustache leading into bushy beard, a bandanna tied around his head, nearly obscuring the ponytail at the back. With his worn-out heavy metal T-shirt over bulging biceps, and his jean jacket with the sleeves torn off, he looked like he'd walked right off a movie set about motorcycle gangs in the 1980s.

"Wow," said Jude, nodding as she turned back to the table. Despite whatever she might have thought about herself, the answer came to her immediately, and with ease. "Uh, honestly, my guess is American flag boxers."

Eliana chortled as she took another drink. "I like it, I like it. But you know, I've seen his type before. All that masculinity— it's almost *too much*, you know? So I'm gonna go with…purple polka dots. Briefs."

Jude couldn't tell if she was serious or not, but she laughed anyway. They picked out a few more people and made their guesses, and with each one they did, Jude felt her internal stigma slip a little farther into background noise.

It took Fisher a few minutes to get back, but eventually he sidled up to their table again, carrying three beers with him. Jude glanced down at the half-full glass in her hand, uncertain, before she felt Eliana nudge her with her finger.

"Wanna race?"

She hesitated only a moment. She'd already committed to everything else; this was nothing. Fisher counted down for them, and they both slammed their drinks together, gulping them down in record time. Jude wasn't sure if it was from the alcohol, or throwing her head back, or merely the psychological effect of committing to the night, but she started to feel a little light-headed as soon as their glasses hit the table.

And already, Fisher was pushing their next round over.

"Fisher!" Eliana announced a bit too loudly. She pointed toward the biker stereotype at the pool table, who was now watching his competition make their play. "Make your judgment on Mr. Meatloaf over there."

Fisher slammed his glass on the table and spun all the way around, making a quick survey of the entire scene before landing back where he started.

"I judge him—unsatisfactory!" He made a pointing motion up towards the ceiling, as if he expected it to speak up and agree with him. "As for my guess—I'm going lumberjack plaid, but on the softest silk you ever did touch."

"And how the hell are we supposed to figure out what it *feels* like, good sir?" Eliana's tone was accusatory, the words "good sir" spitting from her mouth like a curse.

"That's easy," said Fisher, setting his drink down decisively. "We'll have Li burn off the rest of his clothes. Then during the ensuing confusion—"

"We grope the biker?" Eliana offered pointedly.

"Did I say 'easy?' I meant suicidal."

"Why don't you leave the battle plans to me, huh?"

Fisher turned his head to Jude, eyebrows raised expectantly. "What do you think, newbie? Time for a fire fight?"

Jude didn't love his choice of nickname, but she briefly enjoyed his inclusion of her…until she remembered what they were voting for.

"Uh—I'm gonna go with the option that's less likely to burn down the bar before we get the next round."

Fisher considered her point and nodded. "You're right. I

would hate to have to walk five more blocks the next time we go out." Surreptitiously this time, he turned his gaze back on the biker, scanning him for a few extra seconds before ducking his head. "Sorry to say it, but it looks like newbie takes the first round today. The biker is a stars-and-stripes man."

Eliana raised her glass in salute. "To Jude! Ever adding to her considerable list of skills."

"Or her beginner's luck, depending on how you look at it," said Fisher, without bite. He offered Jude a reluctant smile before raising his glass up in toast, as well.

Jude wasn't sure how she felt about winning this game, but she held up her glass anyway, and all three clinked in toast.

Perhaps that was the moment it all shifted. Perhaps, on her successful inclusion in the game, her wins up to that point ceased to be individual anomalies and instead became the proof of her belonging with them, the proof of her place in the big leagues.

Or perhaps it was later, when Fisher revealed that he'd secreted a few phials of potion out of headquarters at some point, and the three of them decided to take them all at once. Or perhaps it was when the potion took effect, and Jude began to find it harder and harder to distinguish one moment from the rest.

When all was said and done, she couldn't really be sure. Nor could she be certain that her already tenuous grasp on the events of the night wouldn't slip further and further from view, the more time came between her present self and the night in question.

All she could really be sure of was that when the night finally came to a forcible end, owing to the inexorable press of the coming dawn, she wasn't ready for it to be over.

"I don't even feel tired yet, you guys," she drawled as they trudged up the cement stairs of the apartment building, up to the third floor.

"Honestly, I'm not either," said Eliana, giving her a sideways glance. "But it's…oh, wow, yeah, it's 6:00am. We need to at least try to get some sleep, before—"

"Before what?"

Ahead of them, Fisher had stopped dead. Eliana took a moment to notice, so she kept walking, nearly running him over as she bumped into him. Then she stopped dead, too.

Jude had a few more steps to go before she could understand why. Then she took in the rest of the scene.

An Adept of the Order of Shadows stood on the landing in front of them, her severe black uniform giving her away. Her arms were crossed over her chest, and her face was set with a deep frown. Jude glanced at the other two just long enough to take in the sheer terror on their faces.

"There's been an incident," said the Adept sharply, taking a few steps toward them, her unforgiving expression static on her face. "When you couldn't be raised, I volunteered to collect you." She spared a glance for Jude before directing a particularly sharp look at Eliana. "Your presence is requested immediately. Your *guest* must remain behind."

Was it just Jude's imagination, or did she say the word guest like she was flinging mud off her shoe?

"Yes, ma'am," said Eliana, her back straightening as she gave a quick salute. "I just need a minute to let my guest back into the apartment."

The Adept gave a quick nod. "You have two. I'll wait for you downstairs."

All three of them scrambled out of the way as the Adept strode toward, and then right past, them. Fisher managed to give Jude a lascivious wink before following after her, leaving Jude and Eliana alone for a moment. Eliana motioned for Jude to follow her as she unlocked the apartment and stepped inside the narrow entrance hallway.

"I'll leave you my keys," she said, pressing them into Jude's hand. "So, if you need to go out for any reason, you can still get back in. If we're actually getting pulled into a mission now, then I don't really know how long we'll be gone. And if we're about to get punished—well, I don't know how long we'll be gone then, either."

"Oh—okay," said Jude, taking the keys with a small amount of reluctance. She didn't really want to sit around Eliana's tiny borrowed apartment all by herself all day, but it didn't seem like she had much of a choice. "Uh, is there anything I can do?"

Eliana smiled ruefully and shook her head. "It's sweet of you to offer, but I don't think so. It's probably best if you just stay here."

"Okay, I can do that."

Eliana reached out and brushed her hair back—then leaned in and kissed her, briefly, on the mouth. "See you soon. I hope."

With that, she slipped out the door and disappeared.

The sun had already gone down by the time they got back to Logan's apartment building, a little after 5:00pm. The days were getting shorter as they tumbled into winter, which in Seattle meant moderate cold and constant gray, an endless supply of rainy days, and shorter and shorter stretches of daylight. Of course, in recent years, there had been more than a few variations from the norm. Logan was starting to suspect she might need to buy an actual winter coat sometime soon.

As Logan was relatively lobby-averse, she guided Alexei down into the parking lot beneath the building to get to the elevator. She made sure to guide them past her own parking spot so she could say a silent 'hello' to her bright green Kawasaki Ninja motorcycle. The colder and wetter it got, the more dangerous it would be to ride. Still, she could feel it in her bones how badly she wanted to take it out. She hadn't had a chance to go on a ride in weeks, since before the Summit at the Order of Shadows. Before everything had gone to hell.

She sighed, feeling briefly overwhelmed by the guilt of how much empty fun she had had today. She should have been training, or talking to Rossi, or doing research into all known mystical bronze artifacts—

"Everything alright over there?" Alexei asked quietly. Logan glanced over at him in time to see that he had been watching her out of the corner of his eye, mild concern in his face. "Feels like you went somewhere."

Logan looked him in the eye, letting her right eyebrow raise.

"How long have I been walking in total silence?"

"Oh, just—10 straight minutes, tops."

Logan nodded and started walking again, heading in the direction of the elevator.

"Sorry. Lost in thought, I guess." She shifted around some of the bags in her hands, more to give herself something to do than anything else. After the first store of the day, Alexei was the only one who'd bought anything, but by now, Logan was carrying the majority of the bags. The longer they'd walked, the more weight she'd insisted on carrying. She felt like it gave her a purpose, and it helped alleviate some of her guilt over taking leisure time. Some, but not all.

"Good thought, or bad?"

Logan glanced down at her hand, unnecessarily, as it pressed the button to call the elevator down.

"Complicated thought." She shrugged her shoulders back, more as a way to work the muscles than as a gesture of nonchalance. "There are a lot of things I probably should have done today."

"Like what?" he asked, incredulously. He glanced around the parking structure, clearly making sure that they were alone. "You already got the demon from your vision. What more were you supposed to do today?"

The elevator opened, and she stepped inside.

The field only reveals.

"The work is never done," she said. Her voice was quiet; she felt like she was only half there, and the other half of her was far away. She could see the image of the Wolf in her mind's eye, feel the threat he represented begging to take center stage. She could feel the storm, too, as if it were now instead of somewhere in the nebulous future—and the skin of the universe, and how badly she wanted it to tear—

"H.C., do you know what a workaholic is?"

She snapped back to the present to raise an eyebrow at him.

"I take your implication, and I resent it."

Alexei chuckled. "It's the truth. You spent one *day* having fun with me. And you're, what, stewing in the guilt now?"

Logan's gaze settled almost unconsciously on the spot where her tattoo was currently covered up by jacket. It burned into her.

"It's not just a job for me," she said quietly. "It's...an obligation. A duty. I...I don't know *why* I have the Key, but as long as I have it...I have to earn it."

Alexei's voice was quiet, too.

"But you did, H.C. You got the demon."

That wasn't the only vision, she thought but didn't say. The elevator came to a stop before she had to say anything, and the doors slid open.

"I should probably check in with Knatt," she said. "Go drop your stuff in the guest room, and I'll meet you back at the closet."

"Ah, if only you knew how often I'd heard that," he muttered wistfully. She dropped his bags somewhat unceremoniously in the hallway before grabbing the one item she'd bought and taking it back to her room, where she could safely shut out the world for a minute or two.

She hadn't told Alexei about her other vision—nor had she spoken to him about how they'd woken up that morning, with her hand resting against his bare chest. Instead, she'd let herself get slightly drunk at breakfast and spent the rest of the day indulging his flirtation. She wasn't sure which part of that made her feel worse.

It stops here, she told herself firmly. She still hadn't decided what 'it' was, but the phrase came close to making her feel better, so she repeated it a few more times before stepping out of the room again.

Unsurprisingly, she made it back to the front hallway before Alexei. Tugging the collar of her motorcycle jacket, she couldn't help but think about her Ninja downstairs, real longing filling her heart. It had been so long…

"Ready to go?" asked Alexei as he cleared the corner.

She glanced down the hallway through her living room, to the sliding glass doors that led out to the balcony and the cold but clear night sky. Not a cloud in sight.

"You know, it's not raining right now, so we could—"

"Oh, no. I am not climbing on that deathtrap, thank you."

"My motorcycle is perfectly safe. Most of the time."

"Absolutely not."

"Well, obviously, if you're afraid, I have to respect that. We can take the easy way."

Alexei folded his arms across his chest.

"I am not scared. It's nighttime in November, and it's freezing out. Only an idiot would want to get on a motorcycle right now."

"Hey, no judgment. There's no shame in admitting your fears. Only strength."

The sides of his mouth folded into a scowl.

"The only thing I'm *scared* of is an overconfident ass hole letting her hands go numb and losing her grip on the handlebars."

"So…you *are* scared."

"Jesus, are you done being a teenage boy yet?"

Demon adolescence, she thought to herself. The words were beginning to sound less like a taunt and more like truth.

"Yeah, I think I'm done. Let's get going."

She turned the skeleton key that stuck out of her hallway closet door. This door was one of only three fixed exits from the traveling room back at the estate, but it only served as an entrance when this *particular* skeleton key was used to open it. When she pulled it open now, they were treated to the sight of the large, echoing marble chamber on the other side—the one and only traveling room. They stepped through, and immediately traversed the thirty miles that stood between her apartment and the Logan estate.

As soon as Logan took a deep breath on the other side, she could tell something was wrong. It took her a moment to pinpoint what it was. Then it hit her: she could smell fresh, cold air, somewhere nearby.

"Someone must have left a window open," she muttered, vaguely. She started walking toward the hallway.

"You can tell that from here?" Alexei looked around at the windowless room they had just entered, as if he could see what she meant.

As soon as she opened the door to the hallway, Logan knew she was right.

"I can smell it," she answered simply, striding forward once more.

They'd barely made it ten feet down the hall when her suspicions were abruptly confirmed.

A loud crashing sound exploded from a room deeper in the house. Someone had broken in.

Or someone had broken out.

Chapter Nine
Unveiled Threat

For one full minute, Jude stood alone in the center of the tiny living room, wondering what she should do next. She didn't feel like sleeping, what with her heart still hammering away inside her chest and her feet still burning to move. Eventually, she decided to pull out the strange book Adele had given her before she left and see what there was to see about it. She went back into Eliana's bedroom and pulled the book out of her backpack, curling up just under the pillow to read it.

She barely got two paragraphs in before she fell asleep, right on the page. By the time she woke up again, the natural light in the room had blossomed, suggesting the dawn had long since come and gone. When she finally found her cell phone, she saw that it was about two in the afternoon.

With a start, she leapt to her feet. Surely Eliana and Fisher had been back for hours by now; she'd practically slept the day away already. She leapt across the short distance from the bed to the door and pulled it open.

But the rest of the apartment was empty. She peeked her head into Fisher's room—it looked, impossibly, even smaller than

Eliana's—but it was empty, too. They were still gone.

With a sigh, she checked her phone again, even though she already knew she had no messages there. Nothing. She slipped it back into her pocket.

As she did, her stomach let out an aggressive growl. She had a vague memory of sharing a hot dog from a street vendor with Eliana and Fisher around three in the morning, but nothing after that.

Eliana's keys weighed heavy in her pocket. With a thrill that was equal parts excitement and terror, she realized that this was her first chance to explore New York City all on her own.

And Logan had given her spending money.

She didn't think about it long. Less than a minute later, she was locking up the apartment and venturing out into the world. Ten minutes after that, she was ducking into the very first delicatessen she saw.

With an inexplicable anxiety, she made careful study of the ordering etiquette of the people before her in line, while also making sure to scan as much of the chalkboard above the counter as she could—despite the nearly illegible scrawl of handwritten chalk marks there. She eventually determined that she wanted an everything bagel with chive and onion cream cheese, tomatoes, red onion, banana peppers, and a slice of cheddar. When her turn finally came up, she copied the other patrons and barked her order loud enough to be heard over the small television behind the counter, which appeared to be tuned to a basketball game. On sudden impulse, she added an iced tea to her order. Then she handed her cash over to the appropriate employee and stood giddily behind the others, awaiting the arrival of her food.

As quickly as it began, it was over again. She took her bottle of tea and her bagel sandwich, wrapped skillfully in folded wax paper and heavy as a stone in her hand. Through a clear corner in the counter, she'd been able to watch as the deli man piled the veggies high before smashing them down again with the top of the bagel.

Though she wasn't sure if she was brave enough to eat alone in public, she didn't want to go back inside yet. So, she picked a direction and started walking, keeping track of where she was by counting the blocks. Logically, of course, she knew the street would eventually end and she'd be forced to turn or head back, but it felt like she could have walked forever if she wanted to. And she almost did.

Everywhere she looked, she saw corner delis and convenience stores and apartment buildings and cafes and hipster-chic restaurants. She was tempted to check out one that promised pho, which she'd heard of but never tasted, despite the fact that she literally already carried her lunch in her hands. It was about there that she decided it was time to turn around and make her way back to the apartment. She was too hungry to keep exploring without a pit stop, and she was a little too intimidated to rest anywhere for long.

So instead, she crossed over one block and began her journey back, intent on taking in the street on the other side this time. By the time she made it back to the right apartment building, she was starting to feel like she'd taken in a broader look at the human condition within the last hour than she had during her entire life leading up to that.

In short, she was beginning to feel exhausted.

Once back inside the apartment, she gratefully closed and locked the door behind her. Though the living room immediately felt more restful than the outside world, there was almost no natural light, since the only winders were in the bedrooms. So, instead of setting herself up on the couch, she went back into Eliana's room and took a seat on the wide ledge beneath the window.

The curtains had been closed before, so she opened them now. She wasn't surprised to find that the bedroom window looked out onto an alley between apartment buildings, primarily affording her a view of brick walls and small windows. As she crossed her legs and leaned back against the wall, she spotted a cat across the way. It was one story down and watching her movements intently. She waved.

When she finally bit down into her first New York bagel, she could have sworn it was the best thing she'd ever tasted. She turned out to be far hungrier than she'd realized, and she devoured it entirely too quickly. She finished it off with her iced tea, but all too soon, that was gone, too. With a sigh, she glanced back down at the other window, only to find that even the cat had vanished.

She stood up somewhat reluctantly and made her way back into the living room. It didn't take long to find the trash and recycling, and to dispose of all the evidence of the time she'd just spent, all on her own, in New York City. On a final impulse, she kept the plastic cap to the tea, rinsed and wiped it off, and stowed it in a pocket of her backpack.

Then she curled up on the living room couch with the book Adele had left her, and went back to reading.

They heard a loud crash from down the hallway. Without so much as a backward glance at Alexei, Logan took off sprinting toward the sound as fast as she could. All she could think was that she didn't know where Knatt was, and she'd left him all alone, and someone could get the jump on him before he had a chance to fight back—

As she got closer to it, she realized where it had come from: the library, on the other side of the house. She let instinct and memory take over as she rocketed through the hallways at top speed until she crashed through the library doors, which already stood slightly ajar.

What greeted her was not the scene she feared. Instead of finding Knatt alone and helpless with a dangerous intruder…she saw her father. He was huddled in an overstuffed armchair, eyes wide with fear, while Rossi stood a few feet away, rifling through their collection of books and tossing them aside when they failed to please him. From the looks of it, he'd overturned another shelf entirely in his zeal.

Logan stepped into the room, suppressing the urge to let loose her spikes.

"You know, if I'd found you in the kitchen, I would have understood." Her voice was even and calm. The calm came easier than she expected. "But what have the books done to deserve this?"

Rossi held another book in his hand as he turned around to face her.

"What can I say?" An empty smile pressed onto his face. "I am a seeker of knowledge."

Logan's right eyebrow rose.

"And what *knowledge* would that be?"

Rossi's smile dripped with menace.

"Did you think I would be so easy, girl?"

"I did. Still do, in fact."

Barely had she let the words fly before she sprang into action, leaping right over the table that stood between them. All the erstwhile worry about her demon side fell away as she seamlessly transitioned her movement into an attack, throwing her weight into the blow she leveled at Rossi's head. He flew sideways, slamming into the bookshelf behind him and upsetting a whole new row of books.

His recovery was swifter than she would have expected from a man who'd been locked in a cage for nearly 48 hours. He rebounded on her and immediately accessed his Bound abilities, transforming into a half-monster right before her eyes. With inhuman strength, he unleashed one blow, and then another, hitting her with such force that she staggered backward until she hit the table behind her. She took that opportunity to knee him in the groin, making him double over. Before he recovered, she let fly three quick jabs, aimed right at the center of his face. She wasn't terribly surprised to see that the blood that poured forth from his nose looked darker and more viscous than it should have—as if it were somewhere between human and demon.

He got in another good hit to her ribs, but she could already feel his strength starting to wane. She, on the other hand, seemed to be better fueled by rich food and a sense of guilt than she ever would have guessed. With a few more well-aimed strikes, including one particularly brutal one to his wrist, it was all over. She had him pinned against the wall, her arm pressed tight against his windpipe, his badly injured wrist hanging limply to one side while she kept the other one locked down.

"You got one way out of this, buddy," she muttered, her voice coming out in a rasp.

Before he could answer, a voice she'd almost forgotten was there chose to make itself heard.

"Henrietta, you must not let him go," her father cried. He sounded absolutely terrified. "He bears the mark of the beast, and if you allow him to escape—"

Logan kept her eyeroll to herself.

"I *got* this, Charles." She didn't bother to look over at him. Redirecting her attention back to the escaped prisoner, she continued. "I don't want to hurt you, Rossi. All I want is to know what you were looking for. Hell, if you can give me something valuable, I might not even hand you over to the Order after this is all done. Wouldn't that be nice?"

Rossi narrowed his eyes at her. It was probably one of the few things he could manage while he still struggled to breathe under the arm she held against his neck.

"You think I would betray my master on as feeble a promise as that?"

"I think a lot of things come into perspective when your life is on the line." She allowed herself a cold smile, letting it curl through her lips like a snake. "Not to mention your freedom. Or have you been having a grand old time, locked up in my basement?"

"Henrietta, *please!*" Her father's voice had grown more insistent and frantic. He sounded like he was on the verge of a panic attack. "Please, he *must* be destroyed! You cannot suffer the beast to live!"

Despite herself, Logan shook her head in exasperation.

"Where do you get this shit, old man? Look, we can just bring him back down to his cell, and this time, we'll actually guard him while he's in there—"

When her father spoke again, he sounded like a different person altogether.

"I'm sorry, Henrietta. You leave me no choice." He paused only a moment, then gave a shout so loud it echoed in her ears.

"*Valkyrie!*"

Just like that, the world turned on its axis. Time seemed to slow down—but Logan had the experience to tell her that what that indicated was a massive spike of adrenaline, surging through her body without warning. About half a second too late, she realized what a mistake it was to use her forearm to pin Rossi down.

As if of their own accord, every single one of her spikes slid out of their spots. She watched in slow motion as the middle two tore through his skin, ripping open his throat.

"No!" She pressed her other hand to his neck, trying uselessly to keep his slightly too-thick blood from slipping through her fingers. "Wait—I didn't mean—I don't want—"

She watched as his hand raised up, one finger pointed accusingly at her father.

Then it went limp again. His legs gave out, and she felt the full weight of him crash against her. He was dead.

The surge of adrenaline immediately began to fade. With considerable effort, she forced her spikes back under her skin. She did her best not to stare too long at the damage they left behind.

Not that it matters now.

With all the care she could manage, she laid Rossi down on

the floor. Her fingers were shaking; horror coursed through her body, a river flooding its banks. She felt like something alien had crept inside her, turned her into a puppet. Used her to its own ends.

But it wasn't an alien.

Slowly, she stood back up and turned to face Charles where he stood. He had jumped up out of the armchair when he'd yelled out his command, or whatever it was, and now he stood frozen in front of her, arms raised in the air like he was performing a cast. His eyes came up to meet hers. They were full of an unsettling mixture of satisfaction and fear.

She was unsurprised to see Alexei standing in the doorway behind him, his face impassive as he took in the scene.

It was her father she addressed.

"What did you do?" Her own voice sounded like venom.

His arms dropped first, followed by his gaze. "It was for the best. He was a beast."

"Oh yes, of course. *Everything* you do is for the best, isn't it?" She shook her head at him. She found it difficult not to vomit. This hollow feeling inside, like someone had emptied her out and turned her shell into a weapon, had a quality to it that was almost too disturbing to name: it felt *familiar*.

"How many times have you done that to me?"

Her words dropped into the silence like pebbles in a still pond. Charles hardly seemed to notice.

"How many…it was—little ducks, in a row—makes you safe. Can't you see? Must be safe."

Logan glanced over his shoulder at Alexei. "Can you find Knatt for me? He might answer his cell."

"Of course." With that, Alexei disappeared into the hallway beyond. Logan felt some small relief to watch him go. She could feel Rossi's blood dripping down her arm, and she didn't want to have to think too long about how much Alexei had witnessed, or what he might be feeling, after what he'd seen.

Once he was gone, she dropped down into a squat near Rossi's still body. He'd been holding a book before she flew at him, and in the shuffle, it had landed a few feet from where his head now lay. She picked it up.

The title printed on the spine read *Rare Objects of the Arcana*. From the looks of it, it was likely one of the many obscure tomes her father had managed to collect over the years. She was fairly certain he'd stolen at least some of the books in this library, if not most. If she had to guess, she'd say he either stole them from the Order itself, or from the occasional oblivious client. Charles held the opinion that one should take as much advantage as possible from every situation that might arise, even if it meant bending one's moral code. Whether or not he, personally, had one was up for debate.

Standing up straight again, she began to flip through the pages of the book. Luckily for her, this one came complete with illustrations of almost every item it discussed. After a few minutes, her search came to an end. She wondered if Rossi knew he'd found the right book before she killed him, or if he'd only hoped.

She placed the book down on the table before glancing across the room. Her father had collapsed back into his armchair, looking like he'd shrunk down several sizes in the interim.

She would address him soon. For now, she pulled her cell phone out of her pocket and dialed the most recent number in her call history: Marion Clément.

She picked up on the third ring.

"Miss Logan." Right off the bat, Clément sounded tired. Logan might even have said *exhausted*. "Our crew should arrive in the early hours of—"

"Change it to a clean-up crew," said Logan brusquely, failing to care that she was cutting the other woman off. "Rossi got out of his cage, and he nearly killed my father. So I did what had to be done."

She paused to let Clément react to that, wondering if it might cost her.

"I see." Clément sounded, if possible, even more tired, and perhaps a touch put-out. But she didn't sound angry or upset. "Well, that is unfortunate. Was anyone else injured?"

Logan spared a withering glance toward her father and his armchair.

"Just a bookshelf or two."

"Indeed. Well, I am pleased to hear that nobody was hurt. I will, of course, make the necessary changes in our arrangements. Are you expecting any trouble from the authorities?"

Logan glanced down at the body. It occurred to her that she would need to take certain steps to obscure what had really caused Rossi's wounds.

"No, I'm not. The center should hold until tomorrow."

"That is good to hear. Once again, Miss Logan, we thank you for your cooperation in this matter—"

"I have one more request."

She could practically hear the gears turning in Clément's head in the brief silence that followed.

"And that would be?"

"An audience with you, in person." She looked over at her father again, wondering where they were going to hide him if Clément agreed. "I have something I need to discuss with you."

The book still lay open on the table beside her. She ran her finger over the pertinent image, which looked like it had been copied from an engraving.

Clément let out a sigh.

"Yes, of course. I wanted to introduce you to someone anyway, and I might as well do it in person. We shall see you tomorrow morning, then."

Without giving Logan a chance to push her luck any further, Clément hung up the phone.

Logan looked down at the book. Beneath her finger lay an image she could have traced from memory if she'd needed to. It was the funny bronze sculpture from her vision.

The Wolf wanted that artifact, and she was going to do everything in her power to keep it from him. Even if that meant she had to work with the Order one more time.

Jude was still on the couch when she woke with a start, driven abruptly back into consciousness by the slamming of an apartment door. In the small space, it echoed malignantly.

Jude blinked several times as she slowly pushed herself into a sitting position, the sudden glare of the overhead lights doing nothing to ease her confusion.

"Oh, sorry, did we wake you up?"

Two figures came into view: Eliana and Ian. Twin smirks danced on their faces, and Jude couldn't quite fight the feeling that she'd woken up in the aftermath of a joke at her own expense.

"Didn't mean to fall asleep," said Jude, groggily. "What time is it?"

"It's past dinnertime, is what time it is," said Ian abruptly, before Eliana had a chance to say anything at all. "I'm calling in pizza. You got any dietary restrictions, newbie?"

"Not that I know of."

"Good. I'm in a mood to fuck with pepperoni futures."

"What?"

"Ignore him," said Eliana, waving him away as he pulled out a cell phone and disappeared into the kitchen. "Are you okay? I'm sorry we left you alone for so long."

"Oh, don't worry about it," said Jude, shrugging her shoulders. She tried to seem as nonchalant as possible while she closed up Adele's book and slid it partway inside her jacket. "I can take care of myself. Actually, I had a really nice day, just walking around the neighborhood."

Thanks to the apartment's limited space, she managed to slip back into Eliana's bedroom as the last word left her lips, and within a moment, her book was hidden away in the depths of her backpack once more. She turned back to glance at Eliana through the open door.

"Honestly, don't worry about it." She stepped back out into the living room. "I just wanna know what you guys have been doing all day. God, I hope they haven't just been punishing you this whole time."

"Oh, no, they wouldn't consider that efficient," said Eliana, with a wave of her hand. "A punishment from the Order is more like…getting relocated from Hawaii to Siberia." With a smile, she added, "I mean, unless you like a challenge."

"Right." Jude smiled and nodded, and shut the bedroom door behind her. "So?"

Eliana gave her a strange, somewhat disconcerting smile and glanced over at the kitchen, where Fisher stood hidden behind a wall.

That was when Jude fully registered how strange the whole thing felt. She couldn't quite put her finger on what it was, but there was something *off* about the atmosphere. Eliana's smile cemented it.

"Fisher's almost off the phone. We should probably tell it together."

"Uh…okay."

For a moment longer, they stood awkwardly in the ill-defined space that made up the apartment's primary living quarters. Jude felt strangely stricken, like Fisher's part in this conversation had fundamentally crippled her own.

Then he walked back into the room.

"The food cometh!" he announced, shaking his phone above his head like a trophy. "Tonight, we feast as gods!"

"Excellent!" said Eliana, practically high-fiving her fellow Adept for his ability to place an order. "Now the real party can start."

Jude glanced between the two of them. They looked too smug, too pleased with themselves. Something was definitely wrong.

"Well, so?" she prompted, feeling desperate. "What happened at the Order?"

Eliana and Ian glanced at each other, twin smirks dancing on their faces.

"You sure you wanna know?" asked Ian. The tease in his voice was more than she could bear.

"Of course I fucking do! Will you just tell me already?"

Another smirk was exchanged; Jude wasn't sure which of them she wanted to punch first.

"Commendations all around," said Ian, shrugging, like it was old news. "Even for you, newbie."

"What? What are you talking about?"

"Jude, relax," said Eliana, walking over to her and reaching out to take her hand. "We didn't get in trouble. Not at all. The opposite, in fact." She reached one hand up to push a stray piece of hair out of Jude's face. "I told you everything would be fine, didn't I? I wouldn't lie to you."

Jude wanted to enjoy the feeling of Eliana's hand on her face, but the pit in her stomach refused to ease. None of this made sense, and none of it felt real.

"I—but—how?"

Eliana and Fisher exchanged another glance, but this one was different. It was wary and uncertain. This one wasn't sure it trusted her. Eliana's hand dropped away.

"So, I know I told you this mission wasn't sanctioned, and that is true—but it's also only sorta true." The look on Eliana's face told Jude she might not like what she was about to hear. "Once you've graduated, well, the Order makes it pretty clear that…as long as you have a good, solid plan, and you can get away clean…you kind of have blanket permission to…well…"

"Go on random demon raids, however you see fit?" Jude

heard the words leave her lips before she registered the conscious decision to say them. And yet, the decision had been made.

"Think of it like a hunting license," said Fisher, with an easy shrug. He sounded unconcerned. "And all the special *parts* we net them as a result are like...the fee to keep it."

The irahu bodies we brought back to the van...we weren't just disposing of supernatural evidence, were we?

"You were collecting trophies?" The pit in her stomach tightened with disgust.

"No, no, it's not like that," said Eliana quickly, waving her hand dismissively. She'd probably meant it to be reassuring, but that wasn't how Jude took it. "Some irahu parts are really valuable, not to mention useful—the ichor and the pincers, in particular. The Order has a whole research department devoted to experimenting with different uses of demonic material. That's how I knew that even if we went out unsanctioned, we wouldn't get in trouble—so long as we brought back a good haul."

"What—what is the Order going to *do* with the—with the parts?"

"Well, some of it will get sold off to donors for an outrageous price." Eliana chuckled, but Jude found herself unable to join her, and she noticed. Clearing her throat, she continued. "I mean, gotta keep the lights on, you know? And, uh, you can use the ichor in all kinds of casts. Works *way* better than human blood, and it means we don't have to cut ourselves every single time."

Jude gaped at her. This information came as a complete surprise to her, though she got the impression that it wasn't supposed to be.

"You use demon blood for your casts?"

"Well…yeah." Eliana and Fisher exchanged a look, like they were second-guessing including her in all of this. "That's how we stay ahead of the demons, Jude. You just…you gotta be ruthless when you're fighting monsters, you know?"

For a moment, Jude stood perfectly still. Every cell in her body felt uncomfortably alive. Suddenly, she understood all too well why Logan was so apprehensive about the Order of Shadows. If they ever found out about her…wouldn't her blood make a perfect target?

Slowly, numbly, she nodded.

"Is that it?" she asked, keeping her face as impassive as possible. "Do you do anything else with…with the bodies?"

Eliana shrugged. "I don't know the specifics. We give it all to the researchers and the scientists. And I am definitely *not* a scientist."

Experiments. They'll use it for experiments. Is that what they would do to Logan?

"I think we should all refocus on the important thing here," said Ian, glancing between the others with a timid smile on his face. "We didn't get in trouble! And we're *done* with work for the day, so why don't we just do something fun?"

For a moment, his words fell into echoing silence. Then Jude cleared her throat and pulled herself together.

"Yeah, totally," she said, and plastered on a smile. "I'm super glad we're not in trouble. And you said there's pizza on the way?"

"Hell yeah, there is!" said Fisher, practically whooping. "And even better than that—I've got *Warlords of the Apocalypse 2* and three controllers! You guys think you're up for it?"

Eliana gave Jude a beseeching smile. She looked grateful for the change of topic.

"What do you think? Wanna help me kick Fisher's ass right into the ground?"

Jude smiled back at her and tried to ignore how hollow it felt.

"Yeah," she said. "Let's do it."

She hoped that would be enough.

In the dream, Logan could see herself. It was like one of those dreams where you watch your life—or, more accurately, a strangely disproportionate accounting of your life—playing out on a screen, turning you into protagonist and spectator all at once. In the dream, she saw herself walking out of an unmarked door on a sunny day, laughing with the dark-haired man beside her.

The other Logan marched with speed and confidence, keeping up her conversation with the man all the while. Eventually, they disappeared inside a department store. Her spectator vantage point shifted then, almost as if she'd shifted rooms. When next she saw herself, it seemed almost like she was hovering in midair, and the world came to her through a haze of smoke. On her view screen, now a little harder to make out, the other Logan was dancing. Dancing, and laughing, and crashing—

The world shifted, and now the other Logan was walking out into the street again, one arm hooked through the arm of the handsome man as she leaned in to tell him a joke or whisper a secret—

Her view shifted, and she realized this wasn't a dream at all— she was simply seeing the world from someone else's point of view. Whoever's body she inhabited stepped back from the window and retreated deeper into the building, heading toward the elevator.

The hall he passed through had a mirror on the wall, and he looked right at it as he passed it.

In the glass, Casimir Volkov's eyes stared back at her.

Logan woke up face-down on the floor next to her bed, feeling like someone had poured gasoline on her back and dropped a match. With a gasp, she pushed herself into an upright position and clambered up onto the edge of her bed. Her breathing came in short, hard gulps as she tried to get her heartbeat to slow down.

After a moment, she heard a knock at her door.

"Come in," she called. There was a glass of water on her bedside table, and by the time the door swung open, she'd nearly drained it.

"Are you okay?" Alexei leaned in her doorway. "I heard a noise."

She let herself take a second to finish off the water. The burning on her back made her sweat.

"He was watching us," she said quietly, putting the glass down.

"He?"

"Volkov. *The Wolf.* He was watching us today." She stood up abruptly, crossing to the nearest window and pulling back the curtain. She felt like she could see him out there, if she could only look hard enough.

"Well, fuck. That's…creepy as hell." Alexei took a few steps into the room, making sure to maintain a careful distance. "You don't—you don't think he's watching us *now*, do you?"

"Not unless he can fly." She didn't live in the tallest building in the city—far from it—but in her particular neighborhood, there weren't any other buildings high enough to get a good vantage point into her apartment. "If I had to guess, I'd say he probably set up shop in view of the front door and followed us when we left." She glanced back at Alexei, now only a few feet away. She felt an overwhelming sense of responsibility for the fact that, were it not for her, he probably wouldn't be on Volkov's radar at all.

What have I gotten you into?

"Should we sweep the place for bugs?"

"You're joking, but that's exactly what we should do." She dropped the curtain and turned back to him. "You know, it seems stupid now that I thought I could just hand Rossi to the Order and wash my hands of it. I guess I should have known he wouldn't give me that kind of choice." She gave Alexei an appraising look, filled with an anxiety she couldn't name. "Now would be a good time for you to jump ship and head back to San Francisco, you know."

Alexei answered her with a shake of his head.

"No, I think that opportunity passed me by a long time ago." He gave her a mournful smile. "Besides, I can't let you have *all* the fun."

Logan sighed.

"Let me know when we get to the *fun* part, will you?"

Chapter Ten
House on Fire

As it turned out, Eliana and Fisher kept more beer on hand than food, which Fisher chose to make up for by ordering no less than six pizzas. Jude had no trouble deciding to accept one beer and nurse it all night long. It had been an unexpectedly strange day, and she didn't think alcohol could make it feel any more normal.

Jude didn't have a ton of experience playing video games, since her parents had refused to let her buy any and the select few friends she had in high school didn't have them either. Fortunately for her, this gave Eliana a chance to teach her how to play, which seemed to ease the awkwardness between them,

She wasn't about to forget their conversation, of course. The back of her mind kept wondering what Logan would think, how much Logan knew. But she made a determined effort to silence that voice.

I don't really know what it means, she told herself. *I can't make a judgment. They're just monsters. We kill monsters all the time.*

About an hour into the game and half an hour after the six pizzas had shown up, Jude started to realize that Eliana wasn't drinking much more than she was. While Fisher was on his third or fourth can, Eliana had only barely moved onto her second, and she didn't look too interested in it. Jude felt comforted by this. She let it tell her what she wanted to hear.

Of course, Eliana's attempts to teach her weren't quite enough to make up for the years of practice that Eliana and Fisher had. They both beat her soundly, though Fisher was the victor most often. She supposed that his particular Binding didn't hurt when it came to the necessary hand-eye coordination—though it was also likely that he spent much more time playing than Eliana did.

He celebrated each of his victories with more beer and pizza, eventually doing away with two whole pies entirely on his own. A little over two hours into play, he passed out on the couch between them.

Eliana wasted no time in catching Jude's eye and motioning toward the front hall with her thumb. Jude nodded, and they both proceeded to extricate themselves from the couch as carefully as possible, leaving Fisher to sleep off his pizza gluttony on his own.

Once they were both safely out of the living room and in the kitchen, Eliana leaned close to whisper to Jude.

"I've got a key to the roof, if you wanna go up and talk for a while."

Even after the strangeness of the day, Jude was more than a little intrigued at the thought of heading up to a rooftop alone with Eliana. They both grabbed their jackets and slipped out of the apartment.

"Probably better to let Ian sleep," said Eliana as they climbed the rickety stairs. "Between almost getting himself killed last night, and our dead silent car ride into headquarters this morning…he's had it rough."

Jude paused, staring at Eliana's retreating back.

"Does that mean you *didn't* know this morning that you weren't gonna get in trouble?" The difference this made was small, but Jude clung to it nonetheless.

Eliana turned back and gave her a short, sheepish look.

"Not 100%, no," she said with a shrug. "We, uh, hadn't actually done it before, so…we were kinda going off what more senior Adepts had told us. Fisher definitely had his doubts about it, but we both figured the reward would be worth it…if it paid off. I mean, if we'd been kicked out barely a week after graduating, neither of us would live it down. But, on the other hand, if we bring in a good haul just a week after getting our pins?" She grinned wildly, clearly still flush with the excitement of victory. "Well, then you're on your way to legendary status."

Jude immediately recalled her conversation with Fisher in the van—how hungry he was to prove himself, how uncertain he was of his place. How afraid of failure. She'd empathized at the time. She still did, now, even if it made her a little uneasy, too.

Looking up at Eliana's lit-up face, Jude realized that the pedestal she'd put her on had kept her from seeing a basic truth: Eliana wanted to prove herself, too. *Of course she does. Why else would she work hard enough to become Champion of the Gauntlet? Nobody trains that much if they don't have something to prove.*

They had to climb a short ladder to get to the roof access, though fortunately it featured a real landing and door at the top. They came out onto a short walkway, and Eliana shoved a brick into place to keep the door from shutting closed.

Once outside, Jude felt the clear, calming onrush of early

winter air. A part of her wanted to shrink back from it, but a part of her wanted it to wash her clean. She chose the latter impulse and pressed forward, to the very edge of the space, and leaned over the rampart-like stone wall on the outer side. It came just up to her waist, offering her a decent view of the surrounding neighborhood.

"Wow," she breathed, watching lights blinking in every direction. She knew they weren't in a particularly glamorous area, but after a lifetime of nights that yielded only a single street-lamp and nothing but trees on all sides, this little neighborhood was breathtaking. There was so much *life* here, even in the dark.

"It's not bad, right?" said Eliana, taking a step closer as she pulled her arms around herself for warmth. "If I wanted to live in New York long-term, I wouldn't mind a set up like this."

"Does that mean you *don't* want to live in New York?"

"Don't get me wrong—I'm not *against* it." Eliana's tone was teasing and mysterious. "But I had something else in mind."

Jude felt a funny, floating kind of anxiety somewhere in the upper region of her chest, though she wasn't quite sure why. The words she wanted to say seemed to stick in her throat. She gave a small cough, hoping to clear it.

"Wh—uh—what did you have in mind?"

Mischief blossomed in Eliana's eyes.

"You have to promise not to tell anyone."

"Of course," said Jude, though the words pulled at her.

With one hip against the stone wall beside them, Eliana leaned her upper body closer to Jude's. When she spoke, her voice had dropped to a conspiratorial whisper.

"It hasn't been announced officially yet, but…the Order is

opening a new field office in Washington State, and I've requested assignment there. And I, uh, got word from my new superior this morning—I was approved."

Jude felt her eyes widen as a series of loud and panic-stricken thoughts raced through her mind. *Eliana's coming to my state. And so is the Order. We don't have to do the long-distance thing. And the Order will be in Logan's backyard. Wait, what thing are we doing anyway? Are we dating? Is she my girlfriend?*

Logan's not gonna like this.

After a full two seconds, Jude realized that Eliana's usual cocky attitude seemed a little deflated, concern now dotting her mischief—

"Oh, my god!" she said suddenly, rushing to fill the dead air up with the first sounds she could think of. "Are—are you serious?"

"Like a hurricane," said Eliana, her voice strained and jerky. "Is—is that alright? Are you—are you mad I didn't talk to you first?"

"What? No! Not at all, I—sorry, I was just shocked. But I'm—I'm not mad, I'm excited! You were really approved?"

"Yeah," Eliana's voice sounded like a sigh of relief. "Fisher, too. The new office isn't ready yet, so I'm not sure when the transfer happens, but…it will happen."

Jude smiled and did her best to bury her sense of dread. She knew she should be happy. She wanted to be happy—and she wanted Eliana to think she was happy.

"That's amazing," she said. With sudden inspiration, she reached out and touched Eliana's arm, then let it linger there a little too long. She ducked her head until she met Eliana's eyes.

The vulnerability she saw there reverberated through her.

"Glad you think so," said Eliana, her voice barely even a whisper now. She was leaning closer and closer. The space between them shrank into nothing.

The moment their lips met, Jude had the curious sensation that she had traveled back to the night before—to the moment she had reached into eira and felt it reach back, the moment it had come alive inside her. She felt powerful and out of control, all at once. It hurt, but she didn't understand why.

Then her clarity dispersed, and all she could feel was the hand in her hair and the other at her waist. She pulled Eliana closer, and she let herself believe that everything would work out fine.

Under her skin, a fire raged.

Charles Logan lay in his bed, holding a cup of herbal tea and looking for all the world like someone's infirm grandfather. If Logan had been capable of feeling sorry for him, she might have.

Knatt sat in a chair beside the bed, his own tea abandoned on a nearby table. Logan, on the other hand, stood against the far wall, practically as far as she could get without leaving the room. The room was Charles's old bedroom, which had gone largely untouched—apart from the occasional dusting—since they'd sent him to the nursing home years before. The walls were lined with messy bookshelves, and at the moment, the only light source in the room was a small desk lamp on the bedside table. Logan stood mostly in shadow, and as she leaned back against the spare bit of empty wall behind her, she closed her eyes just long enough to let her mind go blank.

With the same effort it took to breathe, she called the

shadows to her. In an instant, she felt herself fade into the darkness, almost invisible to the naked eye. The action brought with it a deep sense of comfort.

"Charles, did you hear what I just said?"

Logan's father tilted his head toward his old friend, his eyes looking a little glassy.

"Hugh, is that you?"

"Yes, it's me. Charles, can you tell me about the trigger?"

"The trigger."

"Yes. How did you do it? How did you create the trigger you used on Henrietta?"

"Trigger?"

Knatt let out the barest hint of an exasperated sigh. "Yes, the trigger—you know, the word you shouted earlier that activated Henrietta's abilities? How did you create it?"

Even from across the room, Logan could see the vacant expression in Charles's eyes as he turned them on Knatt.

"Magic, of course."

To his credit, Knatt refrained from groaning.

"But *what* magic, Charles? What was the cast you used?"

Charles giggled.

"Made it myself." Knatt's eyes flickered back to where he knew Logan was standing, but only for a moment. "Do you know, the young people call that DIY? DIY. So many *names* for things these days."

"How did you make the spell, Charles?"

Charles looked dreamy for a moment, his gaze failing to focus on anything in particular. Then, all of a sudden, he sharpened and sat up straight, like he'd heard a sudden noise.

"Is she here? I can't see her."

In the shadows, Logan allowed herself a small smile.

"Focus on me, Charles. Does anyone else know about the trigger? Did you tell anyone about it?"

Like, say, Volkov, perhaps?

"I can keep my secrets, Hugh. You, of anyone, should know that."

"Are you saying you didn't tell anyone about it?"

"I never tell."

"Do you remember the young man who used to visit you, Casimir Volkov? The one who called himself the Wolf?"

Charles Logan's expression changed on a dime. He looked terrified…and ashamed. With one hand, he gathered up the quilt he was under and tried to pull it closer to himself. Perhaps he, too, was trying to disappear. He glanced around the room, eyes wild.

"Is he coming back?"

"No, he's not coming back. You're safe here. Just tell me— did you tell him about the trigger? The word you used on Henrietta earlier? Does the Wolf know about it?"

Charles's eyes grew wide as he stared at Knatt in horror. Ever so slowly, he shook his head. Far from feeling relieved, Logan felt only irritated with him—and the whole situation. How could she *ever* trust what he had to say about it? He might be lying— or he might simply not remember. This whole exercise felt more pointless than anything else they'd done so far.

In a bout of exasperation, she kicked off the wall and strode forward, making sure her footsteps echoed through the room before she let the shadows dispel. She knew what it would look like to anyone watching her: like she'd just incorporated on the spot. To Charles, she must have looked like a ghost out of the gathering mists, in the middle of his bedroom.

When she spoke, her voice rang with the clarity of a bell.

"Tell me about the Choronzon artifacts."

She'd pulled out the book inside her jacket—the one she'd found beside Rossi's corpse, *Objects of the Arcana*. She dropped it open to the page in question and watched him take it in.

The page depicted a small bronze pyramid, just like the one she'd seen in her vision. The caption underneath read, "*Pictured: pyramid in bronze, the only known example of one of the artifacts of the Choronzon, the purposes of which have never been proven.*"

He gaped at the book, then up at her.

"How did you find that?" he asked.

"Pulled it off the man I killed. What does the object do?"

"Please—I shouldn't speak of it—I should never have spoken—"

"We're way past that, Charles," said Logan. Her irritation was getting the best of her. "You *already* spoke it, now you need to speak it *to me*. What does the object *do*?"

Charles turned his pathetic, beseeching gaze toward Knatt, but Knatt only shrugged. Charles's gaze fell to the floor, his shoulders slumped in defeat.

"I...I don't know."

Logan scoffed and threw up her arms, then turned to Knatt.

"This is fucking pointless. We should just take him back to the home and let the Wolf have him. At least then, I won't waste any more of my energy babysitting him."

Knatt raised a placating hand.

"Let's not be too hasty," he said, his withering gaze narrowing in on the other man. "I'm sure I can find Charles's notes on the experiments he used to do on truth casts. Sure, they've an even chance of scattering his mind to the four corners, but if nothing else, we'll get a laugh out of it."

Logan rounded on her father again. She wanted to savor the look on his face.

Then she shrugged.

"It's as good an idea as any. Let's do it."

"Wait!" Charles voice was panicked—and quite clear. "Wait. You'll get more out of me now than—well—"

"If we use one of your own casts on you?" Logan blinked innocently at him.

"Yes," he admitted in grunt. "The truth is, I don't know much. But I'll tell you what I know."

"So…start already."

He sighed, straightened his shoulders, and weakly cleared his throat.

"Everything there is to know about the artifacts of the Choronzon is hearsay, at best," he began. He no longer sounded like the feeble, addled old man she left in the nursing home up north. Instead, he sounded more like the stern, proudly intellectual disciplinarian she'd known in her youth. It nearly made her sick. "The Choronzon are believed to be an old magic order, long since faded out of this world. You know the theory of ebb and flow, yes?"

Logan blinked at him, barely able to comprehend his last few words. She looked over at Knatt, who stared right back at her. She had the eerie feeling they were both having the same thought.

All this time, Charles has known more about the Choronzon than we did.

"Does that mean you don't know about ebb and flow? Hugh, what have you been teaching this child?"

Both Logan and Hugh snapped back to look at Charles at the exact same time. He sounded so much like his former self, she felt like she'd been pulled back in time.

She cleared her throat to give herself a moment to absorb what he was asking.

"The ebb and—oh, uh, it's the theory that magic isn't static. It comes and goes from the world, and so it follows that there have been multiple different ages of magic, which may have each had distinct capabilities."

She blinked and realized she'd answered him just like she used to do, when he used to give her homework and quiz her on it.

"Correct." He smiled in approval at her. She ignored that.

"You're saying the Choronzon are an older order of magic, way older than letha and eira."

"And quite extinct, yes."

"But they left behind artifacts? Like this pyramid thing?"

"Yes. The pyramid, the obelisk, the labyrinth. Here." He grabbed the book and pulled it toward him, flipped a few pages, then stabbed at it with his finger as he pushed it back toward her. "There's a list. It might not be accurate. But it's the best I can offer you."

She pulled the book over, scanned the pertinent part of the page, then handed it over to Knatt.

"What could they do, the Choronzon?"

"There are many theories. Most of them quite outlandish." He looked at the book that now lay in Knatt's hands. "That one tells a fairy tale about a people who held dominion over heaven and hell…which you can interpret any way you like."

Logan nodded. "Is that it? Is that all you know?"

He turned his sad gaze back toward her, and she got the distinct impression that she wouldn't like what came next.

"I *had* to do what I did, Henrietta. I want you to know that."

Logan blinked, momentarily stunned.

"You have to understand the position I was in. The way your—the way you came to me, I had no idea what you—how you were going to grow up. I had to *do* something. I didn't have a choice."

She had the curious sensation that she could no longer feel her extremities. Was that a pricking at her skin, just under the black diamond nearest her wrist?

"What I was going to become."

"What?"

"You were going to say you had no idea *what I was going to become*. Isn't that right?"

Charles let out a long sigh, like he was struggling to figure out how to explain something complex to a child.

"You have so much power, Henrietta."

"And you wish I didn't."

"And whether you'll admit it or not, it's a power rooted in darkness," he snarled, one fist clenching over his old man's blanket. "And, if you'll remember, I used to be a man who fought darkness. You might even call me an expert."

Logan's blood went cold. She remembered the cold of the

lower basement, the staleness of the air. The cell where she'd kept Rossi. Had she seen a little of her father there, when she closed the door?

She remembered Rossi's blood soaking into her clothes.

"Such a special man, aren't you?" Her voice sounded like glass. "With your special burdens. Do they even make rules for men like you?"

He stared at her blankly. Like he didn't understand a word.

"I had to do it."

"No, you didn't," said Knatt quietly. Logan turned to look at him, glad for the reason to look away from her father. "You *chose* to do it. And you were wrong." He stood up abruptly, closing the book and holding it to his chest. "Miss Logan, I believe we've got what we came for. Unless you still want to administer a truth cast."

Logan shrugged.

"I'm bored here. Maybe another day."

They both turned away from him and began to head for the door to leave him behind. Logan had almost made it out when she heard her father speak again.

"Let me know…if you start to remember. Will you?"

Logan left her father's room in a fugue state. She had made it halfway down the hall before she returned to her body, and the moment she did, a venomous rage began to bleed from her heart, infecting the whole system. She managed to turn a corner out of the hallway before it crested to a point. Then she slammed her arm into the wall as hard as she could. The crumbling of drywall made a satisfying crunch.

If you start to remember.

With one arm still against the wall, she closed her eyes and took a deep, slow breath. She wished she could be anywhere else right now. This house was a prison, trapping her in the past. After all this time, she'd started to believe her father no longer had any influence over her. But the truth was that she had never escaped him. She'd never gotten back the memories he'd wiped from her mind, and as it turned out, he'd held onto one last secret—this ability to expose her at any time he wished, with a single word trigger. In one moment, he could turn her into a weapon and reveal the truth about her for anyone to see. For the Order to see, if it lined up right.

Not to mention the dead man in the library.

"Are you all right?"

It was Knatt's voice asking. She took another deep breath before yanking her arm from the wall, out of the indent she'd left in it.

"Sorry about the wall," she muttered. The sleeve of her jacket had protected her skin, and she couldn't feel anything beyond that. Maybe it hadn't hurt her at all.

"I don't care about that," said Knatt, gently. "Are you all right?"

Logan turned around slowly, then almost immediately wished she hadn't. The tender care on his face was too much for her to bear.

"I'm fine."

"You say the word, and I'll bring him back to the home. The Wolf can have him."

"You know we can't do that. If he hasn't told him yet, we'd be opening ourselves up."

Knatt nodded thoughtfully.

"Perhaps I could call Adele. They have…facilities at T'eira'han. They could take him in."

"You don't have to protect me, you know. I'm all grown up now."

"I know. But I also know you don't owe him anything. We don't have to keep him here."

Logan let out a sigh and shook her head.

"I'll settle for you promising never to ask me to talk him again. How's that?"

Knatt let out a quiet, sad laugh.

"Agreed. I solemnly promise I will never ask you to speak to that man again." He took a few steps forward, toward the nearest staircase back down to the main floor. "I believe Mr. Marin is waiting for us in the kitchen. Shall we join him?"

"Right behind you."

She watched him walk down the first few stairs as she took another deep breath. In her mind's eye, she could see her sixteen-year-old self on the day she figured out what her father had done to her. She remembered wondering why, if it was Tuesday, she couldn't remember Monday. She remembered the bruises on her body, and the sharp pain in her ribs if she turned too fast. She remembered the basement, and the door she thought she'd never seen. And she remembered the slow-dawning horror on Knatt's face as he realized that she knew.

And she remembered how he'd helped her pack, how he'd bought her a bus ticket, how he'd snuck sandwiches into her bag when she wasn't looking. She straightened her shoulders and stretched them, forcing some of the tightness there to ease. With one last deep breath, she followed Knatt down the stairs, towards the sweet smell that wafted up from the kitchen.

She entered the kitchen to find Alexei poring over something on the counter, his back to them. After a moment, he turned toward them, carrying a tray with three steaming mugs on it, which he placed delicately on the island.

"Perfect timing," he said as he straightened up. "Knatt, I've made tea for us. And H.C., I made you a caramel latte. I know it's a bit late for caffeine, but—"

"It's never too late for caffeine," said Logan. She felt nothing but gratitude as she took her mug off the tray. Then she noticed the funny design in the foam. "Did you draw me a crescent moon?"

Alexei tilted his head to the side. "Well, I meant to do a heart, but I can see now that I failed."

"It's beautiful." She took a sip, savoring the sugary caramel she rarely let herself indulge in. Warmth spread through her. "Thank you."

"Yes, thank you," said Knatt, picking up one of the other mugs.

"Least I could do." Alexei sat down on one of the stools around the island and motioned for the others to do the same. "So, what did you learn up there?"

Knatt and Logan exchanged a glance. Logan let out a sigh.

"Not as much as we would have liked." She sat down on another stool and took a second sip. "He claims he didn't tell the Wolf about the trigger, but…it's just impossible to say. Maybe he's telling the truth, maybe he's lying. Maybe he doesn't remember."

"He did give us a lead on one thing, though." Knatt produced the tome from the library. "If Charles and this book are to be believed...we may have just learned something about the origin of the Choronzon Key."

"Really?" Alexei looked over at the book with interest. "Care to share?"

"The Choronzon may have been an ancient magic order," said Logan. Knatt seemed reluctant to hand over the book this soon, so she figured it was better to speak. "According to some...they went extinct centuries ago, but they left behind an unknown number of artifacts."

"Plural?" Alexei raised his eyebrows. "Can they all do what the Key can do?"

Logan glanced over at Knatt. "What does the book say?"

Knatt scanned the page he had open, and then turned it and scanned the next.

"The Key is referenced, but...ah, here we go—*though little is known about the artifacts, it is believed that they each possess inherent magical traits which may reveal themselves to a worthy soul. What those traits may be, or what constitutes a worthy soul,* seems up for debate."

A worthy soul. As determined by a rock. Sure.

"But there may be others out there, like H.C., who have been...well, imprinted with one?"

One of Logan's long held suspicions rose to the surface.

"I may actually know someone else who has one," she mumbled, before quickly taking another deep drink from her latte.

Both Knatt and Alexei's heads snapped in her direction.

"Who?" asked Alexei. "And what can they do?"

Logan sighed. "I'm not at liberty to say."

"Seriously?"

"Not my secret." Logan shrugged. "That's not what we should be focusing on, anyway. I think the Wolf knows about the Choronzon, too. Rossi was looking for this book—he had it with him by the time I got there." Knatt had turned the page back, so the image of the pyramidal object was visible again. She motioned toward it. "And I had a vision about that artifact. In the vision, the Wolf had it. He was using it somehow, but...I'm not totally sure what he was trying to do."

That was the easier way to say it. Somehow, she had trouble saying the words: *it made me want to destroy the world.*

Knatt looked at her sharply.

"When did you have this vision?"

"Recently." She took another drink.

"So, we just have to keep him from getting his hands on that, right?" asked Alexei, glancing between the other two. "Which I guess is easier said than done if we don't have any idea where it is."

"I have a guess," said Logan. "Something Rossi said...that the Order wouldn't be able to stop him. I think the Order of Shadows has it. And he knows they have it."

Knatt and Alexei exchanged a look. Logan knew that neither of them had any love for the Order, but she also knew that neither of them had as much to fear from them as she did.

"I suppose that leaves us with few options," said Knatt slowly. "If we are to keep the artifact out of Mr. Volkov's hands..."

"We have to work with them," said Alexei. He was gazing at

Logan with an expression she wasn't sure how to interpret. "We should try to find out how much they know about the Choronzon. Without, you know…"

"Spilling all my secrets? I'd like that, yeah." Logan shrugged and took one last, long drink from her cup, draining it completely. "They'll be here tomorrow, anyway. For the body." She glanced over at Knatt. "There's one last thing we have to do before then."

Knatt returned her look with curiosity. "And that is?"

"We have to test the trigger. We have to see if anyone other than Charles can activate it."

Alexei immediately shook his head.

"No, no way. The Wolf probably doesn't even—"

"I can't take that chance." Logan's voice was firm, but it wasn't Alexei she was looking at. "I *have* to know."

"H.C., there's no way in hell I would ever—"

"I'll do it," said Knatt, cutting him off. "It ought to be me, anyway."

Logan let out an internal sigh of relief, though it was tinged with regret. She'd known he would do it. But it still pained her to ask.

Alexei looked back and forth between the two of them, bewildered and angry.

"You can't be serious. How could *either* of you—"

"How could I *not*?" asked Logan, finally meeting his eyes again. "How could I go into battle beside you and not know? I pose too much of a danger to you as it is."

Alexei just stared at her, dismayed. Slowly, he shook his head. Beside him, Knatt cleared his throat.

"Whatever our ultimate course of action," he said, in his unnervingly calm, steely-eyed tone, "our first step must be research."

Despite everything, Logan found herself comforted by that thought. If she could look at it as research, perhaps she could take away some of the power of that feeling—the feeling of complete helplessness as her father had taken over her body...

"It's just research," she said out loud, to convince herself as much as Alexei. "And I *have* to do it. I have to know."

Alexei shook his head again.

"You do what you need to do, H.C. But I can't be party to it. I'll...I'll be back at the apartment, if you need me."

Without another word, he stood up and left the room. Logan felt a part of herself go with him. Then she looked back at Knatt. The look in his eyes mirrored her heart.

"We don't have to start right away," he said gently. She wished he weren't so kind. "Take all the time you need."

But Logan shook her head.

"No, we should do it now. Before I lose my nerve."

So they did.

Chapter Eleven
Schism

When Logan went back to her apartment, the thought occurred to her that she could go knock on the guest room door and speak to Alexei. The thought occurred, and then she brushed it away. She felt like a contagion, dangerous to anyone with whom she came into contact. She took the skeleton key out of the door that connected to the traveling room to make sure she wouldn't be followed, and then she marched right back to her own bedroom and quietly shut the door.

The adrenaline that rushed through her body every time her spikes came out had worn out her muscles the same as if she'd run 20 miles. She still felt nauseous from the last attempt, but she hoped that would fade with time. She tore off her shirt as she crossed the room, dropping it on the floor before sitting on the side of her bed.

A small black pipe lay on her bedside table, its bowl partially full. She let her gaze linger a moment before she picked it up. While alcohol had never done anything for her, she'd had no such trouble with most other substances.

She told herself she just needed an anesthetic. In a way, it was true.

A few minutes later, she heard a soft knock on the door.

"H.C.?" His voice was soft, barely loud enough to hear. "You in there?"

She stared hard at the empty space of her room before clearing her throat.

"I'm here."

"Oh." He paused, and she could almost feel him trying to think of what to say. "Well, I…if you want to talk…about anything…I'm here. I mean, I'm still up, so…yeah, just let me know."

She lit the pipe again and took another drag.

"Will do."

"Okay."

Down below, she could hear the ever-present sounds of city traffic, the white noise of life. She closed her eyes and waited. Eventually, she heard his footsteps, leading away from her. The click of a door, opened and then shut. The minor sigh he let out as he sat down on the bed.

She pulled back. She hadn't meant to focus in on him so closely. It felt like a transgression.

She knew he was sincere, and she knew it would be good for her to take him up on it. But she didn't have it in her. The walk to his door felt a million miles long, and her feet felt cemented to the floor. She took another hit on her pipe instead.

It was hours until she finally fell asleep. She dreamed of cold cliffsides.

Logan woke early, despite her exhaustion from the day before. She needed to be ready for the Order of Shadows well before they actually arrived, and that meant waking up early. She was sure it wouldn't be the last unpleasant part of her day.

For his part, Alexei begged off the meeting, saying he'd have a better time watching television in her apartment than dancing around the Order higher-ups with her at the estate.

So, it was just Logan and Knatt in the kitchen that morning, silently drinking their respective coffee and tea as they waited for Clément and her delegation to arrive. The silence lay heavily between them, laden with the weight of the night before.

It was Knatt who had completed a final inspection of the body, sometime in the early hours of the morning, to make sure Rossi's wounds looked consistent with the knife Logan had picked as the murder weapon. Restating his caveat that he was hardly a trained forensics investigator, he'd told her it looked believable to him. They would both have to hope that was enough.

Logan was on her third cup of coffee by the time she heard them coming up the drive.

"They're here," she told Knatt. "Sounds like two cars. I'm guessing Clément doesn't want to ride with the body."

"Can't say I blame her," said Knatt. He took a sip of his tea.

Logan listened as the cars pulled up in front of the house and came to a stop. She heard several pairs of boots hit the ground first, and then the sound of softer footfalls—at least two people in dress shoes. They ascended the short set of stairs to the front door and knocked.

With one last, deep drink, she hopped out of her chair and headed for the door, Knatt following close behind. She pulled anxiously at the hem of her dress shirt, like she was headed for an inspection. Then she opened the door.

Marion Clément stood on the other side, the silver at her cuffs and neckline glinting in the cold early winter sun. The rest of her outfit was completely black: crisp black dress pants with a perfectly fitted black uniform jacket befitting a general. Of course, that was exactly what she was.

Just behind her stood a woman Logan didn't recognize. She was Black, likely in her late 40s, her hair pulled back into a tight bun, with the same upright posture as Clément and nearly an identical uniform—except she only had two bands of silver on her wrist cuff, not three, and none on her collar. Behind them swarmed a small team of foot soldiers—the cleanup crew.

"Hi," said Logan, nodding at the two women. "Welcome to the Logan estate."

Clément's mouth was set in a hard, thin line. She nodded.

"Pleasure to see you Miss Logan, Mr. Knatt. Though I do wish we could meet under more auspicious circumstances."

"We must all play the hand we are dealt," said Knatt, his expression guarded.

"Quite," answered Clément with a nod. She gestured to the woman beside her. "I'd like you both to meet my colleague, Dolores Marlowe. Dolores, this is Logan, the one I told you about."

Marlowe looked Logan up-and-down, the calculation in her expression obvious and unguarded.

"The shadow summoner," she said, her tone cold. Logan couldn't be sure, but she thought she heard a hint of disgust there. "Your reputation proceeds you."

Though she'd never met this woman before, she couldn't say that she hadn't been expecting her. In fact, Dolores Marlowe was exactly what Logan always expected when she dealt with the

Order: somewhere between a rival and an open threat. Logan let out an internal sigh and steeled herself.

"Can't say the same, unfortunately." She relaxed her posture and shoved one hand in her back pocket, exuding calm as she gripped the small blade hidden there. "But don't take it personally; I just don't get out much. So, you guys wanna see the corpse?"

She allowed herself a small moment of pleasure as she watched Marlowe work to cover a flinch. Clément didn't react at all.

"Of course," she said, perfectly professional. "Please, lead the way."

Logan headed in without another word, letting them follow behind her. She wondered what they might have looked like to the uninitiated: a group of almost universally black-clad people traipsing through a mansion that had been built to look a century older than it was, on their way to see the dead body in the library.

Bunch of freaks, she thought.

When they reached the double doors to the library, Logan and Knatt pushed them open and pointed the others inside, toward the lumpy blanket in the center of the room. Rossi lay silently underneath.

Clément motioned for the others to stay back a moment, while she went on ahead. Gingerly, she knelt down and reached for the cloth. It was only as she finally pulled back the corner and revealed Rossi's now-closed eyes that Logan remembered that they had been Seers together, likely for many years. Granted, he had turned out to be a traitor who directly contributed to the death of the High Prophet, James Atherton, and a number of other Order Adepts. But that didn't mean Clément wouldn't mourn him.

If she still mourned him now, however, it didn't show on her face. She pulled on a pair of latex gloves and performed a brief clinical exam of his face and wounds, nodding to herself like she was taking mental notes. A few minutes later, she stood up again and waved the rest of the team forward.

"Take him directly to cold storage," she instructed as the lower-level Adepts swarmed around the body. "He might be useful to us, yet."

Logan's heart jumped in her chest. *Useful, as in, you can prove I'm a murderer?*

"Useful, how?" she asked out loud, making her voice blunt and careless.

Clément turned her eyes on Logan, her expression still perfectly clinical and detached.

"We've never been able to study one who has undergone this Binding before," she answered coolly. "You may find it crass, but the Order uses every possible opportunity to learn. Even a tragic one."

Logan shrugged. "Doesn't matter to me what you do with him."

Logan, Knatt, and the two senior Order officials stood to the side while the team of Adepts transferred Rossi into a body bag and marched him out of the library. They took the blanket he'd been covered in, too.

After a moment of silence, Knatt cleared his throat.

"Would anyone like some tea?"

Logan could feel Marlowe's gaze on her as they seated themselves in the primary living room. She picked an armchair to sit in so she wouldn't have to be too close to anyone, then watched Marlowe take the seat directly across from her. There was something inherently confrontational in the straight rod of her spine, the taut set of her jaw. Knatt brought out the coffee first, giving one to Logan and one to Marlowe, then two lovely, dainty teacups on saucers for himself and Clément.

"I hope it's not rude of me to inquire," he said, directing himself at Clément, "but I'm quite curious how the, er, *regime transition* is progressing within the Order."

"It is not rude at all," answered Clément, though her voice still sounded so detached that Logan could only guess what her real reaction was. If *blank* was an option, she might have been that. "It's hasn't been smooth, to say the least, but we limp along. We hope to select a new High Prophet as early as next week."

"In the meantime, duty doesn't sleep," added Marlowe. "The mission carries on." Her gaze stayed fixed on Logan as she sipped her black coffee. Unabashed, Logan looked right back at her, and offered up an ostentatious wink. Marlowe sneered, then turned back to Clément.

"Indeed, the mission carries on," said Clément, sounding contemplative. She took a dainty sip of tea and cleared her throat. "Prior to Atherton's death, our Council had set in motion a plan which has continued forward in his absence. In point of fact, that is why Dolores is here with me today."

"I had wondered," said Logan, smiling serenely at Marlowe.

"Yes. As our highest-ranking Adept not yet assigned to run a field office, she was our first choice to head the new one."

"Wait—a new field office?"

"Indeed. We're finally opening a new office in this quadrant of Washington State—right in the heart of Seattle, as a matter of fact."

Logan blinked.

"Downtown Seattle?"

"Well, the prices are a bit steep for the amount of space we need," said Clément.

"We're renting out a warehouse in the industrial district," said Marlowe.

Right in my backyard. She did her best to keep her face blank, but her right eyebrow rose of its own accord.

"Is that so?" Her voice was a glassy surface over turbulent waters.

"It is," said Marlowe. Her voice was half growl, half warning.

"We're still putting together the team, of course," said Clément impassively, apparently unaware of the tension building in the room, "but I suspect you might find some familiar faces there. I believe you know Miss Blake?"

"I do." Logan didn't like Blake, but she wouldn't like anyone else they could have chosen, either.

"She was first to request the assignment, and as the current Champion, she earned a priority draw. I imagine you'll see her soon."

"Fantastic," said Logan out loud. She was sure she sounded less than enthusiastic. "Will I know anyone else?" She was trying to ascertain how big the team would be without asking outright.

To her surprise, Clément and Marlowe exchanged wearied glances.

"Ian Fisher, also from the new class," muttered Marlowe. "The third post is…yet to be filled."

Logan sensed resentment in her tone. She looked from one Order official to the other, sizing up their predicament.

"You're having trouble finding someone," she said. "Why?"

Clément sighed. "New cadets are hungry to prove themselves."

"They all think this is a soft posting," said Marlowe. "Because the *shadow summoner* already has this area covered." Her disdain was evident.

Logan shrugged.

"And yet, you're opening an office here anyway."

As soon as the words were out of her mouth, she realized how antagonistic she sounded. It wasn't her intention, but it seemed harder and harder to avoid.

"It seems prudent, given the current climate," said Clément, carefully.

"Keeping an eye on me?"

"Keeping an eye on the Wolf."

"And the Wolf is obsessed with the shadow summoner," said Marlowe, now outright glaring at Logan. There was no mistaking the accusation in her tone. "Wonder why that is."

Logan put her mug down on the table beside her and leaned back in her chair.

"I'm not responsible for anyone but myself," she replied.

"You were seen fraternizing with him at the Gauntlet Ball." From the satisfaction in her voice, Logan got the impression that this was the real reason Marlowe had come. "Can you explain that?"

Again, Logan shrugged.

"I didn't know who he was then," she answered easily. "It was my understanding that he was there on special invitation from the Order itself. Would you care to explain how that happened?"

"You were also alone with him after the battle." Marlowe's voice was ice. "And we have only your word to tell us what happened then. How can we know for sure that you didn't help him escape?"

Logan laughed. "Are you suggesting I know how to manipulate the dimensional magic at headquarters?" Her eyes narrowed. "And here I thought only the Order's own scholars knew that."

"You've been in suspicious situations before, though, haven't you?" Marlowe had leaned forward in her seat, like she'd finally gotten to the good part of the movie. "Last summer, you were responsible for the death of Todd Phillips, whom you accused of being in cahoots with the Wolf. Yet again, we have no evidence for that but your word."

"And the multiple other people who saw him fighting alongside the Wolf."

"Both of whom are your own accomplices."

"Accomplices?"

"Confidants, then."

"Well, we sure are throwing around some words, aren't we?"

"Before that, you went to investigate a murder in a small town, and somehow, your chief suspect ended up dead. How convenient for you, that anyone who might testify against you ends up in the ground."

"Not at the moment, it isn't."

"That's enough," Clément cut in. Her tone was harsh, and she sent Marlowe an obvious warning look. Marlowe shrank back into her chair, but the look in her eyes was unrepentant. "Miss Logan, you are not on trial here."

"Could have fooled me."

"I apologize on behalf of Adept Marlowe," Clément said evenly. "Her background is in investigation, not diplomacy. I hope you'll forgive her lack of tact."

Logan's eyebrow twitched, and she crossed her arms over her chest.

"Well, as long we're talking about Volkov," she threw a significant glance at Knatt, who nodded and stood up. "There's something we wanted to show you."

Knatt went out of the room, then came back holding a folder with a single piece of paper in it. Before the Order Adepts had arrived, Knatt had done an impressively accurate sketch of the picture from the book. Logan wanted to hold back the book itself as a bargaining chip, though she had yet to find out if it would be effective as such.

Knatt handed the folder to Clément. Logan watched her face intently as she opened it. Her eyes widened in unmistakable recognition...and concern. She passed it to Marlowe, whose reaction was similar.

"Where did you see this?" asked Clément.

"Rossi had it."

Concern stretched into a moment of panic on her face. "You don't mean he had the object in his possession?"

"No," said Logan calmly. "It was in a book. What does it do?"

Marlowe closed the folder with a snap and passed it back to Clément. "That's privileged information."

"May I see the book?" asked Clément.

"That really depends on if you answer my questions." Settling back into her seat, Logan crossed her arms over her chest. "I found Rossi in my library, holding a book, opened to that page." That part was a lie, but they didn't need to know that. She would take the easy, self-preserving lies where she could get them. "During my brief conversation with him, it became clear that Volkov is after that artifact, whatever it is. He also gave me reason to believe that it may currently be in the possession of the Order of Shadows. So. Are you going to tell me what you know about the artifact, or not?"

A moment of stunned silence greeted her words. She could see Clément considering the question, weighing the pros and cons of letting her in. And she could see Marlowe resolutely shake her head.

"Absolutely not," said Marlowe. "You're an outsider. We have no reason to trust you with that kind of information."

"Fine," shrugged Logan, making a point of looking unconcerned. "You won't share information with me. And I won't help you keep this out of Volkov's hands. I'll just leave you to deal with him on your own, since that's worked out so well for you this far."

Clément let out a heavy sigh and set her saucer and teacup down on the low coffee table, along with the folder.

"It may do nothing. Or it may bring about the end of the world."

"Marion, are you really going to let this *contractor* determine our policies?"

"Not at all. For the time being, *I* determine our policies, which you might do well to remember." Marlowe shook her head in disbelief, but Clément barely took notice, and directed herself at Logan instead. "I can't say for certain what it does. The literature we have on it is both ominous and entirely unspecific.

What I can tell you is that we have the artifact. It is in a safe house, whose location remains undisclosed to all but the most senior—"

She froze in mid-sentence, horror dawning on her face.

"The most senior Order members? Like, say, Savino Rossi and Zilla Ulric?" Logan offered. She felt oddly calm; she'd known this was a possibility, after all.

"Not Savino, but—" Clément shook her head, pulling out a cell phone and pressing rapidly on the screen before holding it up to her ear. "It was last moved over a month ago. I can't know for sure if she—ah, hello Carl, it's the interim Prophet speaking. Yes, quite. Unfortunately it looks like we've run into a Code Black scenario." Clément paused while the person on the other end spoke. "Item 52 bravo-delta. Yes. Move it to the beta site as soon as you can, and call in every one of your alternates to meet you there. If anyone is on duty with you, bring them along. Yes, you'll have to leave the alpha site unguarded. Don't worry, I'll send someone to cover within the hour. Leave immediately, yes. Thank you." With that, she hung up the phone and turned back to Logan. "That should buy us a bit of time, though I can't be certain how much."

"He'll figure it out eventually," said Logan, her next idea already formed. "You should take me there. Whatever you've got in store for him, he could have anticipated it. Especially with Ulric around. But he's much less likely to expect to find me there, ready for him."

Clément didn't hesitate. "I agree. We must try to gain the upper hand, however we can." She looked Logan square in the face, her expression open. "The magic that the artifact belongs to is ancient and lost. The Order has been studying it for a long time." Picking up her cup again, she took a quick sip. "We have never been able to activate it, one way or the other. And we have tried."

Logan nodded, remembering her vision of Volkov, and the destructive desire it unleashed within her. She had a feeling she knew what piece of the puzzle was missing—and Volkov probably did, too.

"The Wolf may know how to activate it," she said, quietly. "Based on what Rossi said, anyway."

"In that case, there are a few more arrangements to be made." Setting her cup down once more, Clément stood and pulled out her phone again. "Marlowe, I'm pulling in your new team, and I'm putting you in charge of this mission. I'll have them here within the hour, and then you can all leave for the beta site together." She looked pointedly between the two of them. "Perhaps it will be best if you take separate cars."

With that, she spirited out of the room, apparently to call in whatever arrangements she needed to set up instantaneous transport across the entire breadth of the United States. Logan knew the Order had that capability, of course, but it would be interesting to see it in action. She'd always wondered what similarities it might have with the functions of the traveling room.

"I think I'll go make some more tea," said Knatt, standing hurriedly. Logan got the distinct impression that he didn't want to stand as the only barrier between Marlowe and herself. He was gone in seconds.

The silence between them stretched like a swamp, waiting to

pull them in. Marlowe offered up a grim smile as her only warning.

"I suppose I should congratulate you," she said. There was danger in her voice; she sounded too pleased with herself.

"Congratulate me for what?"

"For the success of your protege, of course."

"What are you talking about?"

Marlowe smiled pleasantly. "Your protege, the young Miss Judith Li, engaged in the successful raid of a demon nest the other night, along with Adepts Blake and Fisher. A large one, from what I'm told. Didn't you know?"

Logan did her best not to let her surprise show on her face, but she wasn't sure how well she succeeded. "Oh, *that*. Just— just waiting to hear all the details when she gets back."

Marlowe's smile widened into a self-satisfied grin; Logan hadn't convinced her. "Well, be sure you do. It's a fantastic story. Hell, after that performance, the Order might need to think about recruiting her. Wouldn't want to step on your toes, of course." She stood up, making sure to look down her nose at Logan as she did. "I'm going to see if Marion needs any assistance. Excuse me."

Logan nodded but kept her mouth shut. An uncontrollable rage was coursing through her veins, and she didn't know how it might manifest if she didn't lock it down. She wasn't sure what she was angrier at: Marlowe's smugness or Jude's casual betrayal.

It's not a betrayal, she told herself. *Just disobedience.*

She took a deep breath. She'd let Jude travel across the country to visit with her friend, and she'd told herself that she was doing the right thing. She was giving Jude a chance to have some fun, and by physically removing her from herself, she was making her safer—after all, it was Logan the Wolf was after. Jude was only a target as a side effect of their association.

And this is how she pays me back. By putting herself in as much danger as possible.

But a voice at the back of her head put up a protest.

Were you really trying to make her safe? Or did you just want a break from protecting her?

Logan's anger redoubled, but she couldn't say who it was aimed at. Marlowe's footsteps were fading down the hallway. Marlowe would have made an easy target for the anger, but for some reason, she couldn't make it work.

We might need to think about recruiting her, Marlowe had said. Logan let out a heavy sigh.

Perhaps I should let you.

As it turned out, Clément had one more item of business to attend to. When she came back inside, she began by informing Logan that a delegation would be arriving in the backyard within the hour. Then she pivoted to what she really wanted to discuss.

"We don't think it's a coincidence that Rossi went after Charles Logan not once, but twice," she said, with little preamble. Marlowe was fortunately out of the room, as was Knatt—leaving the two of them completely alone. "I'd like a chance to interview him, if you'd permit me."

Logan had poured herself a second cup of coffee, and she took a drink from it now to give herself a moment to consider how to phrase the answer. She wasn't about to give the Order direct access to her father, not when she had no idea which of her secrets he might give up at any moment, but she also didn't want to raise their suspicion when she turned them down.

Eventually, however, she had to say something.

"My father has already been through quite an ordeal in the past 24 hours." She made sure to put as much care and concern into her voice as she could. It helped to pretend she was talking about Knatt, instead. "He's been disoriented since we took him out of the nursing home, and Rossi's attack only exacerbated that. I'm sorry, I just don't think I can put him through another high-stress situation right now."

"I assure you, I would take the utmost care—"

"As a matter of fact," said a voice from the shadow of the doorway, "Mr. Logan is currently sound asleep." Knatt stepped forward into the light from the living room windows. "I've just been up to check on him. After the night he's had, I would say it is *imperative* we let him rest. Perhaps you can send someone back in a few days, when he's had some time to recover."

Clément straightened, an unhappy but resigned look on her face. Logan felt all but confirmed in her suspicion that Clément was more desperate for her help than she would let on. Otherwise, she was sure she would push this matter with considerably more force.

"Very well," she said. "Dolores can handle things from here. I'll be sure to send her back your way, once your father is able enough to speak to her."

Logan cursed silently, annoyed that she'd managed to get her way *and* somehow end up with a worse bargain at the same time. Outwardly, she smiled.

Having the Order of Shadows in her backyard was already proving a nightmare.

Chapter Twelve
Where We Turn

Less than an hour later, Logan stood out on the deck behind the house, Clément and Marlowe on one side, and Knatt and Alexei on the other. She'd placed a discreet call to Alexei after her one-on-one conversation with Clément, and about ten minutes later, he'd sauntered into the living room. She knew he'd come prepared with a story about sleeping in one of the numerous guest rooms upstairs—but neither Marlowe nor Clément asked a single question about it. Apparently, they'd found nothing at all unusual about another random, lowly contractor strolling through the Logan estate. This was not to say that Marlowe, at least, didn't immediately regard Alexei with the same unrelenting disdain and suspicion she'd already displayed toward Logan. Logan was starting to wonder if, perhaps, Marlowe had a problem with everyone who wasn't a card-carrying member of the Order of Shadows.

The spatial fold the Order used for their instant travel was a fascinating thing to behold on this side of the divide. A shimmering piece of light appeared in the middle of the open air, about seven feet above the ground. Then it arced outward in one smooth motion, like an invisible hand drawing a perfect, partial oval. After that, the sky itself formed a door that swung forward, revealing a completely different landscape on the other side. Out of the doorway in the sky walked a tall, muscular man that Logan had never seen before, followed by Eliana Blake and her friend Fisher—and then by a stunned-looking Judith Li.

Beside her, Alexei shifted on his feet, grazing her arm with his, and Logan felt an entirely inappropriate shiver run down her spine.

Keep your shit together, she told herself.

One more down the line, Knatt stepped forward, grinning at Jude as he walked toward her. Logan just barely recognized that look on his face: it was the one he used to have on the rare occasions when he got to pick her up from school for a reason *other* than a disciplinary measure. Knatt half-jogged across the lawn as he waved, and a mirror-image grin broke across Jude's face. The kid would never be good at poker. The next moment they were locked in a hug, as if it had been weeks since they'd seen each other, instead of a few short days. Logan might have been touched if her rage had allowed it.

Blake, Fisher, and their unnamed teammate moved straight for their superiors, ending in a militaristic formation, right hands clasped over their chests in what Logan could only assume was the Order's version of a salute.

"Dolores, you have it from here," said Clément, stepping off the back deck and moving back toward the portal. She paused to toss a glance back at Logan. "I left the GPS coordinates you need on your kitchen counter. If you leave quickly, you should be able to get there before nightfall."

Logan nodded and performed a quick mock-salute before Clément could turn away. The French woman humored her with a wry smile and a shake of her head. A moment later, she was gone, and the portal was, too.

Until now, Logan had managed to avoid looking directly at Jude's face. But now, out of the corner of her eye, she saw her turn toward her, raising her arms just slightly—like she planned to ask for a hug. Before she could finish the movement, Logan turned back toward the house and marched forward, motioning for the rest to follow her.

She refused to look back and see Jude's disappointment, but she could still *feel* it—that sense of rejection and defeat. If she hadn't been sure she was doing the right thing, she might have felt bad about it.

Once inside, Logan made a beeline for the kitchen counter, where a slim piece of paper lay tucked beneath the pepper shaker. She picked it up. Emblazoned across the top were the words "Storage Locker," followed by, as Clément had said, a set of coordinates. Logan made quick work of memorizing the numbers, as she had a guess that Marlowe would likely destroy the paper.

Sure enough, when Marlowe walked in, her direction was terse.

"You'll be handing that back to me once you're done with it," she said. "Which should be in about 60 seconds."

Logan gave it one last glance before passing it over.

"Already got what I needed." A brief mirthless smile passed over her face. Marlowe took the paper silently, disgust still written on hers.

"We're moving out, team," said Marlowe, turning back

around the other Order members, now coming through the back door. "Car's in front. Follow me."

Logan watched them go—first Marlowe, then the unnamed male Adept with the bulky build and buzz cut, and then bespectacled Fisher, who looked out-of-place in his crisp Adept uniform.

Just a kid pretending to be a soldier. Hope he knows they're playing with a loaded gun.

Last came Eliana Blake, who looked like she was intentionally lagging behind the others. As Logan watched, Jude rushed forward to follow after her. Logan's anger flared.

Blake is the reason she lied to you. That girl is the reason she went into a demon's nest without clearance.

Another deep breath.

Knatt and Alexei had come back inside, too, closing the door behind them. Though it wasn't yet noon, the gray sky had already begun to darken, as if a storm were on its way. Of course, Logan knew what winters were like in Washington. Sometimes darker clouds only meant darker clouds.

"Perhaps I should make some hot chocolate before you go," said Knatt, still smiling merrily. Logan wished she could enjoy how happy he was at having the kid back in the house again; he'd be unlikely to admit it on his own, but she knew he loved having someone to take care of. And she knew she'd been a poor recipient of his care for a long time.

"It's the season for it," said Alexei, sounding uncertain. Logan glanced over at him and was startled to find him staring at her, his questioning eyes roaming her face. She raised an eyebrow at him, and watched as he mouthed, *What's wrong?*

Nothing, she mouthed back, looking away before she could see his reaction. Why did he have to choose *now* to be perceptive? Couldn't he let her stew in peace?

Knatt, for his part, seemed oblivious to this silent interaction. He kept his back turned as he started pulling down ingredients for his own personal hot chocolate recipe. She'd only gotten to try it once as a kid before Knatt figured out her sugar thing. Apparently he hadn't fancied taking care of a drunk eight-year-old.

I suppose I should be grateful that at least one parent didn't see everything about me as a new chance to run an experiment. She drummed her fingernails against the counter-top in front of her and recited the coordinates to herself one more time.

On the west side of the house, she could hear the front door finally close, and someone—Jude—sliding the lock into place. She listened to the last of the footsteps disappearing into a car, and she listened to the roar of the engine as it carried the Adepts away toward the designated coordinates.

Jude's steps came back down the hall, toward them. Logan's anger began to swell, but she took another breath, deeper this time. This time, she counted down as she let it out, going as slowly as she could. And she did her best to pretend she couldn't see the look Alexei gave her.

Then Jude walked through the door.

"Hey guys," she said, waving awkwardly at the room. Her gaze levitated unmistakably toward Logan, who pretended not to notice. "Uh, so, sounds like there's a mission. Should we, like, start getting ready to go?"

"Yes, we should." Logan's voice was crystal clear as she finally met Jude's eyes. "But not you."

"What?"

"Alexei and I are going. You're staying here." She glanced over at Knatt. "Do you mind staying to watch her?"

"Of course not," said Knatt, easily and smoothly, though she caught a hint of uncertainty in his eyes.

Jude's confusion gave way to shock. "But—I—I don't understand. Am I not allowed to go?"

"Sounds like you understand just fine."

"But—why?"

"I know about your 'mission' in New York." Logan watched Jude's face impassively. Understanding came first, then the panic of being caught. "That's right. I know that you, Blake, and Fisher went demon hunting all on your own, without consulting either us or the Order. That nice Order lady got to rub it in my face a few minutes ago."

"Is this true, Jude?" asked Knatt. He used his special wounded tone, which Logan happened to know he'd perfected back when she was a teenager. She could admire it now.

Jude hung her head.

"Yeah, it's true," she said, sounding abashed, but still defiant. "But, there's some mitigating stuff that you don't—"

"I don't care," said Logan. "You had no idea what the level of danger was, and you didn't bother to check in with us—or even tell us about it after the fact. We *trusted* you to go on that trip by yourself. And you proved that trust to be a mistake."

"I—uh—okay. Look, I know I didn't make a great decision—"

"There's no room for discussion here. If I can't trust you on your own, then I can't trust you." She turned to her right. "Alexei, you and I should head to the armory—"

"Hey, wait!" Jude jumped forward, one arm outstretched toward Logan, her eyes pleading. "I'm sorry I didn't tell you, okay? I'm really sorry. But—but you can *use* me on this mission, all right? You shouldn't leave me here, because I can *help* now—"

Logan waved her hand dismissively. Her rage turned cold in her chest.

"No, you can't."

"But—but you don't understand—I was really good! I mean, I know I shouldn't have gone, but—but it worked out! I kept myself safe, I swear. I—I managed this really strong eira summon, and I killed a whole bunch of the irahu, and if I hadn't gone, I don't think Eliana and Fisher would have even made it—"

"So, what? You think you did the right thing?" Her fingers clenched hard over her elbows, like she was physically trying to hold herself in. "You think it was *worth* it?" She gave Jude a long, hard look, letting her squirm for as long a moment as possible. "You would do it all again?"

"I—that's not what I—"

She watched the last of Jude's resolve wither away. Suddenly she found it unbearable to remain in the room with her. She shook her head.

"I can't use a fighter I can't trust. So, I have no use for you."

She watched the balloon of Jude's ego and hope, recklessly intertwined, deflate in front of her. Motioning to Alexei, she turned to go.

"We're going. Knatt, call me if you need anything."

Logan decided against the armory at the estate and steered them toward the traveling room, so they could stop by her apartment instead. This turned out to be in Alexei's favor, since he preferred to use his own weapons, anyway. Not for any practical reason, but because he believed they worked better with his outfit. Meanwhile, Logan's favorite holsters all lived in her own closet, not on the estate.

Despite the fact that Logan had to remove more clothing than Alexei did in order to equip herself, she still managed to take less time to get ready. She waited for him at the erstwhile doorway to her front hall closet, currently holding open the connection between the apartment and the estate. By the time he arrived, her reflexive nervous grip on her own arm had begun to leave a bruise.

"Sorry," he said simply as he sidled up to her. "Had to redo the hair."

"Your hair looks the same."

"Exactly."

Logan rolled her eyes and pushed forward, heading through the portal and in the direction of the garage. From the approximate location of the coordinates, the estate was a significantly more efficient starting point than the middle of the city, and, besides, she hadn't yet convinced Alexei that riding on the back of her bike was safe. So, she settled for Knatt's sedan, instead.

They had just about reached the door to the garage when she heard Knatt calling her from down the hall. She sighed.

"Can you get the car started?" she asked, handing Alexei the keys.

"Of course."

"I'm still driving."

"I know."

"Just wanted to make sure."

A moment later, Alexei was out of sight, and Logan had turned back down the hall to meet Knatt halfway.

"If you're gonna try to get me to bring Jude, don't bother."

"Not at all," said Knatt, his tone light and unconcerned. "I think it's good to teach her that there are consequences for her actions."

"I agree."

"Besides which, as the primary fighter, and the person who recruited her, you are ultimately the one who shoulders the responsibility for her safety. For the time being, at least."

"Yep."

"We can't always know, as guardians, what the full effect of our decisions will be."

"Right." Logan cleared her throat. She felt increasingly uncomfortable.

"But that's not what I want to talk to you about."

"Okay."

"I wanted to talk to you about…your father."

Logan blinked. On some level, she knew she should have expected this, but in her rage at Jude, she'd nearly forgotten all about it.

"Okay."

"Your father…doesn't know you."

"Well, yeah, we aren't exactly buds—"

"That's not what I mean. What I mean is…what he said, that your power is rooted in darkness…he doesn't *know* that. He believes it, but he doesn't know it. It's not a fact, it's an opinion. And a bloody misinformed one, if you ask me."

Logan blinked again.

"Knatt, your British is showing."

"I'm aware." He frowned at her. "You weren't born evil, Henrietta. Nobody is born evil. Your father was *absurd* to think so. Do you understand that?"

"Yes."

He sighed. "But do you *believe* it?"

She saw the image of herself in the vision, felt the burning rage that made her want to tear the world open. It had to be real, didn't it? The Choronzon Key had never lied to her.

"I don't know." She shook her head. "Nobody else was ever born like me. Unless there's a secret half-demon support group out there that I've just never found…I'm the only one like me. Maybe I *was* born different."

Knatt put his hand on her shoulder.

"You were a child. You were a *wonderful* child." He let out the saddest sound she'd ever heard from him. "You were, and are, full of love, and wonder, and laughter. You are the best thing that ever happened to me. And I'm so sorry if I ever let you think differently."

Logan's throat burned, and she felt something pricking at her eye. She swallowed hard.

"I…I gotta get going. Um, stay safe here, okay?"

Knatt nodded.

"Of course."

She swallowed again. Then she reached out and touched him briefly on the elbow. She didn't know how it could, but she hoped it conveyed to him how she felt.

Without another word, she left.

By Logan's estimate, it would take them somewhere between two and three hours to get to their destination, no matter how fast she went. Her plan, of course, was to break the speed limit as much as she could get away with: her preternaturally good eyesight was generally a boon when it came to spotting cop cars hiding along the freeway, which meant she could always slow down just in time.

Even so, they were looking at a long drive. This mysterious "beta site" they were headed to appeared to be deep in the middle of nowhere, hovering just northeast of the center of Washington state.

This, unfortunately, left them plenty of time for conversation. She could practically hear Alexei gearing himself up to ask her something as he flipped around between radio stations, uncharacteristically quiet for far too long.

They had been driving for nearly 30 minutes when he finally cleared his throat.

"So…that was intense."

Logan let out a slow sigh and, spying something suspicious just around the bed, pressed her foot gently against the brake.

"We're lucky they haven't closed the pass yet," she said. "And that Knatt already fitted the tires with chains. Could snow while we're on the other side of the mountains."

Out of the corner of her eye, she saw Alexei give a sad shake of his head.

"We've got hours, H.C. You think you can stall me out that long?"

For a moment, Logan said nothing. The rage was going out, and it left her feeling empty.

"What do you want me to say?" The words came out of her like a sigh.

Alexei shifted in his seat, the fine fabric of his pants barely a whisper against the upholstery.

"I guess I'd like to know what I missed," he said.

"All right. You know I met with the Order. Clément and that new woman, Marlowe. And you know what we discussed." Sometimes she wondered how well a steering wheel could hold up under her grip. "Eventually, Clément left to make a call, leaving me alone with Marlowe. I get the impression she doesn't like me very much. When we were alone, she congratulated me on Jude's unsanctioned mission. Which I knew nothing about, because Jude didn't tell me about it. Sounds like it was probably Eliana Blake's idea. And Jude just…went along with it, no hesitation. She could have been killed."

"Yeah, she could have been. I take it she wasn't?"

"No, Marlowe said they were successful. And she…made a joke that the Order might try to recruit her."

Alexei nodded, mulling that over. "Do you think she meant it?"

"I don't know. Maybe she was just trying to goad me." Logan felt her hand clench in frustration again, and she allowed herself a moment to clench it as hard as she could…then forced herself to let go. "But that's exactly the problem. We don't really know what the Order might do in any given moment. The only thing I know for *sure* about them…is that they want to preserve their own power, at all costs." She shook her head, feeling that particular kind of helplessness that only came over her when she had to deal with the machinations of bureaucracy, instead of demons. "How can I protect her if I'm not even sure what I'm protecting her from?"

Alexei let out a small laugh.

"Look, I'm no expert, but I think that's just what *parenting* is." She could feel him watching her, and she turned in time to catch the amusement shining warmly in his eyes.

"Jude is a legal adult. I'm not her parent."

"A kindly aunt, then," said Alexei, amusement in his voice. "A young, *attractive*, kindly aunt."

Logan let out a low chuckle.

"Okay, smart ass. I'm a kindly aunt." She let out a rough sigh. "It's just hard not to think that I might have done the wrong thing, dragging her into this."

"Because of…demons and shit?"

"Because I'm a mess and I shouldn't be in charge of anything." She was gripping too hard on the steering wheel again.

"I don't think you're a mess."

"You sure about that? I just killed someone and tampered with the evidence."

"There were some extenuating circumstances there."

"Oh, yes. The magic word that can turn me into a weapon at any time. That's reassuring, on the mess front." She shook her head and tried to loosen her grip on the steering wheel. "Sorry. I'm not looking for pity. Just trying to be honest."

Beside her, Alexei leaned back into his chair and contemplated her silently for a moment. His eyes were soft and warm, and full of compassion. After what felt like a very long time, he spoke.

"Have I ever told you how I ended up in this line of work?"

"I don't think so."

"Well, it wasn't my proudest moment." He let out a long sigh and settled in. "My mother was always adamant I go to college. I think she thought that would straighten me out, in more ways than one. It won't shock you to learn I had a troubled adolescence."

"It won't, no."

"It continued into college. Turns out Mom was wrong about that one." He smiled wistfully to himself. "I found my group of like-minded miscreants pretty quickly. Boys who liked to drink and, you know, fuck anything that moved. Including each other."

Logan chuckled. "Also not a surprise."

"Mostly it was all stuff I'd done before. But there was this one thing they did that was totally new to me."

"Magic?"

"Magic." He drummed his nails against the fabric of his nice pants. Was he nervous? "I was never a gifted caster. None of us were, except…except for Shawn. Shawn was special. Any cast that anyone came up with, he could do it. He was hot, too."

"You were sleeping with him."

He glanced at her. "I was sleeping with all of them. But I *liked* him. That was the danger." He sighed again. "We all liked him. He was better than all of us, and we knew it. He knew it, too. So, one night, I stay up drinking with one of the others, a guy named Nick. And, I mean, we get *wasted*—the level of wasted where it seems like a great idea to jump off the roof, you know? Only we're magic users, not frat boys. So what do we do? We decide to do a cast, of course. See, Nick, he reveals that he found a book about casting in Shawn's room. He thinks that book is how Shawn manages to be so much better than the rest of us—

and he announces that he's going to steal that book. Now, obviously, I didn't take him that seriously. Hell, I didn't think *either* of us would remember by morning. So, I tell him…I tell him that if he steals the book, then I'll help him do whatever cast he wants from it. Twenty-four hours later, this motherfucker is standing at my door, book in hand."

"Of course."

"And you know me. I'm a man of my word. I tell him to pick a cast. Two guesses what he picked."

"A demon summon?"

"Right on the money." He gave a sad little shake of his head. "You know, it was only later that I found out Shawn *intended* for one of us to find the book. At the time, I just…well. I agreed to help Nick. And I had poor enough sense to think that meant I couldn't back out. So, together, we head out in the woods to do the cast. Naturally, we bring along our liquid courage, because if anything helps with casting, it's incoherent drunkenness. God, we were such idiots."

"Did the summon work?"

"Oh, it worked. Lucky for me, the only cast I'd mastered up to that point was a yurok letha summon. Poison spray. So, when this demon came screaming into the world, I was just barely able to protect myself. Nick wasn't."

"Oh god."

"Turns out Shawn had been watching us, waiting to see if we could do it. He ran out of the trees just in time to save me, but not Nick." Alexei's expression darkened. "The whole fucking thing was a test. Shawn was a plant, sent by the Order of Shadows. Apparently, it's a common recruitment tactic of theirs."

"Christ."

"And *lucky me*, I passed the test. Shawn asked me if I wanted to join up with the Order, see what heights I could reach with them. He let me know it would be a paying position, of course."

"What'd you say?"

"I asked him how many other potential recruits had ended up like Nick. And then I asked him to leave me alone."

Logan let out a long breath. She, too, wondered how many other recruits had ended up like Alexei's friend. The Order was so good at cleaning up their tracks, she'd probably never know. She felt her right hand travel instinctively to her face—to the scar Zilla Ulric had left, straight down the right side of her face.

Beside her, Alexei cleared his throat.

"So, my advice." He caught her eyes in the mirror. "I think you're right to keep an eye on Jude whenever they're around. I think we'd all be wise to do the same. And maybe end this…*partnership* with them, as soon as we can."

His words hit home. They confirmed the dread she'd already built.

"Let's hope this *is* the end of it."

Chapter Thirteen
Into the Waiting Dark

When Alexei and Logan arrived at what appeared to be a barn in the middle of the Washington woods, she got the distinct impression that swift action had recently been taken, perhaps only minutes before they'd arrived. Deep tread marks led away from the barn door, curving sharply away from the main path and into the shadows on the far side of the building.

As she pulled up to the front, a camouflaged garage door opened automatically just to the right, leading the way into a dark interior.

"Does that look ominous to you?" Alexei's hand grasped the top of his panther-headed cane, which now lay across his lap.

Logan shifted into reverse, then steered toward this new door.

"I'm more interested in the tire marks over there," she motioned behind them. "Wondering what they thought was important enough to hustle up and hide. And where it could have gone."

"Back to the alpha site, maybe?"

"Or on to the gamma."

As she steered the car into the building, the door began to

shut automatically behind them. No sooner had she come to a stop than several blindingly bright floodlights came on. Her eyes had automatically dilated to make out as much of the darkened space as she could, and the sudden onslaught of light burned her. She shut her eyes and ducked her head below the wheel.

"Christ," muttered Alexei from the seat next to her. "This seems unnecessary."

"Oh, I'm sure Marlowe's enjoying herself." Blinking furiously, she finished cutting the engine and unbuckling her seat belt, making sure she had one hand on a hidden throwing knife before she opened the door. "Ready?"

"As ever."

With that, they stepped out into the overwhelming bright.

Logan stood with her arms crossed, staring down at the table in the center of the room. It held a to-scale representation of the compound in which they stood, complete with moveable figures, mostly in the shape of the Order's sun-and-sword symbol. The two shapes that represented Alexei and herself were the only outliers: two nondescript rectangles floating across the board.

She didn't want to sign on to this plan, but she didn't see many other options.

Marlowe had taken the lead early, and Logan had acquiesced, sensing that Marlowe's pride had taken a hit the moment Clément had ordered her to bring Logan along in the first place. She just wanted to get through this—preferably without dying.

Marlowe pushed one more figurine into place before standing up straight.

"So, does everyone understand their assignment?"

The room was full of unknown Order faces, and every single one of them looked to Marlowe with absolute reverence. Blake and her friend were the only ones Logan recognized, though she'd picked up a few other names during the course of Marlowe's speech.

Heads around the room began to nod, each Order soldier looking like they might strain their back with the effort to straighten it.

Logan cleared her throat.

"Uh, quick question…shouldn't one of us actually go downstairs and guard the vault? And by 'one of us,' I mean me."

"No," said Marlowe, sharply and without hesitation. "I won't send anyone down there unless it's absolutely necessary. Besides, the Wolf can't get down there without getting through the rest of us first. Which is not going to happen."

Logan pressed her lips into a hard line.

"If you say so, captain."

Marlowe shot her a look, but said nothing. Instead, she turned her attention back to the rest.

"If there are no more questions, you're all dismissed. Get to your posts."

Logan stood her ground, arms crossed, watching the others filter out toward their destinations. Including the three Adepts she knew, there were 13 of them in total. Since Marlowe saw fit to keep her as far back from the front line as possible, she could only hope that they were all skilled enough to keep themselves safe…or that Volkov was uninterested in killing anyone else on his way to the artifact.

Her eyes were fixated on Blake's departing back when she sensed someone walking toward her. She shifted her gaze, finding it landing…on the bespectacled Ian Fisher. Blake's friend.

"Can I help you?" She did her best to keep the aggravated edge out of her voice, to mixed results.

"Uh—I—uh—I think we're—assigned to the same spot," he managed, his left eye twitching slightly with each word. He looked as nervous as if he were asking her to prom.

"Basement door?"

"Yeah, basement door."

"Okay, kid," she said, shrugging. "Lead the way."

Before she followed after him, Logan took one last look at the three-dimensional map on the table. She couldn't help but let her eyes linger on the parts that had clearly been intentionally obscured, either given significantly less detail or simply blacked out completely. The largest one seemed to be an area in the basement, not terribly far from the vault. Right where she wanted to be, one way or another.

She let out a sigh and walked after Fisher.

Priorities.

The last time Jude had spent time alone stewing in her own anger in her bedroom, she had lived in a different house. This time, she felt split about everything. Equal parts angry and resentful…and abashed and uncertain. Equally angry at Logan as herself. She *could* have called, couldn't she? She could have done something different than what she did.

But did she have to? She was over 18, which made her legally an adult. And she no longer lived with her parents. But what did that make Logan and Knatt? When she'd agreed to come with

Logan, she'd accepted that Logan was the boss. Had they ever really agreed out loud on how far that power went?

As she lay on her bed, on the navy striped comforter either Logan or Knatt had bought for her, her hands curled into fists.

I wasn't trying to rebel. I just wanted Eliana to think I was cool.

Even as she thought it, she felt something within her deflate. If her only aim was to get a girl to think she was cool, wasn't that proof enough of her immaturity? *Act like a teenager, get treated like a teenager.*

She reached above her head until her hand found Mortimor the moose, and she dragged him down to her chest. Feeling his floppy, bean-filled little body collapse against her collar bone brought her an unexplainable level of peace. She'd anthropomorphized him for so many years, he felt almost like a real pet.

"What do you think, boy? Did I do it bad?"

Mortimor waited on her chest, quietly reassuring her with his slight weight.

If I hadn't gone with them, I wouldn't have summoned the fire, she thought. *It might have taken me months to figure it out without a real danger to fight.*

Dangerous. Maybe that was the whole point.

She remembered the look of those shiny irahu bodies as they advanced on Fisher, as they threatened to engulf him. She remembered the way they screamed when they ran toward her. And she remembered the way they lay lifeless afterward, when Eliana and Ian started gathering them up.

Suddenly, she sat bolt upright. She hadn't told Knatt or Logan about the directive to collect as much demon material as possible. Whatever else she kept to herself, that seemed like something that needed to be shared. Setting Mortimor aside, she got up and left the warm confines of her bedroom behind, in search of Knatt.

It didn't take her long to find him. He was down in the overly large living room, sitting in an armchair in the small ring of light from a floor lamp, reading a book. A part of her wondered how many times teenage Logan had stomped down from her bedroom and found him exactly like that.

"Hey, Knatt?" she said tentatively. She wasn't sure if he was as upset with her as Logan was, and she didn't want another fight.

But he just smiled beatifically at her and put the book down.

"Jude," he said, warmly. "I was just thinking of putting the kettle on. Would you like some tea?"

An immense pressure seemed to release from her chest. Whatever Logan's feelings were, Knatt, at least, didn't hate her.

"Yes, please."

Knatt nodded and stood, motioning toward the kitchen.

"Shall we?"

He led the way, and Jude followed. She picked out the kind of tea she wanted, Earl Grey, and then seated herself at the island counter while he put together a tray as the water boiled. He picked out little cookies and poured some cream into a pitcher, and she watched his careful movements with the twin feelings of fascination and relief residing within her.

She jumped a little when the kettle finally let out its high-pitched squeal; it reminded her too much of the incessant screams of the irahu. She could only hope that memory would fade fast. A moment later, Knatt brought over the tea tray and set it between them.

"Did you wish to speak to me about something?" he asked as he poured his own cup.

Jude nodded. "Yeah. It's about the Order. I, uh, kinda…learned something about them, when I…well, when I went on that mission with them." She winced, expecting blow back.

But again, Knatt simply nodded encouragingly.

"Go on."

"They…they gather up the bodies of demons and bring them back to do experiments on them." Even saying the words out loud felt morbid. She knew they were just demons, and dead ones to boot, but it still felt strange to her, wrong even. "That's why they were fine with us doing a mission off-book. Eliana and Ian brought back a good enough haul that…that they didn't care they weren't sanctioned to do it. And…Eliana said she knew they wouldn't care, because…because they never do. I—I thought you should know."

Knatt nodded, his expression unreadable.

"Thank you for telling me." He paused for a moment to blow across the top of his cup. "That does confirm a suspicion."

"It does?"

"Yes, it does." He put his mug down on the counter and stared at it for a moment, seemingly lost in thought. Then he cleared his throat. "For centuries, the Order has managed to maintain their edge on everyone else by pushing the limits of letha casting through experimentation. Over time, a good number of their experiments have proven unethical, and those are just the ones that have come to light. Much like Logan's father…they have used human test subjects in the past."

"They're pretty familiar with guns, too," said Jude, thinking back to their fight, and the look in Eliana's eyes as she fired her weapon, over and over.

"Yes, those can work on certain smaller demons. Do you remember what kind you fought?"

"Yeah." She wished she didn't. "Irahu."

"Ah. You would have to have quite good aim, but yes, that could work." He sounded like he was speaking more to himself than to her.

"Fisher requested enhanced vision for his Binding," she explained immediately. "I think it helps with his aim." She stared down into her own cup for several seconds. She hoped she'd forget the inhuman gleam of their dark and unmoving bodies, too. "We didn't really have a plan. We just went in, with almost no recon to go on. With literal guns blazing."

"That sounds quite reckless."

"It was." She held her cup with both hands, still staring down at it, willing herself to say the rest. "Knatt…if I tell you something, will you promise not to tell Logan? I don't want her to be even more mad at me."

He reached out a hand to lay it over her own. His eyes looked sad.

"Without knowing what it is you want to tell me, I can't make that promise." He gave another encouraging smile. "We only want to keep you safe, Jude. Both Henrietta and I."

Jude swallowed, hard.

"Right. Well…Fisher kinda…almost died on the mission."

Knatt's eyebrows shot up in surprise. "So, Fisher used his enhanced vision to look at the nest, and we thought we'd accounted for all of them, so nobody panicked when we ran out of bullets, and then Fisher rushed forward to kill what we thought was the last one, and—and all these irahu just swarmed out of this hole in the wall that we didn't even know was there—"

"Dear lord. Was he injured?"

"Well, a little, but—well, that's when I did my summon. I summoned this, like, wave of fire and it just—it just burned them away."

Knatt nodded slowly, taking this all in as he took another sip. Finally, he fixed her with a look.

"You killed the rest of the demons with a fire summon?"

"Y-yeah."

"Have you summoned anything since?"

He sounded tense, almost alarmed. She felt her stomach already beginning to clench.

"No, I haven't."

"Perhaps it's better that you refrain until Adele returns to us," he said carefully; she could just barely pick up on the restrained concern beneath his veneer. "It can be quite dangerous to perform eira without balance. The element you call has an effect on you. If you lean too heavily on an element like fire…its euphoric properties can become addictive. It can…warp the mind, as it were."

"Warp the mind? Has that happened before?"

"Oh, yes. You would not be the first."

Jude let out a slow breath, like a balloon hissing out air.

"Well, this just keeps getting better and better. Jeez, can I do anything right?"

"Don't get me wrong—it is a *good* thing that you saved young Mr. Fisher's life. When faced with that kind of situation, it is better to act. But I don't want you to push too hard without the proper guidance. I don't want to throw you in the deep end, as it were."

You mean you don't want to do what Logan's dad did, she thought but didn't say. Instead, she gave a terse nod.

"Right."

In the silence that followed, Jude found herself drinking her tea with new urgency. She felt strange and restless, inexplicably *off*—like she had right after the demon fight. It was like the fire was calling to her, just like she had called to it. Was that what Knatt was talking about?

Across from her, Knatt cleared his throat and gazed at her with serious intent.

"Power can be intoxicating," he said. He sounded weary, like he knew it all too well. "But it is not without its costs. You must always remember that, Jude."

Jude nodded, though she felt like there was something under his words that she was missing. It was difficult to concentrate on it, though. Her restlessness had settled into her bones. She doubted she could sit still much longer.

What she wanted, of course, was to be in the fight. She wanted to be where the action was.

But Logan had said no. Logan said she couldn't be trusted.

"I think I should go for a walk," she said, standing up abruptly. She drank the rest of her tea in one gulp. "Is that okay?"

"Of course," said Knatt. He sounded relaxed, but he looked concerned. "Just make sure you're back before dark, all right?

And we'll order take-away from town, hm?"

"That sounds good." She was already moving toward the door, her hands ready to grab her coat off its hook. "I'll see you in a little bit."

"Don't stray too far," he said as she rounded the corner. "And bring your cell phone, and your whistle!"

For a moment, Jude stopped in her tracks, her jacket already halfway on. She felt an impulse to refuse his request, felt a sudden unaccountable resentment that he'd even made it. She shook her head at herself, then forced her arms to finish pulling on her coat.

Stop being an idiot, she told herself. *Act like a child and you'll get treated like a child, remember?*

She managed to hold her tongue until she walked out the back door, closing it tight behind her. When the cold, damp air hit her face, the fire eased a little. She wasn't even sure why she'd been annoyed at all a moment ago. After all, she rarely went anywhere without the cell phone, and the whistle already sat in her jacket pocket. His requests were reasonable, if a little motherly. But what was wrong with that?

She took a few steps out into the yard and tried to breathe in as much of the winter air as she could. For a moment, it seemed to work…then, out of nowhere, she remembered that there was a second car still sitting in the garage. If she wanted, she could take the keys and slip away, go join the fight—

Cut that out, she thought, giving herself a shake.

And then, not a moment later, *why should I?*

The fingers on her right hand flexed. She was relatively certain that she could summon the fire again right now, if she wanted to.

But what did Knatt just *tell you?*

She took a steadying breath and picked forward. The fire was burning in her veins, calling to her still. All she wanted to do was summon it, feel it lighting her up the way it had that night.

Instead, she picked up the pace and set out at a light jog. That would have to do for now.

Though it was still afternoon, the sky was dark and gray. It had been cold but bright in New York this morning. She nearly flinched as she remembered her strange trip home, surrounded by the Order in their neat black uniforms, only to find Logan waiting for her, angrier than she'd ever seen her...

I should turn back. I should go watch a movie with Knatt.

Then a voice, that only barely sounded like her own, whispered, *No. I should be in the fight. I should be with them now.*

She could feel the outline of her thoughts and the tight spiral they seemed to be caught in just as sure as she could feel the wind on her face. Everything had felt so clear and easy when she was fighting with Eliana and Ian. A kind of mindless joy had taken over. It had all seemed so clear cut.

Now the world seemed fuzzy and vague and uncertain. Even looking back, the certainty seemed like a lie, one way or the other. She'd believed it because she wanted to.

The world around her was quiet. She jogged a few more paces, then slowed as she reached the trees beyond the property line. She could feel the quiet in her bones.

Except there was a disturbance in her quiet. For just a moment, she heard a rustling that hadn't been there before.

Her first impulse was to freeze, but she didn't let herself. If someone was there, trying to keep quiet, then she didn't want them to know she knew.

Ever so slowly, she came to a halt, her hands resting in her pockets, her gaze drifting aimlessly through the trees. It would look, for all the world, like she was deep in contemplation. Then she slowly began to turn around and head back to the house.

She hadn't gone two steps back when she heard the rustle again, a little louder this time. She did her best to pick up her pace without looking like she was doing so.

The third time she heard the rustle, there could be no mistaking it. Whoever was out there no longer seemed to care if she knew. She broke into a run, and she heard them break into a run behind her.

Right as her hand brought the whistle from her pocket to her lips, they collided with her.

The world went dark.

It began to rain. Thousands of tiny raindrops came down on the false wood roof, which rested somewhere above the real metal one. Logan could hear them all. In the 20 minutes that had passed since her arrival, she'd only gotten a half-decent look around the place, but it didn't seem like she needed much more. It was a giant warehouse, with rooms along three of the walls to make up the offices, including the control room with the 3D map, and not-so-secret storage rooms with classified content.

And then there was the door she stood in front of now, which led down into the basement. It was closer to the center of the space than the others, which automatically made it stand out a little. The main floor was empty in the center, though some strange, ominous looking devices dangled down from the high ceiling. Logan didn't think it was too far-fetched a guess to venture that those were likely used to help them restrain demons they hadn't killed yet. But, of course, to say so out loud would be tantamount to an accusation, so she kept her thoughts to herself. And she pretended not to notice the dark stains on the floor.

She glanced at her compatriot, who stood a few feet away and started nervously at every little sound. She let out a sigh.

"Your name's Fisher, right?" she said gently, trying not to startle him. He jumped a little, anyway.

"Y-yeah," he nodded. He tugged at the hem of his uniform jacket, like he was readying himself for inspection.

Logan shifted her weight from one foot to the other. She was trying to be friendly, but it was hard enough to make casual conversation with any Order Adept, let alone one who looked like he was openly afraid of her. She cleared her throat.

"So…uh…you…enjoy your work here?" She gestured vaguely at the general space of the warehouse.

"I've never actually been here before," he said, still sounding apprehensive. "This is, uh, my first official mission off-base."

"Oh."

"Sorry."

"What?"

"Uh—sorry you got stuck with a nobody like me."

Logan chuckled.

"Oh, don't worry about it. You're all nobodies to me." He blinked at her, eyes wide and nonreactive. "That was a joke."

"Oh!" For a moment, he looked like he was going to force a laugh, but the attempt died before it ever formed.

Logan cleared her throat again, feeling more awkward with every passing moment. Another minute passed in silence before she tried again.

"So…you all get Bound when you graduate, right?"

Fisher gave her a shifty glance, then nodded.

"What power did you get?"

At long last, a hint of a smile broke on his face. He tapped his glasses while he turned to her.

"Enhanced vision," he said. She detected the barest hint of pride in his voice. "I can see through walls. And my aim is perfect."

"Enhanced vision, huh?" She gave him an appraising look, an idea occurring to her. "Do you know what demon they used to draw that from?"

"Didn't ask," he answered with a shrug. "Does it make a difference?"

"Generally, yes," she said. "But perhaps not at the moment. Watch this."

Once his eyes were on her, she closed her own and reached into the easiest well of knowledge she had. She conjured up the cool, comforting embrace of the endless dark, and felt the unnecessary parts of herself fall away, evaporating into ether.

"Holy shit." At last, an emotion unhindered by anxiety: awe. His special eyes stared vaguely in her direction, and she watched as they nearly managed to focus on her—only to stumble at the last moment, lost to the swim once more.

She took one small step to the left. She counted to 10, then 15. Finally, his eyes found her again, though they still couldn't quite reach focus.

"How are you doing that?" he asked. He sounded a little

breathless. "Why can't I pin you down?"

"Don't feel bad." As she spoke, his eyes sharpened, briefly figuring her out again. "You're doing better than most."

"Is this…is this your shadow summon?"

"Yep." Her amusement at his predicament was fading more quickly into irritation than she'd thought it would. She turned away from him, back toward the front entrance of the warehouse barn. "You might want to ease up, kid. You'll give yourself a headache before the fight even starts."

"Oh. Right." He shook his head slightly and turned back toward the front. After only a few seconds, he shot another uncertain glance at where he'd last seen her, so fast it was almost like a nervous tick.

"Don't worry. I won't leave you alone. Without saying something first."

"Uh…right." He didn't look reassured, but that wasn't really her problem.

The next few moments passed in dull quiet, with nothing but the sound of rain to punctuate the nothingness. As she waited in Fisher's unimpressive company, she began to regret her decision to leave Jude behind. It wasn't Fisher's fault, really. She simply would have preferred backup from the rookie she already knew.

The nothingness stretched a little while longer, letting dread yawn its way into the late afternoon. It was barely past three, yet Logan knew it was already dark outside. This far north, evening came early in the winter. And the rain had helped it along.

At long last, she heard a rumble, echoing through the evergreens all around them. It might have come from halfway across the state, or it might have come from 40 feet away. The rain seemed to have flattened all sense of time and distance.

After a few moments, she began to isolate the sound from the surrounding echoes of weather hitting the hollow wood-and-metal structure above them.

It sounded like a howl.

Chapter Fourteen
Avalanche

"Can you hear that?" Logan asked, keeping her voice low. Fisher jumped.

"Shit," he muttered, visibly pulling himself together again. "Man, it's weird having you wobbling around in my peripheral vision like that. Uh, what'd you say?"

"Do you hear that?" she asked, voice still low. It had gotten closer.

Fisher's eyes widened in fear before closing and scrunching up, like a child's concept of deep concentration.

"No…wait, yeah. Fuck, what is that? It sounds…big."

Logan made a quick assessment of the room, taking her third note of all points of egress to make sure she hadn't missed any.

"Could be any number of things," she replied. She decided not to shrug, since either he wouldn't see it, or it would freak him out even more. "I've fought all kinds of demons out here."

"But you…you always kill them, don't you?"

"Generally speaking, yes. And yet, *somehow*, I never seem to run out."

He narrowed his eyes again, this time focusing them on the false door ahead.

"I can't see anything," he said, his voice barely a whisper. "So, it—it must still be far away…"

"It's probably just a distraction," she muttered, more to herself than to him. She flexed her wrists, fighting down the urge to let her spikes fly loose. It wouldn't do to expose herself to the Order—not now, not ever.

She heard the howl again, closer this time.

"Wait—I can see something now," said Fisher, his voice lower now, almost panicky. "It's just an outline, but…it looks big."

"Keep your wits about you," said Logan, glancing at him out of the corner of her eye. She wondered what the chances were that he would bolt, leaving her on her own…and giving her an opportunity to slip off and explore all those unmarked places on the map. Still, it wouldn't be a good idea to let him run off on his own in the middle of these woods. "Leave the outside demons to the front line, okay? We don't have to worry about that until we're called."

Fisher's face collapsed in a frown, his eyes dark and resentful.

"You think I'm a coward, don't you?" He turned to her, his eyes still comically unable to focus on her exact position. "You think I want to run."

"Didn't say that." *Even if I did think it.*

Outside, several people began to shout at once, alerting the rest of the front line. The beast had come.

It howled again: the excited sound of a beast lighting on its prey.

Beside her, Fisher shuffled his feet and gripped the gun at his waist. Logan doubted a gun would have much use against whatever had just arrived, but she wasn't about to tell him that. He cleared his throat.

"Yeah, well—I don't, okay?" he muttered. His brow furrowed as he gazed through the door, at the action she couldn't see. "What I *want* is to be out there. To fight and to prove my worth. To die, if I have to. What I *don't* want is to be stuck in here, waiting around to see if I'll finally get a chance to be useful." He crossed his arms as he finished, casting his gaze around the room, like a teenager sulking from a grounding. It reminded her of Jude.

"You can be plenty useful in here." She turned away from him, scanning the wide room around them again. "Just keep your eyes open. All right?"

His response was more of a grumble than an actual answer. Nevertheless, he turned his eyes back to the front. She let her own gaze linger a moment on him. Was he really so eager to die for his cause? Did the Order train all their Adepts that way, no matter how young?

Am I doing the same thing to Jude?

She heard the howling again. It was right outside, and it sounded…joyous.

She sympathized with the kid, of course. This interminable waiting was hateful in a way the fight itself never was. Action always felt better than inaction, even when she got hurt. Maybe it always would, up until the end.

A few minutes later, she heard the fight outside getting louder, more desperate. The Adepts did not sound like they were winning. She saw Fisher narrow his eyes as he noticed the same thing. Then his eyes widened in surprise.

He cleared his throat, looking uncertain. He reached for the radio at his hip and lifted the mouthpiece. He spoke into it without pressing the button, and his voice was barely a whisper.

"Hey, Miss Logan? I think I…I'm having that same problem I was having a few minutes ago. Uh, you remember that?"

He was speaking in code, and pretending he was alone. Her ears pricked up.

There was someone else in the room with them. Or, at least, he believed there was. Someone he couldn't quite see, just like he couldn't quite see her.

"The pinning down problem, you mean?" her voice was barely a whisper as she moved almost silently past him, tapping him lightly on the shoulder so he could keep track of her movement. He flinched involuntarily, then gave a quick nod to indicate he understood.

"That's the one," he hissed, then pointed. "That way."

His finger indicated one of the side doors, not twenty feet ahead of them. One of the points of egress.

Logan took a deep breath and steadied her mind, refocusing her senses. Her eyes came to a close. There would be no point trying to look for the intruder; instead, she decided to listen for them. She had already tuned out the sounds of the rain, so now she let all sounds from outside the room fall away, listening only to the vibrations within. She waited for the barest hint of an unnatural sound.

There it was. A quiet scraping, like—

Like a door, opening.

She turned just in time to see the door to the basement, and the largest block of blacked-out area from the map, sliding shut once more.

Well, they weren't in the room anymore. She took hold of Fisher's arm so he would know where she was.

"We have to go into the basement," she said tersely, already moving in the direction and, thanks to her strength, pulling him along with her.

"What? But I'm not supposed to let—we're supposed to stay *up here*, and just wait to see if there's a breach—"

"The breach has already happened, Fisher. Someone just closed the basement door, which means they first opened it and went inside. So, tell me, is it more important to keep *me* from seeing what's down there, or the Wolf?"

He gulped audibly, straight panic writ large on his features. He hadn't anticipated the possibility of this, and neither had the orders he'd been given.

Bunch of idiots in this place.

"Look, I'm going down there, with or without you," she said, releasing his arm at last. "It's up to you to decide if you want to be useful today or not."

Within a few seconds, she'd reached the door and yanked it open. She didn't have to look back to know that he'd followed her.

"Don't you people know about locks?" she muttered as they started down the darkened stairwell. The only lighting emanated from a thin strip by their feet, like a movie theater.

"That door *was* locked," said Fisher, sounding incredulous.

"Hm. Volkov and his many talents." *All of which map bizarrely well onto mine.* She'd known how to pick a lock since she was 16.

The stairs leading down seemed to stretch forever, reminding her more than a little of the stairs on the estate leading into the lower basement. It had been cool inside the building to begin with, but as they descended further into the earth, the minimal heat dropped away. She touched the handle of the blade hidden up her left sleeve and doubled down on her suppression of the urge to let her spikes loose.

At long last, they reached the bottom stair. The map had somewhat prepared her for the labyrinthine nature of the subterranean level, if not for the fact that, like the stairs, its only source of light came from track lighting along the floor.

Lucky we've both got good eyes, she thought.

"You take left, I'll take right," she whispered. "Last one to catch an invisible man loses."

Fisher nodded, a little green around the edges, and headed in his assigned direction. A part of her wished she managed to offer him some kind of reassurance before she let him go. The rest of her had no idea what that reassurance might have looked like.

She had spent a lot of time inside creepy subterranean spaces before, but this one outdid them all. A few feet in, the slim hallway she'd been traveling down opened up, revealing a new corridor to her left, which seemed to emit a strange glow from its very walls. After a second, she realized it wasn't walls she was looking at, but a series of tanks.

Each one held a different demon, suspended in liquid. Each one glowed softly in the dark. This one had horns growing out of a lumpy forehead. Another looked like it was primarily composed of tentacles, with a small cluster of suckers puckering against the glass. It might have looked like an exhibit at an old freak show if it weren't for the high-tech look of the tanks and lighting. A modern-day museum of the macabre.

As she stared down the corridor, the image before her changed. Like in a dream, she saw herself suspended there, in one of those tanks. What would the markings on her skin look like under that blue light?

She gave herself a shake and moved on. There was no one down there, no reason to linger. Volkov, if it was him, would be deeper in. She continued down the main passage.

The next few moments passed in silence. She had to assume that the silence meant Fisher hadn't yet run into trouble. She couldn't risk letting Volkov get away by going to check on him, and she needed to stay as quiet as possible if she hoped to take him by surprise. As she walked, she picked up the occasional gurgle from the tanks in the adjoining halls, but apart from that, nothing. Her own footfalls were silent, and so, it would seem, were Volkov's.

It was in this silence that she heard the creature, well before she saw where it had come from. It was a slithering, slippery sound, like a salamander moving over wet rock. The sound echoed in the dark tunnels all around her, preventing her from locating its source. She kept moving forward.

At the next corridor she crossed, she met a disturbing sight: one of the tanks stood open. The covering at the top had been removed, and whatever had once been inside now roamed free. Logan slid her hidden knife into her waiting hand, anticipation crackling up her spine.

She had barely taken another step when she heard it again. The soft, wet sound of its movement reminded her of cave dwellers. It was nearer now, but she still couldn't see it. Perhaps it was as invisible as the rest of them.

The thought had barely passed through her mind when she felt something drip down onto her shoulder, splattering on her jacket. She had just enough time to look up before it attacked.

All she could see was a mass of gleaming teeth and slimy, milk-white skin before something sharp sank into her arm, which seemed to have thrown itself in front of her face of its own accord. The next few seconds passed in a tornado of motion. The creature bit down hard enough to nearly pierce the leather, but she hardly noticed. Instead, she pushed all her might into the motion of slamming it against the wall beside her, pinning it down with the arm it still held in its mouth. The hard crunch of the impact told her she had broken its jaw. With her left hand, she brought her battle knife to its throat and cut straight through to bone. Black ichor gushed forward, oddly shimmery in the low blue lighting. The demon went limp, its grip on her arm melting away in an instant.

She let it drop to the floor and shook out her arm. It hadn't quite torn the leather, and as she checked her arm, she saw that it hadn't broken the skin, either. In fact, it was rather small. Gazing down at it, she couldn't help but be taken aback by *how* small it was. It felt more like she'd killed an iguana than a demon.

Doesn't matter now. She forced her feet to move again. She had to get to Volkov. She had to stop him.

She kept going.

The next hallway she passed featured another open, empty tank. She ignored it. If it was like the last, Fisher could handle it on his own. These demons were small enough to handle with a gun.

She followed the curve in the corridor, remembering what it looked like on the map. The curve meant she was closing in on the center…and the biggest of the blacked-out sections. Without thinking, she reached a hand out to the wall on her right, half expecting to meet the rough, cold surface of a cave wall. She didn't, of course. Instead the wall her hand found was sickly smooth, unnatural and inhuman. She came to a stop and closed her eyes, letting her other senses reach out into the world around her.

He was close. She could feel it. She could almost taste it. His scent was familiar to her. It reminded her of smoke.

You wouldn't hurt me, would you?

She could see him in her mind's eye, standing just on the other side of a shimmering barrier. She'd been more than willing to hurt him then; in fact, she'd wanted to do it.

So, tell me, summoner, are we all damned just the same?

She had his scent now. Treading lightly, she dropped her hand from the wall and pressed forward.

She could see him as soon as she rounded the corner. He was standing in front of a thick metal door, which featured neither a lock nor a visible handle. He faced away from her, his white hair blue in the light. As per usual, he was clad in all black. Just like the Order. Just like her.

He dropped the shadow summon, if that's what he was doing. She tried her best not to think about the fact that she'd never met someone else who could do that summon as well as she could. Out of some antediluvian concept of fairness, she automatically considering dropping her own summon to even the playing field. Then she remembered where she was, and who she was looking at. She stepped forward silently, leaving herself cloaked in shadow.

"I know you're here somewhere," he muttered to himself. She froze in her tracks, but he didn't turn around. She watched him pat himself down, evidently searching for something. "Come, now, darling, where—ah, there you are."

He produced a strange silver object that looked almost exactly like the Order's sun-and-sword symbol. If she'd had to guess, she'd say he probably picked it off an unsuspecting Adept on his way into the building.

It's what I would have done.

She stepped closer still, making sure to move as softly and silently as possible.

"Honestly, I can hardly believe how easy this is." When he spoke, his voice was so quiet she wasn't sure human ears would have heard him.

He raised the sun-and-sword up to the heavy door, placing it against the metal at the very center. She watched with no small amount of fascination as the silver object seemed to press into the door, melding into it until the seam between the two metals disappeared. She had to guess that this was magic, not tech, but she had no idea what kind of cast might have made such an object.

Add it to the ever-expanding list of Order secrets and move along, she told herself. She took another inching step.

Volkov began to chuckle to himself as he watched the heavy door open of its own accord. She imagined he saw this as his moment of triumph.

Her knife slid into her palm with ease. She waited until he

raised his hand before she moved her own. In one smooth movement, she threw the knife with precision. With a dull thud, it slid through the flesh of his outstretched hand, right in the very center, pinning it to the door frame.

"Aaargh—what the—"

His hand still stuck to the wall, Volkov whipped around.

"*Shadow summoner*. Christ, I should have known."

She said nothing, but watched silently as he gripped the handle of the knife and tried to wrench it free. On his third attempt, it finally moved, sliding with painful lethargy out of the wall and his flesh.

He tossed the knife to the ground in disgust.

"You know, in polite society, we say hello with words."

"Good thing neither of us is polite, then."

His pale eyes bore into her, searching, beseeching. Her right hand rested on the second knife. At long last, he spoke.

"I suppose it's too much to hope you've come here to join me." His voice was sorrowful. Almost regretful. "In fact, I imagine you're here to stop me."

Logan shrugged.

"The door's open. Why don't you look inside?"

He looked at her uncertainly, then slowly turned around to the now-open door to the Order's top-secret vault. He stepped inside.

It only took him a moment. Then he came back out into the main room, gazing at her with astonishment and disappointment.

"It's gone," he muttered, vaguely shaking his head. "But how?"

Logan allowed herself a small smile. Her left hand automatically flexed.

"You sent your man after me, and he told me everything I needed to know." She could still feel the warmth that had spilled out of him, but she tried not to think about it. "It was easy."

Recognition mixed with something else passed over Volkov's face.

"Or perhaps you had a little help." He took a step closer to her, then gestured at the empty vault behind him. "He couldn't have told you what it does, of course. Do you know?"

"Doesn't matter. All that matters is that you don't have it." This, more than the lineup upstairs, was the crux of their plan. In point of fact, she didn't know exactly where the artifact was at the moment.

"But can't you *feel* it, Henrietta?" He took another step. "Did they let you see it, before they took it away? I'm so curious. Did it call to you?"

She felt her brow furrowing.

"It's an object," she said stubbornly. "I didn't give it my phone number."

He chuckled. "That's too bad. So, tell me, did you kill Rossi?"

She pressed her mouth into a thin line. "Had to protect my own."

"I see." Volkov glanced down at his hand, still bleeding and useless against his chest. "Zilla will be sorry to hear it. But I suppose I don't blame you. We all have to make difficult choices sometimes, don't we?"

It took her a moment to recognize the expression on his face. It was sympathy. She cleared her throat, suddenly uncomfortable.

"You know I can't let you leave this place," she said. "You have to be held accountable for the things you've done."

"Well, you've certainly got me at a disadvantage," he nodded down at his hand. "But perhaps not as great a one as you might think. *Solvo specula.*"

As he hissed those last two words, he released a pinch of powder she hadn't realized he'd been holding. An unnatural, high-pitched sound emitted from him, filling the room: he had used the blood from his wound to catalyze a letha summon. *Fuck. I forgot you were clever.*

Behind her, she heard the earth-shattering crash of multiple glass cages breaking open and spilling their contents. The sound echoed ominously through the cavernous dark. Any number of caged demons had just been freed, and it was only a matter of time before they converged here, on the two nearest humans and the smell of blood.

"That won't save you," she muttered. She unhooked the top strap on her ax sheath and slid the second knife into her hand.

"Perhaps not." With a determined, demented look, Volkov gazed into the wound on his palm and pressed into it, forcing out more blood. Then he smiled, and flicked his hand in her direction—showering her with a fine spray of blood droplets. "But it will slow you down."

Before she could respond, the first wave of slithery, slimy demons flooded into the room. Logan threw her knife straight into the nearest one's head, then pulled her ax free of its sheath. She didn't have enough knives to get them all. Backing away from the entrance, she readied herself for the assault. No fewer than a dozen writhing, centipede-like demons the size of cats slithered into the room, each one tasting the air for blood. Some headed for Volkov, while the rest headed right for her.

She shrugged her shoulders twice, trying to get the blood moving before it was time to attack. When the first one reached her, she wasted no time. One clean strike cleaved it in two, and she bounced back to her starting position. Just behind it, two came at her at once, so she listed to the side to let them line up, then delivered two swift, fatal blows in succession. Just as the next one lined up in her sights, she heard Volkov perform his cast again: another unnatural noise filled the air, followed by more glass breaking. The waves of demons would never end. She could only hope they'd all be as easy as these.

While she took out another, a fifth circled around her and managed to jump on her back. She wrenched it free with one hand in a slick, easy motion, and threw it as hard as she could against the wall. A sickening crack resounded through the chamber.

Her adrenaline rose to the challenge, filling her with strength. It felt like a game. She picked up her pace, moving faster and faster as she went, splattering the ground with ichor like it was paint on a canvas. On the other side of the room, Volkov had unsheathed his sword and downed several of his own. She could see him scrambling along the wall, searching for another exit. She still stood between him and the only one visible.

She had smashed through another layer of demon onslaught when she heard a different sound: a human voice, calling to her.

"Logan?" It was Fisher, sounding panicked. "I thought I heard an explosion—"

"Get backup!" she called back to him. "Volkov let all your pets out of their cages!"

She wasn't sure if he heard her. At the moment, she couldn't concentrate on it. Another, larger demon had just entered the room, eyes focused in on her. This one stood upright on two legs, pincers dragging along the floor as it lumbered toward her. She readied herself for its attack, planting her feet and raising her ax—only to feel a sudden pain at her ankle, sharper than she could have expected.

She glanced down, and was shocked to see a snake-like beast, partially wrapped around her leg, with its jaw clenched around her ankle, fangs sunk through her skin. From the burning sensation now spreading out from the bite, she guessed it was likely venomous.

The next few moments passed in a fog. Barely conscious of what she was doing, Logan grabbed hold of the beast and tore it from her body, holding it out from her in her right hand. She squeezed her grip tighter and tighter, until she felt its body burst under her inhuman strength. Then she tossed its empty form aside and wiped her hand on her jeans.

She tried to take a step forward, but the ankle that had been bitten didn't want to move. She looked down at it, bemused, and tried again. She could still bend her knee, but when her foot met the ground again, another stab of pain shot through her. So, instead of trying to move forward, she planted her feet again and waited for the lumbering demon to come to her.

It swung a long, pincer-ended arm at her, and she swung back at it with her ax, deflecting if not hurting it. Time felt like it was slowing down, or maybe it was just the demon that was slow. It swung at her again, and she met it again, this time with more force. She heard the metal clang of ax against exoskeleton, and then—

"Logan?" Fisher stumbled into the room, gun out and pointed toward the floor. He fired once, and the sound of it echoed in her ears over and over and over. The lumbering demon turned toward the noise.

Logan gave herself a shake and raised her ax again. She had to take advantage of the moment. While the demon's back was turned, she willed herself to ignore the pain in her leg, creeping steadily upward, and leapt forward, ax swinging. She brought it down on the back of its neck and watched it tumble to the ground, like a marionette with cut strings. Her landing sent another shock wave through her body.

"Watch out for the snakes," she called to Fisher, though she wasn't sure how clear her words were. The world seemed to be fading in and out.

"Snakes?" Fisher asked, still sounding panicked. "Were you bitten?"

She turned in time to see something slithering toward him, and she ran forward to beat it. In an instant, she swung her ax again, cutting another monster down before she even had time to register its shape. Out of instinct, she reached for Fisher with her right arm and pinned him back against the wall behind her, trying to keep him safe.

No sooner had she made contact with him than she caught Volkov's eye again. He was smiling at her, eyes alight with excitement.

"I only want to set you free, Henrietta."

Awful understanding broke over her like a flood. She couldn't have said how she understood, only that she did: Volkov knew about the trigger word, and he was going to use it. She was trapped. If she didn't want Fisher's blood on her hands, there was only one option.

Right as Volkov's voice rang out, she leapt away from the wall, holding her arms clear of the Order Adept—and in full view.

"Valkyrie!"

Adrenaline exploded within her, driving out all other sensation. All eight spikes shot out of her arms at once, tearing right through her jacket. She stood frozen in place, fixed on display, right in the center of Order territory.

She met Fisher's eyes, and she knew he had seen it. There was no going back.

The adrenaline vanished as soon as it had come, and with it, all her strength. The venom from the snake-demon had finally caught up with her, now of all moments.

She felt her knees hit the ground before the world went black.

Chapter Fifteen
On Silent Seas

When Logan briefly woke, she had lost all sense of time and space. She felt like she was floating, rocked back and forth by invisible waves. Movement was the only thing that was certain. An impossible sky stretched out before her, and she thought she might retch.

She glimpsed something in the periphery, saw a face in outline but couldn't make it out.

"Knatt?" she heard her voice ask.

Then she disappeared again.

The images that came were disjointed; sometimes connected to sounds, sometimes not. Sometimes her father was there, haunting her like a ghost. Sometimes she was alone. She dreamed of the estate, but it was twisted and wild, turned into something new. Sometimes the places she dreamed of didn't seem to exist at all.

She knew she was dreaming as soon as the dream began. She stood inside a warehouse so cavernous she couldn't see both sides of it at once. As she neared one, the other disappeared entirely.

It was cold in the warehouse, but her veins felt like they were on fire. Distantly, she remembered that something bad had happened to her, but it seemed far away now. Unimportant.

She walked forward, her footsteps echoing unnaturally through the chamber. Eventually, she could start to make out the metal wall before her. Archways were set along it at regular intervals, stretching out in both directions. She headed for the first one she saw, but as she approached it, a sense of unease crept up her spine. Her feet slowed to a halt, unwilling to travel any further. She could just make out the view on the other side: it looked like the front of the Logan estate, with its artificially ancient facade and its rolling lawn, and the driveway that curved in a giant U shape.

"I don't want to go there," she said out loud, though she wasn't sure why.

"That's up to you," a voice answered. She turned around, to where she believed the source was, but there was nothing behind her but more echoing space. So she continued turning until she faced forward again—and there stood her aunt Adele, smiling pleasantly at her.

"Have I been here before?"

"You've always had the option to come."

Logan nodded slowly, then started walking forward again, this time toward the next archway down the line. This one opened on a cliff, its edge only a few feet away. She came to a stop just beside it.

"Am I dying?" she asked, turning back to her aunt.

Adele laughed.

"You don't have to die to come here, Henri. This place belongs to you."

"Funny, I don't remember buying an infinite warehouse."

"Oh, you couldn't buy this if you tried."

Logan nodded. She knew Adele was right, even though she didn't know what that meant. She started walking again, past more archways. Each one let out into a completely different physical space—some of them seemed ripped right from her past, while some were completely unfamiliar to her. In one, she was fairly certain she could see giants as big as mountains, moving slowly in the distance.

Even though she walked in a straight line, somehow she ended up at the archway to the estate again.

"I don't want to go there," she repeated, her voice quiet.

"Are you sure?"

"It doesn't have what I want."

"Maybe not. But that isn't why you go."

Logan turned to look at her aunt, but she was gone. Somehow, she'd known she would be.

"I thought you said I had a choice."

Her feet moved her forward, drawn inexorably into the past. When she crossed the threshold, it wasn't at all what she'd expected. She could feel someone else with her, someone she couldn't see—but it wasn't Adele. It was more like a specter.

Even in the dream, her body ached. It reminded her of something. Home, perhaps.

She walked forward, and she felt the specter follow her. Though she'd thought she would come out on the lawn in front of the estate, instead she now walked through a forest. It was unlike any forest she'd ever seen in real life. The trees stretched upward forever, and there was no sky. Dread became a liquid in her stomach, ice-cold and demanding.

I didn't want to come here.

She kept going. The specter in her mind grew louder.

When the acrid smell of blood hit her nose, it was enough to make her vomit. She didn't know where it had come from, but now it was everywhere, all at once. It was on her hands, on her clothes, on the ground. She closed her eyes and kept going.

The specter grew louder until it was right behind her; she could feel its breath on her neck. And even though she knew it was coming, she still let out a gasp when it grabbed hold of her. She felt its grip tighten into a fist.

The hand on her shoulder steered her forward. Its strength was iron clad.

"Are you ready now, Henrietta?"

The voice that rasped at her was a menace. She knew it well.

She opened her eyes. She stood now in the middle of a wide circle—like a stage, or a sacrificial altar.

"I'm only trying to make you better, Henrietta."

Beyond the circle in which she stood, dark figures moved. One of them would come for her, eventually. One of them always came.

"This is the way it's done, you know. I'm only doing for you what my father would have done for me. I'm only trying to prepare you. Don't you want to be a good girl, Henrietta?"

One of the figures shifted out of the shadows, stepping into the low illumination of the ring. Its face was long and oddly square, like a horse. It had the wings of a bat, stretching out toward the sky. It stepped forward and stretched out a talon.

She couldn't remember how, but she knew exactly what to

do, without even thinking about it. Her body dropped into a fighter's stance, low and loose and ready to move. Her hands formed fists and drifted in front of her face.

And four long spikes slid out of each arm. She had been marked by the same spoiled brush as the beast before her. They were one and the same.

"Are you going to make me proud, Henrietta?"

At long last, her father relinquished his iron-tight grip on her shoulder.

The fight had already begun.

She was a child, and her father was driving the car.

She wasn't sure how she'd gotten there. She'd simply woken up already in the car, fully strapped in, her father at the wheel beside her. Miles and miles of evergreen trees zoomed past the window.

"Where are we going?" she asked groggily.

"Somewhere very special," he answered, authoritatively, reassuringly. "I'll tell you all about it when we get there."

She was a child, and her father was driving the car. So, when he reassured her, she believed him. She slipped back into sleep, never once thinking how strange it was that they were driving so fast in the middle of the night. Never once wondering why he hadn't given her a straight answer.

When she woke up again, they had already arrived. Her father was rousing her, hurrying her along, already out of the car and far ahead. She rushed to keep up. As she went, she felt her hair getting damp from the rain, and she realized that he had put boots on her. She felt grateful that he'd remembered to do that—then stopped in her tracks, briefly certain that he'd forgotten once before. But what did that mean? She'd never been here before.

Her memory skipped the track and came back in somewhere down the line. Her father had set up a tarp over their heads to keep the rain off. Beneath their feet was wet cement, old and cracked.

"It's an old military base," her father explained. He was tending to the fire he'd built. It smelled funny to her, like something more than wood was burning there. "They used to load up a large gun here. Took them 50 men to do it. Not to worry, though. We won't need 50 men for our purposes."

He gave her a small bag of crystals to hold, told her they were likely to resonate well here, told her to focus on them as hard as she could. Once she was good and focused, he made a small cut on the inside of her arm. She wanted to scream, but she bit down on her tongue instead.

"There's a good girl," he murmured as he caught her blood in a small vial. "Have I told you about the weak spots, Henrietta?"

She shook her head. She was afraid that if she tried to speak out loud, she would cry.

"The weak spots are a theory, and we're here to test that theory. You see, there were men a long time ago who did a special kind of magic that we've long since forgotten. And I'm going to see if we can bring it back. You'd like to be a part of something special like that, wouldn't you?"

She nodded, but what she really wanted was to go home. It was cold out here, and her arm hurt. He seemed to sense at least some of what she felt, because he patted her reassuringly on her shoulder.

"Remember to be a good girl, Henrietta. I promise I'll make it quick. And when I'm successful, we can go home and never come back here. All right?"

But what a lie that was.

The same scene played out again and again in her memories. She could lay them side-by-side if she wanted to. It was almost like looking at alternate time lines: every little girl had been altered in her own way, and each of them believed she was the only one. But she wasn't.

The shining constant that united them all was her father. He was a liar every time.

Logan woke up in a darkened room. For several minutes, she knew neither where she was, nor who she was. It was like her slate had been wiped clean. Then it all crashed in on her, a million tiny waves eating away at the shore. A mountain of memory sat in the center of her mind, but she wasn't ready to go there yet.

She understood, vaguely, that Alexei had driven her back to the estate, though she couldn't remember getting into or out of the car. And as she looked around, her eyes adjusting to the low light, she could see that she was on a couch in the living room. Someone had pulled her boots off and put a blanket over her, though she noticed that nobody had removed her jacket. Perhaps no one could.

Though she would consciously have chosen to sleep just about anywhere else, she didn't blame anyone for putting her here. Frankly, she was impressed the others could carry her even this far, and she couldn't help but wonder how many of them it had taken, and what the effort had looked like. She'd met plenty of people over the years who thought they'd be able to pick her up without aid; not a one of them could.

There was almost no light in the room, but she could see a sliver of light bleeding in from the hallway. She pulled back the blanket and swung her feet over the edge of the couch, pulling her boots on as fast as she could. At the moment, she couldn't stand to be barefoot.

Once she felt secure in her laced-up boots, she took a deep breath and looked around the room. Something felt wrong, but she didn't know what. Maybe she'd overheard something in her sleep, or…maybe it was the hushed voices she could hear now, coming from the other room. She stood up.

The voices were in the kitchen. She closed her eyes and listened.

"—least we still have the artifact."

"Yes, I'm sure that will be a worthy consolation."

"Not a consolation. Leverage."

"Hmm. If the Order will allow it."

"Well, seeing as I conveniently *forgot* to give it back to them in my rush to get her back home, I don't see how they have a choice in the matter."

"Did you really? And how did you manage that?"

"With my incredible stealth and charisma, of course."

"What's going on?" Logan found herself suddenly on the other side of the door, barely even aware of having made the decision to walk across the room and step through the threshold.

"Henrietta," said Knatt, with quiet surprise. He stood on one side of the island counter, while Alexei sat on a stool on the other. Two cups of tea and a small plate of scones sat between them. Knatt indicated the plate as he spoke again. "They're savory, if you're hungry. I wasn't sure when last you'd eaten."

As he spoke, the smell of them hit her, and she heard her stomach give an audible grumble. She wasn't sure when last she'd eaten, either. In fact, she wasn't even sure what time it was.

"How long have I been out?" She closed the distance between herself and food in an instant and brought the first one she could reach up to her nose. With one deep inhale, she noted the overwhelming smell of jalapeño and cheddar, and the slightly softer notes of butter and scallion. Even in the midst of the frightening swirl of emotions currently laying waste to the interior of her mind, she had to take a moment to appreciate Knatt's mastery of baked goods. Then she took a bite, and for a split second, all conscious thought was obliterated.

"Ah—well, about a day," said Knatt, forming each syllable with care. As she was still in the thrall of her food, it took her several seconds to absorb the words. She made sure to swallow before she spoke.

"A fucking day?" she rasped, the lovely but dry crumbles of scone soaking up what little moisture there was to be had in her throat. She watched in some amazement as Knatt jumped into action, grabbing a glass from the cabinet and filling it up with water, only to hand it over to her. She drank the whole thing in about four seconds, then coughed. "Thanks. A day?"

Knatt glanced over at Alexei. "Perhaps you should start."

"Right," said Alexei, nodding as he took a quick sip from his teacup before setting it down. "So, uh, things were a little chaotic when I got back to the beta site. There was a gigantic dead demon outside, for starters. It looked like the Order had just barely managed to take it down."

"Were there any casualties?"

"Definitely a lot of injuries, some pretty bad. To be honest, I was more concerned about finding you than getting a clear picture." A weary sigh escaped his lips, and she took in the bags under his eyes and the slightly rumpled quality of his shirt. She got the impression he hadn't gotten much sleep since all this had happened. "The whole thing was a mess. The first few people I talked to had no idea where you were, and then someone ran by shouting that the Wolf was there, and something about you—"

"What'd they say?" were the words that Logan attempted to form through her first bite of her second scone. What came out was closer to: "*Wha dey shey?*"

"They said you were dead," he answered bluntly. There was something in his eyes as he said the words. She wondered how long he'd believed them. "Eventually I got hold of Marlowe, and she brought me to you. You were in a first-aid room, unconscious. They said you'd been injected with demon venom, and they didn't know if you were going to survive."

A cold anxiety gripped her.

"Did they…do you know if they—"

"The medical facilities there were pretty crude," he answered. "I don't think they took any blood. They gave you the antivenom they had on hand, and they hoped for the best."

Logan swallowed hard and nodded.

"Fisher was there, too—the kid with the glasses," Alexei continued. "He said you *had* seen Volkov, but that he escaped after the demon took you down."

"Almost had him, too." She let out a sigh. "He can summon shadows, like me. He was nearly invisible when he snuck into the base. I'm guessing he did it again on the way out." She picked up a third scone and bit into it. "Do we have any protein in the house? Maybe I should order food. What time is it?"

"I've got some field roast," said Knatt, springing into action again. "I'll make you a sandwich."

She watched him as he set to work. There was something comforting about Knatt trying to feed her, so for a moment, she allowed herself to be comforted. Then she remembered her feeling that something was wrong, and the snippet of conversation she'd taken in before she'd stepped through the door. A dark suspicion overthrew her.

"Where's Jude?"

Knatt and Alexei exchanged a look. Ever so slowly, Alexei let his eyes slide back over to her.

"So, uh...I took the artifact, just like we planned, and I started driving along the route we mapped out. And not half an hour in, I got a phone call. From here."

"It was my fault," said Knatt, somberly. He was facing away from them, toward the counter, and his movements came to a stop. "I told her she could go on a walk in the woods, as long as she came back before dinner. But she didn't come back."

Knatt's voice faded out. Both Logan and Alexei watched his back muscles contract and release, and after a moment, he began working on the food once more. Alexei's gaze turned to Logan.

"He went out to look for her, and he found this instead."

He pulled something out of his pocket and laid it on the counter. It was a small piece of carved wood, in the shape of a Wolf's head.

Logan blinked, taking it in. It all made perfect sense. Way too much sense, in fact.

"Ulric." Her voice sounded hollow. "Had to be Ulric. Either a contingency plan, or…or the main plan. And I played right into it."

"It's not your fault," said Knatt, still facing away from her. "It's mine."

"How about it's the fault of the person who took her?" said Alexei. He sounded angry. "How about we all agree that everyone's responsible for their own actions, and we just focus on what we're gonna do next, hm?"

For a moment, Logan said nothing. She wished someone would yell at her. She wished one of them would take her to task for leaving Jude behind, leaving her on her own. It was her fault, whether they would admit it or not. She'd let her anger make that decision—and maybe her pride, too. She'd thought Jude was acting ungrateful, and she'd wanted to punish her.

Just like dear old Dad. The thought threatened to crush her under its weight.

In the silence, Knatt had finished putting together the sandwich, and he turned around to hand it to her. She reached out her hand to pull it closer, and as she did, she noticed the slightest tremor. Her fingers curled around the edges of the plate and froze there, uninterested in moving further.

In the tremor of her hand, she could see sands shifting, just beneath the foundation. Her whole life had just been laid bare to her, and she did not yet know what to make of it.

"You're right," she said, finally. "We have to focus on getting her back. So…how do we do that? I'm open to suggestions."

"Well," said Alexei, glancing uncertainly over at Knatt. "It's not a full plan, but…we may have some leverage."

"Go on."

"We have the artifact."

"The other—the Choronzon artifact?"

"Yep. There was just enough chaos there, with all the wounded and with you nearly dying—I managed to drive away before Marlowe could demand it back."

"Good." Logan took a bite of the sandwich and chewed as quickly as she could, then swallowed. On some level, she recognized the taste of it, but for the most part, it was more a means to an end by now. "If it's here, we should probably—"

"It's not here," said Knatt easily, straightening his spine where he stood. "I have any number of friends in the city. It would be quite difficult to locate them all, even with the resources at the Order's disposal."

"Also good." She took another bite of the sandwich, trying to finish as much of it as she could. "So, just to make sure we've got all our ducks—the wolf head was the *only* thing you found, right? No note or anything else?"

"Correct," said Knatt with a sigh. "We've combed the area twice now, but to no avail."

"What are you thinking, H.C.?" asked Alexei.

"I'm thinking that the Wolf still doesn't have what he really wants." She swallowed another bite. She could feel her strength returning to her, bit by bit. The venom may have taken her down, but she was starting to feel like the rest had been good for her. "He *did* intend to find the artifact there. He wants to use it for something. Grabbing Jude was probably just…"

As she trailed off, she felt her hand reach up and back, touching the edge of the Choronzon Key under her jacket.

"Maybe they do the same thing," she mused. "Or he just thinks they do."

Alexei tapped impatiently on the counter.

"Care to let us in on the reverie?"

Logan nodded, then took another large bite before she spoke. The sandwich was almost done now. "Jude was a contingency plan, in case we figured him out. But the Order wouldn't care about Jude—not enough to make a deal with him, anyway. So it was a contingency plan meant specifically for *me*."

She paused, giving them a moment to figure it out. They stared blankly at her.

"Which means?" asked Alexei.

"Which means he either knows or suspects I have the Choronzon Key. And he believes that it will suit his purposes just as well as the other artifact." She glanced at the little red lights above the oven which told the time: 8:37pm. "He's going to set up an ambush, and then he's going to use Jude to lure me into it. So, we have two questions we need to answer before he has a chance to complete his setup: *where* has he taken her? And what does he think the artifacts of the Choronzon will do?"

Knatt nodded. "I agree. Those are the questions we need answered. But how do we answer them?"

Logan let out a long, slow sigh.

"I have to talk to Dad again."

Logan was unsurprised to find her father awake in his room, nestled safely under the quilt on his bed. Though it should have been easy for her to forget he was there, considering how little noise he made and how little she consented to interact with him, somehow she never did. He sat like a spider in the corner of her mind.

In some ways, he looked just like the man she remembered from her youth—confidant and demanding, with an air of righteousness that was hard to fake. But in other ways, he looked like he had long since wasted away; a shrunken version of his former self, skinny and frail and gray all over.

She entered without knocking and she shut the door behind her. Charles Logan looked up at her in surprise, but as he saw her face, his own softened into recognition.

"Good evening, Henrietta. How are you?"

For a moment, she didn't answer, taking a quick inventory of the room instead. Eventually, she saw her target: the overstuffed armchair in the corner. Though she could have easily picked it up, she chose to drag it over, letting it scrape noisily along the hardwood floors. When it was close enough to the bed to maintain eye contact but still far enough that she was out of physical reach, she plopped down into it.

"Hi, Dad." She sat outside of the warm glow of his lamp, so she couldn't say how well he could see her. But she could see him just fine.

"I thought you might come back here."

"Yeah, well. Technically I own this place, remember?" He had signed the estate's deed over to her a few years ago, back when they first brought him up to the nursing home. It had seemed like a good idea at the time.

"I remember that, yes," he said, nodding.

"Good. I hope that means you're having a lucid day."

"I believe I am." He plucked a bookmark off his nightstand

and slipped it into the book he was reading, and then closed it tight. "Did you wish to speak with me?"

"I was hoping you could confirm a couple of theories of mine."

"I'll certainly try."

Logan let out a deep breath she wasn't aware she'd been holding. Why was this part so hard? Hadn't she waited all her life to accuse him of the things he'd done? Or had some part of her held onto the hope that if she never asked him out loud, she could make them untrue?

Not that it mattered now.

"It was you who let Savino Rossi out of the cage in the basement." Her voice was steady and clear, like a well-struck gong. "Wasn't it?"

In the dim but warm glow of the lamp, she watched the surprise register on Charles' face, The shame that followed told her she was right.

"Yes. I let him out. How did you know?"

She sighed. Once the words hit the open air, there would be no swallowing them back up. They'd be irretrievable.

"It was just a feeling, at first. Locked him in there myself, after all. And then…and then I began to remember. It started when you used that word on me. Like you'd knocked something loose. I could remember spending hours down there, banging on that door. Begging you to let me out. Rossi may have been Bound, but…he wasn't stronger than me. And even I couldn't get through that door."

As she looked at him now, she did her best to take stock. It was long past time to lose the image of him from her childhood.

He was no longer some inescapable genius on the verge of his next great discovery. He was an old man who hadn't taken very good care of himself.

On his face now, comprehension looked like horror.

"How much can you remember?"

"Not sure. Everything's a patchwork. If I…push my way through the memories I know are there, sometimes…sometimes I can see new ones, hidden underneath—only they aren't new. They're as old as the other ones, but…they used to be gaps, and now they aren't." She blinked and gave her head a small shake. If she looked too hard, the memories threatened to engulf her.

She jumped a little when she heard him speak.

"I lost track. Didn't know what year it was." His voice was a tremor. She hated it. "I thought I'd locked you in again. Thought I'd put you in there and forgotten to take you back out. Again."

She could press him now, if she wanted to. She could throw all her accusations at him, demand he hold himself accountable. But she already knew he would never give her what she really wanted. So, what would have been the point?

When she spoke, there was no anger.

"It's funny, the things that make you question your assumptions. You tried to make everything seem simple when I was a kid, but…that's not really the way things work, is it?"

His expression soured, some of his pride returning.

"I was trying to teach you how to survive." His gaze fell, coming to rest on the book in his lap. She had a feeling she knew what book it was. "The same as my father taught me."

"Great. We're a walking family tragedy." She let out her breath in a huff, vaguely wishing she'd brought a cigarette.

"Well, I guess that's it for palling around. I want you to tell me everything you know about the Choronzon. And this time, I do mean everything."

Charles Logan raised his eyebrow at her, an eerie mirror of her own favored facial expression.

"That almost sounds like a threat, Henrietta."

"It is. See, Volkov has taken one of my friends hostage. And if you don't answer me to my satisfaction, I'm going to offer to trade you to him, in exchange for her."

She was happy to hear the steady certainty in her voice, the ruthless clarity. Whether he believed her or not, she was believable.

"I see." Charles tapped his fingertips against the hard cover of the book, considering this. "I suppose I have no choice. I'll tell you what I can. But you have to understand, there are gaps, here and there. I'm not the man I was."

"I certainly hope not."

Charles gave her a sad, resigned smile.

"Well, I suppose I should start with the obvious. I know that you are in possession of the labyrinth."

Logan stiffened. She'd suspected he knew, but it still felt strange to hear it.

"And how do you know that?"

"I bugged Hugh's rooms, of course—bedroom and office. After you ran away from home, and he refused to tell me where you'd gone, I didn't see that I had much of a choice. How else was I going to keep track of my family?"

"Did it ever occur to you that maybe you didn't have a right to keep track of me, after what you did?"

"Nonsense. Family is forever."

She could feel a headache coming on, so she pinched the bridge of her nose.

"Okay. So you bugged Knatt's room. And you heard about the Key?"

"Ah, yes. The Key. Why *do* you call it that?"

"Hey, it's my question time, not yours. If I find your answers satisfactory, maybe I'll tell you at the end."

"Fine, fine. Yes, I heard him discuss it with someone—Adele, I think. Imagine my surprise. To have spent so much time trying to study this elusive ancient magic…only for my daughter to stumble upon it entirely by accident."

"Shit happens, I guess. What else do you know about them?"

Charles stretched back in his seat, folding his hands together and bringing them behind his head.

"I came across the name by chance, in a little bookshop in London," he said. "A charming little bookshop, with a charming little bookkeeper. I was researching some demon or other when I saw the name for the first time." He chuckled to himself. "At the ripe old age of 24, I was sure I'd heard of everything. But here was this little sentence that read: '*The only known Masters of the Gates of Hell were the ancient Choronzon, long since perished from this World.*' This damn little book blew my mind. Naturally, I became obsessed. For a little while."

"A little while?"

"Yes. Nothing dampens the spirit quite like repeated failure." He let out a deep sigh. "After years of exhaustive research, the facts I can tell you are these: the Choronzon were an ancient mystical order. It is believed that some unknown cataclysmic event wiped them out, although there is no proof of that. And they left behind a number of artifacts which are believed to have mystical powers, bestowed on them as the final legacy of the Choronzon themselves. There are at least five artifacts. No one knows for sure what they do, but...I wager a guess that it has something to do with travel to other dimensions, other worlds. Of course, my main proof for that is no proof at all—it's simply the fact that, over and over again, they are referred to as the keepers of the gates to hell."

Logan blinked at him.

"You don't think maybe they were *literally* the keepers of the gates to hell?"

"Well, what is hell but an alternate world to our own?"

"Right."

"There is one other thing."

"And that is?"

"There are at least five artifacts. But one of them may be...more powerful than the others." He fixed her with a penetrating stare. "The labyrinth. The Key, as you call it."

Chapter Sixteen
A New Wind

A sudden chill ran down Logan's spine.

"In what *way* is it more powerful?"

"Impossible to say." A smirk crossed his features. "But shouldn't you know? You have the labyrinth. All that time I spent searching for it, and it came to you. What does it *do*? Surely, you can tell me that now. Hasn't it ever shown you another world?"

Slowly, Logan shook her head.

"Nope. This is the only world I've ever been to." She shrugged. "It sends me visions of people in trouble. That's what it does. If you hadn't told me this gates of hell stuff...I'd assume the Choronzon could just see the future or something. That's all the Key does."

"Oh." Charles looked visibly disappointed.

Logan clasped her hands together, thinking for a moment. *Was* that all the Key could do? Or had she somehow been using it wrong, and it was meant to do something else entirely?

"You were obsessed with the Choronzon," she said quietly, slowly pulling more of the pieces together. "And you've always been a tinkerer. Have you tried to recreate their magic? Did you ever try to walk between worlds?"

"Yes, I have. Over the years, I managed to weave some of the rumors and legends together, and I came to believe that the Knights of the Choronzon used a kind of intersecting grid to guide their magic. You might call them ley lines, of a sort. And the places where the most powerful ley lines intersect—that's where the veil between worlds is thinnest. Those would be the best kinds of places to try to break through to the other side."

"But you didn't have any Choronzon artifacts to help you, did you?"

"No, I didn't." He looked her square in the eyes now, and something about the bare, desperate determination on his face gave her a chill. "But I did have something that I knew originated in another world. At least, in part."

With terrible certainty, she realized what he meant.

"You had me." Her voice was quiet, barely audible. "Those road trips you brought me on. To faraway places at first, and then...then that old army base on the peninsula. Over and over. The way you would...cut my skin and use the blood. You summoned demons."

Charles let out a slow sigh, his head finally drooping.

"That wasn't my intent, but...yes. I tried to part the veil, to make it to the other side, and I failed. And my failures carried consequences. Yes, I summoned demons. And you fought and killed them all—well, almost. The first time it happened, I was taken by surprise and nearly killed—but your instinct took over. You kept us alive, if only just. Bought me just enough time to remember my best summon, and together, we destroyed the beast." He looked her right in the eye without remorse. "That was how I knew you were ready to be tested."

She felt a kind of sinking sensation in her core. *I should have known he'd find a way to make it my fault.* She cleared her throat and wished she could clear her mind as easily.

"So, you failed, then. You never crossed over."

"No, I never did. Eventually I accepted it was impossible. Without any of the Choronzon artifacts, that is. And I never did get my hands on one." His gaze narrowed on her again. "But you did."

She felt herself return, suddenly and without warning, to the physicality of her own body. She could feel the Key, cold and inert on her back. Could it really do what he thought it could?

"You told Volkov. You told him about the—the labyrinth."

"I think so. I...I didn't understand what he wanted, at first. He came to me asking for help with some research into a demon, said he had reason to think I would know. He was...reverent." Charles stumbled then, confusion crossing his face. "This is where the gaps are. He...he did something to me, made me forget...." He trailed off, his gaze falling to the side. It was like he had stepped in an unseen hole and fallen in. "Wolves at the gate..."

"Charles, focus on me. We're talking about Volkov. What did you tell him?"

His eyes seem to swim their way back to her. He focused on her, but only just.

"I can't remember."

"He knows I have the Key. Does he think he can use it to go to another world?"

Charles gazed at her, his expression blank. For several seconds, he said nothing at all.

"Is that you, Henrietta?"

A deep sigh escaped her lips. They'd gotten so far, but he couldn't quite make it to the finish line. She supposed there was a kind of symmetry here: he'd taken her memories, and Volkov had taken his, in turn. *Hell, he probably learned the cast from Charles in the first place.*

"Yeah, it's me, Charles. I think we're just about done here."

Without warning, he leaned forward and reached out his hand, just far enough to touch her knee. She glanced into his face, and she saw something like panic there.

"Do you hate me, Henrietta?"

If he had been anybody else, this would have been the moment that she pitied him. Instead, she felt nothing. She was as blank as his memory. She touched his hand where it sat on her knee.

"I don't hate you, old man. I don't think about you often enough for that." She released his hand and stood. "Good night, Charles."

With that, she left the room, and she didn't look back.

When she got back to the kitchen, it was empty. Running primarily on the twin needs to keep her hands moving and to accomplish something, she set about the task of making coffee. Knatt kept an automatic coffee maker in the house, but she was so used to the manual process of French press coffee that it always took her a moment to remember how to use it.

So much more complicated than it needs to be, she thought as she located the coffee filters in a nearby cabinet, almost, but not quite, out of her reach. She plucked out the top one and slid it into the strange plastic mold of the coffee maker. It struck her as strangely appropriate that this method of brewing coffee, the common method among most Americans, was both the most complicated and the most expensive. Aside from paying someone else to do it, of course.

Unfortunately for her, it still wasn't complicated enough to create more than a few moments of activity. The slow drip of liquid through finely ground beans offered her little distraction.

There was a short pile of dishes waiting in the sink, so she got to work. The clank of ceramic and metal filled the empty room.

"Was it the brief coma that left you with an urge to help out around the house?"

Knatt had materialized in the doorway, quieter than she was.

"Just trying to keep things interesting," she replied. "Don't want to be too predictable."

"No danger of that."

She felt, more than saw, him lean against the island counter, a lean so casual she was sure he nearly believed it. But the tremor in his voice gave him away.

"Did you speak to him?"

"Yes."

In the pregnant pause, she could feel the weight of decades. She picked up another plate—the one she'd used earlier.

"And did you get what you needed?"

His voice was quiet, like he was afraid of taking up too much aural space.

"I got some information. And an idea for what to do next."

There was a spot on the dish, though she didn't know how it had gotten there.

"But was it what you needed?"

She took a moment to dry it. The dish that had held the sandwich he'd made for her. The automatic instinct he held, to care for her, at every turn.

"I was never going to get that from him." She put the dish away and showed him her face, so he could understand her. "But that's why I had you."

His own face crumpled in shame.

"I should have taken you away from him when you were still a child. I should have found a way to protect you—"

"Stop." She took a step forward. She almost reached her hand out toward him, but at the last moment, she let it come to rest on the counter instead. "You did what you could with what you had. I am only alive because of you. I've never forgotten that."

With cultivated gentleness, he closed the rest of the gap and placed his hand on top of hers, right where it lay on the counter.

"I need you to hear me when I say this, Henrietta." His gaze matched his voice for seriousness. She forced herself not to make a joke, not to break the moment by cowering away from it. "You were not *born* a monster. Nobody is ever born a monster."

She nodded, but the fingers of her left hand formed a fist.

"But some people are *made* into monsters," she whispered.

Knatt let out a slow sigh.

"I won't deny that Charles did his best to turn you into one. He did. But he failed. He never understood your *true* strength. Every time you make your choice, he fails. Do you see that? Do you believe it?"

A war still raged within her, and she stood at the frayed edges of it. She was two things at once. She was both. She would always be both.

"I want to believe it," she said. "I want to."

Knatt squeezed her hand.

"Perhaps that is enough."

It started simply, then it grew.

Her desire to remove herself from the physical premises of the Logan estate burst open like a water balloon as soon as she finished up with Knatt. Even as she made her way down the hall to the traveling room, she could feel the promise of relief building, and once she crossed the threshold into her own front hallway, that relief washed over her. There were no words big enough to describe it. Here, she could be herself again. She could breathe again, now that she was alone.

Of course, she wasn't really alone. Alexei had left the estate before her, and there was only one place he could have gone. As she'd made her way to the traveling room, she'd told herself that he was probably asleep already. One step into her apartment shattered that illusion. She could hear him in the kitchen, dropping ice into a glass. Probably waiting for her. Possibly waiting to drink with her.

That will lead to no good. I should go straight to bed.

Shouldn't even stop to say hi.

She closed the door, cutting off the estate and announcing her presence all at once. She took a deep breath, thinking it might be steadying, and immediately inhaled the lingering scent of him—roses, cedar, a hint of smoke and sweat. Like the prelude to a good time.

She took a few steps down the hall, moving slowly to give herself a moment. As vague as the memory was, her mind decided to drag out the last moment she'd spent alone with him—the feel of his chest against her body as he helped place her in the back seat of the car—the feel of his hand brushing the hair from her face—

Her breath stopped short as she rounded the corner. There he stood, like an oil painting come to life. His black hair perfectly tousled, his dark skin perfectly smooth. Had he dabbed rose oil on his wrists?

"Hi." She swallowed hard, trying to reel herself in. "I, uh—I wanted to say thank you…for bringing me back to the house, and for securing the artifact."

"No need to thank me," he answered easily, giving her a sly wink that she pretended not to notice. "It's only a matter of time before they figure that one out. Frankly, I'm shocked it hasn't happened yet."

"Well, nevertheless. It was a good move. Might help us."

"Speaking of…I don't suppose you've figured out a plan for what to do next? How we get Jude back, that sort of thing?"

Logan came back down to earth with a thump. Her eyes strayed to her forearms, even though they were inert.

"I've got an idea. I just…"

Her left hand went for her right arm, feeling automatically for the small black diamond, where the last spike would come out. She could still feel the way her body seized up when—

With a quick shake of her head, she turned away from the kitchen and headed toward the living room, toward a small box she kept on an ordinary shelf.

"Am I allowed to follow you?" Alexei called from behind her.

"Yes," she called back. Already she had the box open. Already she had the joint stuck between her fingers. "I'm going out to the balcony. You might want a jacket."

In another step, she had the sliding door pulled wide, and in the next one after that, she stood out in the frigid air, a faint mist blowing against her face. She breathed it in, letting its light, cool touch deliver a calm that little else could. Then she slid the lighter out of her pocket. Tugging up the collar of her jacket, she ducked face, lighter, and joint behind it, providing just barely enough protection against the rain to get it lit.

She heard Alexei step down behind her, heard the faint rustle of a fine suit jacket as he pulled it straight.

"Why didn't you just light it inside?"

"Needed to get out. Sorry I was abrupt."

"No offense taken."

She took another pull, moving the flame around to the other side. Finally, it caught even, and she slipped the lighter away and turned to face him.

Now that the November air had poured cold water on her libido, she saw him a little more clearly. She saw that his eyes still looked tired, his hair still a step away from perfect. But he'd changed clothes. His shirt was now a light blue, almost white, and wrinkle-free. His suit jacket was a dark blue plaid, with lapels of solid dark green. She knew without asking that it would be the latest fashion.

It started simply.

"When's the last time you slept?" She took in some smoke and held it. She wanted to feel the harsh edges of things fading, blurring out. She wanted a soft focus for a little while.

"Oh, there was sleep in there somewhere. Around 6:00am. For at least…fifteen minutes or so."

"Well, that sounds healthy."

"You're one to talk."

"Hey, I've been asleep for a whole day. I think I've earned a late night."

He didn't respond immediately. He just looked at her for a long minute. She couldn't interpret his expression, but she suspected it might have unsettled her if the blur hadn't started to take effect.

That's good. A small knot of tension in her shoulders released.

He shoved his hands in his pockets, which she guessed was a defense against the cold. She wanted to tell him to go put on a warmer jacket, but something stopped her.

"I can't believe you have a nicer apartment than me," he said, sounding amused. It took a moment for his words to sink in for her. She rarely thought about the relative luxury of different living spaces. After all the time she'd spent sleeping beneath overpasses or huddled around a dying fire in the woods or in rat-infested, small-town motels…at a certain point, the degree of "niceness" ceased to matter.

But Alexei knew about luxury. So if he said it, it must be true. She shrugged.

"Hey, if you want to trade rich, shitty parents, you just say the word. I'm game."

"Not sure I would have survived your childhood. Not always sure I survived mine."

Then it grew.

She offered out her hand, two fingers crooked.

"You want?"

He raised an eyebrow at her.

"Why do I get the feeling that *your* weed would knock me on my ass?"

She pulled her hand back and brought it straight to her lips.

"Are you suggesting, Mr. Marin, that I'm trying to roofie you?" The blur began to spread down her neck, into her torso. The wind pricked at her back, but she could hardly tell.

"Not at all. Just wondering if, perhaps, your tolerance might be higher than mine."

Logan shrugged again.

"Who knows? Can't really be bothered to keep up with the fragility of you precious mortals, you know?"

"I think I'll pass, then," he said, with an easy smile. "Besides, I just shot-gunned a gin and tonic so I could follow you out here. Don't want to press my luck."

"Suit yourself." She took another pull, though she had nearly reached the perfect balance. She held it in for a long moment. "I've started to remember things."

This time, both of Alexei's eyebrows shot up.

"You have? What things?"

"The gaps I used to have, in my memory. They're filling in. I think it's the trigger word, pulling them out somehow." She took another drag, fueled by need. "Volkov used it on me, back at the warehouse. I didn't hurt anyone, but…that kid, Fisher, saw me. At least…I'm pretty sure he did."

Alexei's expression softened to concern.

"Do you think he'll tell his superiors?"

"I don't know. Probably. Unless...unless he doesn't understand what he saw." The ash had grown into a long stem, and she flicked it onto the wet cement of the balcony floor. "He might just think I'm Bound."

"Which is still illegal, in the eyes of the Order."

"Indeed." She let out a sigh. "It's definitely good we've got that artifact. Might be the only thing keeping me safe."

"Ah, you're just saying that to let me feel useful for once."

"You're always useful to me, Alexei. Why do you think I keep you around?" As soon as the words tumbled forth, she had to laugh. "You know, that sounded less mercenary in my head."

"What could be mercenary about that?" He grinned at her, then reached out his hand. "On second thought, maybe I wouldn't mind getting knocked on my ass."

She knocked a little more ash off before handing it over to him. Silence descended as he took a hit, and she let out a sigh.

"I really do hope Jude is alright," she said.

Alexei coughed into his hand as he passed the joint back to her.

"Volkov needs her alive." His voice was scratchy, so he cleared his throat. "She might not be comfortable, but...she's alive. She wouldn't make good leverage if she weren't."

Logan nodded slowly. She had to believe he was right. If Jude died, and it was all her fault...she wasn't sure that was something she could live with.

"I think he's pragmatic enough for that. He's got to be."

"He is, H.C. It'll be okay."

Backlit from the light spilling through the halls in her apartment, his perfect features softened in a romantic haze, he looked more than beautiful. He tempted her to forget everything else, in favor of pure aestheticism. She gazed at him long enough to take all of him in—the hands shoved back in his pockets and the slight hunch against the wind did nothing to detract from his well-tailored clothes and the curving shapes of muscle beneath.

"You must be cold." The words came out more breathlessly than she'd intended. She reached out with her right hand, touching him lightly on the arm. "Maybe we should go inside."

As if to illustrate her point, the faint mist chose that moment to turn into actual rain.

"No argument from me," he said, already ducking back inside.

She pressed the burning tip of the joint against the metal railing until it went out. It was a little damp now, but there was still a third of it left. Before following him, she tilted her head back and let the ice-cold rain fall on her face and drip into her hair. It felt honest. Then she straightened back up and shook her head, letting her too-long hair flip shake dry before she went inside. She shut the glass door tight and threw the lock, then left the partial joint in the open box on the mantle.

"Well, that was bracing," said Alexei as he turned back around to face her. His shirt was now speckled with raindrops, causing it to stick even tighter to his skin. "I think I might make myself another drink. You want anything?"

That's a mistake, she thought.

"Sure," she said. "I think I've got some hot chocolate powder somewhere…"

"Yeah, I saw it earlier." He turned toward the kitchen. "I'll go start the water."

A few minutes later, they stood facing each other, leaning

against opposite counter tops, with steaming mugs clutched in their hands. Logan had added chili powder to her hot chocolate, while Alexei had added gin to his.

She was doing her best not to look at him too long, which only seemed to add to the awkward tension between them. After a few short sips, she could feel the burn the sugar produced in her veins. Alexei cleared his throat.

"So." He looked at her with amusement. "You decorate the place yourself?"

Logan shook her head. "Hired a decorator. Told her I wanted something minimalist. After she left...I donated a couple of things."

"You wanted more minimal than minimalist, huh?"

Logan shrugged and took another sip. "I like things to be clean."

"I noticed."

She could feel her resolve slipping, and she found her gaze lingering on him longer than she meant it to.

"Alexei...do you ever..." She realized what she was asking only after she'd begun, and it brought her to a halt.

"Do I ever what, H.C.?"

His voice was gentle but insistent. She let her gaze, open and honest, narrow in on him.

"Do you ever think about the first time we met?"

The corner of his mouth twitched.

"Only when I'm alone, and the curtains are drawn."

She felt a flush on her neck, though she didn't know if it was visible beneath the hardened purplish markings. *What did I think he would say?*

She forced herself to look down at her cup.

"Jude's gonna be pissed she missed out on hot chocolate bonding time." She knew he would see right through her, but she did it anyway.

Alexei gave her a long look, his mouth still caught in an almost smile, his eyes questioning. Then he took a deep drink from his mug before setting it in the sink.

"Maybe we should both get some sleep," he said. She couldn't get a read on his tone. "I'm sure we'll feel better in the morning, hm?"

"Uh—yeah," said Logan automatically. She felt like she'd lost her footing somehow. She downed the rest of her drink, then placed it next to his. "You're probably right. We should go to bed."

The different phrasing escaped her lips before she could stop it, but she pretended not to notice. Instead, she motioned for him to go ahead of her and flipped the lights off behind them.

He paused at the door to her room, waiting a moment for her to catch up. The door to her room was already open, so she leaned against the frame. He let the quiet linger before he spoke.

"Guess this is goodnight, then."

It had all started out so simply. But now she felt a cacophony in her veins.

"Alexei...I'm not tired." Fixed him with an honest stare. "Are you?"

He stepped closer and leaned his shoulders against the other half of the door frame, and crossed his arms over his chest.

"Tell me what you want, H.C." A dare, but also a plea.

She knew what she wanted, even if she didn't want to admit

it. She just didn't know if she was ready to let herself have it. She acted anyway.

An actual step was unnecessary. As soon as her arm touched the crook of his slightly wet jacket sleeve, his arms began to slip open, defenses disappearing. All she had to do was lean forward. Her right hand moved from his sleeve to his chest, pushing aside the dark green lapel and resting just underneath it. Her left hand reached up to cup the side of his face, and she pressed her lips to his.

She pulled back almost immediately, but she didn't go far.

"Am I being clear?"

His lips grazed the side of her cheek.

"Not sure," he whispered in her ear, with mock earnestness. "You'd better try again."

So she did.

Chapter Seventeen
Unbalanced

Jude woke up in a darkened and unfamiliar room. The first sensation she felt was the cold. She opened her eyes to see where she was, but it made no difference. She couldn't see anything. She reached out automatically with her hand, groping for the pull on the lamp near her bed. But her hand swiped through the air, coming into contact with nothing. What was going on?

She felt fuzzy. It took her mind several seconds to piece her reality back together. She remembered talking to Knatt, and feeling restless, and putting on her coat, and walking out into the cold. As she patted herself down, she felt slightly relieved to discover that she still wore her coat. Somehow that made her feel a touch less vulnerable. But that feeling faded away again as she remembered walking through the trees, and the growing certainty that she was not alone.

Something, or someone, had taken her. But where?

She felt herself breathe in sharply as she blinked again, trying in vain to will her vision to work in the absolute dark. Maybe if she had Logan's eyes, or even Fisher's, she could have done it. But no matter how hard she tried, she couldn't change her human weakness. She could not see.

Panic rose like molten lava in her chest, but she took another breath, forcing herself to concentrate. She had to find out what she could, even if she couldn't see.

She pressed her hands onto the surface beneath her, and was surprised to find a funny kind of fabric there. It wasn't particularly soft; she might have described it as similar to plastic, or something else slightly unnatural....

Like the top of a bare mattress, she thought, pressing her hand down and feeling the cushion give. She rolled her body, ever so slightly, from side to side to confirm it. It was true.

Do most kidnappers bother with this level of nicety? It seemed almost quaint. She started inching her right hand outward, searching for the edge. She found it almost immediately. With a silent grimace, she pushed down her anxiety one more time. Before she could think herself out of it, she dropped her arm over the edge to see if she could feel the ground.

Her hand came into abrupt contact with a cold, smooth surface, and as she moved her fingers, she heard a quiet crinkly noise. In her mind's eye, she saw an image of the room she was in: cold dirt walls covered in a plastic tarp, then a bare mattress on the floor. And on it, her own unconscious body. Suddenly the mattress lost its quaintness.

Don't panic, she told herself, though she knew it was useless. *At least my hands aren't bound, right? And...and I can probably still summon.*

But should I?

One of the last things Knatt had told her, before she'd gotten herself kidnapped, was to make sure she didn't perform another eira summon without proper supervision. He said the fire could be addictive. It could take her down a path. Change her.

So what am I supposed to do, just lay here and die, when I might have the power to free myself? Who's that gonna help?

The panic was rising again, flooding through her torso like radiation. She felt like a child, brought to sit in the darkened den, blindfolded, until her mother decided it was time to mete out punishment. The very thought of her mother was nearly enough to push her over the edge—

"I gotta do something." She jumped at the sound of her own voice. She hadn't intended to say what she was thinking out loud. And yet something about actually *saying* the words soothed her. It felt like a command. Almost like it came from someone else—like someone else was giving her permission.

And permission was all she needed. She closed her eyes, though it made little difference in the dark, and she let herself reach into the fire. The fire was already right there, just beneath the surface. It only needed an entrance.

She brought her hands together, forming a circle she couldn't see. She could feel the essence of the fire, and she whispered its egress into the center of her hands—

For one brilliant moment, the whole room lit up, thrown into sharp relief by the burning light in her hands. She opened her eyes wide, taking in as much visual information as she could. For an instant, everything was fine—then her hands exploded in pain. Though it had done her no harm before, the fire now burned her, like it wished to consume her along with everything else. She released the summon immediately, though the damage had been done.

In the darkness, a rainbow afterimage of the room danced before her eyes. She held her hands above her still, shuddering as she felt the skin blister. She tried to bend her fingers, but even the slightest movement sent a shock wave of pain down her arm. Eventually, she let her hands fall limply to the side, wishing the cold would do more to numb the feeling.

The light from the fire had shown her just enough to give her an idea of what the room looked like—and she wasn't sure she wanted more than that. Her suspicion about the plastic had proved true—the floor and walls both appeared to be covered in layers of semi-opaque plastic sheeting. If she had to guess, she'd say the foundation under the plastic was either stone or cement. The color of it looked splotchy and uneven, with large dark spots clearly visible. They looked, rather unfortunately, like mold…or blood.

To say the room was sparsely furnished would have been an understatement. Apart from the mattress she now lay on, Jude had seen nothing but a suspicious-looking bucket in the far corner. The cell was larger than she would have guessed, though that was far from comforting. It was large enough to feel cavernous, and it was only the precise right-angled corners that told her she wasn't in a cave.

And if there's that much space around to waste on me, I'm guessing there's nobody near enough to hear me scream….

She shook her head at herself, willing her mind to stay focused. It was cold and damp in here. Did that mean she was still somewhere near Seattle, or had they simply taken her to a *different* cold, damp place?

She took another deep breath, then made herself still. She had to keep a cool head, had to stay ready to—

What was that?

She'd heard a noise. Was there someone outside? Someone coming to get her? After a moment, she heard another noise, and this time she was fairly certain it was the soft thud of a footfall—

One terrible scraping sound later, a thin, weak sliver of light broke into the room, accompanied by a fresh burst of cold air.

"Did the little girl wake up from her nap?"

The voice was surprisingly high-pitched and feminine. A woman.

Jude elected not to answer her, her face tilted away from the door, her eyes wide. She was trying to force them to accustom themselves to the light, before—

She whipped her head toward the door, her eyes narrowing on the source of the light. She could just about make out the wall beyond: it looked like a dark gray cement wall, and then a piece of dark sky—

"Oh, how delightful. She wakes."

The woman in the doorway pushed the door wider for just a moment, dragging something behind her as she came inside. As she shut the door behind her, she pressed a button on the device she held in her hand, and a cold, bluish light filled the space.

Jude silently cursed herself. Despite her best efforts, she was no closer to learning anything of importance. Wherever she was, it was made of cement. And the door to her cell appeared to be made of metal—old but impossibly thick and heavy. If she wanted to burn her way out of here, she'd have to melt through several inches of that metal. Suffice it to say, she'd never done anything like that before. And with her hands still smarting from her last summon, she was far from sure such a thing was possible.

"I've met you before, haven't I?" asked the woman. Jude directed her attention back to her just in time to see her shake out a metal folding chair and seat herself in it. The device she had held in the other hand appeared to be some kind of lantern; its sickly hued light turned the room an unnatural color and cast deep shadows along the walls. She placed it on the ground next to her.

Jude sat up straight on the mattress, careful to keep her still-burning hands from touching anything, and folding her legs into a half-lotus as she turned to face her captor—or, perhaps, *one* of her captors. The woman was surprisingly small, with long black hair falling in a thick sheath around her body. Her skin, already pale, looked almost purple in the light, and the circles under her eyes made them look more like sockets in a skull than working eyeballs.

They *had* met before, albeit briefly.

"You're Zilla Ulric." She remembered her face well enough, though she had been a bit drunk when she'd seen it. She'd come to the estate to ask Logan to attend the Summit. Jude had thought then that she looked like a witch; now she looked more like a ghost. "You're the Seer who turned traitor."

She heard the spite in her words before she realized she felt it. She hardly knew this woman, but for some reason, she couldn't help but hate her. Hate her, with the passion of—

Fire, she thought, feeling the fingers of her right hand automatically flexing. As they did, pain shot up her arm, and she barely kept herself from cringing. She let her eyes glance down long enough to take in the damage, and even in the ghostly bluish light, her skin appeared an angry shade of purplish red.

"That is my name, yes," said the woman, her large eyes wide as they stared Jude down. "Though whether one can truly betray an organization that betrays its own people is…up for debate, I should say. And you would be the shadow summoner's little pet, isn't that right? Can't remember the name. Probably a Chan or a Chang, hm?"

Jude blinked at her.

"You're the Wolf's errand boy." The one nice thing about the anger burning inside her, echoed by the dull ache of burn in her hands, was that it kept her focused. She didn't feel scared or intimidated. She just felt *hate*. "Did you bring me here on his orders?"

Ulric offered her an empty smirk and leaned back in her chair, like she was considering her.

"The order wasn't for you, specifically. My personal preference would have been the senior Logan, but then you made yourself so incredibly easy to catch. Rather stupid of you, don't you think?"

The pain in Jude's hand kept her from clenching it.

"I try not to live my life assuming there's a psycho bitch hiding behind every tree."

"And how's that working out for you?"

Jude let out a long, slow breath. Her hands lay open, just beneath her knees, and she hoped that Ulric didn't look too far down. She told herself this was restraint, not impotence.

Ahead of her, Ulric let out a sigh, slowly shaking her head.

"You have to understand, this is nothing personal." She sounded almost professional. Almost detached. As Jude watched, she pulled a long, thin blade out of her pocket, holding it in her hand like she was about to sit down to a meal. It gave off an eerie shine in the blueish light. "This is just the way the world is. Matters like this, well…they can be hard to understand when you're a child."

The cold, hard edge of the knife in this terrible blue light was enough to send a chill down her spine. It was enough to quiet her anger, if only for a moment. She found the plea escaping her lips before she'd made a conscious choice to do it.

"If it's nothing personal, then why don't you just let me go?" She felt suddenly very aware of how little space stood between the blade and her. The fire had never seemed farther from her reach.

A smile lived and died on Ulric's face.

"Well, I should be clear—it's nothing personal against *you*. But that doesn't mean you can't be useful to us. Your problem, little girl, is that you decided to take up with the shadow summoner. I can't think of a more dangerous choice you could have made. And, to be quite honest, I'm not sure it's the kind of thing I can simply look past."

Jude shook her head. She felt like she'd walked into the middle of a play in progress, and she didn't know any of her lines.

"What are you talking about? What has Logan ever done to you?"

Ulric shrugged, disdain coloring her features.

"It's not about what she's done. It's about what she *represents*." The way she moved the knife in front of her face gave Jude the impression of someone gazing into a handheld mirror. "Yes, the shadow summoner primarily functions as an upholder of the status quo. Most of her complicity is unconscious. But her *corruption* runs far deeper than that."

Her already unpleasant expression became distorted, an inhuman rage momentarily possessing her features. Though it faded as soon as it had come, Jude felt like she could see the echo of it still, like it had burned an afterimage into the space it had occupied.

"Why do you hate her so much?"

Ulric's mouth twisted in an ugly grin.

"It's not about hate, little girl. It's about power. The Order has never understood the extent of the shadow summoner's power, not as the Wolf has. And though it is unnatural and inhuman, it would be foolish to ignore it. A power like that must be *harnessed* for a greater cause. Power like that must be controlled—"

"Enslaved, you mean." Jude was beginning to see her a little more clearly.

Ulric glanced up from her reflection in the knife. Her expression was one of pity.

"You idolize her, don't you? Do you know what she is?"

"I know *who* she is."

Ulric's eyes lit up with silent laughter, her head tilting knowingly to the side.

"I think you *do* know what she is. Tell me, do you think every demon should get a fair trial? Should we start asking for names and identification before we carry out our orders? Before we exterminate the vermin?"

An eerie calm came over Jude. Her blistered hands still burned raw, but she could ignore them. The person sitting before her was not a ghost, nor any more a witch than Jude was. She was just another authority figure, scrabbling desperately for power. Jude had known plenty of them.

"Logan already knows your name. She won't need to ask."

Ulric's pose remained relaxed, but Jude saw her eyes narrow, her smirk freezing in place. She caught Jude's look and, holding her gaze, turned the knife over in her hand, letting it reflect the light. When she smiled, she revealed a row of teeth as sharp and shiny as the blade. Her eyes, above them, were fathomless.

"Did you know that every Seer in the Order has to choose a specialty in which to focus our talents? Would you like to know what mine was?"

Jude felt the overwhelming urge to shake her head and crawl backwards, putting as much distance between the two of them as she could. But instead she held her ground, and despite the blisters on her skin, she let each hand start to curve, and tried to reach inside herself, to where she was sure she could still find the fire. If she could just reach it—

Before her, Ulric's face looked inhuman.

"Dissection. I like to find out what's underneath." She turned her head casually, almost lazily, to the left, and called out. "Boys?"

Before Jude could react, the door burst open again, and three burly young men she didn't recognize barreled in, heading right for her. She tried desperately to call the fire, but it already felt like plunging her blistered fingers into a pot of boiling water, her fingers closing on nothing—

Two large sets of hands clamped down on each of her arms, pulling her vulnerable hands out into the open and immediately shattering her illusions of summoning the fire. The third man, rippling with muscle and covered in black, spidery veins all over his skin, wielded a sharp, ominous object, pointing it at her like a weapon. She heard her own voice crying out like it was coming from far away, though she could still feel her arms and legs kicking, ignoring the burn, striking out, trying to break free—

All the while, Ulric sat quietly in the background, watching her struggle.

In a moment, it was all over. Just as Jude realized that the third man was holding a needle of some kind, it made contact with her skin. She watched helplessly as he pushed the plunger down.

The effect was immediate. She felt her muscles relaxing, against her will. The fire, such as it was, faded into nothing. Her ability to struggle, or even remain upright, melted away, and just like that, they were laying her down on the mattress, flat on her back and unable to change position. Her gaze was fixed on the oddly luminescent, plastic-covered ceiling when Ulric swam back into view.

Jude hated how pleased with herself she looked.

"What's this?"

Jude felt Ulric's bony fingers close around her wrist, felt her hand as it was raised up in front of her.

She cried out as Ulric dug her fingernails hard into Jude's palm, raking them across her blistered skin. It felt like she was ripping her flesh right from the bone. Jude couldn't pull her arm back from Ulric's grip, but she found she could still scream just fine.

"Oh, my, yes. I think I'm going to have fun with you. Miss Jude Li."

She said my name. Jude barely had time to register the thought before the wide jaws of pain opened once more, and swallowed her whole.

Time in the cell didn't seem to pass in a straight line. Jude could no longer remember what questions Ulric had asked, nor how many times her answers had failed to satisfy. She couldn't even remember when her left eye had swelled up, preventing it from opening again.

There were still a few specific questions that stood out to her though. Questions like: *Has the shadow summoner ever told you what kind of demon she is?* And: *What do you know about the Choronzon Order?*

And the strangest one of all: *Has the shadow summoner ever told you about travel between dimensions?*

Jude was just starting to think that their session would never end, when something unexpected happened. The door opened up again, and a new person stepped through. She tried to look up to see who it was, but her head had rolled slightly forward, obscuring what was left of her vision.

"Zilla, what are the boys doing down here? I told you I didn't want the prisoner harmed." This voice sounded male, and slightly accented.

"Not to worry, sir. No lasting harm has been done."

"What is that supposed to mean? What have you done here?"

Jude heard a kind of hushed silence descend above her as somebody new knelt down. She felt hands moving her clothes around, and she wanted to wriggle away from them, but she could still barely move. After a moment, her clothes were back in place anyway.

The voice that spoke sounded deadly.

"Zilla...I need you to remove yourself from this room before I become angry. Take the boys with you."

"But—master, I—I was only trying to get the information you wanted—"

"I said *GET OUT!*"

If Jude could have moved, she would have jumped at the scream that curdled the air. She heard people moving around her, heard the scrape of the metal chair, heard feet scrambling for purchase as they sputtered toward the door.

Then, for several minutes, she heard nothing. She'd been left alone, with nothing but the dull, throbbing pain of Ulric's interrogation tactics to keep her company. A part of her wondered, vaguely, what her face looked like with one swollen eye. The rest of her didn't want to know.

At long last, she heard movement again. Someone knelt down beside her, and the next moment, oddly gentle hands turned her over onto her back. Her one good eye could see the world again.

Before her sat a young man with white-blond hair and a concerned look on his face. She knew him, too, though they had never technically met.

"Volkov," she rasped, her voice barely able to form the necessary sounds.

"When you're able to sit up, I've brought you a glass of water." Jude was pretty sure his accent was British, but she wouldn't bet on any of her own assumptions right now. "In the meantime, do you mind if I place this over your eye?"

He held up what appeared to be an ice pack.

"Nothing I can do to stop you," said Jude, wincing at her own voice.

Volkov looked inexpressibly sad as he placed the ice pack on her face.

"I'm terribly sorry about all this. I knew Zilla had some doubts about my methodology, but I didn't think she would come down here without my knowledge. That's not an excuse, mind you. I ought to know my own people better than that."

Jude looked at him blankly. In the long run, the ice pack was probably a good idea, but in the short run, it made it easier to focus on all the other pains dotted throughout her body. After a moment, she cleared her throat.

"If you expect me to believe that bullshit…" she felt herself rumble to a stop and cleared her throat again. "Then you're dumber than I thought."

"No, I don't expect you to believe me. I only hope you will let me help you. Tell me, if I were to move you over to the wall so that you might sit up and lean against it, would you let me do that?"

Jude let her one eye close. She wanted the dignity of sitting upright more than anything, but she wouldn't willingly give him an inch. She said nothing.

"Well…I'm going to try. Let me know if it hurts."

It did hurt, but she wasn't about to tell him that. With surprising ease, he lifted her up and turned her around on the mattress, putting her back down so that her back lay flat against the wall behind her. Before she was even done taking that in, Volkov knelt before her, holding the promised glass of water up to her lips. She closed her eye again as she tilted her head back, letting him tip water into her mouth. In moments, she had emptied the glass.

"Would you like another?"

He held the empty glass up before her, as if she needed a visual aid. She let her head fall back against the wall, saying nothing. After a moment, he gave her a contemplative nod, then jumped up and walked over to the heavy door, opening it just enough to poke his head out. In her mind's eye, she imagined jumping up and running after him, bowling him down on her way out the door...but she knew she couldn't. Her muscles refused to do what she wanted them to do, and that was to say nothing of the still-blossoming pain in nearly every part of her body.

A moment later, Volkov was back, holding out a second glass of water for her. She took a deep breath, then put all her effort into lifting up her right hand to take it from him. To her surprise, it obeyed her. She took the glass, and she made sure to drink this one more slowly. She kept her eyes open and trained on him the whole time. Eventually, she put the glass down beside her and let out a small cough to clear her throat.

"So. What are you gonna do to me now?"

Volkov let out a slow sigh, sadly shaking his head.

"Oh, Miss Li. You've got entirely the wrong idea about me. I don't want to hurt you. Hell, I don't want to hurt Logan either. All I want is for her to realize her true potential. And you're going to help me do that."

"How exactly am I going to do that?"

"You're already doing it." Smiling happily at her, he seated himself near her feet, stretching his legs out before him and nonchalantly crossing one ankle in front of the other. "See, she may not want to admit it, but the truth is, I already know Logan pretty well. The kind of person she is, the way she'll likely respond to any given situation. It's written into everything she does." He gave her an audacious wink. "And you, my dear, are the perfect bait for her."

Jude felt a flutter in her stomach, the first signs of building dread. She got the impression that Volkov *did* understand Logan—well enough, at least.

"You want her to come and rescue me," she said, feeling her now-empty right hand clench into a fist again, despite the pain. It hardly mattered compared to the rest of the pain, anyway. "Why? What do you think will happen then?"

"Oh, nothing too serious," said Volkov, sounding absolutely delighted. "Just the first step in a revolution. The revolution to end all revolutions, you might say."

Jude blinked at him. All at once, she felt incredibly tired.

"Can we cut it out with this cryptic shit? What's your plan, dude?"

Just then, the giant metal door creaked open again, and another burly young man came inside. Jude couldn't be sure if he was one of the ones who had beaten her up or not. They all had an unsettling sameness about them, though she couldn't quite name it at first.

This one carried what appeared to be a large metal box, which he placed on the ground a few feet away. He turned a knob on the side and it spluttered to life, emitting a kind of low humming sound.

"Thank you, Billy," said Volkov, never taking his eyes off Jude. "You may return to your post."

The bulky man-child grunted in response, then lumbered out

the door, shutting it firmly behind him. It wasn't until Jude felt a small gasp of warm air drift over her shins that she realized what it was.

"Is that a heater?" She did her best to sound neutral.

"Indeed, it is." He still sounded so goddamn pleased with himself. She could feel her anger starting to burn again, and this time, she didn't think it had anything to do with her unbalanced fire summon. "I told you, I don't want you harmed. I haven't brought you here to torture you. I want you to be absolutely as comfortable as possible. Unfortunately, our current base of operations is…a little *inherently* uncomfortable. But we'll make do as we can, hm?"

Jude clucked her tongue and reached for the water glass again, giving herself a moment of quiet. A part of her brain couldn't help but think that maybe the presence of the heater might help her somehow—that maybe she could use it to help her reconnect with the fire. When she put the glass down, she jumped a little to see that Volkov had leaned forward, holding out the ice pack for her once more. She placed the glass gently on the ground before taking the pack from him and holding it over her eye. She flinched automatically as it touched the tender skin there, but it only took a moment for her to feel its soothing effect. Eventually she cleared her throat, trying once more to keep to the task at hand.

"You really want to make this place comfortable for me?"

"I do."

"You wanna tell me *where* this place actually is?"

The side of his mouth twitched in amusement.

"Perhaps I will. Tomorrow, maybe."

"Great." She glanced down at the water glass. "I don't suppose you got anything else where that water came from?"

"I might." He tilted his head to the side, gazing at her with something like fondness. "What do you need?"

"A sandwich maybe. Not picky, just…haven't eaten in a while."

"Of course." The way he leaned back on his hands as he looked at her, she almost got the impression that they were nothing more than two friends on a sleepover. Granted, it was probably the worst sleepover she could think of. "I'll make sure to have one of the boys get you something. And in return for my generosity, I don't suppose you'd deign to answer a question for me? Just one, I promise."

She didn't notice any shift in tone or demeanor from him; it still felt like they were friends having a chat, nothing more. Which made her all the more suspicious of his intentions.

"Depends on the question, I guess," she answered, thoughtfully.

"Oh, it's harmless, I assure you." His eyes glittered like sharp diamonds. "I've just been wondering…what do *you* know about the Choronzon Key?"

Her eyes automatically widened in surprise, but she did her best to mute any expression beyond that. She could feel his gaze searching her face for every possible clue, and she had no idea what she might be giving away without knowing it. The last thing she wanted to do was betray any of Logan's secrets. She swallowed, hard.

"Not a lot," she answered, as truthfully as she could. "I know that…that nobody's ever proven it really exists."

"But you know it *does* exist, don't you?" His gaze was clear, focused, and certain. "You've seen it, haven't you?"

She swallowed again, saying nothing. Or maybe saying everything. Why had none of her training included instructions on how to bluff?

Maybe Logan didn't think that would be the best thing to train an 18-year-old to do, she thought, more to distract herself than anything else. She couldn't shake the feeling that she was failing somehow, just by having this conversation.

"I—I've seen pictures—"

"Oh, come now. Must you stain us with a lie? It's all right, you know. I already know about Logan. There's absolutely *nothing* you can say that would surprise me."

Oh, I'm really not too sure about that, she thought but didn't say. She shook her head at him, then immediately regretted it as a fresh stab of pain radiated through her skull.

"Sorry, dude. I can't help you."

A patient smile slowly spread over his face.

"You don't trust me." If she didn't know better, she would have said he sounded sad about that. "I suppose that's understandable, unfortunately. He gave her a long look before he spoke again, and she found herself squirming under the intensity of his gaze. "I wish I could show you my vision. You'd understand it all, then. Well, tell me. Is there anything at all I can do to help you trust me?"

Jude gripped the ice pack tighter, steeling herself.

"You could let me go."

Volkov's smile dissolved in an instant, replaced by something uglier. He recovered himself, but not quickly enough for her to miss it: the unadulterated rage that lay just beneath the surface.

The smile that popped back into place was as false and flimsy as cardboard.

"But if I let you go, how would you ever see my vision?"

Jude let her neck muscles relax until her head leaned back against the plastic sheeting on the wall behind her. She could feel herself starting to slip. Without the fire to sustain her, the drug and her exhaustion were clearing her out.

"I'll settle for the sandwich then," she heard herself mumble, as if from far away. She was starting to drift.

"Consider it done." She heard him moving around and realized that her eye had slid shut. "I think I'll let you get some rest now."

She was only vaguely aware of him leaving the room, and after that, only vaguely aware of the ice pack slipping from her hand as her body slid down the wall, landing semi-sprawled across the mattress.

He left the heater here.

The warmth enveloped her as she disappeared into the dark.

Chapter Eighteen
Mobilized

Somewhere, in the dark, she began to dream. Her dream formed a distant shoreline—one she'd never seen before, but one that looked undeniably familiar. She wasn't sure it really existed, but at the same time, she knew it had *always* existed. It was permanent, and it was safe. She *knew* she was safe here, though she didn't know how. The background noise of her own unease began to fade. This was a place she could come to, if everything else was stripped away from her.

But it did not belong to her.

In the distance, a dark figure approached. As she gazed at it, her surroundings began to fill themselves in. Before, the shore had stood alone, an abstract idea in a sea of nothingness. But now the sea took form. To her right stood an impossibly high cliff, the dark rock of its surface informing her in no uncertain terms that any attempt to climb it would prove disastrous for her. And to her left stood a deep, gray ocean, more dark rocks forming a cold island in the distance. Everything was shades of black and gray.

And before her, a figure. Moving ever closer.

She stepped toward it, and as soon as she did, the distance between them vanished. They stood face-to-face.

Jude had never been so happy to see that face.

"How did you find me?"

Logan gave her a sad smile.

"Sorry, kid. I haven't found you yet."

Jude looked around, taking in the scene one more time. Then it clicked.

"This isn't real, is it?"

"Not really, no. It's the mind-space, the one we tried to connect to before. I, uh…I wasn't ready to let you in then." She glanced around them, indicating the ominous sea, the forbidding cliff. "I don't think most people would like it here."

"Well, it's better than…wherever the hell I am."

Logan motioned to Jude's right, toward the cliff.

"Shall we sit?"

Suddenly, Jude noticed the roaring fire, accompanied by two puffy floor cushions, only a few feet away from them. She was absolutely certain they hadn't been there a moment ago, but she supposed she ought to accept that anything around her could change at any time.

"Did you make those?"

"I borrowed them."

Jude nodded, though she didn't know what that meant, and sat down on the nearer pillow. Logan took the other, immediately folding her legs into a perfect lotus.

Jude tried to place her hands beneath her, but immediately pulled them back as her raw skin brushed the very real-feeling fabric.

"Shit. I didn't think this could hurt here."

Logan tilted her head at Jude's hands, her expression curious.

"You bring your outside self in here with you. Here, give me your hands." Jude offered them without hesitation, and Logan took them in her own. Jude was prepared to flinch on contact, but it didn't hurt. After a few seconds, Logan let go, and Jude brought her hands up to her face. They didn't hurt anymore, and there was no evidence of the burn on them, either.

"How did you do that?"

"I've been coming here a while, so I've got a few tricks. Don't be too impressed, though. I didn't really *heal* them, so they'll hurt again as soon as you wake up."

"Well, I'll worry about that then." She watched her hands as they fell into her lap, still amazed. When she looked up, she saw Logan was still staring at her with concern. "What?"

"Should I fix your eye, too?"

"Oh, sure. I guess I forgot about it because I can see just fine here."

Logan let out a sigh, then leaned forward and waved her hand over Jude's face. The small amount of discomfort Jude hadn't even noticed disappeared.

"Did the Wolf do this to you?"

Jude chuckled. Somehow, none of it seemed so bad now that she was removed from it, though she was sure that would change as soon as she woke up.

"Actually, most of it was Ulric. The hands I did to myself."

"Ah. You tried to summon fire again?"

"Yeah. Knatt warned me not to, but…I thought maybe I could escape, somehow." She let her air out in a huff and slumped her shoulders. "There's no chance of that, though. The cell I'm in is made of cement, I think. And there's a solid metal door, like three inches thick. No way am I getting through that."

Logan's right eyebrow quirked upward.

"Cement, huh? Can you tell me anything else about where you are?"

Jude's heart leaped: Logan was going to rescue her. But then it fell just as quickly, as she remembered what Volkov had said: he was using her as bait.

"Logan—you can't come after me."

"What?"

"You can't come here. You can't try to find me. The Wolf, he's using you—he wants to use you. I don't...I don't really get what for, but—he *really* seems to think he can do it. And he *knows* things, Logan. He knows so much. You just—you can't come here. It's not safe."

But Logan just shook her head.

"Don't worry about that, Jude. I can handle the Wolf. Just tell me what you can see."

Jude gave her a long look. One part of her wanted nothing more than to convince Logan that she wasn't worth the risk— but another part of her wanted Logan to save her, and more than that...she believed that she could. After all, hadn't she essentially based her whole life around her belief in what Logan could do? If she didn't have her belief in her friends, what did she have?

She let out a long, slow breath, and gave herself over.

"Okay. I can tell you that it's cold and damp here, just like on the estate—although I guess he could have taken me anywhere that's cold and damp."

"Not necessarily." Logan looked contemplative. "He would no longer have access to the Order's spatial warping ability. That only exists inside of Headquarters, and there's no way he or Ulric have gotten back in there. My guess is he's at most a few hours away from here."

"Okay. Well, I can't see outside much. But, like I said, this room seems to be made of cement. And...the metal of the door is old, and kinda rusty. And the cell itself is pretty big. I don't think they're too worried about space. Oh—and someone put tarps or plastic sheeting all over the walls and the floor. I don't know if that helps."

Logan's brows knitted together in thought, and she sat quietly for several moments. Her dark eyes reflected the light of the fire—a flicker of brightness in the dark. Jude took note of the scar that ran along her face—the one Zilla Ulric had left her, possibly made with the same blade she'd pulled out of her pocket earlier that night. At long last, Logan nodded.

"It helps enough. You might want to get some rest. You can fall asleep here, if you'd like." Logan glanced around them, and then waved her hand to indicate a space on the other side of the fire.

When Jude looked in that direction, she saw a thin but soft-looking mat, complete with a pillow and blanket. Her exhaustion hit her all at once.

"Is it safe to sleep here?"

"It's safe. You'll wake up in the cell, of course."

"Okay. I think I'll do that.

"I'll stay until you fall asleep. And then I'm coming to get you."

Logan woke in advance of the sun. Before she opened her eyes, she sensed the presence next to her, and for just a moment, she braced herself for an attack. Then she remembered.

Her eyes blinked slowly open. Dim moonlight striped the ceiling above her, let in by a small crack in her dark gray curtains. Refusing to let her head turn to the right, where his presence lay sleeping, she let it fall to the left instead. Her carpet was a light, cool toned gray, and a dark gray chair sat next to the window. Against all that monotone, the vibrantly blue and green plaid jacket laying rumpled on her floor stood out. She couldn't ignore it, as much as she wanted to.

Her gaze returned to the ceiling, and she made herself count to ten before letting it fall to the other side.

There he was, sleeping peacefully. The perfect angles of his face shone in the moonlight. His hair was slightly more mussed than usual. He looked so perfect, so vulnerable. If she let herself, she could still feel the weight of his hand on her cheek, the soft press of his lips against hers. Everything about him was soft and inviting. She wanted to reach out and touch him, but she couldn't risk losing herself in his light. She couldn't risk waking him up, either.

There was work left to be done. She let herself linger for only a moment, making sure to take in every pane of his sleeping face, before slowly maneuvering herself out of bed, into the cold, empty dark of her bedroom. Her first order of business was to locate her pants, which had somehow ended up underneath the bed.

Sometime later, she was back in her kitchen, brewing coffee and getting ready to make another phone call she didn't want to make. This time, it was to Marlowe. She hoped against hope that Fisher hadn't managed to tell her anything yet, and she chose to proceed as if this were the case.

The voice that answered was cold and unamused.

"Well, isn't this a surprise."

"I've got a new plan, if you're ready to listen."

"Oh, boy! Let me think about that one. Mm, no."

"Just hear me out."

"Miss Logan, Marion Clément convinced me to deal with you two days ago, and in return for the trust she placed in you, you stole a valuable artifact from us. And now you want me to repeat her mistake?"

"Well, for starters, you can hardly blame me for something that happened while I was unconscious."

"I have absolutely no doubt that Mr. Marin acted with your blessing, if not under your direct order. Besides, the artifact has not been returned to us, has it?"

"You'll get it back, all right? I'm going to give you exactly what you want, but this is only going to work if you agree to a few things first, and if we *all* agree to go along with my plan. It's the only way we're going to catch the Wolf off-guard."

The woman on the other end was silent for several seconds. Then Logan heard a sigh.

"What's the plan?"

"Well, just to be upfront…the first caveat is that I can't tell you everything."

"That's a promising start."

"It'll be worth it. Money back guarantee." Logan took a deep breath and reached over to push the plunger down on the French press, as if the promise of impending coffee could give her strength. "I know where the Wolf is. I'm going to take you to him."

When she hung up the phone a short while later, she could already hear Alexei heading toward her from the bedroom.

No, not hear, she thought. *I can* smell *him. Great.*

Though the coffee was still piping hot, she tipped her head back and began to drink it down as fast as she could. She'd been desperately hoping that he would sleep in, and she'd have a little bit more time to examine how she felt. What she wanted to do next.

"Good morning." His voice sounded as warm and sweet as honey. It made her want to claw her own eyes out. "Were you just on the phone?"

"Yeah, with Marlowe."

"From the Order?"

"Yeah. We've got a plan, and we're moving forward with it. There's coffee on the counter if you want some. I'm gonna go hop in the shower and let Knatt know what's going on."

She had already set her mug down in the sink and taken a step toward the door when he reached out to touch her arm.

"Hey. Could you maybe tell *me* what's going on? A basic outline would be good."

Logan blinked and nodded. Her feet still wanted to move out of the room, but she forced them to stay still.

"Right. Uh, we're gonna meet the Order down in SoDo, at their unfinished base. And then we're gonna go rescue Jude. Sound good?"

"Of course."

She paused for just a moment. She could see in his face that he wanted to talk about what happened. But she wasn't ready yet. She couldn't do it.

"Okay. See you in a few."

With that, she spun around and disappeared down the hall.

She took her motorcycle to the location Marlowe had provided. It was uncomfortably close to her apartment building, only a short ride south if the stadiums were empty. Already she hated the feeling of the Order right in her backyard, close enough to watch every move she made.

Still, that was beside the point, for now. She had to work with them. Their omnipresence had left her with few other choices.

The address they'd given her turned out to be another warehouse, although this one had not been made up to look like a barn. It was just another warehouse within the sea of warehouses that populated this part of the city. She pulled into the unmarked parking lot and brought her bike to a stop as near to the building as she could, then hopped off. There were no other cars in the entire lot, and there weren't even any little yellow lines indicating where vehicles should be placed. In fact, the building was largely unmarked, too. There was nothing to indicate she'd actually found the right spot.

Knatt pulled up a few minutes later, guiding his little red four-door into the spot roughly adjacent to Logan's bike. Alexei sat in the passenger's seat, having traveled back to the estate to avoid a ride on her motorcycle.

"I don't know if anyone's here yet," she said as the other two came to stand beside her. "I suppose we could try knocking on the door."

"Might as well start somewhere." Knatt looked up and all around, then pointed to the left. "That way, perhaps?"

"Sure, why not?"

They marched leftward, toward what looked like the outline of a door in the side of the blank white building in front of them. Logan reached it first, and she reached out and rapped her knuckles against it three times.

They waited for several seconds, but no one came. Logan tried again, but still nobody appeared. Finally, she reached down for the door knob and began to jiggle it. She might have tried breaking the door down, if a little voice in her head hadn't suggested that there might be cameras hidden on the premises.

"Well, what do you think?"

Knatt cleared his throat and was about to reply when they heard something further down the wall to their right.

"Hey, over here!"

All three of them looked over to see Ian Fisher poking his head out of the wall, apparently leaning out of a door they hadn't seen. Logan raised her eyebrow at him.

"You guys really don't want to deal with solicitors, do you?"

For a brief moment, she locked eyes with Fisher. Her brow furrowed automatically as she searched for any clues in his face. He looked nervous for a moment, but then he grinned at her.

"Marlowe says I can only keep this door open for 60 seconds. So, are you guys coming or not?"

Beside her, Alexei chuckled and started forward. Knatt followed him, and Logan allowed them both to get a few feet ahead of her before joining them. She still wasn't sure how to take Fisher, but she supposed she'd find out shortly if the Order was planning to arrest her as soon as she got behind that door.

Sure would put a crimp in the plan.

She hesitated one last second just before the threshold, but then crossed over it. The door shut with a bang behind her, and though she made no visible movement, internally, she flinched.

Several seconds passed, and no handcuffs materialized to lock her down. Fisher led them into another bright, open space—this one set up more like a garage, or an airplane hangar. A small fleet of vans stood off to the side, each one looking like it was prepped for the apocalypse. Several of them appeared to have small cannons set into the top, and they all had blacked-out windows everywhere but the windshield.

This looks like the makings of a private demon-fighting militia. Didn't Clément say the Seattle team would only have four members?

She decided to put that thought in the back of her mind, since it would have little bearing on the fight at hand. Refocusing on her current purpose, she turned her attention to where Fisher was leading them.

Marlowe stood waiting, flanked by Eliana Blake, the fourth team member whose name Logan still didn't know, and two other Order Adepts Logan didn't recognize. Her heart sank a little as she took them in.

"Is this all we've got?" she asked, giving their small group a once-over. She took a quick look around the rest of the space, in case she'd missed anything, but she didn't see anyone else in there.

Marlowe clucked her tongue and folded her arms over her chest.

"You've got what we can spare. After the disaster at the beta site, this is all Headquarters would authorize. Especially considering that we cannot prove that whatever Volkov is doing now is any threat to us."

"Did you tell them that he kidnapped Jude and is probably, you know, trying to open a portal to another world to let an untold number of demons through?"

Marlow's face remained impassive. "I did. But as I can neither substantiate nor disprove your theory, it remains just that—a theory. The Order is not in the habit of acting on mere theory, despite what Clément's recent decision may have led you to believe."

Logan's fist curled into a ball, but she managed to keep her arms at her sides. *It's still more people than if you hadn't told them*, she thought.

"Fine. I guess I'll take what I can get." She took a short but deep breath and did her best to release her frustration into the ether as she let it out. "Did you need me to go over the formation again, or are we ready to roll?"

The amount of satisfaction she got from the annoyance that flashed over Marlowe's features was small, but it would have to see her through.

"Ready when you are, shadow summoner."

"Great. Go team."

With that, she turned away from the Order Adepts and headed back out into the light.

They were setting out as early as they could, but Logan knew the coming winter had already started shortening the days, and the gray sky above them didn't bode well for long light. Still, she couldn't leave Jude alone out there for one more night or give the Wolf that much more time to pull together the rest of his plan. So what other choice did she have?

She rode out first, like a sentinel on her Ninja. The ferry was the fastest option at this time of day, so that was the way they took. As she pulled her bike into its allotted slot near the front of the first car level, she realized that the last time she'd been on the ferry, she'd had Jude with her. She remembered the look on her face as she saw the city shrinking away from them for the very first time.

Maybe I should have gone with her to New York, she thought to herself. *She just wanted to see a big city. I should have been happy to show her one. Would that have made a difference?*

She waited on the car level, amidst the lingering fumes, until she saw Knatt's little car pull in just ahead of the Order's large, unmarked, windowless black van. She didn't think it was one of the ones with a cannon, unless the cannons were retractable somehow. Still, how they'd been allowed on without a thorough search was beyond her.

Just as she was about to head toward the staircase, she caught Alexei's look through the windshield of Knatt's car. She could have gotten lost in that look, if she'd let herself. It asked her a question, and a part of her longed to answer it.

Instead, she headed upstairs in search of coffee. It had been hours now since she'd had any.

She ran into Knatt in the small cafeteria above deck. He appeared to have brought his own tea bags, and he was filling up a lined cardboard cup with hot water.

"I'm not sure I'm convinced of all this," he said as she came up next to him. She put her own cup under the coffee spout. "Or, I should say, I'm not sure how I feel about letting you take the lion's share of the responsibility. We already know Volkov can…you know."

Use the trigger. Logan appreciated Knatt's reluctance to say it out loud, but it echoed in her head nonetheless.

"And now I know that, and how to deal with it." She left just enough room for cream at the top, and she smiled to see that they'd supplied actual half-and-half and not that strange powdered stuff that gave her headaches. "He's a one-trick pony. And he already used up the trick."

That wasn't exactly what she thought, but it wasn't quite a lie, either. And that was good enough for now.

"If you say so," said Knatt, making no attempt to hide his uncertainty. "Well. I think I shall find myself a seat on the sun deck and meditate awhile. You may join me, if you wish."

Logan felt a half smile fade across her face.

"Something I should do first."

Knatt nodded vaguely at her, then wandered off to find a cashier. Logan decided to take a deep drink of her coffee and fill it up again before paying.

It didn't take her long to find him, though his scent was significantly harder to locate between the layered smells of saltwater, fish, exhaust, and the small midday crowd of people. He still had a tendency to stand out, wherever he was.

The suit was new, and just as loud as every other she'd seen him wear. This one was a three piece of bright azure, and the faintest of lavender for the collared shirt beneath. He had a floor-length black trench-coat with him, but it hung draped over his arm.

He was standing near the rear of the second-floor deck, leaning against the rail and staring back at the city behind them. It wasn't far from where she'd stood with Jude. She came up and leaned against the railing right next to him, and stood there quietly for a whole minute before she said anything. Her coffee was half gone when she finally spoke.

"You probably think I'm avoiding you." Her voice sounded slightly husky, even to her own ears.

"The thought had crossed my mind." His sounded smooth and calm, like the surface of a crystal ball.

"I kind of am."

"Well. Points for honesty, I guess." She heard the hurt in his voice, and she winced.

"Sorry, I didn't mean it like that." They were near the back of the boat, and below, the Sound was roiling and churning like a living thing. "We've been friends a long time, Alexei."

"I'm aware of that."

"What I mean is…you mean something to me. Something kind of…hard to express. But Jude is out there, right now. Which means I have to focus on the mission." She let out a slow breath, readying herself. "And I care about you too much to give you less than my full attention. So, if it's okay with you, can we talk about it tomorrow, instead?"

He stayed quiet long enough to make her squirm.

"Tomorrow. You promise?"

"It would take an act of god to stop me."

"Well, now you're tempting fate."

"I promise. Okay?"

"All right. I can wait. Until tomorrow."

"Thank you."

He turned to look at her, and the smile he gave her could have outshone the sun.

She rode out first, and she didn't bother to see if the caravan could keep up. This was part of the plan: on her own, she could travel faster than the rest, so she would. A scouting party of one. If the Order had agreed to send in more troops, she suspected they might have objected to this course of action. But with barely more than Marlowe's small team assigned to them, they seemed to be letting Marlowe herself call the shots. And she was more than willing to risk Logan's life first. Whatever her reasons, Logan was glad she'd get a chance to do it her own way.

The ferry let out into the small tourist town of Bainbridge Island. Fortunately for Logan, she only had to sit through two relatively short lights before she reached a stretch of open road. Nothing made her feel more antsy and uncertain than sitting through a red light on the Ninja. She felt like a raging ball of energy, chained by arbitrary symbolism and human law. But then the light turned green and the lock broke loose.

Though it was still afternoon, the sun hadn't quite broken through the clouds all day, and she could already see its wan presence starting to fade. *Storm clouds.* Under the visor on her helmet, she shifted her nose around and took a deep breath, taking in all the scents on the air. Past the exhaust fumes and the evergreen pine, she could just about taste the coming rain. It was hard to say how long rains on the peninsula would last; the winds shifted enough that even deep clouds might pass along in a few minutes, heading out to the Sound or south to deeper forests.

She knew these roads like the back of her hand. She'd come out here so many times over the years, either at the bequest of a client, or because she'd had a vision...or, on occasion, just to go hunting. The Olympic rainforest stretched the length of the peninsula, and within lived an endless well of secrets and monsters. Sometimes they swam out of its depths and headed too close to human territory—but, more often, it was humans who dove too far deep into theirs. Of course, by Order dictate, the monsters themselves had no rights, no territory. They were always, without exception, executed without trial.

But she wasn't headed deep into the rainforest this time. Granted, trees still outnumbered people here, so one was never *far* from the edge of the forest. But they were headed for concrete—to an abandoned army base just along the shore of the Sound.

That's where they were going. She'd remembered it, all at once, when she'd gotten her memories back. It was where her father used to take her, when he thought he could break through to another world. It was one of his "weak spots." That was where the Wolf would be.

She felt an unfamiliar thrill at the thought of the Wolf. He was still a murderer, of course. She wouldn't forget that, but she had questions now. Questions like, what did he know about the Choronzon Key that she still did not?

And how could she get it out of him?

First things first: she had to get there. There was another stoplight a few miles out of town, but after that, she burst out into open road. Traffic was light this time of day, and soon enough, she zoomed around what little of it there was and entered into lonely country. Out here, the biggest danger on the roads was the deer.

As the crow flies, the shortest route to the military base would take her through Port Townsend, but that way required slowing down for laws and pedestrians, so she went around it. She wanted to mask her approach anyway, so it would be better to go on the old abandoned route her father used to take. It came to her with shocking ease. She hadn't known how many times she'd *really* been out here until a day ago, so it took her by surprise when her mind stumbled into sense memory and began to guide the way.

The way turned out to be a gravel road through the trees west of town. She rode along the bumpy path as it narrowed and gave way to dirt, ducking beneath low-hanging branches and swerving to avoid potholes. The Sound was getting closer; she could smell the saltwater, even if she couldn't taste it yet.

Eventually, the road sputtered out and vanished. She brought the Ninja to a stop and threw the kickstand, then removed her helmet and placed it on the handlebars. She already had her arms and legs strapped with throwing knives, but she clicked open the hidden compartment on the bike and pulled out a belt and a machete to hang around her waist, then the ax harness that pulled over her shoulders. And with that, she was ready.

The first few raindrops slipped through the evergreens and landed on the top of her head as she was streaming through the underbrush, flying like a cougar over the mushy, mossy terrain. She knew without looking that her boots would be caked with mud by the time she hit the concrete.

But even in the cold and damp, she could feel her muscles come alive as she ran. She felt the demon in her stretching its wings, excited for the fight it knew was coming. It called to the forest, and the forest called back to it. When it came time for her to vanish into shadow, she was met with no resistance. The sight of her faded into nothing, absorbed into the dark like a river into the ocean.

She met the edge of the forest faster than she would have

liked. Her feet kept pounding onward as she emerged from the tree line, still entirely obscured.

Out before her stretched the gray cement remains of an abandoned military base—and a potential point of egress into another world.

Chapter Nineteen
An Unearthly Mist

Logan kept her eyes open wide as she ran, trying to take in as much of the layout as possible. The rain was coming down in earnest now: she could hear the waves lapping against the shore on the other side of the base, frothing into a frenzy as the winds riled the tide. With her eyes trained on the top level of the hollow structure, just barely visible from her low vantage point, she saw a sudden flash of light illuminate the dark, stormy sky. If she'd been any farther away, she would have said it was lightning. But natural lightning, in her experience, rarely contained so many colors.

Whatever Volkov was planning to do out here, it seemed he had already begun.

Her feet landed loud on the first stretch of concrete, and, momentarily afraid someone might hear the sound and come to investigate, she located a row of thick stone pillars and slipped into the shadow of the first one.

She had come out into an open hallway that stretched along the southern end of the structure, old metal piping all along the ceilings and concrete stairways leading up to the higher levels.

Despite the general air of dereliction and decay, artificial lighting, in the form of presumably battery-operated lanterns, had been placed at regular intervals along the corridor, and Logan suspected they could be found throughout as well.

She knew her shadow cover would keep her hidden from most eyes, but nevertheless, she waited behind the pillar, craning her neck just enough to peek around the corner. It didn't take long for her to spy a dark shape passing in front of the cold lantern light. The shape looked roughly human, but too large and strangely bulky. Once Logan's eyes adjusted to the strange blue light, she realized what she was actually looking at: a Bound human, displaying the full height of his Bound powers. He was a giant of a man, his head completely shaved and somewhat bumpy, with tell-tale spidery black veins spreading out from his eyes over the rest of his face and down his bare shoulders. Apparently immune to the cold, he walked through the corridor in army fatigue pants and no shirt. She couldn't tell if it was the artificial light or the Binding that made his skin look so sickly pale and inhuman, but whatever it was, it was effective.

She held her breath as he passed by. Once he was safely out of sight, she slipped out from her cover and crept further down the passage, ducking behind more stone pillars along the way. As she passed an especially wide doorway leading to a cavernous space beyond, something made her pause. On the other end of the space stood a curving tunnel, disappearing into the depths of the underground structure, inviting her inside. She walked a few feet into the space, then took a deep breath of the air coming out of the deeper well. What she sensed there made her shudder. Something smelled *wrong* down there—like sewage and blood.

It smelled like the living essence of dread.

She stood still for several seconds, frozen in indecision. Uncertainty lay like an irresistible lure before her. Eventually she gave in and started down the tunnel.

I have to know.

There were no battery-powered lanterns in here, so the shadows would only grow more absolute the farther in she went. She no longer had any fear that a human, Bound or otherwise, could catch her. Compelled by some unknown instinct, she pressed onward until she met the lip of the tunnel. The right angles where the walls met each other were all that reminded her that, technically, this structure was completely man-made. Everything else about it felt more akin to a naturally occurring cave. She kept her footfalls soft as she crept through the darkness.

The scent called her deeper and deeper in, and she felt her eyes dilating as her vision came into sharp focus. The tunnel was wide, made of the same aged cement as everything else. A handful of rusted metal doors sat at odd intervals, all closed. As she walked, she felt the air grow colder, like a great chill welled outward from the bowels of the earth.

She'd been walking along the gently curving path for a full minute when she slowed to a stop. The smell had gotten abruptly worse. Bracing herself, she took another deep breath, trying to see if she could identify the smell. There were a few demons whose smell she recognized—primarily the ones more common to the Pacific Northwest. When she'd first lived on her own, camping out in the mountains, she'd *had* to learn them just to survive. It was never a good idea to set up camp in teteran territory…and an even worse one to fall asleep there.

She took a few more tentative steps, belatedly realizing that she walked through total darkness now. If her eyes had been human, she'd be lost.

At long last, she came to a rest in front of another thick metal door. The stench was strongest here. A demon lurked behind this door; she could feel it with every fiber of her being. She felt an irresistible impulse to reach out and touch the metal, and as her hand began to drift toward it, she became convinced that the creature on the other side knew she was there, too—

Just before her hand made contact, she stopped herself and pulled back. Her gaze fell to the floor just in time to see a strange mist seeping out through the crack, spreading like a thin layer of fog over the ground. *It lured me here.*

She glanced to her right, where the corridor twisted even further into the earth. There were more doors down there, rusted and waiting in the dark. Every single one held something within its keep; she could scent them all from here.

We're walking into an ambush.

With one heal-point turn, she headed back out the corridor, moving significantly faster this time. She had no idea what kind of demon was behind that door, nor what demons waited behind the others, but she knew without a shadow of a doubt that she had to get Jude *out* of here. Their plan hinged on catching Volkov off-guard; it didn't account for *this*, whatever it was.

There was nothing left to do but flee.

Once she was out of the tunnel and a few feet away, her senses returned to normal. Based on what Jude had told her about the room she was in, Logan guessed she'd be on one of the lower levels...which was for the best, since Volkov himself was likely up above. She decided her best course of action was to stick to the shadows and do her best to locate Jude as quickly as possible...then get everyone out of there.

She was nearing the end of the open corridor when she heard movement just around the corner. There was no time to slip behind a pillar, so instead she stilled, letting shadows wreath her form entirely. Another Bound rounded the corner, and passed her without so much as a glance.

She marveled at his ugliness as she paused, though on some level, it made her feel like a hypocrite. Would she look like him someday? Lumpy, covered in visible veins, and inhuman? Would there come a time when she could no longer pass as normal?

When he was gone, she let those thoughts go with him. She had to focus on the task at hand.

The rest of the way to Jude's cell was relatively uneventful. She pressed on to a slightly separated section of the structure, climbed up a short ladder to get to it, and ducked down as she passed over an upper level of concrete. After that, two stairways led her back down to a single rusted door. She could just about make out a human smell beneath the overwhelm of the old, weathered metal, and the giant padlock looped through the ancient lock on the door told her she was right. With one last look around to make sure there was no one else in sight, she took hold of the lock and pulled as hard as she could. The older metal broke first, and the entire lock mechanism yanked free of the door. She placed it quietly on the ground before pulling the handle on the now unlocked door. The metal screeched on its hinges, but it opened easily.

The cell was dark, but surprisingly warm.

"Who's there?"

The dim light from the outside was enough for Logan, and she recognized Jude's form even as she heard her speak.

"It's me. I'm getting you out."

"Logan?"

Jude was laying on the spare mattress on the floor, and as she spoke, she pulled herself into a sitting position. In here, the cement walls had all been covered in a thick plastic sheeting. Logan supposed that was easier than trying to clean out half a century of mold and decay, but it made for unsettling decor.

Jude's face was even more unsettling. She looked like a living bruise, her right eye swelled shut and angry red burns on her hands.

"Fuck." Logan crossed the room and knelt down on the floor in front of her, the plastic crinkling loudly with her movements. She reached out one hand to the side of Jude's face, taking care to be as gentle as she could, and tilted it toward the light. "Are you okay?"

"I've been better," said Jude, smiling mirthlessly. "But I'll be fine once we get home."

Logan nodded and leaned back on her heels. The faster they were, the better.

"Can you run?"

"Yes." Jude checked the laces on her sneakers, which were already caked in dried mud. "I can fight, too, if you've got a weapon for me. Not, uh, not sure I can really eira summon at the moment—"

She held out one of her burn-marked hands as explanation.

"No, don't even try to. Our objective is to flee." She hopped back up and glanced outside, searching her sight-line for Volkov and his confederates. No one yet. She motioned to Jude to follow her up. "We need to get you out of here. Can you make it to the tree line at a straight run?"

Jude's eyes went wide in the dim light.

"Shouldn't we help you fight?"

Logan shook her head. "Volkov is way farther along in his plans than we thought. He's got a small horde of demons waiting for us already." She paused a moment, her recent sense memory coming back to her, filling her head with an alien urge. "And they're *hungry*." She glanced back up the steps where she had come. She could hear footsteps in the distance, but they didn't seem to be headed this way. They had to go, now. "Follow me, and keep as quiet as you can."

Together, they made their way back toward the exit. This time, it was Jude who slipped behind pillars, while Logan checked to see if the way was clear. Finally, they made it to the stretch where Logan had first entered.

"Just keep low to the ground, head for the trees, and don't look back. Okay?"

"Okay."

She offered Jude a smile, and one quick, reassuring shoulder-squeeze for the road.

"You'll be okay. I'll be right behind you."

"Okay." Jude looked a little like a lost child, but her eyes were determined. Suddenly, a much heartier grin broke across her face, and she threw her arms around Logan, wrapping her in a hug. "I knew you would come for me."

Logan felt her eyes close as she returned the hug. It would be so easy to follow her now. So easy to run away.

"I'll always come back for you, Jude. Always." She gave her one last squeeze before letting go. "Alright. Are you ready?"

"Totally."

She did one last visual sweep, but they were still in the clear.

"Remember, don't look back. Now go!"

Jude took off like a light, flying over the damp ground with almost unbelievable speed.

Logan watched her almost all the way. She never did look back.

"Stay safe, kid."

With that, she turned toward the complex once more, and headed back inside.

Once her feet left the pavement, Jude started running. She ran as fast as she could go, years of soccer and months of training on the estate coming back to her in an instant. Rain slicked her hair down to her head, but she didn't care. She just kept running, propelled by her desire to put as much space between herself and Zilla Ulric as possible. Adrenaline took over, helping to mute the throbbing in her head and hands.

She had nearly reached the forest when she felt an unexpected change in the air. She could still hear the rain, but somehow it seemed like it was farther away. As she slowly drifted to a stop mere feet away from the tree line, her gaze fell to the ground. A strange, thick mist was wrapping around her feet. As she watched, it began to rise and expand.

"Wh-what's going on?"

She whipped around, looking for Logan to explain what was

happening—but there was nobody behind her.

"Logan?"

She strained her eyes, thinking maybe somehow Logan had simply fallen behind—but she could still make out enough of the path she had just traveled to see that it was empty. Logan had not followed her. She was alone.

The mist, if that's what it was, already obscured most of the base. Where she stood, it rose rapidly to chest level and kept going. She turned back to the tree line, but it was already hard to say for sure where it was. Still, she moved toward where it had been a moment ago, hoping maybe if she just kept going, she'd be able to see again.

Why hadn't Logan come with her? She found herself glancing over her shoulder automatically, as if the alien fog behind her might reveal an answer at any moment. She knew the answer already, of course: Logan had decided to go it alone. Against the ambush she'd said they weren't prepared for.

It took Jude a full minute to realize the rain was gone. By then, she could no longer see more than a few feet in front of her. This was the thickest fog she'd ever seen in her life. She could no longer see where she was going, or what obstacles might be in her path.

A chill ran up her spine. If anyone or anything tried to get the jump on her now, she'd have almost no way of knowing. She kept moving forward anyway, taking small steps and keeping her hands out in front of her to guide her way.

I don't think this is a natural fog.

She tried to keep that thought at bay, but once it had broken over her, there was no taking it back. It haunted her tiny, careful steps. She kept her ears focused for every possible sound, but somehow, even those seemed muffled. It was as though someone had wrapped gauze around all her senses.

When her hand alighted on the rough bark of a tree, she drew as close to it as she could, grateful for anything solid to hold onto. She was still fairly certain that she was headed in the right direction—away from the army base instead of toward it—but she had no evidence of that. The whole world had turned blank.

If I could summon the fire…maybe I could burn some of this away. But as if in answer to that thought, her damaged hands sent a spasm of pain up her arms. She wouldn't be summoning anything today.

She was just about to start walking again when she heard a noise, only a few feet away. It sounded like footsteps in the wet underbrush. She pushed her back against the tree, simultaneously looking for a place to hide and to minimize the chances that something could sneak up on her…though that was a losing battle.

The noise came again, louder this time. Her heart began to race. Trying to keep as still as possible, she slipped her hands fruitlessly in the pockets of her coat, wishing for any kind of letha aid so she could at least try to defend herself. The footsteps were getting louder and faster, like someone was running right at her—

"Hey, slow down!"

The voice was familiar, but—

"Hurry up, I saw something moving over here!"

"Why is that a *good* thing?"

Jude stepped out from behind the tree.

"Eliana?" she called, tentatively. She was pretty certain she recognized that voice, but without being able to see her face—

"Newbie!" Ian Fisher burst into view, barely three feet away from her. "I knew I saw something. Blake, get over here!"

Not a moment later, Eliana Blake materialized within the fog, too. The three of them stood in a tight circle with the tree, creating a miniature oasis in this ocean of mist.

"We found you! Well, sort of." Eliana gave her a crooked smile, then glanced uncertainly over at Fisher. "We were, uh, betting on whether or not we think this fog is natural, or, you know, a demon thing."

"I'm gonna put my money on demon thing," said Jude, casting her gaze around the impenetrable wall all around them. "Although I guess I can't say for sure." She pointed over at Fisher, afraid subtler gestures might be lost. "Can you see through it?"

"Better than you two, but that's not saying much." He peered past her—toward where she believed the abandoned base was. "I think my range is about ten or fifteen feet. Does it get any better where you came from?"

"I can't be sure," said Jude, shaking her head. "It came up kinda suddenly. I was already almost to the trees before I noticed it, and then it was everywhere."

"Well, I guess we'll just have to go see for ourselves," said Eliana, turning her standard cocky smile on the other two—though Jude noticed that it seemed turned to a lower wattage than normal. She took a step forward.

"No, we can't," said Jude, reaching out to grab Eliana's arm and pulling her up short. "Logan broke me out, and she told me to run. We have to get out of here—she said there's an ambush waiting for us."

Eliana looked at her quizzically.

"Where is Logan? Is she with you?"

"Well—not at the moment—but she said we had to go!" Jude tugged lightly at Eliana's arm, in the opposite direction from the base.

Fisher and Eliana exchanged nervous glances. Jude saw real fear there; maybe hearing that the shadow summoner believed they were out of their depth actually gave them pause. And yet, neither one of them moved.

"Marlowe's already gone ahead," said Eliana. Her voice sounded smaller than normal, too. "And we…don't actually know where your friend Alexei is. If it really is that bad, and we just leave them behind—"

"They're toast," said Fisher.

Jude took a deep breath and bit her lip. On some level, it felt like history was repeating itself—here she was, considering going against Logan's wishes at the behest of her new friends. Logan had explicitly told her to flee, that the operation had gone south before it had begun. But…Logan herself had turned back. If she hadn't followed Jude, that could only mean one thing. She'd intended for them to leave her behind; she intended to confront the Wolf alone.

But now, Jude had no way to relay that message to the rest of the team, which had already ventured into the fog. A team that included Alexei. Jude let her breath out as slow as she could.

"Well. Anyone got an extra weapon I can borrow?"

Shortly after she turned away from Jude and back toward the base, Logan noticed a distinct change in the air. An unearthly chill which seemed to swell toward her, welling up from the depths of the earth. She had nearly reached the first stone stairway when she smelled it—rot and sewage, the smell of death. The smell of the demon Volkov had chained down in that dark corridor. She looked to her left, toward where the tunnel lay.

The mist she'd seen seeping out from under the door now spilled out at an alarming rate, spreading like a thick carpet over the cement in every direction. She had a feeling it wouldn't end with the perimeter of the base, but she had no idea how to stop it. She could only hope that Jude reached the others in time, and that they all made the sensible decision to leave. So, she continued up the stairs, in search of the Wolf.

Knatt would tell me I'm being reckless, she thought. *Maybe I am. But Volkov isn't going to stop.*

This is the only way.

She pressed forward, heading southward, back toward Jude's erstwhile cell. The base was something of a labyrinth, with multiple ladders and stairways heading in different directions, some leading back to each other and some not. Eventually she found a hidden ladder she'd passed earlier, now slick with rain. She held tight as she climbed it, mindful that one wrong move would alert Volkov's men to her presence. Once up top again, she opted to leave the cement for the stretch of tall, overgrown grass that would lead her to the central base of the structure once more. The mists hadn't seemed to reach this level yet, which meant the rain still fell heavily up here. By the time she pushed her hair back from her face, it was already soaking wet.

She saw another Bound up ahead, and she dropped low to the ground, waiting for him to turn another corner. As he did so, she noticed that he'd come out of what looked like an old guard post—a small chamber, elevated slightly above the rest of the top level. She waited only a moment, listening for more footfalls, before darting right for the entrance.

The old guard post was empty of people, but a whole wall had been filled up with crates of supplies. One deep breath told her that these would be mostly casting supplies, likely the very ones they had used to summon the horde of demons waiting below.

She also discovered another ladder, this one even more rusty and hazardous than the last, leading to the roof of the post. She grabbed it with both hands, briefly testing its strength and its slipperiness, then zipped up it as fast as she could. Once she was on the small roof, she flattened herself out, snaking between empty cement cylinders that once held gun turrets. For now, they would aid her cover. Whichever parts of her that had still been dry seemed to disappear in an instant, but she willed herself to pay it no mind. She crawled to the edge of the roof and peered out.

The floor just below her was the highest full level of the structure, lined with a railed-in path along the side, but it gave way to the true center of the base: a sunken chamber, open to the elements, with a tiered depression in the middle. If she hadn't known better, she might have thought it was an open-air amphitheater with limited seating. She did know what it was, of course, because her father had told her, years ago: this was where the soldiers had kept the battery, in the unlikely event of an invasion.

She'd been here before. She could remember her father

performing his experiments, right out there. It was a memory Volkov had helped return to her, when he used the trigger word and unwittingly helped crack the cast underlying it.

She could see Volkov. He stood in the exact same place Charles had once stood.

He seemed deeply engrossed in some kind of work—probably a cast, possibly another demon summon. Inching even closer to the edge, she took a deep breath, and scented a few more Bound in the air. She couldn't quite tell how many there were; the rain interfered with her precision.

The Bound would be easier to kill than the demons below…but could she really bring herself to kill them? And *should* she?

They're pawns in Volkov's scheme. None of them would be here if it weren't for him.

But what violence might they be capable of, if I let them live?

She gave herself a tiny, invisible shake, and reminded herself of one important thing: she'd already gotten Jude out. The only immediate threat they represented was to her. It would be harder to take them out without killing them, yes. But maybe it was better to see that as a challenge. She liked challenges, didn't she?

With hardly a sound, she dropped from the guard post roof and headed toward the edge.

Toward Volkov.

Chapter Twenty
Empty Images

With Fisher leading the way, their three-person unit made slow but steady progress through the shifting mists. Jude carried a borrowed machete in a sheath on her waist, but while it gave her a small degree of comfort, she still jumped at every unexpected sound, every tiny movement just visible enough to catch her eye. She couldn't shake the feeling that they were inching their way toward inevitable doom. Logan's urgent warning to run away rang in her ears.

"I think I can hear something, up ahead," said Eliana, nodding toward the direction they believed the old army base still stood. "Sounds like fighting."

Jude turned her head slightly to strain her ears, but to no avail. All she could hear was the oppressive false silence of the fog. It was like a blanket had been draped over the world, muffling every single one of her senses.

"I can't hear it," she whispered back.

Eliana cast her a worried glance. "Maybe we should walk a little closer together," she said. Her own voice was not quite a whisper, but it was nearly low enough for one. "It's safer that way."

Fisher came to an abrupt stop and turned to face the other two, his supernaturally gifted eyes flashing.

"Did we come here to be safe, or did we come here to fight?" he asked, impatiently, crossing his arms over his chest and narrowing his eyes at them.

"I came here to fight what I can *see*," said Eliana. "Not to get eaten by invisible monsters because you're too hyped up to be cautious."

Fisher practically rolled his eyes at her.

"You're just jealous because I've got the advantage for once."

Eliana shook her head and straightened her back, coming to her full, impressive height.

"Ian, I'm not messing around here. We have to be careful in this place. If the shadow summoner thinks this is a bad idea—"

"Is *that* what this is about? The shadow summoner tells us to run, so you start shaking in your boots?" He shook his head and rolled his eyes. "Come on, this is our perfect opportunity! We can finally show everyone in the Order—and, yeah, the shadow summoner, too—what we're really made of! We can *prove* how much we're worth by going in there and kicking ass, just like we do on our raids. This is finally the big leagues, Blake. No more back of the pack guard duty with a goddamn babysitter. Not for me."

He stared hard at the ground, resentment pouring off him in waves. Jude glanced at Eliana, who met her gaze, eyes wide with understanding. Jude knew without asking that it was only Fisher, and not Eliana, who was given those lower-rung duties. This meant something to him that it didn't to her.

And with all that hunger to prove himself going unmitigated… he might just get them all killed.

"Hey, nobody's saying we need to turn back," said Jude slowly, feeling her way through this minefield with care. She knew where he was coming from, after all. "Let's just…walk a little closer together on the way, all right?"

Fisher let out a huffy sigh and rolled his eyes again, then shrugged.

"Fine. You two—just…just keep up with me, okay?"

With that, he turned on his heel and started moving again. Eliana gave Jude a quick, worried glance, then grabbed her hand and took off after him once more.

They kept their pace up to prevent too much space developing between them, which meant that Jude tripped over an unseen obstacle more than once. The third time it happened, she lost her balance entirely and went crashing to the ground, her hand ripping out of Eliana's in the process.

"Ian, stop!" she heard Eliana's panicked whisper from somewhere above her. The wind had been knocked out of her, but she could still feel the dark wetness of the ground below. "Jude, are you okay?"

Jude planted her hands in the unnervingly soft earth.

"I've been better, but I think I'll be—"

Her voice died in her throat as something dark and slimy slithered across the top of her hand before disappearing into the fog once more. With a small yelp, she leapt back to her feet.

"There's something down there," she whispered, and frantically wiped the back of her hand against her jeans. "I think a demon got out of its cage."

Not 20 feet ahead of them, a rustling sound seemed to prove her right immediately.

"Maybe more than one," said Eliana, inching closer to Jude. "Uh, hey, you know what would be great right now? A big, roaring fire to burn away all this damned mist."

Jude's heart sank right to her feet as her anxiety soared. "I told you, if I try to summon right now—"

"Yeah, I know, it's just…well, you're right. Shouldn't focus on what we don't have. You still got that knife, though, right?"

She gripped the hilt where it stuck out of the sheath.

"Hell yeah, I do."

Ian cleared his throat, glancing at the other two with obvious skepticism. He'd taken a step closer, but he was still standing significantly further from them than they were from each other.

"Maybe I should scout ahead," he said. "Come back and give you two the low-down."

Eliana looked stricken at the suggestion.

"Ian, no. That doesn't sound safe at all. Look, Captain Marlowe is stuck in the same fog that we're in, and she doesn't have your special eyes to get her there faster—"

"All the more reason for me to go on ahead and see if I can help her," answered Fisher, a smug smile spreading beneath his glasses. He offered them a quick double thumbs up as he took a step backward, further away from them and deeper into the mist. "Don't worry. I'll be back before you know it."

And with that, he disappeared before either of them could stop him. Eliana's hand shot out and grabbed Jude's, giving her a light squeeze. Jude squeezed back.

"We should keep moving," she said, forcing a confidence into her voice that she could not feel. "If we keep moving forward, then he won't get as far away from us, and we can still—"

"Come to his rescue if he needs it? Might as well try, I guess."

As they started walking again, Jude did her best not to think about large glistening slugs darting over their feet on the obscured ground below. They walked a few minutes in that strange, oppressive quiet before a thought occurred to her.

"Eliana," she said, keeping her voice low, afraid of what might hear her, "I think we've been walking too long."

Eliana cast her a look and squeezed her hand. "What do you mean?"

"I think—maybe we've gone off course. If we were really retracing my footsteps…I think we should have reached the base by now."

Eliana looked ahead of them, toward where Ian had disappeared.

"Fisher," she hissed, with urgency, "what do you see?"

If he heard her well enough to respond, he never got the chance. Right at that moment, a terrible, unearthly cry rent the air. It sounded somewhere between the screech of an animal and the screeching of metal ripping apart.

The two of them froze where they stood, momentarily too terrified to move. Jude tried her best not to think about all the deep dark holes she'd passed on her way out of the base. She failed.

Another cry ripped through the air, but this one seemed to unfreeze them. They moved forward as one. Eliana and Jude dropped their hand-hold simultaneously, each of them reaching for their respective weapon. For a few glorious moments, Jude felt like they were moving inexorably forth together, ready to take on whatever the mists had to offer.

Then everything went to hell all at once.

The first one went down quick. She materialized right behind him and sucker-punched him in the back of the head. He wobbled for a moment, but then he went down without another sound. She dragged his body back several feet, took a deep breath, and kept going.

Logan knew they wouldn't all be that easy, and she wasn't confident she knew how many there were. But she also knew they tended to be a little slow, perhaps unaccustomed to their new-found bulk, and she hoped she'd be able to use that to her advantage.

She gathered the shadows before edging along the catwalk, hurrying away from him. She couldn't be sure whether the others had heard the thump of his body as it fell—not until she rounded the corner—

She saw the outline of another right as she reached it, and fell back immediately, disappearing into the dark. He didn't seem to have heard anything. She took a deep breath, then reached out to the metal railing on her left, and gave it the quietest tap.

That he did hear. She watched his outline perk up as he turned toward the source of the noise. As he lumbered roughly in her direction, she flattened against the wall and waited for him to pass. He was nearly level with her when he paused to look around in all directions. She kept her breathing quiet. After one long moment, he took a few more steps forward. She waited just long enough, then slipped out behind him and used the outer railing to propel herself upward, landing on his back and catching him immediately in a sleeper hold. He nearly managed to cry out—but his voice lost all power as she cut off his oxygen, and soon he collapsed to his knees. She caught him just before his body fell forward, then lowered him slowly to the ground.

Then she continued onward.

She slowed as she reached the corner. She had to assume that Volkov's ability to call the shadows worked just the way hers did—that, though he could make himself invisible, he had no special ability to see through her summon. Until now, she'd never had a real opportunity to test that assumption. So, with great care, she stepped around the corner, onto the section of catwalk that directly overlooked the scene.

Volkov still stood inside the sunken circle, pouring over a large, leather-bound book on a reading stand and chanting in a low voice. She clocked at least two Bound on the far side of the enclosure, as well as a familiar figure a little behind Volkov—one with long, dark hair and pale skin.

Zilla Ulric. Logan felt herself snarl. She repressed the urge to touch the scar across her brow, from where Ulric had cut her at the Order's headquarters. She wouldn't say she was exactly fond of her.

As if he were reading her mind, Volkov turned to address Ulric.

"Zilla." His tone sounded sweet, even from this far away. "Would you perhaps go and fetch our guest? I think she might like to see this part."

"Of course."

Ulric made a heal-point turn and marched away from him, disappearing underneath the catwalk Logan had just traversed.

Volkov took a moment to watch her go, and as he turned back to his work, his gaze drifted slightly upward. Logan remained as still as she could, declining even to breathe, as his gaze crested over her. After what felt like a very long moment, his eyes returned to the ground, and he turned back to the reading stand. Logan slowly let the air out of her lungs.

A few quick seconds later, Logan reached the ladder. She squatted down next to it and reached out with one hand to test it—both its strength and its level of slickness. It was, indeed, exceptionally slick—but it seemed about as sturdy as the last ladder, which suggested it should, at least, be able to hold her weight.

Even if it didn't, she supposed it didn't matter. She had to get down there one way or another. She only hoped to do so with some manner of stealth, instead of announcing herself with a crash. So, she grabbed the first rung and lowered herself down, as slowly and quietly as she could.

To her relief, she made it all the way to the lower level without incident. Then, as soon as her feet landed softly on the wet ground below, she froze—a Bound stood guard not three feet away. She held her breath, waiting to see if he would notice her. One second passed, then two.

He remained as he was, staring straight ahead like a marble statue—a strangely veiny marble statue. Logan let her breath out in a slow, steady stream before turning around to take in the scene again.

Volkov had returned to his chanting, apparently guided by the book on the stand. It was angled away from her at the moment, so she couldn't see inside. He had begun combining catalysts in a small stone bowl as he read.

Apart from the one she'd already taken out and the marble man standing only feet away from her, there were two other Bound in sight—though she had to acknowledge there could be more she couldn't see. If Volkov had already summoned a whole horde of demons down below, there was no way of knowing how many Bound he had already recruited, as well.

Still, three isn't bad. I can deal with three.

She turned to the statue man and made a few calculations. There was no way of bringing all this to a stop without calling attention to herself, so she might as well begin with the easiest target...or, rather, the nearest.

The setup was simple enough. After all, she'd essentially just done a practice run. So, she lined herself up carefully behind him, did a quick check of her weapons, and let out a silent prayer that this wasn't exactly the wrong thing to do. And then she sucker-punched the marble man in the back of the head.

Several things happened at once. The punched Bound man let out an impressively strangled cry as he stumbled forward, the Wolf's chanting and muttering ceased, and three sets of eyes narrowed in on her location, alerted by the sound of the cry as well as the loud snap of her fist colliding with a bare skull.

Make that four pairs of eyes, she corrected silently as she took in the scene ahead of her. A Bound man not included in her original count stepped out of a door on the other side of the small enclosure she now stood in.

In the half second it took her to pull back her foot and let fly a swift kick, she re-assessed the field. From one perspective, it certainly looked like a stage, the perfect place to perform a letha ritual, with its high back wall, and the sunken, circular section in the center, with perfect concentric rows of steps leading outward, like rows of seats. But taken from another perspective—say, the perspective of one staring down the inevitability of battle—it looked more like an arena.

The Bound man wobbled, but he didn't fall down. Instead he turned on her with a growl, while in the background, three other hulking figures began to circle. She ignored them, and used her momentum to swing herself into an immediate second kick, which brought him down. Still, she got the uncomfortable impression that he wasn't quite unconscious…

But there was no time to think about it now. She jumped backwards, creating distance while keeping an eye on the rest of her opponents. To her chagrin, their gazes followed her—falteringly, but they did it. Her concealment was broken, predictably sapped by the combination of sound and her own fractured concentration.

She heard Volkov's hiss at 20 yards.

"*Shadow summoner.*" He sounded pleased, almost delighted. Briefly, his gaze locked with hers before she had to turn away.

The next Bound was already upon her. His bulky arm flew through the air, but she dropped beneath it and spun out behind him. From there, she let fly a spinning kick to his rib cage before dancing out of his reach again.

Kicks to the ribs weren't gonna do it, though. In this case, it didn't even slow him down. He rebounded immediately, faster than she expected, and came at her with full force. His fist connected with her abdomen before she could stop it. The pain that accompanied it was shocking in intensity, but she didn't let that slow her down. She moved with the blow, letting its momentum flow through her, before whipping around and planting her feet, and throwing up an arm to block his next attack.

On the heals of pain came a burst of anger, accompanied by the sound of her father's voice.

Be a good girl, Henrietta.

It was his voice that begged the worst of her. His voice, in the back of her mind, reminding her that the simplest solution to this was still available. Life was a singular thing, and the power to extract it lay within her.

Instead, she played the match. Let her fists fly with furious speed, unleashing a brief but intense torrent of blows aimed at her slightly slower opponent's torso, stealing the wind from his sails instead of the breath from his lungs.

He wheeled back, slipping away from her just before she could deliver her intended final blow. Right at that moment, the third Bound man appeared directly in front of her without warning. His oversized right hook landed squarely in the middle of her face, and she went sprawling backwards.

A part of her brain recognized, logically, that her nose had sprung a leak of some sickly thick fluid with a coppery tang. But her conscious self barely had the space to acknowledge it. Instead, her focus went to turning the fall into a roll, rolling into a crouch, and launching up from the crouch, right at the source of her trouble.

She rained down a lightning fast series of blows, absorbed another from him, and whirled herself around into a flying kick. As he reeled from that, she turned back on her other opponent and landed another kick across his jaw, finally sending him down to his knees. She had just swung her knee up into his face and was still watching him crumble when she felt the other grab her from behind and swing her around, releasing her to crash into the cement wall behind them.

The fourth Bound was already approaching, but she couldn't stop to think about that. This time, she used the wall at her back as her launching pad, springing with inhuman force at the Bound who had thrown her.

To her surprise, he opted not to engage and instead stepped swiftly to the side, letting her stumble several paces past him, arms swinging wildly at her missed target.

As her left foot made contact with the ground, she felt something in the air change. An unaccountable red glow came over everything in sight—and she could feel the Choronzon Key blaze white-hot at her back.

What the fuck?

The glow was coming from the ground. She looked down at her feet and found a pattern stretching out beneath her, emitting an unnatural red light. It looked like—

"The Choronzon Key," came Volkov's booming, triumphant voice. Logan felt a terrible understanding beginning to slide into place. "Tell me, Henrietta…would you say I understand you now?"

Even if she'd wanted to reply, she wouldn't have had time. The Bound she'd rushed past was at her heels. She ducked just in time and unhooked a small throwing knife from her ankle as she tumbled away. She couldn't throw it at anything vital, but perhaps she could injure him enough to slow him down.

Her movement stopped just long enough for her to aim, then her knife went flying, landing squarely in his forearm, near the wrist. The shock of it was enough to freeze him in place, if only for a moment—but a moment was all she needed. She rushed toward him and, before he could think to stop her, grabbed his hand and pushed the blade down, twisting it along the way. While he let out a cry of pain, she ripped the knife back out and gripped the weakened wrist between her two arms before giving a powerful, fearful twist. She felt an ugly satisfaction when she heard the bones snap.

Cradling his broken arm, he fell away from her, backing up over the red glow on the ground. She watched him stumble onto unmarked ground, and she found herself transfixed. She had a sneaking suspicion that she knew exactly what would happen next.

Still, she had to know for sure.

She walked forward, toward her now-prone opponent, traveling over the markings beneath her feet. She stepped right up to the edge, and she reached out a hand. It met with something invisible but completely solid, and apparently immovable. Though the Bound had crossed the threshold with ease, she pressed against it with all her might and found it would not yield. There was a wall there, all right, and it seemed to travel all along the length of the Choronzon Key that had been painted on the ground.

And she was trapped inside it, with no way out.

Almost as soon as Jude had steadied the battle knife in her hand, she felt something begin to crawl up her leg—in fact, she felt multiple somethings sliming their way up over her feet, onto the hems of her pants, sliding higher—

Trying to keep her head cool enough to avoid cutting away her own pants, Jude looked down and took a big swipe at the highest creepy crawly. Her aim was true, and her knife cut cleanly through an obscenely large slug, just like the one she'd seen crawl across her hand—only her knife met no resistance. It slipped right through the creature—and as it did, the creature vanished from sight. Like it had never been.

"Eliana—I just—I think I just hallucinated a demon."

"You just *what*?"

"I just had a pretty full-blown hallucination of a giant slug crawling up my pants." As another bug demon, which she was reasonably sure was also not real, slimed up over her knee, she swiped at it with confidence. It disappeared, too. "Yeah, I'm gonna go out on a limb and say that either there's a demon nearby who can make us see shit, or the fucking mist has driven me insane."

She could still see just far enough to observe Eliana's careful, calculating gaze as it fell on her.

"Are you sure?"

"Yeah, I'm sure." She looked ahead, toward where they had last seen Ian before he disappeared. "If I'm hallucinating...you and Fisher might be, too."

With a grimace, Eliana spun away from her and took a few steps forward.

"Fisher, will you get back here? Our eyes are playing tricks on us, man."

Though her voice rang out with clarity, he did not respond.

"Fisher? Ian!"

Still nothing. They were alone. Jude felt her apprehension slowly shift into dread.

"This isn't good," she muttered, more to herself than to Eliana. She felt another slug on her knee, but instead of swiping at it, she simply gave a hard kick at nothing. Once again, it disappeared, slipping away into nothingness.

She'd expected to hear that awful cry again, but the next sound they heard was different. It was a kind of slithering sound, like a snake moving rapidly through tall grass. Eliana set her jaw as she raised her gun, steadying it with her other hand before taking another step. Jude fell in line just behind, re-gripping the knife. For the first time in her life, she wished she had a gun. Stuck without access to her fire summoning power and holding nothing but a knife…she couldn't help but think she'd feel less vulnerable if she had the same firepower Eliana did.

The slithering sound gathered speed, like it was heading right toward them. Just as it reached a fever pitch, something broke through the mist—something massive and misshapen, rising upward, like a giant snake rising to strike. While Jude gripped her knife harder than ever, Eliana didn't hesitate. She fired two quick rounds, right at the snake-creature's gaping maw. It froze in place and hovered a moment—then it melted into vapor before their eyes.

"What the fuck was that?" The naked uncertainty in Eliana's voice gave away her calm exterior.

"I think—I think it's the same thing as the slugs crawling up my legs. It's all an illusion."

"An illusion caused by *what*?" She sounded panicked now.

"Some kind of demon? One of the ones Logan said they have locked up here."

"Did she say…how *many* demons?"

Jude swallowed, hard.

"She just said a lot."

Eliana lowered her gun for a moment, glancing at it uncertainly. "But that thing I just shot…it wasn't even a demon, right? We're out here just…fighting hallucinations."

Jude heard the slithering sound start up again, even closer this time.

"And we've got another one incoming," she said, gripping the knife and raising it up in defensive posture. Eliana pulled her gun back up, too.

Jude barely had time to register that the sound seemed like it was coming from more than one place before two giant snakes burst through the mist, coming right for them. Eliana shot the one on their right directly through the middle, but she couldn't shoot them both at once. Jude's feet seemed to move of their own accord, compelled by training and impulse, and she found herself meeting the demon with her knife outstretched. She plunged it directly into the snake's eye—only to watch its form immediately dissipate, vanishing into the vapor from which it had come.

Jude blinked, taking in what she'd just seen.

"It's the same as the fog," she said, aware that she sounded somewhat dazed and dreamy as she tried to bring her idea into words.

"What?"

"The illusions—it's like they're forming out of the fog. It's all the same thing."

Eliana blinked at her.

"You mean…the mist isn't real either?"

Jude took a deep breath.

"I don't think so."

Eliana regripped her weapon and closed the distance between them again.

"Well, isn't that just wonderful?"

The slithering started up again, and they turned to face it. Again, two demons came out of the mist, and again, they cut them down. Jude exhaled a strangled sigh of relief as her knife cut cleanly through demon flesh, which promptly melted into mist.

They barely had a moment to catch their breath before three new illusions appeared before them. And as soon as these were vanquished, new forms took their place. The pace of battle had become relentless, and both Jude and Eliana rose to meet it. Jude quickly realized that she didn't need to aim for a traditional killing blow to turn the illusions back into fog, so she began swinging wildly, trying to take out as many as she could reach with a single thrust. Eliana paused only when her clip emptied, and she replaced it so fast Jude could barely register the movement.

Eventually, Jude lost count of how many illusions they'd taken out. She felt her arms growing weary, felt the knife seem to get heavier and heavier with each new movement. She wondered how many bullets Eliana was carrying.

At long last, the flow seemed to slow down. And then, quite suddenly, it stopped. Jude took an extra swing, automatically moving on the assumption that more were coming, and nearly toppled over as she hit empty air.

In the silence that followed, Jude and Eliana automatically moved back closer together, their backs to each other so they could each keep an eye on one side. Jude heard the pounding of her heart, the heaving of her breath—and Eliana's similarly heavy breathing just behind her.

They waited. And waited. After what might have been two minutes or an hour, Jude heard Eliana clear her throat.

"Do you think that's it?"

"I don't know."

"Should we start moving toward the base?"

"I don't know. Maybe."

But before either of them could move, they heard another sound, coming from Eliana's side. Jude whipped around, knife held aloft. For a moment, Jude thought it sounded different from the last wave, but the difference was so small, she forgot the thought nearly as soon as it had come.

Then one lone giant snake burst through the mist, and Eliana fired a single round, right at the center. The beast froze in place.

As its image began to melt into mist, Jude felt a growing wrongness in the core of her being. This time, the snake didn't disappear—it changed.

It took Jude a moment to understand what she was looking at. Ian Fisher stood before them, staring in disbelief at the growing dark spot in the middle of his torso.

Beside her, Eliana dropped her gun and rushed forward.

"Fisher—Fisher—"

"Hey—Blake—"

Jude stood transfixed, lost in numb incomprehension. She watched Ian drop to his knees as Eliana reached him, watched Eliana catch him in her arms. She laid him carefully on the ground and placed both her hands on his wound, applying pressure like they were probably trained to do at the Order.

Jude's feet stumbled forward, and she found herself picking up the gun Eliana had dropped. A voice was telling her that there might be more of them, that she needed to keep her guard up.

Another voice told her that Fisher was dying.

But he couldn't be. It had happened too fast—she hadn't really seen what she saw, or maybe it was another illusion—

"Ian, stay with me." Eliana's voice sounded different, not panicky like it was right after the first false demon had come. Now she sounded far too calm. Like she was determined not to see.

Ian's voice sounded thick, like a syrup that had cooked too long.

"Blake...hey, Blake...do you think...did I made the right choice? When I picked...my eyes?"

"Yeah, Fisher, you did." She sounded like an alien, like someone Jude had never met. "Keep—keep talking—just, just keep talking—"

Jude could see her hands over the wound, already covered in blood. There was just so much of it. She had never realized how dark blood could look. Fisher's whole jacket was dark with it now, too.

"Did I make...an impression?"

Jude watched his hand rise an inch before it dropped back down.

"Ian?"

The feeling of wrongness in her core seemed to deepen, seeping out of its hole and into the rest of her body. Why did Ian's body look so *off*?

His chest had stopped moving.

"Ian? Fisher, man, come back—wake up. Fisher, wake up." Eliana's hands remained firmly in place, but the rest of her seemed to vibrate. "Fisher, wake up. Jude, I can't move—can you—can you wake him up?"

Jude blinked. She stared hard at the back of Eliana's head. Eliana's eyes seemed glued to Ian's very still face, unable to look away. And yet…

Slowly, Jude closed the distance and dropped down on Ian's other side. She put the gun down, right by her feet. Slowly, she let her eyes come to rest on his still face, his unmoving lips—

"What do you want me to do?" she asked, her voice barely more than a whisper.

"Just—just wake him up, okay?"

Jude blinked again, stealing herself. She reached out and touched his shoulder. Grabbing a tenuous hold of it, she gave a weak shake. His head rolled limply to the side, and she recoiled immediately. The feeling of wrongness now screamed from every part of her body. How did they get here? Why couldn't they just go back? If she could rewind the clock, only a few minutes—

The sound of Eliana's gun firing rang through her mind and made her flinch.

"I can't, Eliana," she whispered. The words didn't want to form, but she made them anyway. "He's gone."

Chapter Twenty-One
An Unknown Quantity

Logan stood on top of the painted Choronzon Key, one hand stretched out against an invisible wall she could not penetrate. The false Key glowed, but the one on her back burned white-hot. Somehow, she knew it was the conjunction of the two that held her captive.

As if to confirm it for her, out of the corner of her eye she saw the Bound man she hadn't faced yet, grinning wildly at her, reach across the threshold with no problem. Almost immediately, he headed toward her—only on the other side of the barrier, where she couldn't touch him.

She could see his plan without asking, too: he could hit her through the barrier, and she would be unable to return the attack. So, out of necessity, she stepped back from border, out of his reach, drawing herself deeper into the trap. The Bound stopped before his feet crossed over. His grin never slipped.

"So," said a voice that sounded far too pleased, "*this* is what it takes to get you alone."

Logan planted her feet, still glaring at the Bound she couldn't touch.

"Not really. Most people just buy me a drink." As she turned, she did her best to take in as much of her surroundings as she could. She didn't need any more surprises now. "It's only murderers who have to set a trap."

Their eyes met, and Volkov gave her an easy, self-assured smile. His hands were folded neatly in front of him, as if he were about to conduct a simple business transaction. He wore a crisp black suit and leather shoes. Were it not for the white-blond hair slicked back with rain and sweat and the overpowering smell of blood radiating off him, he might have been a stock broker.

Logan found herself flexing her left hand, yet again resisting the urge to end the fight before it began. She could still taste her own blood in her mouth, though her nose had stopped dripping. Zilla Ulric had not yet returned, but that was far from Logan's only concern. A series of old, rusted metal doors had been set into the curved wall behind Volkov, and based on the sounds emanating from their concealed interiors, she had a pretty good guess what might be inside.

Volkov took a step across the dais, moving closer to her.

"Such loyalty," he said approvingly, as if he were appraising an employee. "You came for the girl, yes? I thought you might. After all, you are her *mentor*. If anything were to happen to her…it would be your fault, wouldn't it?"

In his mouth, *mentor* sounded like an insult.

"Nothing's going to happen to her," said Logan, with a shrug. "If I were you, I'd be much more concerned about myself right now."

He might have been a teacher, about to give a lecture. His easy smile remained.

"Not to worry. Miss Li has already served her purpose."

"And that would be?"

"She brought you to me, of course."

It was obvious, and it was exactly what she'd expected him to say. And yet she still couldn't see the rest of his plan. *Why* did he want her here? And what magic had he done that now held her trapped in an invisible cage?

"I'd like to tell you a story, if I may." His smile fell short of a leer.

She shrugged. What other choice was there?

"Yeah, fine. Tell me a story." She kept her feet planted, ready to draw her weapon at a moment's notice.

"Did Charles ever tell you his theory that different magics have come and gone from the world, some more powerful than others?"

"He has."

"Good. Well, as you may have guessed, he is far from the only Order associate who has ever held such a belief. My father was another. And my father was obsessed with one long-lost form of magic in particular."

"Let me guess. The Choronzon."

Volkov's smile widened.

"Why, yes. Very good, Henrietta." He was lucky she was still too far away from him to throw a punch. "Little is known about the Choronzon, of course. Many Order scholars have studied them, and most have come to their own conclusions with very little evidence. My father happened to believe that the Choronzon knew the secret to eternal life—and that if he could only learn what they once knew, he could make himself immortal. As you might imagine, he became a man obsessed."

Logan felt her eyebrow raise of its own accord.

"He made most of his money doing research for the Order, and his position earned him certain privileges—such as access to the Order's private library. Very few outside the Order ever get to see it, and he had high hopes that it would give him an advantage in his quest to revive the Choronzon magic."

"Did it?"

"No. As it turns out, even the Order has almost no knowledge of them. Or, if they do, it's hidden somewhere even deeper than that. He learned almost nothing from them. Not that that stopped him, or even slowed him down. You see, what I eventually realized about my father is that…he was a fool."

Logan felt a jolt of recognition, of unwilling empathy. She knew that tone, knew that feeling.

"What did your father do to you?"

"Same thing as anyone, I suppose," said Volkov, almost wistfully. At long last, his smile slipped. He turned away from her and cast his gaze at the wall of closed metal doors behind him. His hands contracted into fists. "He turned me into a monster."

Volkov's pronouncement was followed by several long moments of silence as Logan waited for him to continue. After a moment, she became impatient.

"So, is that, like, he *metaphorically* made you a monster, or…?"

Volkov cast her a disdainful look over his shoulder.

"No, I mean it quite literally. You see, after years of study, my father finally found exactly one text within the Order's library that made mention of the Choronzon. It said that though the Choronzon had begun as an order of some power, they made their greatest achievements when they found a way to connect to a demon—known only as the Choronzon demon, though it is unclear whether that is truly the demon's name, or simply its designation due to its association with the Choronzon and their magic. Of course, my father became convinced that this *must* be the key to finding the answers he sought. His focus, accordingly, shifted to searching for this demon, and for any possible way to contact it."

Logan had the terrible feeling that she knew exactly where this story was headed.

"He wanted to make a deal with the demon," she said. "The same deal he believed the Choronzon had made."

"The very same," Volkov, still turned away from her, nodded. "He began the way any researcher for the Order of Shadows would do: he made a list of every demon known to be intelligent enough to communicate with men, and from there, a list of those believed to strike deals from time to time. It wasn't a very long list." Slowly, Volkov turned to face her once more, and she watched a brief change come and go on his face, so fast that human eyes might not have caught it. It looked like veins, gone as fast as they had come. "He never did get what he wanted, of course. But he managed to get something else."

Her suspicion solidified into certainty.

"He had you Bound," she said. "That's how he turned you into a monster, isn't it?"

"He got my mother killed first," said Volkov, a bitter edge to his voice. She saw his fingers flex and clench again. Behind her, she could hear the other Bound man beginning to move around the edge of the circle. "And then, yes, he Bound me with the heart of the demon. He didn't even know its name, but still he used it to Bind me. I was twelve."

A small shock went through her.

"I've never heard of anyone being Bound so young."

"Indeed. Even the Order considers it inhumane to Bind anyone who cannot consent. Though I imagine that might change if they ever came to believe they could gain something from it. As it stands, they don't seem to think the pre-pubescent have much to offer them, and I'm inclined to agree." He began to pace, tracing a path along the edge of the Choronzon Key beneath them. Logan took the opportunity to move as well, matching her stride to his so that they circled each other. As she walked, she noted that the nameless final Bound had come to stand by the first metal door in the wall, looking as though he were awaiting his next order.

Volkov continued his speech.

"The effect the Binding had on me was…terrible and savage. I began to feel…such rage. Uncontrollable rage. And for the first time in my young life, I had the power to do something about it." He flexed again, and this time, a tangle of black veins spread over his hands before disappearing up his jacket sleeve. "I began to lash out violently over the slightest upsets, to give in to my darkest desires…and my father only encouraged it. As I said, he was a fool."

Logan took in a short breath.

"You killed him. Didn't you?"

Volkov nodded, a wistful smile on his face. "The day I realized his life's mission had been a failure from the beginning.

You could argue I put him out of his misery."

"I wouldn't, though." She felt cold, but it had nothing to do with the rain.

He didn't seem to hear her.

"He never understood the power he sought, you see. But by virtue of the horrors he visited upon me, I did understand." As she watched, he ceased his pacing and dropped into a squat, hands spread wide as he placed them on the glowing Choronzon Key beneath them, which seemed to hum expectantly in return. "Where he lacked, I will prevail. Where he failed, I will triumph." He glanced up at her, and his features seemed to soften. The resulting expression looked alien on his face.

"Tell me, Henrietta…if I offered you the world, would you take it?"

Logan felt her right eyebrow threaten to disappear into her hairline. This wasn't exactly how she'd expected things to go.

"What do you mean?"

"Exactly what I said." In the faint red glow of the false Choronzon Key, his face twisted darkly. "Letha is limited and weak. I've already taken from it what I can, and for you, it offers nothing. Eira is far stronger, of course, but it takes a lifetime to master, and even then, only if you're quite lucky. A single catastrophe could easily wipe its few true practitioners from the face the of the earth." He cracked his face open wide in a rictus grin. "But you and I could be so much more than any of that. You and I could bring back the true power of the Choronzon. And in so doing, we would become the two most powerful people in the world."

His gaze was expectant. She could read the naked desire there, the reckless hope. How badly he'd misjudged her.

"Right." Her gaze bounced between him and the Bound as she sized up her chances and wondered how long she could keep him talking. "So, in the course of your research…did you ever find out what the Choronzon could actually do?"

Volkov only smiled, pressing his hand harder into the false Key, letting its off-putting red illumination flood the planes of his face.

"The easier question is what they couldn't do. But you already *feel* that to be true, don't you?"

The urge to reach back and touch the Key rose within her, but she resisted it. Her mind replayed for her the vision she'd had only a few days ago: standing under the rain, staring Volkov down, and the dark desire to rip the world apart. Did the desire originate with the Key itself? Was the Choronzon Key capable of *wanting*? And did that mean that it trapped her here, now, because it wanted to?

A part of her wanted to say yes to Volkov—not because she wanted the undefined power he offered, but because she wanted to *know* what that power actually was. After all this time, the Key had still revealed so little of itself to her.

But she knew that Volkov's way of getting those answers could not be her way. She shook her head.

"You can't tell me what it is because you don't know." Her fingers brushed a knife hidden in her sleeve. "And unfortunately for you, I'm not much of a gambler."

Volkov let out a heavy sigh, pitching his weight forward onto his outstretched hand as he prepared to stand. When he came to his full height, he looked worn.

"On some level, you must understand that you don't really have a choice." He took a step toward her, closing some of the distance, but his expression remained friendly. "You *need* this power, as much as I do." He waved his hand in the general direction from which she had come. "They will come after you. You must know that."

Logan relaxed her eyebrow so she could raise it again.

"Who, now?"

"The Order, of course." He shook his head, as if in disbelief. "When they find out the truth about you, they will come for you. The power you have is already a threat to them, and they don't know the half of it. But they will. One way or another, they'll find out. And they will hunt you down. They will *erase* you, and then they'll erase the very memory of you." He shook his head, his expression regretful. "To the man, every one of them will do what it takes to maintain their power. And it will be so easy to convince themselves that what it takes…is getting rid of you."

The glow flared up again, like it was illustrating his point. She didn't disagree with him. The Order's primary goal had always been the maintenance and increase of their own power.

But they were a known quantity. As long as they operated in their favored shadows, there was a limit to what they could really do. For now, in effect, all they did was train a few half-formed legal adults how to kill demons and send them out into the world. Maybe there were worse things.

"I know they will," she said, and watched his face light up with that vacant alien smile. She had to wonder to what extent he believed his own rhetoric. "But my answer is still no."

His face crumpled, brow furrowing.

"I'm offering you the power to neutralize any threat the Order could ever pose to you."

"Yes. And I'm rejecting your offer."

"But why?"

"The price is too high."

"But you would be in control. I would be your only equal; no one else could touch us. We could rule the world."

"Pass."

"Pass?"

"Pass. Thanks, but no thanks. I've got all the power I can stand."

He shook his head, his expression one of pure disappointment.

"I don't want to hurt you, Henrietta. But I will, if I have to."

Logan smiled, the ecstasy of clarity spreading through her body.

"Hm. You sound just like my father."

Volkov drew his knife first, but Logan's was ready in her hand within a second. He gave a swift nod to the Bound man beyond the circle—the one standing right next to the first heavy cell door. The Bound unlocked the giant padlock holding it in place and swung the door open wide, and its old rusty hinges let out a frightful scream.

From within the darkened chamber, a dark growl rumbled out to meet them.

The fight had begun at last.

Jude didn't know how long they had sat in silence. They sat still but alert, Ian's body square between them. She had picked up the gun again, though she knew she couldn't use it. It felt too dangerous to use, too unpredictable—but it also felt too dangerous to leave on the ground. She held it loosely in her left hand, while her right remained gripped on the knife in its holster. Her eyes stayed trained on the ground. She was too afraid to look at him.

Between them, the silence stretched and stretched. She had lost all sense of time; they might have been stranded in the mist forever, or they might have never been there at all. If it weren't for Fisher, of course.

He's probably getting cold. He's probably cold already. We should get him inside somewhere—it's not right to leave him out here like this. But—but where do we take him?

She couldn't look around for an answer. Her eyes might fall to the wrong place. What was she thinking, anyway? It was only a matter of time before the next threat revealed itself.

"We have to do something," said Eliana, shattering the glass. Her voice sounded far away.

"I know," said Jude. She didn't know what she sounded like.

Eliana said nothing to that. Silence returned again.

After an indeterminate amount of time, she heard a new sound. It sounded like shuffling, or footsteps. Her right hand still gripped the knife, but she didn't move. Her eyes were on the gun, lying useless in her limp hand.

The footsteps came up behind her, then traveled around. She watched as human feet, clad in very old boots, came into view.

"Jude?"

Hugh Knatt knelt down in front of her. At long last, she let go of the gun. She felt, more than saw, his hand reach out and come to rest on her shoulder.

"Are you alright?"

Jude blinked. "I'm not injured." She glanced in the direction of the body, but her eyes stopped as soon as they saw his still, pale hand. "We don't know what to do."

His hand gave her shoulder a squeeze as his gaze looked just past her.

"Miss Blake, are you hurt?"

Jude heard her clear her throat.

"Sound of mind and body, sir. What are my orders?"

Jude looked up in time to see the heartbreak and worry mingling on his face. His voice was gentle.

"Can either of you tell me what happened here?"

Eliana cleared her throat again. Jude knew without looking that her posture had gone straighter than a board.

"It's my fault, sir. We were fighting illusions in the fog, and I mistook Fisher for one, sir."

"He *looked* like one, Knatt," said Jude, sounding as small as she felt. "It would have been me if she weren't faster."

"I fired the shot, sir." Her voice still had that strange, calm quality to it. "I fired the shot."

Jude watched Knatt's face as he considered this. He moved his hand through the mist, momentarily looking as if he were trying to catch a fistful of it. After a moment, comprehension broke.

"It wasn't your fault, Miss Blake," he said, injecting his voice with as much authority and certainty as Jude had ever heard. "You were fighting a tarnoch demon. Incredibly rare, they are small in stature but quite difficult to kill owing to their ability to create complex illusions for up to one square mile around their physical location."

Jude nodded. It all made a terrible kind of sense.

"The Order has dealt with them before," Knatt continued, his tone gentle but firm. "They have a record of them. Mr. Fisher is not the first Adept to meet this fate."

Jude glanced over at Eliana, who looked like she'd been lost at sea. She cracked a strange smile that somehow looked like it might be the beginning of a cry.

"Damn. He'd be so pissed that he wasn't the first."

The words hit her like a punch in the gut. She felt something inside her crumple and break into a million pieces.

"The tarnoch would be in a dark hole or cave somewhere," said Knatt, taking on his authoritative but comforting tone again. "Can you both walk?"

"Yeah."

"Yes, sir."

"Good. The tarnoch needs to be eliminated as quickly as possible." With one last squeeze of Jude's shoulder, he stood up again, gazing toward the area where Jude believed the base lay. "Where are the others?"

"Captain Marlowe went on ahead," said Eliana, also coming to stand. Just as Jude suspected, her posture was impeccable, even as she clambered to her feet. "We lost her in the fog. Same for Mr. Marin."

Alexei. Jude felt a little shock go through her as she thought of him, though she knew it made perfect sense for him to be there, too. She couldn't help but wonder if someone else had mistaken him for a demon, too...

"And Logan?"

"Haven't seen her since I arrived."

"I have," said Jude. She was still sitting on the ground. Her eyes still rested on the hand that would not move. "She warned us to leave. Said there were too many demons for us to handle. But the others had already gone ahead, so we didn't want to leave them."

Knatt nodded, considering this.

"Do you think the two of you could make it back to the van?"

Jude didn't need to look at Eliana's face to know what it would look like.

"I can't leave my Captain behind, sir. If you're going in, I'm going with you."

Knatt let out a heavy sigh.

"I suppose you'll both be safer with me than on your own."

"No," said Jude, but the word barely seemed to make it past her lips. "I mean…we can't just…leave him here. All alone."

The other two were quiet for a moment. It was almost like a return to that awful silence from before, when she and Eliana were alone, and without purpose.

Knatt knelt in front of her again. She began to pity his knees.

"You've done all you can for him, Jude." He was so gentle, it made her want to scream. "It isn't safe to stay here. You're a waiting target."

"Maybe we could…move him."

"He's too heavy, and there isn't enough time. Come, now. I need you to stand with me." When she still didn't move, he let out a soft sigh. "I promise we'll come back for him, as soon as it is *safe* to do so."

Jude nodded. She knew she was being ridiculous. It was just…a part of her refused to believe he was dead, even with all the evidence staring her in the face. Even though she'd said it herself.

"Okay," she whispered, and she let Knatt take her gently by the elbow and guide her to standing.

With one last worried glance at her, Knatt set his jaw and took a step forward, toward the base.

"Off we go, then."

Jude kept her eyes trained to the front. She figured it was better she not witness the moment that Fisher disappeared into the mist behind them.

Logan took a deep breath and made some quick mental calculations. The first layer of her problem was the unknown magic of the Choronzon Key painted beneath her feet, which held her trapped by the unknown magic of the Choronzon Key permanently adhered to her back. One magic called to the other, and she could not disentangle herself from either. They had become one, as though they shared a single soul between them.

The second layer of her problem was the demon slowly emerging from its own cage, which the Bound had been kind enough to open. She watched as two long, multi-pronged antlers protruded out of the dark hole first, announcing the massive size of the beast that owned them.

The third layer of her problem was Volkov. Now she knew for sure that he was Bound—but she did not know how strong he was in his Bound state. Had she fought him that way before, but been unable to tell because the markers of it were hidden under a mask? Or had she never actually experienced his peak form?

She didn't have much time to ponder the question. The first demon had emerged from its cage.

Its two antlers stood out from an elongated skull of a head, which sat atop a hunchbacked but surprisingly human-shaped body, though Logan had never seen a human being quite so large. It stretched to its full height as it exited the cage, before throwing back its unearthly head and letting loose a full-throated roar. It stretched out hands that were little more than articulated talons, and then it settled its empty-socket eyes on Logan.

A small part of her shivered in horror. The rest of her came alive with adrenaline.

The monster moved faster than she could have imagined. Almost as soon as it looked at her, it was galloping toward her, closing the distance between them with terrifying speed. Still, Logan was ready for it. With one breath, she threw the knife already in her hand, and with her second breath, she reached back and drew her ax, holding it aloft before her. The knife stuck hard in between what may or may not have been the creature's ribs, if it had any, but it didn't seem to notice. Within moments, it came within reach, and she swung hard. The demon reared back, but not quite soon enough. It screamed as her ax took off one of its antlers at the root, spraying dark ichor over the scene.

As she spun away from it to build up her momentum, she caught sight of the Bound man, already unlocking the second cell door. She had just enough time to scan Volkov's face before she sprang into action again. He looked pleased.

The first demon was relentless and unbothered by injury. It swung its long talons her way, and she had to leap to avoid them. A voice inside her head laughed, energized by the thrill of a near miss. When she spun toward it again, she was faster and harder than ever before. A fierce crunch split the air, and in an instant, the fight was over. The creature's head toppled from its body. Logan felt the unwilling but automatic rush of pleasure at her own quick and efficient kill. It was a familiar satisfaction, but the baseness of it sickened her.

Still, now was not the time to chide herself for her imperfect impulses. Instead, she squared her feet, readying herself to stand against the second demon. And just out of the corner of her eye, she thought she could see the painted, glowing Key underneath her beginning to shift....

The second demon lumbered forward on four legs. It looked like an overlarge bear, only rippling with thickly veined muscles, with a protruding ridge of bone shooting out of its spine. If it had eyes, she couldn't discern them.

It reached her even faster than the first. And she slew it even faster, too. A single hard strike with her ax took its head clean off, no preamble necessary.

This time, she dropped into a roll and aimed herself at the body of the first demon. She could hear the Bound man rattling the lock on the third cage, but she needed a moment. And as she threw herself at the ground, she saw it again: fluctuations in the Choronzon Key painted on the ground. It was as if the paint itself had begun to move—begun to swim and shift along the axis of itself.

She grabbed the hilt of her knife from where it stuck out of the first demon's corpse. She pulled hard and swung it free, then stood up to look at Volkov one more time.

He gazed at her openly, a self-satisfied smile set on his face.

He was happy she'd succeeded. He *wanted* her to kill the demons.

She glanced back at the glowing red symbol below. Its movement had ceased, but it looked distinctly brighter now. Then it dawned on her.

It's a sacrifice, she thought. *Killing the demons will activate his cast.*

She had no idea how the Choronzon magic worked, but the look on Volkov's face told her everything. The third cell stood open now, and Volkov stared at it with outright hunger.

There are seven doors. Seven demons. And we're already down two.

This time, Volkov didn't wait for her to initiate the fight. He rushed at the demon himself, letting out a primal scream as he swung at it with his knife. His aim struck true, and another fine spray of dark ichor fell on the ground, but it didn't kill the demon.

For only a moment, Logan stood frozen, calculating her next best move. The Bound was already headed for the next cell, and Volkov was already preparing to redouble on the demon. *To kill it, so he can advance the spell.*

Strange as it seemed, she had to protect the demon.

She rushed forward, knife at the ready, and placed herself between Volkov and the demon. At long last, Volkov's smile faltered.

"Get out of the way!" he called at her, taking a step forward and raising his own knife again. "I don't want to hurt you."

She shook her head. "If you want to get past me, you have to go through me."

His gaze hardened into a glare.

"Why must you always *fight* me? Why not join me?"

Logan was about to answer him when she noticed the movement behind her—the demon, oblivious to her intentions, had advanced upon them. Logan swung immediately to the side, but she was a hair too late. Something sharp sliced through the air, catching her shoulder through her jacket. She heard the tear of leather as white-hot pain shot through her torso, forcing her to her knees. On blind instinct, she dropped and rolled out of reach, the need to protect herself momentarily overriding her goal of protecting the demon.

It was only a momentary lapse, but it was enough. As she lay stunned from the sudden pain, Volkov unsheathed the sword at his waist and swung it at the demon. He moved like a trained swordfighter, leaving deep cuts on its arms and torso while dancing out of the way of its retaliatory strikes. Slowly but surely, the demon began to wind down.

Logan struggled to her knees just in time to see Volkov plunge his sword deep into the beast's chest. It fell over dead a moment later.

Three down.

Even though the fourth demon was already emerging from its cage, Logan didn't yet rise. Instead, she found her gaze pulled inexorably toward the symbol beneath her. It was shifting again. It looked like water moving under a glass surface. It seemed to flicker, like a candle in rain. Her shoulder still burned, and the pain of it reminded her of the feeling she got right before a vision. The symbol moved and twitched, almost a living thing.

In fact, she had the strangest feeling that if she were to touch it with her hand, it would feel alive. She could almost *hear* it whispering to her—asking her, even daring her, to stretch out her hand—to reach out for the heat it promised her...

She felt a sudden shift on the wind. When she looked up, a rock dropped to the pit of her stomach.

The Bound had already unleashed the next *two* demons, and the third was on its way.

Chapter Twenty-Two
Across the Boundary

The fog swathed their movements. Jude moved like in a dream, uncertain each time she put her foot down where it might land. Uncertain of the ground beneath her and the ground ahead, the only thing she was sure was real was the solid outline of Hugh Knatt's back cutting a path for them. Somewhere behind her, Eliana's footsteps sounded, reassuring but not quite real themselves. Maybe her own weren't real, either.

The fog did not dissipate when they finally heard the sounds of human voices once again. Jude became dimly aware that Knatt was calling out to someone, and someone else was answering him. And then Adept Marlowe appeared before them.

They were talking. Jude knew they were talking.

"Mr. Knatt. Is that really you?"

"It is, although I suppose an advanced illusion might say the same. I think we're dealing with a tarnoch demon. Which, as far as I know, are not known to replicate human speech."

"Though I suppose that's exactly what an illusion would say, if it could." It was possible Marlowe was smirking. Jude seemed to have lost the ability to tell. "I've heard of the tarnoch, but I've never seen one in person myself." Her head turned in Jude's direction, then behind her. "I see you found the others. Only…"

"I'm afraid I was a bit late. There's been an accident."

Jude faded out again. A vast emptiness seemed to open before her. She searched for Eliana's face, but her expression was wrong. She didn't look like the same girl.

Voices faded in again.

"I'll keep an eye out. Godspeed, Mr. Knatt."

With that, the solid form of Knatt's breathing, moving body disappeared from view.

"Wait, what's going on?" The words felt thick in her mouth.

Marlowe looked at her with obvious, unbearable pity.

"Mr. Knatt knows how to track the demon. Don't worry, Miss Li. It'll all be over shortly."

The statement did little to comfort her.

And yet, as it turned out, she didn't have to wait too much longer. Or perhaps it was longer than she felt it was—it was hard for her to assess her own experience. In what felt like no time at all, they heard the dying scream of an unseen force. It sounded guttural and shattering. Jude wondered why Ian hadn't screamed like that.

And then the physical appearance of the fog around them began to diminish. It didn't vanish in an instant, but instead melted away, like ice on a summer sidewalk. Eventually the rain came back. Jude could feel it on her face. A pitter patter. A drip drop.

Jude was lost in her own muted wonder when she realized the other two had stood to attention. The vanishing fog had left behind two demons, nearly within striking range of their small group. She hadn't kept the gun from before, and she wasn't sure how she felt about that now.

Without it, she gripped the battle knife. It felt unsteady in her hand, but it was something. But the others were too fast for her. Eliana slashed out with her own knife while Marlowe fired three quick rounds. Both demons dropped to the ground before Jude even had a chance to react.

The illusions had definitely come to an end. These demons didn't disappear, but remained solid where they lay.

"Where's Knatt?" she heard herself ask.

Marlowe shot her a concerned look.

"He'll be back soon, Miss Li."

"I'm right here."

Jude whipped around, turning automatically toward the familiar voice. Knatt was about 15 feet away, looking rain-dampened but otherwise unharmed. Alexei Marin stood beside him.

"And you've located the rest of our party," said Marlowe, sheathing her gun in her hip holster once more. "As long as neither of you is injured, I suggest we get our asses moving on into that base."

"Aye aye, Captain," drawled Alexei, performing a quick salute.

"Wait," said Jude. All eyes turned toward her, and she realized quite suddenly that she had no authority over anyone present. Still, she had to at least try to convey Logan's message. "Logan—Logan wanted us to go. She said…the Wolf is farther along than she thought, and we're walking into an ambush. We have to call off the mission."

She watched her words register with the group. It was Marlowe who spoke first.

"If we're calling off the mission, then where is Logan?"

"She—she went back."

Knatt took a step forward, looking stricken. "She's gone on alone?"

"Of course, she did," sighed Alexei. He shoved his hands in his pockets and shook his head. Jude didn't know how to interpret that.

Marlowe let out a sigh and checked the safety on her gun, before stowing it in her holster. "Well, unfortunately for the shadow summoner, she doesn't actually get to say when I pull my team out of a mission." She motioned to Eliana. "How's your ammo, Adept?"

"I have my backups, sir." Eliana's hand rested on the gun in her holster, but she didn't take it out.

"Then I see no reason not to push forward."

Automatically, Jude searched for Knatt's gaze, and when she found it, it echoed her uncertainty back to her. She knew neither of them wanted to leave Logan on her own, but she also knew that the Order of Shadows would never be her preferred backup.

They barely had time to exchange that glance, let alone express anything out loud, when a new voice interrupted them.

"Oh, good. I'd hoped you wouldn't leave us too early."

The shape it came from was human, with long, dark hair and hollow eyes. Ice formed in Jude's blood, and her breathing quickened.

It was Zilla Ulric. She gave them a smile, and it stretched too wide in her face. With a jolt, Jude realized she had already begun to change into her Bound form.

Marlowe and Eliana both snapped to attention, simultaneously unsheathing their guns and aiming them.

"You've got one shot, Ulric," said Marlowe, advancing a few feet with her weapon drawn. "Surrender to us now, and we'll take you in without incident."

"Surrender?" Ulric let out a short cackle. "Why in the world would I do that?"

"You know the Order's directive is to shoot traitors on sight." As Marlowe took another step, Jude could have sworn she sent Knatt a look. Was that a wink? "Which gives me very little reason to limit my use of lethal force here."

"Oh, yes. In fact, I helped write that one." Ulric's eyes flashed dangerously. Already, she looked larger than her normal self. "Seemed as good an excuse as any at the time. Tell me, Captain Marlowe, had Clément demoted you out to this backwater so soon? I thought she liked you."

"I go where I'm needed." As Marlowe advanced again, Knatt slipped backward and motioned to Jude behind his back, indicating she should follow. "Unlike you, I know my place."

While Knatt stepped quietly to the right, Jude did, too. She stole one last look at Eliana, who had advanced behind Marlowe, only a few steps behind. She looked like a soldier. Her exterior was finely crafted diamond, and beneath it, only echoes. Her posture was straight as ever, and it carried her forward. Jude had spent so much time studying her face, but she'd never seen it do something like this. She wanted to ask her where she was. She wanted to reach out and take Eliana's hand in her own.

She said nothing. Her gaze turned to Knatt, and her feet kept her moving.

"Oh, I think my place is right here." Ulric's voice had now deepened and distorted, and when Jude saw her again, her muscles had all bulged to double their original size, and black veins criss-crossed over every inch of exposed skin.

Jude shuddered involuntarily and followed Knatt another step to the right.

A few quick moves later, she was jogging after Knatt as he headed for the next staircase up. Alexei followed close behind her, checking every few feet that they weren't being followed. The fight between the Order Adepts and Ulric faded out behind them, and a new one loomed ahead.

"I suggest we attempt to follow Ulric's footsteps," said Knatt as he led them up the staircase. "That might be our best chance at finding—"

Just then, a terrible, demonic scream rent the sky. All three of them stopped in their tracks, looking up in the direction from which it had come.

"I suggest we follow that," said Jude.

"Yes, quite."

And they were off again, sprinting up the next flight of stairs as fast as they could. Alexei pulled out ahead, clearly spurred on by the sounds. Jude could feel a pressure rising within her—the twin dread of reaching Logan and whatever she was fighting—and of not reaching her at all.

She kept her feet moving regardless, chasing after Alexei Marin like her own life depended on it. It was the only thing she could do.

At long last, she skidded to a halt, nearly running into Alexei, with Knatt close on her heels. They'd reached the end of open-air corridor and come out into an unexpectedly large opening. Jude surveyed the scene. Everything before them seemed to shine with red light, though she couldn't immediately say why. Another cement wall stood behind a semi-circular depression in the stone floor, with several open metal doors like gaping mouths punctuating its surface, revealing the empty caverns they held.

In between their group and the empty cells stood Logan, Casimir Volkov, and a handful of fantastically giant demons. Three of them—and a fourth emerging from the final cavern. Logan's back was to them, her ax grasped firmly in her hand.

Despite the circumstances, Jude felt a small rush of relief at the sight of her. On some deeper level, a part of her still believed she would always be safe as long as Logan was around.

Jude took in the rest of the scene. There were bodies here— some demon, definitely dead, and some human, less so. She couldn't be too sure about the human bodies, though; she found it hard to look at them long.

She was jerked back to the present moment by an urgent voice to her left.

"H.C., look out!"

Jude grimaced as she saw the nearest lumbering giant of a demon lunge toward Logan, but Logan ducked into a roll and slipped easily out of the way. When she got to her feet again, she jumped back and turned toward them.

"Get out of here!" she called, using her ax to point them back whence they'd come. "I've got this handled."

Before any of them could reply, Volkov's gleeful voice floated over to them.

"Are these your friends, Henrietta? How nice of them to join us."

Jude felt a chill run up her spine. Why did he sound so happy?

He wanted us to come, she thought, with rising terror.

"We should go," she said, only it came out as a whisper. She took an automatic step backward and nearly ran into Knatt.

The others didn't hear her. Instead, they sprang into action.

"I've got the one on the left," Alexei called, gripping his panther-headed cane just beneath the handle and holding it aloft like a club.

"I'll take the far right," Knatt returned, also moving away from her. He glanced back at her for only a moment. "Stay back, Jude."

A part of her wanted to obey him. She still felt numb, paralyzed. But then she looked behind him.

He was turning too slowly; he would see the demon too late. In an instant, everything else melted away, and her body moved of its own accord. Her disrupted mind found the fire so easily— like a death wish finding a bullet.

She threw her still-injured hands out before her, letting blind rage overtake her like a tidal wave.

In the background, she thought she heard Logan calling to her. Her hands felt raw and wrong, but it didn't seem to matter; it was like they belonged to someone else. She had become the fire, and she remembered nothing else.

It surged right past Knatt's head, barely missing him, before blossoming into an ocean and consuming the demon whole. She felt the moment it died, and she felt the delight of the fire—its satiation. Its completion.

And then the monster burned away to nothing, and the fire went out. Jude's body slumped forward, emptied of everything that mattered.

"Jude!" She heard Logan's voice clearly now—as well as her obvious exasperation. Jude popped her head up, eyes searching wildly until they found Logan's blurry outline. "I said *don't kill them!* That's what starts the ritual!"

Jude barely managed to register what Logan was saying before her attention was pulled irrevocably in another direction—toward Volkov, standing behind her, arms thrown wide.

His body had begun to transform into something new.

Four down, three to go.

It happened so quickly. One moment, Logan was telling them to go, to leave the fight to her—and the next, fire poured like lava out of Jude's scarred hands, felling the fourth demon in a single shocking strike. Logan scrambled, screaming at her to stop—but she could already see that Jude had been transported—the eira summon controlling her, rather than the other way around. And then the demon was gone, and Volkov's plan was one step further along the road to completion.

The fire disappeared, and Jude fell to her knees, depleted.

"Jude!" Logan could barely contain her mounting panic. "I said *don't kill them!* That's what starts the ritual!"

She watched Jude's gaze slowly rise to meet her own, saw a moment of recognition there, before her eyes slid out of focus, landing on something behind Logan's head. Logan felt a shiver go up her spine. She turned around.

It was Volkov. He was still grinning madly, but something

about him had begun to look different. He stretched his neck from one side to the other, and she watched as the muscles there bulged to unnatural size. Tell-tale black veins spread out from his eyes and across his face. She heard the fabric of his fine silk shirt begin to tear.

It took her a moment to notice the part of the change that should, perhaps, have caught her attention right off the bat: purplish-black marks scaling the sides of his neck, disappearing under his endangered shirt.

She felt her hand reach automatically for her neck, where her own marks peaked out from her collar.

Understanding struck her like a gut-punch. He hadn't been bound with *any* demon powers. He'd been bound with *hers*—or, rather, the powers she'd inherited from the mother she'd never known. For one desperate moment, her mind searched for another option—surely she'd seen at least one other demon with marks that matched, hadn't she? But she couldn't think of one. She felt the cold pinpricks of the spikes in her arms, begging to come out. Would he have spikes, too? Or would he only have the strength? Or, perhaps—

He can summon the shadows. The thought emerged on its own, without being called. *He's not an eira master, but he can summon shadows.*

With resignation, she realized she'd found an answer to a question she'd never bothered to ask. The shadow summoning *was* a demon trait. It had been all along.

She blinked and forced her focus back to him. Since she had no idea how to stop the ritual that was already in progress, all she had to do was stop him from completing it. And maybe the best way to do that was to incapacitate him—a task made somewhat more difficult by his Bound form.

He looked like he'd tripled in size; the fine suit now hung loosely off his bulging frame, reduced to little more than scraps. His once fine features looked distorted and stretched beneath inhuman veins. He seemed to revel in it; she watched him roll his neck and shoulders in an anticipatory stretch, before he threw his head back and let out a sudden cry. It landed somewhere between a frat boy yell and a werewolf howl.

Before she decided on her next course of action, he turned away from her. Just like that, he was running, jumping, leaping—and landing on the next demon with a sickening crunch.

"Fuck." She leaped to her feet and sprinted after him, but she already knew it was useless. The demon stood just outside the painted Choronzon Key—and, thus, just outside of her reach. Sure enough, as she was about to catch up to him, she crashed right into the invisible barrier pinning her in.

She watched as Volkov's massive new form wielded his sword like a child's plaything. He gave her a wink, and she banged her fist against the boundary in reply.

Volkov's first few strikes with the sword glanced off the monster, doing little more than keeping it off-balance. It was almost like he wanted to put on a show. In fact, Logan was sure he did.

Still, he seemed to remember that time was a factor, and Logan was no longer alone. The fight was over in moments. With one last wink at Logan, he drew his sword up high and brought it down on the creature, slicing right through its skull.

The ground gave another great shake. This time, there was

absolutely no denying that the Choronzon Key beneath her feet had begun to change. It now burned red hot—just like the one on her back.

Five down.

Volkov began to laugh. She could see from the look on his face that he exalted in his kill. As if he felt her watching him, he turned to face her, eyes alight with passion.

"You know, Henrietta, I always wondered why you took up your father's profession, after everything." With an amused quirk of his mouth, he wiped the ichor from his sword on his pant leg. Logan did her best not to shudder. "But I think I'm starting to understand it. It's *fun*, isn't it? Hunting down demons, letting all your violence loose on them. Scratches an itch you can't quite name, doesn't it?"

Logan had an answer on the tip of her tongue, but she held it back. She had the sudden, inescapable feeling that something had gone irrevocably wrong. She felt paralyzed, pinned to the spot—

And the Choronzon Key on her back burst into flames.

Jude watched in horror as Logan fell to the ground, rocked by some unseen force. And yet, miraculously, she barely had time to process it before Logan had jumped to her feet again.

"Stay back!" she yelled, pointing herself right at Jude. Jude recoiled automatically, like a scolded child. Her hands immediately contracted, sending shockwaves of pain down her arms. Still, she forced herself to keep her gaze steady on Logan, and in a moment, she was glad she did. Logan jabbed her ax at the ground, almost like…like she was pointing at something. "*Stay back.*"

Jude's gaze fell to the ground, and she recognized what her mind had barely registered before: the red glow of the scene was coming from the ground, from a giant symbol painted there. It looked like a labyrinth.

No. It looks like the Choronzon Key, she realized with a jump. But what the hell did that mean? She had no idea. Nevertheless, she backed up, making sure she wasn't touching it at all—and she could see both Knatt and Alexei back up a few paces, too. Did they understand it better than she did, or were they going off blind faith, too?

Unfortunately for them, the Key was the least of their worries. There were two demons left, and one of them lumbered right towards them, moving along their side of the painted symbol, far from Logan and the Wolf. It looked like a giant bear with slicked-down fur, its powerful jaws opening wide.

It had already nearly reached Alexei. Jude watched him hesitate and glance back at Logan. How were they supposed to protect themselves if they weren't supposed to kill the demons?

Jude held her useless hands in front of her. Gone was her ability to call to the fire, and gone, too, was her basic ability to hold a knife. She had nothing left, and she wouldn't have known what to do even if she had.

She could already feel herself dissolving in panic when she heard Logan's voice again.

"Take it out!"

Jude's head jerked up in surprise, glancing quickly between Logan on one side, and Alexei and the demon on the other. She saw her give Alexei an affirming nod, and then she saw nothing else of her.

The creature was almost on him now. A part of her braced for impact, but she could not look away.

Then Alexei raised his panther-headed cane in front of him and cried out cast words she didn't know, before slamming the steel tip into the ground beneath.

"*Invoco yakoshum!*"

As soon as his steel met stone, the whole scene changed. Suddenly she wasn't just looking at one Alexei staring down the beast—she was looking at a small band of them. Five new Alexeis appeared out of thin air, each one battle-ready and wielding a cane.

They fell on the bear in twos. The first pair bum-rushed it, causing it to rear back in surprise. They were followed shortly by the next four, one of which—the real one, Jude suspected—managed to land a quick slice on the upper part of the bear-demon's forelimb before leaping out of reach.

The false Alexeis did not let up. They fell on the demon one after the other. Finally, the demon overcame its confusion well enough to aim a heavy swipe right through the center of one—and Jude was certain that if it had managed to hit the real one, it would have caused potentially fatal damage. Instead, however, its arm broke right through the illusion, swinging impotently through empty space.

For a moment, Jude felt a surge of triumph—until she remembered, all at once, the look on Fisher's face as the final illusion faded away. The floor of her stomach gave way, and she nearly heaved.

And yet, the battle before her would not relent. While the Alexei apparitions distracted the demon, Knatt charged forward, his arms already raised in the beginning of a cast. Jude listened closely, but she couldn't hear him chanting any cast words—and she didn't see him raise a knife for a blood catalyst.

Nevertheless, he spread his arms wide, then pulled them down hard in a great contraction. The ancient wall of cement just behind and above the beast cracked open, and a giant piece of it crumbled down. It landed heavily on the demon's torso, on its left side. Jude watched it buckle under the force.

Still, the monster had not been felled. Jude could see it moving, though it could not stand.

Alexei slammed the cane down again, and this time, all his copies vanished. Then he gave the panther's head a strange little twist, and something shiny seemed to pop out of the other end. He darted forward, jabbing the beast a few quick times with the sharp end of the cane. Then he stood back and watched.

Jude watched, too, as the creature's breath slowed, then stopped. She felt something small and unseen drop away from her, too.

Then the world gave a great shake, and ripped wide open.

Be a good girl, Henrietta.

Her father's voice screamed in her ears. For a moment, she couldn't remember where she was. She knew she'd fallen to her knees, but it was hard sorting out her thoughts and her surroundings through all the pain.

Oh, right. The pain.

Her back was still burning, though she'd adjusted to the initial shock of it. She could already feel, if not hear, her friends coming to her—putting themselves at greater risk when all she wanted them to do was leave. She could feel something else, too. It was hard to say exactly what it was, but it felt intimately familiar.

"*Stay back*," she yelled as she jumped to her feet. Despite the fog in her mind, she managed to spin around and narrow her eyes on Jude, where the message needed to go most. "*Stay back.*"

Jude looked uncertain, even a little crestfallen. Logan didn't want to hurt her feelings, but whatever explanations she had were going to have to wait. She made sure Jude was still looking at her as she made a quick circle with the ax.

Stay off of the Key, she thought, even though she knew they couldn't hear her. She could only hope they all understood her anyway.

Her father's voice had fallen to a whisper, but it was still there. In the background, like it *was* the background. Maybe it would always be there—her father's last legacy in her life, lingering long after she had shut him out of it. His last stab at control.

Control.

"It's all about control." As the symbol on her back burned quietly, she dropped into a squat and reached out to touch the one beneath her feet. As soon as her fingers made contact, it lit up, like it was answering her. Welcoming her. The pain on her back had already receded. Now it was only warmth.

She remembered the vision she'd had about this moment, and suddenly, she understood. Volkov may have started the sequence, but how it would end was entirely up to her.

Her eyes still on the Choronzon Key churning beneath her, she stood and turned toward Volkov, and smiled.

There was only so much time, and so many variables. Of the two remaining demons, one was already headed toward her friends—Alexei was closest, and though he held his panther-headed cane in his hand, she could see him backing up out of the corner of her eye, cowed by her last directive. Volkov could wait a moment more.

"Take it out!" she called to Alexei, re-gripping her ax as she caught his eye one last time. He met her gaze, and his uncertainty melted away. *Stay safe*, she mouthed at him—although at this distance, she doubted he could see it. He gave her a curt nod before turning back to the fray, and with relief, she saw that Knatt was already headed toward him.

He'll be fine, she told herself, forcefully. *He can take care of himself. They all can.*

"Are you sure that's wise?" asked Volkov, his voice suddenly much closer than she expected. When she turned back toward him, she could see that he now stood just on the outside of the ring, with nothing but the barrier between them. "Surely by now, you understand how this all works."

"Better than you do," she said. She could see the way the pieces all fit together, and she was ready for them. "I've seen how it all ends, too. I don't think you'll like it."

Volkov scoffed. He slid his sword back into the scabbard at his waist and shoved his hands into his pockets. In what felt like a practiced move, he tilted his head down until a single strand of hair fell into his eyes, then he glanced up at her. He looked like a naughty school boy if she'd ever seen one.

"I've wanted to do this since the moment I knew what it was. I think I'm going to like it just fine."

She felt a sudden swell of pity for him. In another life, she might have been him.

"I know you think that." She shook her head at him. "Your father thought he understood it, too, right?"

For a moment, Volkov looked uncertain—like he had glimpsed into the abyss and finally seen it for what it was. Then he shook his head at her, and his bravado returned.

"I'm nothing like him. I have powers he couldn't dream of."

Logan shrugged. "If you say so. But don't say I didn't warn you."

She had just enough time to see the surprise register on his face before she had to turn and spring away. The other demon had finally slimed its way onto the Choronzon Key—into the arena, with her.

She took a running leap at the demon, ax swinging wide as she did so. It reared back at the last second, pulling up like a cobra to get out of the way of her blade. Still, she heard the slick slice of metal into flesh, and ichor splattered the ground behind her as she landed in a squat on the other side. She'd made contact, even if she hadn't killed the beast. It roared in anger, and she turned in time to see the poison sacks on either side of its head swelling to full size.

Fuck. She dropped into a roll and spun out of the way, just barely avoiding the venom that sailed after her. She had to ditch the ax as she did, leaving her momentarily unarmed—though not entirely.

The demon didn't seem to need much downtime between jets of poison. As she sprung to her feet at the end of the roll, it was already puffing out its sacks again. Lucky for her, she didn't need much downtime either. As it started a new torrent, she got down low and rushed toward it, flinging out her arms and exposing her spikes as she went. At the last second, she dropped even lower before springing up and launching herself over the back half of the beast's body like a missile. She slashed at its flesh with inhuman speed, striking it over and over. She let her last blow sink in deep, using it like a hook on a rappel line. She landed softly on the other side. The demon screamed and writhed and tried to twist toward her, but she was already gone. In the next moment, she had her ax back in her hand and she'd turned on the demon again.

At long last, it seemed slowed, if only just. They were both covered in the deep blue ichor that had sprayed from its wounds, and its head drooped as it followed her. Her grip on the ax was solid when she launched at it one final time.

In a moment, it was all over. Her ax soared clean through its neck, the power of her thrust severing its head cleanly away. In comical fashion, it flew straight toward Volkov and landed with a thud before rolling to his feet. He jumped back from it, which proved a solid instinct when one last stream of poison poured out of its open mouth. He glanced up at her in surprise, even shock. After all this, she had to wonder if her capacity for violence still took him aback.

Well, if it does, then he'd better get used to the feeling.

Staring him dead in the eye, she thrust out her right hand toward him. Her eyes closed as she reached out with her mind, stilling the self until she became a mere observer of her own consciousness, and calling out to the oneness of all things. The wind was in her, and she was in the wind. She called it right out of his chest.

Her eyes popped open in time to see him stumble. She gave him back a little so he didn't faint too early. His feet carried him further forward, almost like he was trying to physically move himself in the direction of the air that had just escaped him.

She moved closer to him, too.

He clawed at his throat and took another step forward. Just like that, she knew she had already won. In another moment, she had given his air right back to him—and closed her real-life hand around his throat.

"You crossed the line," she whispered in his ear. They stood just inside the boundary of the Choronzon Key painted below them. She could feel it pulsating—it pulsated within her, their connection growing stronger by the second. With surprising ease, she pulled Volkov deeper in with her, bringing them both to the very center of the symbol.

Just behind her, her friends were still engaged in battle. She knew she had just as much time as their fight took. Despite herself, she turned on the spot until she could see them.

"What are you doing?" he asked her. She looked back at him, surprised to realize she'd almost forgotten his presence, even with her hand wrapped around his throat.

She shook her head. There wasn't enough time left in the universe to explain it so that he would actually understand.

"You wanted to control the power. But you made a mistake." She gave a shrug. Behind him, the fight had reached a fever pitch. "I *am* the power."

His eyes widened at her, concern turning instantly to fear. She looked away from him, beyond him.

She was just in time to see Alexei strike out with his cane, the sharp end sinking deep into the demon's flesh one last time.

She felt the moment it died. She felt the last piece of the puzzle fall into place, and the Choronzon Key on her back soaring to life.

It felt different, but it felt exactly the same. The power was a part of her. It always had been.

"I told you that you wouldn't like it."

The Key beneath them turned into a beam of pure light as the Key on her back ripped open a tear in the sky in front of her. She knew, without having to ask, that there was only one way to close it.

She stepped through.

Chapter Twenty-Three
A Strange Land

Jude stood transfixed. She might have stopped breathing minutes ago, for all she knew. She was still getting over the shock of seeing a small pack of Alexeis form from thin air to fight a demon—when the fight ended in spectacular fashion, and set off what, for one wild moment, she believed to be a fireworks show erupting from the earth.

The ground gave its third great shake of the evening—only this time, it didn't subside immediately. She felt her body turning as if it were in slow motion. She realized now that it wasn't a fireworks display at all—instead, a giant column of light appeared to have birthed itself out of the ground. Of course, even as Jude's eyes told her that was what was happening, her brain argued that that made even less sense than the first idea.

She could still make out Logan at the center of it all. Logan had one hand on her ax and the other wrapped around Volkov's throat. She didn't look at Jude—didn't seem to see anything around her at all.

And then, just like that, she vanished. The ax and Volkov vanished, too.

Jude blinked several times, momentarily certain that her eyes were playing more tricks. But nothing changed. She felt her feet take an uncertain step forward. The ground gave another shake, causing her to lurch and clench her raw hands. She barely managed to right herself in time to see what looked like a tear forming, right where Logan and Volkov had vanished only moments ago…

And then a demon fell through it.

She could hear a rhythmic rushing sound. The world around her was dark, cold, and wet. The air had a tangy, salty smell to it. The rushing seemed to echo on all sides, or perhaps it was merely loud enough to overwhelm her senses. She was fairly certain she was supposed to do something, but she couldn't remember what.

Wake up.

With a start of recognition, she realized her eyes were closed. She pried them open. A dark gray sky filled her vision, at once familiar and not. Her right hand, now empty, gave a twitch. She felt cold grains of sand slide against her skin. She sat up with a soft grunt.

She was on an isolated beach under a gray sky. For a moment, she entertained the possibility that she'd somehow been thrown to the other side of Fort Worden, toward the beach on the other side. But that didn't quite add up. For one thing, it was day here, and the rain was gone. For another, as she cast her gaze behind her, she saw a sheer cliff face several hundred feet high, which seemed to stretch endlessly in either direction, as far as she could see. With care, she pushed herself up to standing and took a good look around.

Volkov was nowhere to be seen.

In fact, there was no one, anywhere, to be seen. She was completely alone.

And she had absolutely no idea where she was.

Hey there! If you liked this novel and you'd like to get a FREE copy of the Choronzon Chronicles prequel novelette, *Strange Love*, as well as a sneak-peak at Book 4 and notifications when the next *Choronzon Chronicles* novel is released, then click here to sign up for Tess Adair's mailing list: https://www.tessadair.com/mailing-list-signup

Authors live and die by the power of the word; if you enjoyed the book, please consider putting a few words into a review wherever you purchased it. The author thanks you!

About the Author:

Tess Adair has lived in the Midwest and the Northeast, and currently resides in the Pacific Northwest. She enjoys discovering new cafes, making friends with cats, and not hiking. Follow her on her blog at: https://www.tessadair.com/thebodypolitic/